THE IMPORTANCE OF BEING THOROUGH

"This," he said, a little breathlessly as he bent to her, "is my bedchamber. This is my bed. And this is my kiss. Now you see," he continued softly, "I've lured you here and compromised you thoroughly." He smiled in triumph.

"But," Susannah said gently, "I don't see where you've compromised me . . . thoroughly." And she lay back against the pillows, her flaxen hair spread out over them like a silken coverlet, her lovely green gown down to her waist, her white, pink tipped breasts against his cheek, the taste of them burning on his lips.

"Susannah," he said, covering her nakedness with himself, trembling in an agony of desire, "I think I've compromised you fairly thoroughly by now."

"Oh," she said, her mind still scattered by the new things she felt, her senses taking control of her sense, "Have we done that . . . ?"

EDITH LAYTON, one of the most widely read and acclaimed Regency writers, is winner of the 1984 Reviewers Choice and Romantic Times Awards for Best New Regency Author . . . the 1985 Reviewers Choice Award for Best Regency Novel *(Lord of Dishonor)* . . . and the 1986 Reviewers Choice for Best Regency Author. *Love in Disguise* won the Romantic Writers' Association 1987 Golden Leaf Award for best historical novel, and earned Ms. Layton the 1987 Romantic Times Award for Best Regency Author.

SIGNET REGENCY ROMANCE
COMING IN FEBRUARY 1991

Charlotte Louise Dolan
The Substitute Bridegroom

Mary Balogh
A Certain Magic

Dorothy Mack
The Unlikely Chaperone

LOVE
IN DISGUISE

Edith Layton

A SIGNET BOOK

*For Hilary Ross—who dared to
wager on a Black Duke. . . .*

SIGNET
Published by the Penguin Group
Penguin Books USA Inc., 375 Hudson Street,
New York, New York 10014, U.S.A.
Penguin Books Ltd, 27 Wrights Lane,
London W8 5TZ, England
Penguin Books Australia Ltd, Ringwood,
Victoria, Australia
Penguin Books Canada Ltd, 2801 John Street,
Markham, Ontario, Canada L3R 1B4
Penguin Books (N.Z.) Ltd, 182-190 Wairau Road,
Auckland 10, New Zealand

Penguin Books Ltd, Registered Offices:
Harmondsworth, Middlesex, England

First Printing, August, 1987
10 9 8 7 6 5 4

 REGISTERED TRADEMARK—MARCA REGISTRADA

Printed in the United States of America

. . . For what is courtship, but disguise?
True hearts may have dissembling eyes . . .
  —Thomas Campion, "Never Love Unless You Can"

1

The safest way to arrive in London this night would be to arrange to be born there. For a thin, chill, freezing rain glazed the surfaces of the roads so that the teams of horses had to tread like ballerinas to keep their balance and the coaches swayed in their wake, slewing wildly at every misstep, and shaking almost as violently as their terrified passengers did. A trip that ought to have been accomplished in hours now looked as though it might take the night to complete, or else be over at any moment, if completion were to occur with a spill into a ditch. Or so the inside passengers on the *Brighton Thunder* moaned to each other as they clung to their shifting seats.

The outside riders on their lofty rocking seats were taking the hazardous journey far differently. Half of them were whooping and shouting with every wild swing of their lurching ride, because they were just as drunk as the cliché said such young lords were supposed to be. From their elevated outlook they found every danger entrancing, their youth and their condition making death and injury as unreal as the state they were in. The wind carried their gleeful cries away into the night. But since the other four hapless passengers who shared the carriage roof with them were there for economy's, not audacity's, sake, they wished the driving wind would carry the young merrymakers away along with their shouts.

The lead horses mistook a turn in the road and the coach made a long slide to the left, just grazing a milestone, causing the inside passengers to shriek, as a young lord on the coach top rose and brandished his flask to the night and shouted,

"They're off!!" to the winds. He stood there swaying and giggling as the coach shuddered to a halt, its drag pan finally catching in a jagged rut, and the horses came to a steaming stand, trembling, at the road's edge. Then a hard hand came down on the young reveler, and even in his drunken state he saw such rage in the face that glared down at him that he swallowed hard, and under pressure of that heavy hand, as his legs turned to jelly, he sank unresisting to his seat.

"Not another word, you young idiot," a furious voice growled. "There's nothing funny in these proud beasts working their great hearts out. A broken leg's death for them, and their deaths would be more than the little inconvenience yours might be for your family when I tumble you from your seat—as I will, my word on it—if you stand up once more this night."

And the proud young lord, who'd been taught all his privileged life that everyone on earth was inferior to him except for his father and his king, sat very quietly and obediently. Because it had been the coachman who ordered him to, and drunk as he was, the young gentleman knew the rules. The coachman was a law unto himself, and the absolute king of the road.

The sleet continued to hiss down as the coachman conferred with the guard. Then he climbed down and tried the surface of the road with his booted toe and scooped up some of the nubbly bits of sleet that began to bounce off the sheer ice that lay beneath, so as to assess its weight and texture in his gloved palm. He lifted his face to the racing clouds, and when a jagged bit of cloud tore off from the face of the bone-white moon, his eyes were as cold and colorless as the sleet which stung his own ivory face.

"The wind's rising," he said when he took up the reins again. And as he nudged the wheelers so that they might inch up on the leaders to get the coach on its way again, he added for the topside passengers who'd leaned close to hear him, "And the temperature's dropping. It's a skating pond now. Snowdrifts can be forded, my cattle can swim floods, but they're not mountain goats. And we're not the Royal Mail either, gentlemen. We're not sworn to get to London, dead or alive, on schedule. So we'll be inning tonight instead of just changing horses, courtesy of the company. We'll stop at the Silver Swan, not a league ahead, not far from Blindley Heath and Gibbet Hill. Yes, a charming location for an overnight stay," he said on a grin that was nonetheless as grim as his voice, "but better than the grave, I believe. I apologize," he added in a most nonapologetic voice as the four horses inched their way down the treacherous road again, "for the delay, but the *Thunder* will not be rolling on tonight."

And gifted with a quip that was as good as any they'd heard, and quotable at a dozen merry occasions as well, his sporting young gentlemen passengers sat back, content to get to the Silver Swan alive even if it meant not having a tale of their derring-do on the Brighton Road to regale their friends with out of this night's business.

It was such a terrible night that the Swan was almost filled. The *Brighton Fancy* had been the last stagecoach through, at dusk, when the road had just started to freeze. Even now the drivers and passengers of the *Dart* and the *Eagle* and the *Royal George* sat snug within the taproom. Their ranks were swelled by the wealthier owners of various stalled private coaches who now dined and drank as they looked out the Swan's windows to curse the weather, and paid handsomely to do so in comfort. The proprietor of the Silver Swan had a hundred tasks to occupy him as his inn filled, but it was his sense of hospitality, as well as gleeful greed, that caused him to remain near the door.

"A filthy night," he commiserated as he admitted another new guest.

"Aye, a filthy night," agreed the robust, well-set-up gentleman after he'd stepped from his own fine coach, delivering what might have been the password to gain admittance for that night, it was spoken so often.

In a practiced single gesture, the landlord proffered the register and swept into a bow. But he had difficulty straightening up when he chanced to glance at the young female who'd come in on the gentleman's arm, as she pushed back her hood and gazed about the inn. Hundreds of female visitors had graced the Swan, but still the landlord had seen few so stunningly lovely. For her hood fell back to reveal a quantity of cornsilk hair so light and shining it seemed richer and more extravagant than the sable fur that had covered it, and her white skin was the sort only fairy-tale maidens were supposed to have. But there was nothing classical or cool about her fair good looks, not when such liveliness sparkled in those wide brown eyes, not with that saucy pouting mouth she had. Hers was such an expressive, beguiling face, in fact, the landlord thought, that it made a fellow hesitate for a moment before he tried not to gape at her lush form. She took his breath away, and it added to her charm that she didn't seem to notice it.

It wasn't surprising to the landlord that the gentleman carefully signed her name separately on the register as "Miss Logan" to his own "Mr. Logan," as it soon became obvious that they were brother and sister. For when the gentleman took off his high hat, it could be seen that his thinning fair hair was the exact match of hers in color, if not in wavy abundance, and both noses in profile tended to tip upward at the end of their insignificant lengths. And as soon as he'd done writing their names, she grinned, and teased him in the most sisterly fashion.

"What a charming inn," she exclaimed. "Just smell that dinner cooking! Mmm. Poor Charlie, it's too bad, isn't it, because you did say you promised Mary you'd see to slimming?"

"Just so," the heavyset gentleman answered comfortably, "I shall. I'll watch my dinner carefully."

"Oh, Charlie," she laughed, "what a bouncer! You'll only watch to be sure it all gets on your fork! If I didn't know better," she added on a mock sigh, including the landlord in her conspiratorial smile, "I'd vow you scented roast in the wind a mile back and poured ice on the road yourself."

Before they'd done laughing, and even before the young woman's very proper-looking maid staggered in muttering about her young lady catching her death on such a night, the landlord assigned them one of his last best private dining rooms and a pair of his finest bedchambers, for his experienced eye had noticed something else about the pair. The stylishly simple high-waisted gown that hinted, rather than boasted, of the lady's shapely form, had immediately spoken up to him in accents as cultured as any he'd ever heard pronounced, and the gentleman's tailoring had given him as many details as his bank statement could.

No sooner had he seen them snug and safely away from the common herd than the door burst open admitting gusts of cold air and a horde of stamping, blowing, and laughing young men.

"Filthy night," the landlord dutifully informed the private coachload of dashing blades, and getting a strong whiff of alcohol as the gentlemen agreed with him in far more colorful terms, he recklessly consigned the lot of them to his paltriest private parlor when they requested superior accommodations, deciding to keep his best remaining private dining room and bedchambers against the arrival of some nob who'd appreciate it.

But the night drew on, and though incoming stragglers reported that the wind was cutting keen and ice was hardening like a moneylender's heart, no one entered the inn to lay claim to those last best chambers and his finest dining room. The landlord was brooding over lost opportunities, muttering "Filthy night" to a somewhat unsteady gentleman who'd just arrived, when an amused voice said in reply, overriding the gentleman's slurred "Too right, damn filthy":

"Insalubrious, yes."

The landlord's heart picked up even as his head did, and he looked up to try to find the gentleman who'd just unknowingly engaged the best dining room and bedchambers in the Silver Swan for himself and his three companions.

The flustered dandy attempting to extricate himself from his scarf and greatcoat was, from his cut and style, a London smart, at least three bottles to the better already, the landlord judged, quickly gazing past him. His auburn-haired female companion, pretty as a picture and painted up just like one too, was likely earning her keep as she stood there fawning on him. Another young woman, with hair as bright as a buttercup's and about as real as the possibility of one blooming on such a March night too, attempted an air of dignity. But dignity didn't march with such a lavishly rouged face, or such a daringly low-cut gown, so it must have been put on even as the gown had been, to please her escort, who was obviously the one who'd just spoken and engaged their rooms. For she didn't attempt, as her friend did with the other gentleman, to please him by wrapping herself around him. She might have been no better than she should be, the landlord realized, but she was no fool. This wasn't the sort of gentleman who'd take kindly to such public displays, whatever his private pastimes with her involved. This gentleman was, as the innkeeper had instantly recognized, a patrician in every particular.

He was tall and slender, but firmly muscled and evenly proportioned, as his well-cut, closely fitting clothes revealed when he removed his many-caped greatcoat. His dark blue jacket was fitted over a richly embroidered muted peach waistcoat, which had gone on over blindingly white linen. Dun pantaloons fit flawlessly over long legs encased in high gleaming Hessian boots. But anyone with funds could dress as a gentleman. This fellow, the landlord thought with great pleasure as he bowed, could have played the part in rags.

So when the gentleman was handed the register, and his host said, "If you'd be pleased to sign, your lordship," he was surprised when the bosky gentleman muttered instead:

"You do it, Warwick, damned if my hand ain't frozen."

The landlord hadn't even addressed the drunken fellow, and so he only proffered the register to the elegant gentleman again, and said more clearly, "Here you are, your lordship," only to hear him reply:

"Certainly, I'll sign, but my friend is quite right, landlord. It is *Mister*—Mr. Warwick Jones."

And so he signed it, though he styled his friend as "Baron" on the next line. But it made no matter to his host. He knew aristocracy when he saw it, titled or not.

And in fact, the countenance before him was a complex one, that of a voluptuary and an aesthetic intermingled, the sort of face that came from discipline as well as breeding, where intellect had been trained to hold tight rein on strong passions. Soft, shining nut-brown hair was swept back from the thin, high-boned face. The nose was thin as well, but long and high and arched, over full lips that were either sensitive or sensual according to his mood, or the mood of the observer. The lean cheeks tapered inward from the prominent sweep of cheekbones, and his skin was clear and smooth, but of a pale and olive cast. He was clearly a young man, but still it had never been precisely a young face; age was incidental to it. Nor could it be termed a handsome face, not with such a nose dominating it, not with such contradictions in it, not, at least, until one saw, beneath the flyaway brows, the heavy-lidded long eyes, which turned down at their corners, open to bend a surprisingly brilliant sapphire gaze down upon the world. The centers of those large eyes were deepest blue, and the white surround showed all around them, and this was such an arresting feature that the viewer forgot to assess whether it was or wasn't a handsome face when he was caught in that calm, intelligent regard.

It was that quizzical look of appraisal that convinced the innkeeper. This was the easy grace of a man used to respect, command, and instant obedience. Overall, the last, most important touch was evident: he looked as though he knew the reactions he'd caused in his observer and was vastly amused rather than gratified by them. It was the amusement, of course, that set the seal on it. This was a Man of Consequence.

Without a word, the landlord showed the quartet into his finest private dining room. A small fire had been laid in the enormous grate and it crackled merrily as they entered the room. But while his guests settled themselves, the landlord piled logs high until the fire thundered forth the warm welcome he wished he could express himself. Then, not even bothering to take their order, for he'd already decided to send his best to them, he wordlessly bowed his way out.

For a moment the landlord stood in the long common hallway listening to the increasing sounds of merriment from the crowded taproom, knowing that all his private dining rooms were occupied, and in that one small moment he was a man who knew the precise meaning of contentment.

And then a stableboy came dashing into the inn shouting for help, for he cried, "The *Thunder*'s comin' up t' drive! And she's filled t' the sky!"

The stranded coachmen and their guards who'd been taking their ease in the taproom lumbered out at once to aid their brothers. The coachmen were all fine specimens of the breed:

big, thick-shouldered, red-faced men with mighty barrel chests and great burgeoning bellies, fellows who swaggered the earth with a clear regard for their own importance, and it was they who reached the *Thunder* first to help hand down the outside riders into the courtyard of the Swan. They shepherded all the passengers into the inn, congratulating them for arriving whole after such a journey, as the coachman of the *Thunder* coaxed his exhausted teams into the stable.

Only after all the passengers had left his care, after the coach was buffed and dried, and the horses untethered, rubbed down, and soothed, for they, poor creatures, had a short brutish life and deserved that courtesy at least, did the coachman of the *Thunder* finally allow himself to enter the Swan to thaw and seek his own comfort. The landlord saw him unlock his great Benjamin cape from around his shoulders and straighten as he eased it off, understanding his relief only when he saw the amount of encrusted sleet that had weighed it down. He went to help him find a place at the fire to dry it, but paused when he saw Nan, his steady serving wench, come out of the taproom, wipe her hands on her apron, and then run into the coachman's arms with a great cry of joy.

"Oh here now, Nan," the coachman said on a laugh, accepting the warm, wide armful of girl and speaking softly into her tangle of brown hair scented with ale, wood smoke, frying fat, and good laundry soap, "I'm come in from the Brighton Road, love, not from the wars. I haven't been in France, only Brighton. And I'm not wounded, only half-frozen. But yes, love, warm me this way, do."

The girl wrenched herself from his embrace and stepped back, running her hand beneath her nose as she struggled for control. She was a handsome creature, full-bodied and broad-boned, with a wide and open face and a fine pair of flashing hazel eyes to save it from plainness. And, the landlord knew, as he grinned almost as widely as the coachman did, watching her, she was furious with herself for her display of emotion. For Nan was an emotional girl, all right, famous for her tirades, but it was seldom sentiment she showed.

"I dunno what came over me," she said, pushing him away as vigorously as she'd embraced him. "It's only that I knew you was on the job tunnight, but I din't know if you got through or not. But I 'spect you'd of been just as pleased if you'd pulled up at the Crown. Any port in a storm, that's you all over, in'it?''

"The Crown?" mused the coachman in a low, gentle voice as he reached to push a coil of curls gently back from her brow. "Oh yes, that's where that ugly little black-haired wench works, isn't it?"

"Ho!" Nan retorted, throwing her head back and shaking off his hand, glad of a game to cover her lapse, and making much of it to recover her dignity. "I understand there's some gents as don't think her ugly when they stop over at the Crown. I understand there's some as can make the best of it even if they do," she said, eyeing him sidewise.

The landlord smiled and turned away to leave Nan to her love play. He'd a punch to concoct: a tankard black with rum, awash with oranges, dusted with cinnamon, smelling like a spicy tropical sea, hot and buttered to go down as smooth as a summer afternoon—that was the coachman's favorite. And the coachman was a favorite at the Swan.

Before he could take more than a few steps to his mission, the door to the most meager private room flew open, and a tall, thin, chinless gentleman took a wavering step out into the hall, obviously in search of the convenience. When he saw the coachman, he stopped and stared, goggling as though he'd just seen him rise up from a green mist in a churchyard, rather than standing in the lamplight in a hallway of a way-side inn.

Of course, the coachman *was* singular. Indeed, he looked nothing like any others of his profession that the landlord had ever seen before, but he no longer occasioned comment at the Swan because, the innkeeper supposed, as he saw the gentleman continue to gape openmouthed at the driver of the *Thunder*, they were all used to him now.

It wasn't just that he wasn't broad and beefy, like so many of his confederates were. He was, after all, a few inches over average height, and though his frame was slender and articulate, his wide shoulders and flat abdomen spoke of his athleticism and hardihood as well as the overstuffed figures of any of the other coachmen did.

But his complexion was smooth, and even after being

stung by the storm and now warmed by the fire, its color rose only to the most subtle peach radiance of the hearth, and his eyes were so gray that in sunlight he looked blind, though now in the lamplight their troubled expression darkened them to a subtle shade of morning fog. His brow was high, his nose shapely, his mouth sensitive and tender, and his chin determined even though there was a light cleft gracing it. Framing all, his thick overlong hair glowed gold in the lamplight, curling only at its ends where it had gotten damp, and so forming wistful tendrils on his strong young neck. He did not look like a coachman. He looked nothing like a coachman. He looked rather like certain Attic statues or the stuff of maidens' prayers. He was, in brief, quite beautiful.

The chinless gentleman in the doorway squinted and then spoke in a voice of wonder. "My God, it's Hazelton! Damme, if it ain't Hazelton himself. It's been ages, and there he stands as though he were still alive. Come see. Good God, it's Hazelton!"

A disheveled assortment of the gentlemen who were still able staggered to the doorway to peer out at the apparition. The coachman stood and faced them, seemingly at his ease, but something in his stance, something in the way he eyed them, like a man facing a hangman, caused Nan's fists to clench beneath her apron.

"Damme, so it is," cried one of the young gentlemen.

"Hazelton himself," agreed another.

"But what are you doing in that rig," one demanded, "dressed as a coachman? Ho, Hazelton's up to some sport. What a night, by God, what a night. Now, here's Hazelton, cutting up, he's up to something, all right."

"What, Hazelton driving a coach? What a caper! What's the wager?" shouted another gentleman eagerly. "I'll put a pony on it myself."

"Is it down in the betting book at White's?" asked another, looking around wildly. "I didn't see it there. Haven't seen Hazelton in months either, though. Thought he was dead," he whispered loudly.

"Not dead," the coachman answered on a small smile, "only not at the club, Harry."

"Same thing," the young man replied, shrugging.

"See here," the chinless gentleman said, suddenly as serious as only a gravely drunken man can get, "why are you dressed up as a coachman, sir?"

"Because I am one, Bryant," the coachman said calmly. "I drive the *Brighton Thunder* now."

"A coachman?" hooted one of the young men, delighted. "Julian Dylan, fifth Viscount Hazelton, a coachman? Hear that rumbling, chaps? That's all his ancestors turning over at the thought. Come, come, Hazelton, we're friends, jolly good friends, and we're ripe for a spree," he said eagerly. "Let us in on the joke."

"No joke, my friends," the coachman said regretfully, "or rather I suppose it might be considered a howler of one, at that. Because I do actually drive the coach. And I do it for the money. For you see, I haven't a penny piece left to my name. And I've gotten into the sordid habit of eating. I discovered I wasn't astute enough to be a schoolmaster, tactful enough to be a butler, foolhardy enough to attempt to be a prizefighter, or even handy enough with my fives to be a tailor, and no one will pay me for my noblest skills: drinking, dancing, and wenching. But I can drive a coach. And so I do it for my living, not for sport. And," he said into the silence which followed his words, "I'm told I do it rather well. At least I earn quite a nice bit of blunt from it."

There was a moment of absolute silence before weak little comments of "Oh" and "Quite" and "Indeed" were heard, and then, no one of them quite meeting his eyes, some of the gentlemen made ragged, perfunctory bows to him before they turned and stepped back into their parlor, and at the last, the fellow who'd originally spied him said, "Servant, Hazelton," and sketching a bow that almost landed him headfirst on the floor, he staggered back into the room and closed the door behind him.

The landlord rushed to make his tankard of punch, not knowing what other solace to offer. Nan stood with her hands twisting in her apron, as though she sought something there that she could take out and say to him. But then a languid voice commented:

"Shame, Julian. But that's what you get for telling filthy stories in polite company. Yes, my dear," the observer commented, taking his dark blue gaze from the coachman as Nan's head snapped up to stare at him as he stood leaning, elegant and precise, against the door to the finest private room that he'd just left, "he could have told those gentlemen any number of scandalous details about his love life, or his other dealings with your sex, or even other gentlemen, or even their own grannies, I believe, but nothing would be considered so obscene as his talking about money. Or specifically, his complete lack of it. Julian, Julian, out of touch with society for only a few Seasons, and look at you, telling the truth. Is there no hope for you?"

"Warwick!" the coachman cried in delighted recognition.

He strode to the gentleman and put out his hand. Then the two shook hands so hard, grinning at each other so fiercely, that Nan, though used to more tangible signs of affection, stood and smiled tremulously at them, until she caught herself at it, frowned, and stamped away to the taproom, muttering about work not getting done standing gawking.

"Bryant was right," the coachman finally said. "What a night, indeed. It's been ages since I've seen you."

"Oh, I know it," his friend said softly, "because I looked for you, you know. Ah, I see you do know. That's bad, I think. Should I be insulted? Should I leave now? I will, if you'd like," he offered, unsmiling, holding his head to one side as he awaited an answer.

"No," the coachman said, abashed, "please, don't go. I knew you made inquiries, but I was very proud then and much younger than I am now. Five-and-twenty is very young, you'll admit, Warwick, now that we're old codgers with almost a full two more years in our dishes. I didn't want anyone to see how the mighty had fallen. Even so, it was hard to turn away my closest friend then. But now, I think I've fallen on my feet at last. It's good to see you, Warwick. Will you come have a drink with me?"

"Several. But first I have to make my apologies to my companions. No," he said as he cracked the door open, "they're not your sort, my friend. Actually, they're not mine either," he mused, "but loneliness breeds strange bedfellows. Or is it when one is lonely one doesn't find any bedfellows strange? At any rate, Julian," he continued as he eased the door ajar and peered into the dining room, "I haven't changed at all, sad to say, except that once I'd lost my best friends to wedlock and foreign service and coachmen's positions and whatnot, I seemed to lose my best intentions. You see the sot snoring in the corner? None other than the Baron Hyde, and he's just as rackety as he was when you knew him, although, obviously, his capacity's diminished over the years—he's only had a tun of wine and he's done for the night already. And so I suddenly have the uneasy notion that the two delightful females we struck up an acquaintance with in Brighton the other evening, the ones glaring at each other there, are about to draw straws for the use of my pure young body tonight. Perhaps you'd care to join us?" he asked hopefully. "I'll admit I'd have reservations about asking you if I thought I had only the one to cope with, remembering your success with the gender. Well, you can scarcely blame me for not wanting to end up with only the kitchen cat to warm my bed, can you? But now I believe even I might prove insufficient to the task. They do look rather hungry, don't you think?" he asked with a great deal of affected nervousness.

"You haven't changed at all, Warwick." His friend laughed. "Thank you, but as you very well know, I'd rather speak to you alone than cavort with your two light ladies."

"You have changed." The gentleman frowned as he paused at the door.

"No, it's just that I have my own diversions here," the coachman replied merrily.

He stepped out into the hall to wait for his friend to be done with making his excuses to his companions. As he stood musing, he became aware of the scent of honeysuckle before he even heard the hesitant murmured, "Pardon me, please," at his elbow. And so he turned around before the words were done being uttered, to discover himself facing one of the most beautiful young women he'd ever seen, so lovely as to be almost more improbable than anything else he'd encountered in the Swan this improbable night. The top of her flaxen head came only to his shoulder, and he looked down into her wide, dazed dark eyes as she paused and looked up at him. She'd obviously just been trying to negotiate the narrow hallway and hadn't meant to do more than alert him so she could pass by without brushing against him. But she'd been halted in mid-step by his appearance. She was a charming sight as she stopped and stared and the color slowly rose in her pale cheeks. But he was well used to such reactions, and lovely as she was, he'd had his fill of being gaped at this evening.

From her dress and voice, he guessed she was a lady who'd doubtless soon regret her artlessness. And he was light-headed with pleasure at finding his oldest friend again. So he didn't try to suppress a wicked impulse that came over him as suddenly as a sneeze. Instead of ignoring her momentary lapse and frank wide stare as a gentleman ought, or earnestly trying to press his acquaintance as a gentleman oughtn't but a normal man might, he gave her a wide white smile and said as fervently as he was able:

"Anything! Sweetheart, I'll pardon you anything, if only you don't say no to me."

Of course, before he could go on to enumerate the things she should say yes to, she gasped, blinked, and, jolted from her rapt study of him, backed a pace, and then with a burst of bravery shivered past him and fled down the hall. Her form, in retreat, was so entrancing that when she'd opened the door to the private dining room she sought and glanced back, she discovered him still smiling at her bemusedly.

He found the next impulse irresistible as well. As she watched, he bowed as low to her as a cavalier of olden days would have done, sweeping the floor with his imaginary outstretched plumed hat in hand. At that, she wheeled about and so Warwick got to see only the back of her head as she firmly slammed the door on the pair of them.

"Oh, good," Warwick said lightly, "there's hope for me yet. I see there's one female left in the world who's refused you."

"But I didn't get a chance to tell her what I was offering," the viscount explained, grinning.

"You never had to before," his friend corrected him. "Now, can we find a room somewhere in this place where we can talk without distractions or even such diversions as that paragon of a girl? I want to help you, Julian," he said, seriously, at last.

"I know," the viscount said, saddened again, "but you cannot, my friend."

2

The lovely blond girl looked down toward her toes, and from what could be seen of her averted, downcast profile, her lower lip was trembling. Her face had been pale to begin with, but now in her dejection she seemed lost as well as fragile, and as even her high-waisted gown was a study in deepest blue, she could, her guilty brother thought, have posed for the design on a funeral urn. He felt like a brute, and of course he knew he looked like one too.

But all he'd done was chide her after he'd heard her gasp and slam shut the door to their private parlor. He'd turned from taking himself an extra bit of that excellent nut cake when he'd heard her draw in her breath, and had only a momentary glimpse at the gentlemen in the hall before she'd closed the door in their faces.

"Of course you were met with insult, Susannah," he'd said with some heat, after she'd explained. "I don't know why you're surprised, you're lucky it was only a jest you attracted. I told you not to leave the room by yourself, you ought to have called your maid if you wanted to visit the necessary. The landlord said the place was all in a stew tonight, what with everyone and his uncle stranded on the road. Even though it's a decent inn, if you're going to stand like a gapeseed in the hallway, of course you were mocked, you deserved it."

He hadn't even thundered at her, he couldn't. He'd frowned and deepened his voice, but still when he'd spoken he'd sounded more as if he were teasing than threatening her. But really, he thought on a sigh, she was such a charming little creature, it was impossible for him to get angry with her. It had always been that way. His own wife scolded him for it, saying that Susannah could run rings around him, and so she could. But not just because, as his good lady always added on a laugh, she reminded him so much of himself. As if he, a great balding, substantial man, could remotely resemble such a lovely creature, he'd always scoff in reply, although, as ever, there was a little hidden pleasure in the denial, since it was such a pleasant thought. For she was the beauty of the family.

Da had been fair-haired and light-skinned, and Mum had just that sort of delicate features and that heart-shaped face. It was the image of Da's own snub nose that saved her face from perfection, making her beauty touching and human. But neither parent had possessed such cat-shaped eyes nor that impudent mouth, nor such grace and shapeliness in every limb and lineament. No, and neither did he or her other brother, though they both had her coloring and something of the look of her, so it could at least be believed they were related. But only that, for she was unique and as totally surprising in her appearance as she'd been in her initial appearance into the family, coming so late to them, and coming so lovely as well. Hadn't Da himself said that it was as if her Maker had left her as an apology for taking her mum when she'd come? He'd never blamed her for Mum's loss neither, for he'd always sighed that it was a treat to let his eyes rest on her at the end of a wearing day. And in truth, there was little enough beauty in the world, and when one found it, one oughtn't to trample it, so the substantial blond gentleman gazed at the forlorn young woman, cleared his throat, and said, wheedling instead of reproving now:

"Come, I never meant to make you cry. It's only that the fellow likely found you pretty and was having a flirt in the only way he knew. Don't take on, I didn't mean to upset you, and if I did, why, I'm sorry for it, for there was no real harm done, Sukey," he said anxiously when she didn't raise her head, using her pet name to jolly her. "It isn't the end of the world, give us a smile, won't you, puss?"

She gave him more, for when she raised her head it could be seen that she wore a most unrepentant grin, and her eyes sparkled with laughter as she dissolved in giggles and said, as best she was able:

"Oh, Charlie, some things never change. I believe I could have shot that gentleman in the hallway and left him there for dead, and still have gotten you to apologize for scolding me for it. My dear Charlie, Charlie my love, I'm all grown-up now, a great big whopping lass of one-and-twenty, and I have some manners, and know I deserved to be insulted for standing and gawking like a goose in a common public hallway. I was lucky that all the pretty fellow did was to twit me for my rudeness. Dear Charlie," she said more soberly, giving him a warming smile, "will you never learn that your sister can do wrong, aye, and often does, too?"

"Of course I know that," he said at once, seizing on her comment, for whatever his feelings toward his only sister, he was a man of business, and a good one too, and never a fellow to let such a rare opening for advantage get past him. "Isn't that just what I've been saying all night? It's a godsend, this weather, for it stopped us cold in our tracks and gives me an extra day and night to try to talk some sense into you. You don't belong in Tunbridge Wells with Cousin May, no matter that we're bound there, no, you don't, no matter that she writes she needs a companion about the house. For you need a man about the house, Sukey, and that's the whole of it. And for all she says she's got a fine home, she's old as the hills. How many dashing young blades do you think she's got cluttering up her parlor? And though the place is supposed to be a fashionable spa, how many handsome, hardy young gents do you think go there on a repairing lease? No, gout and crotchets is what you'll find in plenty, so if you want a nice old fellow reeking with liniment, why, then, it's the place for you.

"A year in New Haven with Cousin Elizabeth ought to have been enough for you," he said with real grievance, "with nothing to do but help with her brats while her husband was at sea, and no one to talk to but all the other married females whose husbands were at sea. I would've come to drag you away even if you hadn't written when you did," he grumbled. "All the young ensigns she promised me, all the worthy young chaps she raved about . . . 'and all officer material, Charlie,' " he mocked in a brittle soprano. "All the grand young men that never materialized," he sighed.

"Never say she promised *you* a young gentleman too!" his sister cried in mock horror, hoping to turn the subject, for he was getting onto firm ground now and she wanted to divert him. But he was not to be sidetracked,

"You might've gone straightaway to a convent after school for all the good that stay did you," he said angrily. "Blast it, Sukey, you're a rare beauty, don't deny it, for I've eyes. You've a fine education too, out of the ordinary in fact, because that's what Da wanted for you. And he provided for you in abundance, your dowry wouldn't shame a queen. And how do you use it all? By agreeing to keep company to any old female relative that asks you in? It's time to come out into the world, Susannah, it's time to take your rightful place in it," he shouted, bringing his fist down on the table and causing all the dessert plates of cakes and fruit to hop.

His sister remained very still, and then, when he again began to fear he'd wounded her, she spoke. Her voice was low and sober, and filled with such sorrow he realized this time she was beyond mere hurt.

"And just where is that rightful place, Charlie?" she asked, gazing at him steadily.

But now he was ready for her, for it was an old hurt and so it was an old argument that he'd had time to ponder, and though he was doting he was never a fool.

"And how will you know unless you stop hiding and come out to try to find it?" he asked as steadily and seriously as he'd ever spoken to her.

She turned her head to the side to acknowledge the hit.

"A season, only a season in London," he offered at once, pressing his advantage.

"A season?" she asked quizzically, one finely arched eyebrow rising. "Surely you don't mean *the* Season? Just think, the closest I'd get to such a haven for society ladies as Almack's would be if I passed it in a coach, and the nearest I'd come to a come-out ball would be if that coach rolled over someone coming out of one. A Season, Charlie? Not with all my dowry and education and looks rolled up in one, I think. For I'm no lady, Charlie, though I've been given all the trappings of one. I'm still the fishmonger's daughter, and don't forget it, for, believe me, no one will ever let me do so."

"I meant a season, and so I said it," he persisted, refusing to wince at her words, his fair complexion growing ruddy from the force of his emotions, suppressed and expressed. "This spring season in London, and perhaps, if this cousin of ours, this Mrs. Anderson I've turned up, if she's got the sort of connections she says she does, why then, yes, something very much like a *Season* too. Oh, try it, Sukey, just once. For me, if for nothing else," he pleaded, as she averted her head from him and kept to a stubborn silence, just as she'd done all night whenever he'd broached the subject to her.

"Because it pains me," he continued in frustration, using almost all the same words as he had all evening, "it gives me real pain, it does, seeing you wasting yourself. I want to see you meeting fine young gentlemen, eligible men of wit and education and breeding, the sort you were made for. And London's the place for it, never doubt it. Why, those young gents you saw in the hall, they're London stock," he said suddenly, inspired to new efforts by the thought of them. "You'll never find their like in Tunbridge Wells or New Haven. Confess it, would you expect to? Why, take that young Warwick Jones for example, he's top of the trees in London, and there are half a dozen other chaps I know—"

But she cut him off there, turning around at once and asking in surprise, "You know him? The young man I saw in the hallway?"

"Yes," he answered, pausing to watch curiously as her color mounted as he spoke, before he went on to say slowly, as he continued to observe her interest, "As a matter of fact, I do. Capitol chap. From an old family, a fine proud-looking fellow but with not a toplofty bone in his body for all of it. I've done business with him and he's never made me feel the less for it. Oh, you'd like him, my girl, why, it's a wonder I never thought of it before," he said, his enthusiasm mounting even as the flush in her cheeks did, for he was a born salesman, like his Da, and so knew how to shade his speech to suit his audience's response exactly, and catching fire from her kindled interest he went on:

"He's bright as a golden guinea and he's got enough of those, Lord knows. He's rich as Croesus, and getting richer as we speak, for he's got a head on those broad shoulders and knows how to get a bit of silver to sire golden babies with the best of them. And he's the best of them himself, never doubt it."

"But," his sister asked, a frown replacing the wide-eyed attention she'd shown, "then why is he driving a coach?"

"Driving a coach?" Her brother laughed. "Why, I suppose if he does, it's because he belongs to the Four-in-Hand Club, like so many of the young sporting gentlemen do, though I hadn't heard of it. It surprises me, because Mr. Jones isn't the sort of fellow to do the fashionable thing for the sake of it, not much of a clubman, I'd have thought. Bit of a renegade, he is—not," he said hastily, "that he's a rebel, or an upstart, or anything like, no, just his own man, is what he is."

"Oh," she said abruptly, visibly crestfallen, remembering then that some other fellow had come into the hall to join the young fair-haired coachman, "then I mistook you. It was the other gentleman I thought you knew. The one they called a viscount, though I suppose that was just a joke—the nobility don't drive public coaches."

"Some do, especially on the Brighton run, and not just for a joke neither," her brother mused. "It's a fashionable road, lots of the gentry go down to Prinny's new palace and then back again, so I'd imagine the tips are good, since the quality try to outdo each other in everything. As a matter of fact, there's a baron, and a lord, aye, and a marquess's son that I know of, all down on their luck and so up on the coachman's box to earn a penny, for what else are such cubs equipped to do after they've drained the family dry and their creditors are at their heels? No one's going to pay them a farthing to play cricket or fence, taste wine or dance, or do the sort of thing they were raised to do, so driving's as good a way to turn a living for them as any. Yes, he might well be a viscount, at that," he went on, casting a shrewd glance at his sister's complete, arrested attention as he spoke, "and as he's obviously a friend of young Warwick's, I can find out easily enough.

"I tell you what," he said with great vivacity. "If you don't mind sitting here alone for a spell, I'll go and hunt up Warwick Jones and have a word or two with him, and find out the lot. I'd wanted to have a chat with him when I first saw him tonight anyway, but I scarcely could after you'd closed the door in his face."

He left the room immediately, ignoring his usually collected sibling's hesitant, embarrassed protests about not wishing him to bother, "since really it was only an idle thought, since actually it made no matter what the viscount did, really." He decided it would be excellent for her to meet up with Mr. Warwick Jones, and hold a good thought for him while such a meeting was being arranged. Because that gentleman was one of the best that went by that name that he'd ever encountered. And since the fellow had no title, but a great deal of wit, sensitivity, and breeding to make up for it, it became clearer as he thought on it, and he regretted not having thought it sooner, that it was as though Mr. Jones had been made for Susannah.

Although he had no similar wish for her to encounter the unknown viscount, since that sort of young nobleman was just the type of reckless ornamental wastrel and care-for-nothing that he wanted to shield her from, if her interest in the fellow could interest her enough to move her to going to London to learn even more, why then, it was a worthwhile one. For then she could be in a position to meet Mr. Jones and a dozen other similarly worthy young men.

The robust gentleman wore a bright expression as he strolled down the hall to seek out the innkeeper and get Mr. Jones's direction. He'd find out about the unfortunate viscount, he decided, and regale his sister with the story, suitably edited, when he rejoined her. He didn't pause for a moment to worry about whether her interest in the nobleman might be a lasting one, because he was a fair judge of human nature and he didn't believe it to be any deeper than the easy, romantic concern any impressionable young female might feel after seeing such an unusually handsome, ill-fated young gentleman. And at that, his Susannah, he thought smugly, was far more than just any young woman, for she had a first-rate brain in that beautiful head.

But then, he could be forgiven for his complacency, for he was a doting brother, and it had been, after all, a year since he'd seen his sister, and many more than that had passed since he'd really known her.

Because even as he sought information about the noble coachman, his Susannah—his clever, educated, and sensible young sister—sat back in a chair in their private dining parlor and used all the power of the considerable brain her brother had admired to dissect that last smile she'd received from the young man. And in her mind's eye she reviewed it, turning it about and upside down, wondering what else she could read into it. She'd seen charm there, of course, and since the mockery had been so outsize, she discounted it, as its creator had doubtless intended; she found humor instead, along with a merry sort of self-deprecation, and so she reckoned humility was there as well. It was a great deal to infer from just a smile, but then, it had never been just a smile at all. It had been a revelation to her.

She'd been set on joining Cousin May in Tunbridge Wells, one more stop on her journey to a sufficient age to set up housekeeping by herself being much the same as any other to her. Her brother had been right, which was why she hadn't bothered to dispute him: Cousin May looked to be a bore, Cousin Elizabeth had been one, but she hadn't expected anything else from them. She didn't expect much more from her life. She might well have an education, she granted that she had some wit, and though she doubted she was as exquisite a creature as her devoted brother thought, she believed she'd do. It was just that she knew there wasn't any place for her anymore, at least, not in any world she knew.

She supposed it was her father's fault, but even if it were, she couldn't help but be grateful to him anyway. Raised by a fond papa and two older, protective and adoring brothers, she imagined that she might have grown to be a shockingly conceited, spoiled young woman. From earliest days her least frown had brought instant comforting, her largest mischief only indulgent chuckles. She had only to breathe to be admired, and being wrapped in unrelenting love, might have grown to adulthood never knowing or caring about how to win or deserve it. But her father in his wisdom had foreseen that, and wanting to save her from the results of unquestioning love equally as much as he'd wanted to lavish it upon her, he'd taken the harder road for himself and sent her off to school to be educated. It had saved her from conceit. It had also ruined her for the life it prepared her for.

Miss Spring's Academy for Young Women was an excellent school, with lofty tuition fees and a manor to house its students in what was as fine as any nobleman's principal seat. It attracted those who could afford it, and those who wished to be taken for those who could afford it. Miss Spring elevated the academy even more by instituting the discreet policy of letting titled young women in for a reduced fee so that the common young women's families, such as Miss Susannah Logan's, might think their offspring would be equipped to eventually socialize with just that class of person they'd been to school with. It was a clever ploy, and the academy prospered, even if some of its graduates broke their hearts colliding with the real world when they entered it. But this didn't affect the school's reputation at all.

After all, just as Miss Spring envisioned, any scheme that had to do with matters of social climbing and status would be amply protected by the secrecy of all involved. And so it was, for silence was kept on both sides. The unlucky young persons who weren't admitted into select society when they exited the school were hardly likely to want the world to know it, and after graduation, the titled young persons would scarcely let on about how they'd been little more than charity cases at the academy, or mention how many commoners had attended with them. It was an excellent plan, for the school at least. And Miss Susannah Logan did receive quite an education there.

Perhaps living at school would have been difficult for her wherever she went, for she doted on her family just as much as they did on her. Then too, young females didn't usually receive educations outside their homes unless there were unusual circumstances at work, and whatever girls she'd have met at any school would have been young persons with certain difficulties in their homes, and thus in their own lives as well. And of course, human nature being what it is, only the mediocre can sail through childhood without hurt or insult from their peers. An extremely bright and beautiful young girl encounters just as many problems in growing up as an extremely dull and ugly one does, perhaps more, because she'll be more aware of them. And from the first, Susannah was aware.

Lady Mary might be at Miss Spring's Academy because her papa drank, and the Honorable Miss Amelia might be there because her mama sought a new papa for her and so took a great many lovers in the process of elimination, and even simple little Miss Smythe might be sent there because her papa, a suspicious baronet, had decided her red hair proof that his lady had played him false, and with his best friend this time, but none of them had to apologize for any of these family failings for a moment. And Jenny Mason's papa might have been only a man-at-law, even less important than Betty Howard's father, who was a country doctor, and even further down on the scale from Bessie Parsons' mam, who owned a horse farm, and yet they prospered at Miss Spring's. But Susannah Logan's father had started out in life as a fishmonger, and everyone knew it, and no one forgot it.

He was proud of it, and rightly so, for now he had more blunt than anyone else's father at the entire academy, or in the entire county, for that matter. But that didn't make things any easier for his daughter. Because a hundred years earlier he would have remained a fishmonger, hawking eels and waving his mullet under the nose of anyone who dared to challenge its freshness, to the end of his days. Still, a hundred years later, no one could get used to the idea that he was now rich enough, just as he often declared, to buy his own sea to fish in, and name it after himself too, if he'd a notion to.

But then, nothing was stable anymore, not these days. The winds of change were blowing a great many lives off course, for there was a war on and the world was suddenly expanding. Not only were there new inventions being unveiled daily for health and wealth: gas for heat and light, and machines to weave, farm, and cook with—there were new roads to get to new lands to make new trade with, there was talk of someday being able to travel altogether without proper roads, by sailing along tracks in a "Puffing Billy" engine, and those on the coast scanned the skies for the threat of Boney's forces flying cross-Channel in those amazing enormous balloons. Overnight, it seemed, new successful businesses that dealt in these wonders were springing up like the "mushrooms" the quality called the men who made their fortunes from them.

Susannah's Da was a man born for his time. He'd taken his profits in fish and cleverly put them into less ephemeral products: mines, mills, trading companies, and ships. But not one of the gently bred young women, and few of the commoner sort either, could ever forget that the richest young woman in school might have remained firmly in her place in front of her father's fish barrow if he hadn't had the audacity to step out from behind it.

She became a superior student. Books had the power to inspire her, but any hurt they might inflict was a distant, entirely intellectual sort of pain, and they made good companions for an increasingly dreamy girl whose best friends were made of ink and paper. Which was not to say that she shunned the other students. No, she was by nature a gregarious girl. But her living friends were never as close to her as her fictional ones were. Except for Lady Alice, that once, for that long, and then never again.

Lady Alice was exactly Susannah's age. They met at the academy in their first years there, but each was too busy mourning her distant family, and too weary each day from lying awake stifling her sobs every night to pay much attention to each other then. But in time they did. It was only natural, they had so much in common. They both were motherless but home-loving children who enjoyed literature and music and hated the Honorable Miss Mary and their green vegetables and their French mistress, Madame Corday, with an equal passion. Lady Alice was a pretty child with brown ringlets and a merry, open countenance, and when Susannah's Da saw them together one day when he visited the school: two lovely children, one fair, one dark, with their arms around each other's waists, it could be said, just as he was that pleased to always say after, that his heart near broke it was so full from the beautiful sight of it, and as he didn't say, from the pride of it. For he saw the fishmonger's daughter and the duke's own daughter, arm in arm, coming down the stair as though they were equals set on coming on through life together.

It was a friendship that supported both. It helped Lady Alice to bear the fact that she was exiled from her home because of her rakeshame father's depraved entertainments there, and later on, it helped Susannah through the enormous pain of her own father's death. But Lady Alice didn't shed a tear when her papa finally met his end at the hand of a rival for some wench's bed. She only clapped her hands together when she was at last alone with her friend, and said, eyes glowing with sudden joy she'd concealed in all propriety from everyone but her friend of friends:

"Only think, Susannah, now I can go home! But, my dearest, don't frown, for of course, you shall come visit me too. But oh, Sukey, I am free!"

It had been hard for them to separate, they were fifteen and had shared everything for five years of that short span. It was only Lady Alice's promise to have her friend visit during the next summer vacation that kept Susannah's heart high all that long, lonely winter. A dreamer by nature, now a dreamer by reason of necessity, she passed the winter by envisioning the delights of the coming summer: seeing her friend again, and at last meeting her friend's idol, her brother. Susannah knew all about brothers, and took a great deal of what she'd been told about the new duke, newly returned home himself, with a tablespoon of salt. But when he came to the school with his sister to collect Susannah for the promised visit in her six-teenth summer, it was hard for her to fault one wonderful thing she'd been told about him.

He was slender and brown-haired, and if not particularly handsome, with his even features and ready smile, his charm and politeness made up for any lack in his appearance. Best of all, he was all of three-and-twenty, and so was a perfect, safe object of idolatry for Susannah, since he was of an age when he considered all his sister's friends to be infants. In a year he'd seek a wife from their ranks, but in that summer they were still all children to him. And so he spared no effort to be charming to Susannah, for he liked children and she was a particularly lovely one, and his sister's favorite.

It began thrillingly. Their home was a stately one, filled

with the sort of inherited treasures that even Susannah's father had never been able to buy, and it was staffed with a dizzying number of servants who all seemed to have been handed down in the family for ages as well. Lady Alice's aged aunt was a benevolent chaperon, but the house belonged to the new duke and his sister now and they were clearly determined to bring it back to the calm state of grace it had enjoyed before their father's misbehavior had routed them. Though she'd always been cosseted, Susannah's life took on the even tone of privileged leisure that she'd only read and heard about before. She felt as though she were living in an enchanted world where noble, graceful people did even the smallest things with wit and elegance. Every day there were new diversions, as Alice and her brother took their guest on picnics and improvised water parties and led her on riding tours through the neighborhood. The first nights were filled with laughter as Susannah caught Alice up on all the gossip at school, and her friend, in turn, told her all about the neighbors and their peculiarities.

But then, even with their games of cards, and singing and performances at the pianoforte, time, especially on subsequent nights, began to hang heavy. For once the gossip dried up, Susannah realized, there were no exchanges with other people to feed them more. And after those first nights, the young duke, using a young gentleman's prerogative, slipped off into the night to his own diversions.

Each night, then, after those first weeks, the girls went to bed earlier and retired alone, with nothing like the forbidden, deliciously wild giggling sessions that had kept them up half the night, stifling their laughter under their coverlets, at school. Very soon, Susannah thought with disquiet one warm moonlit night as she sat in her room alone, they would be going to bed with the sun, and rising with it, like farmers, not best friends. Yet, she recalled, Alice's letters had been full of local dances, routs, and supper parties. It was then that Susannah began to entertain the most serious doubts about her welcome. She resolved to ask about it first thing in the morning. But she never had to.

For she rose early, before Alice's maid could awaken her, and she slipped into her clothes and went downstairs. She'd worried about how to ask her friend so as to present the matter lightly and avoid the risk of saying anything insulting. She was rehearsing how to put it as she entered the morning room where Lady Alice and her brother were taking coffee after their earlier morning ride and conference. Then she heard them, and so had her answer before she ever had the chance to frame her question.

"Well, Allie, my sweet," the young duke was saying in his usual light, casual tones, "I've racked my brain but I can't think of another place we can safely take her. So if she's truly your friend, I believe the sacrifice of a few weeks of your entertainment is only right. Your beaux must wait, your other friends will understand. She's lovely as a sprite and as clever as you claimed, but there's absolutely no way we can foist our beautiful mermaid on polite society, love, not without disgracing ourselves, and that's all there is to it."

"I do wish you wouldn't persist in calling her that," she heard Alice sigh.

"But, love," the young duke answered, laughing in his gentle, charming fashion, "what else would you call a fishmonger's beautiful daughter?"

Susannah squirmed even now, remembering, even though she sat alone in a parlor of a wayside inn, five years after and a hundred miles away from that place and that one summer's morning moment. But it was a moment that remained evergreen, and appeared whole and clear in her most unsettled dreams, and would, she believed, always.

But on that morning they were all mutually aghast and embarrassed when the young duke spied movement in the corner of his eye and turned in time to see Susannah flee. Being a gentleman, he of course sought her out that very day and apologized handsomely, and being trained to be sensitive to his inferiors, he felt badly about it for a week. But by then she was gone from his home. For being very well-bred herself, she'd accepted his apologies and then given hers to Lady Alice just as nicely when she left two days later, pleading her own brothers' sudden desire to see her home for the summer, after all.

As both girls were extremely polite, having been trained to it in the same classroom, they could never discuss it again, and so after a few stilted letters passed between them, the friendship ended gently, deflating rather than exploding, full of sighs but with no harsh words on either side. Because, Susannah had thought then, as she thought now, what was there to say, after all? She was a fishmonger's daughter, and true gentlemen and ladies of the *ton* were made of older, if not finer, stuff than that.

But she'd been educated as a lady even if she was never to be accepted as one. And when school was done and she came home to live with Charlie and his wife (her other brother living on the Continent, managing their growing businesses' interests there), she found that her education had ruined her for the suitors Charlie brought around. She doubted any of them would have pleased her, but in any case, she scarcely had the opportunity to find out. Although they were impressed by her looks, most of those earnest, rising men of business were dismayed at the amount of her knowledge and the extent of her social graces, fearing she was too far above them, since, having just risen so high, they were not anxious to be brought or thought low in their own homes or bedrooms. Or else they were just the opposite sort, and so, and far worse in her eyes, they were clearly desirous of acquiring her as they would any other souvenir they'd picked up on their travels to the top, and for the same reasons of purely proud show.

The gentlemen she'd dreamed of, and read about, and had been trained to meet and consort with, were not available to her. Unless, of course, they were like those few who'd sought her out even in her obscurity, the sort she'd learned of and scorned even in school: those who were gentlemen born, but out of funds, and so out of desperation willing to sell their names, even to a fishmonger's daughter, in order to live like gentlemen again.

There was no one for her, because she didn't know quite what she was anymore. She had a great deal of knowledge but couldn't be of help with the family business, since all her schooling had to do with things a lady ought to know, such as poetry and art, and she hadn't a grain of skill with math or matters of finance. She'd been told she was beautiful, but if she was, of what use was it? She couldn't be a suitable helpmeet for a man of business, nor could she do more than attract a gentleman's interest. Unable to be a wife, unwilling to be a mistress, there was little else she could think to do except grow old enough to set up her own household.

Ironically, and lately she'd thought it often, she believed she'd become very like the mermaid she'd been named years before. She was, she knew, in some ways just such a hybrid creature, not fitted for one way of life or another. Whatever she was, she was clearly not wholly suitable for the usual sort of life, however she might dream of love, of happiness. That was why she'd refused her brother's latest offer of London for a season with some genteel relative he swore he'd unearthed. That was why she'd been on her way to Tunbridge Wells to live out a few more years in seclusion, until that eventual day when her brothers deemed her old enough to let alone, and let live alone.

Yet tonight she'd had a glimpse of something else. Perhaps because she was still very young, she had not buried hope quite so deep as she'd thought.

She sat back in her chair now, entirely passive, waiting for her brother's return, and she thought of the beautiful young coachman again. If he were truly a gentleman, then he was certainly an unusual one, quite as unusual in his way as she was in hers. For if she were a commoner with the style of a lady, then he was a nobleman taking on the ways of a commoner. But he was more admirable, she thought with sudden painful honesty, for he didn't shrink from the world's opinion as she'd done, as she was now shamed but able to admit she'd done. She took courage from his courage, for she'd overheard his whole encounter with the other young gentlemen, and it was obvious he was willing to work at the most menial chores for his living, though he reaped scorn from his fellows for it.

And so, she thought, picking up that one strand of information she'd gotten and spinning out an entire story from it as daydreamers do, as she always did, surely if such a gentleman wanted a wife, if he hadn't a wife—and he hadn't the look of a married man—he wouldn't think of either money or class in his search. And just like the prince he resembled from all the fairy tales she'd loved, he'd seek out the one lady who suited him, who fitted him as well as her lost slipper fitted her, and he'd love her, whether she were truly a born lady or not.

It was true that this was a great deal to imagine from a very few facts and one small encounter. But she had the time and the imagination and the need to embroider upon it. It was also true that their eyes had met for only a moment, but they had met, and she'd never forget it, so it was not too much to believe that he might remember her if they ever met again. And now she had hopes that they might. Her brother might have been right, she thought: this night might have been a godsend after all. For if nothing else, at least she had hopes again, and if they had any foundation, they were a class above dreams.

She hoped her brother would go about his business discreetly and not embarrass her by betraying her interest. For she decided that she might just go to London after all. It might be that she'd given up too soon on too much. Once, before reality had frightened her away from life, she'd hoped for a great many things. Now it seemed, incredibly enough, as she sat and stared into the firelight and allowed herself to see a certain bright face instead of the flames leaping there, that it might just possibly turn out just the way it did in all her favorite stories, in all her dreams, in all her best, most secret hopes.

3

"Now, this," Warwick Jones said with satisfaction as he strolled into the room, "is much more like it. More like a home than any parlor I've ever seen in an inn, at least," he mused as he seated himself at a planked wooden table and lifted a tankard, twin to the one his seated companion already held to his lips, and raised it to his own. "It makes me quite nostalgic for . . . I'm not quite sure what"—he frowned—"for I'm positive my mama would never have given house room to that pair of chipped china spaniels, much less placed them on the mantel to enchant her guests. Ah well . . . Good God, Julian, what is this concoction?" he asked as he gagged on it, and then, grimacing, wiped his mouth with the back of his hand and demanded, "Have you taken to drinking perfume? I'll swear this is heated bay rum, someone's put a hot poker in a cup of scent. You're supposed to dab it on your cheeks and put it behind your ears, man, to delight the ladies from without, not swill it to destroy yourself from within. You can't be that far down on your luck, Blue Ruin's only a penny a glass, and though it'll make you blind, I believe you'd survive it better than a swallow of this."

He put down his tankard and gazed at his friend, looking very affronted. But the coachman, who had taken off his jacket and high boots, sat relaxed in his shirtsleeves and vest, and only stretched out his legs to the fire to dry the last damp from his pantaloons.

"It's a Jamaican punch our landlord's made in my honor," he replied, unfazed, "and I like it. That's spice and citrus and

38

cinnamon in it, Warwick, but you know it, since as I remember, you're something of an epicurean. And this is his private parlor, and I'm honored, if you're not, that he's lent it to us, because he hasn't a private mousehole left in the Swan tonight, and I told him I wanted some time alone with you. I could hardly ask you to throw your ladies out into the cold."

"You could have asked," the slender gentleman said, laughing. "Oh Lord, Julian," he sighed, "I'm not at all sure I wouldn't have obliged you, too. It's fairly awful having to face what seemed so entrancing face-to-face the night before, the evening after. I should have been thinking back on my little impetuous encounter with the young woman with fond remembrance tonight, instead of actually attempting to converse with her. Which was, by the by, perhaps the only thing I didn't attempt with her last night when we first met. My only excuse is that I'd just passed a dreary week at an aged uncle's bedside. I was spoiling for some merrier sport, I suppose, and went directly to an acquaintance's country home near to my own, by invitation. I won't bother to mention his name, it makes no matter, it turned out the sport there was too merry for me.

"I don't know if I'm too young or too old for orgies," he said on a shrug, "but they don't suit me, so I took off in the night, bound for London, and decided to stop over at the Ship in Brighton. There I met the baron and his young companion, and before I could close my wallet, the other young female showed up. This morning, out of courtesy, I offered them all a ride home with me. By rights, and as a reward for my charity, I ought to have been in London now, with the baron sleeping in his own house, the two young lovelies sleeping with whomever they choose for the night, and I in my own little bed, happily alone at last, sleeping or not. My, whatever has happened to me, Julian?" he asked on a sad smile.

"You didn't used to talk about your young ladies," his friend said from the echoing depths of his tankard, so that only the edges of his grin could be seen above the rim.

"No, and I still don't. It must be quite some time since you've dealt with young ladies, Julian, for I assure you, these two are not of their number," he replied lightly. "No, they are women of business, my dear, I believe one of them even has a card printed up," he mused, as his friend choked on a swallow of punch, "or is it a broadsheet? No matter, the point is that I haven't had much to do with ladies of late, either. Or gentlemen, for that matter. That was why it was so good to see you tonight,"

"Oh yes," the viscount said, his handsome face grown expressionless, "quite a gentleman, driving the Brighton coach and touching my hat to the passengers for a generous tip."

"Is that all you get to touch? Poor lad," Warwick sighed as he won a grin from his companion, "but if a frog can be a prince, I have no trouble recognizing a gentleman in a coachman. It's not the way of it that concerns me, it's the why," he said, fixing his friend with a sudden long and serious stare as he waited for his reply.

"As I said," the golden-haired young man answered, the flickering firelight giving his face its only change of expression, "not a penny to my name, Warwick, I've lost it all, and so, as you see, I wield a whip for the horses and chat up the topside gents for my bread now."

"Driving the Brighton coach after you've driven yourself down the road to perdition? No, I don't see it, Julian. I haven't seen you for a while, true, but you were never a gamester, not a fellow to lose the family home on the turn of a card. And you've always had ample companionship, so you're not a fool to throw it away at the feet of some enticing adventuress, and you look remarkably healthy, so I doubt it was opium-eating that brought you to ruin. I know it wasn't Jamaican punch," he added with a haughty sniff down his long nose at the tankard, "so what was it? You were well enough to grass when last we met."

"No," his friend said slowly, "actually, Warwick, there's the whole of it, I wasn't, I hadn't been for years, you see, only I didn't see, I didn't know."

And then, keeping his voice as calm and steady as he was able, he told his friend all of it. There was little enough to tell, he thought when it was done, and his friend rose and stood against the mantel looking down into the fire, his thin face set, obviously thinking deeply. For it was a simple, trite enough tale, he thought, even as he'd said.

His father had no head for business matters, but even that

was commonplace enough, few gentlemen did, he only needed a good man of business to keep his estates in good heart and his fortune intact. Only, it transpired, his father had engaged a rogue, or at least, to be fair, the fellow had turned into a rogue after decades of good service. He'd run at the last with the last of the funds he could squeeze from the estate, knowing a noose or a transport ship awaited him when his clients found him out, and he'd been entirely successful, for only his body had been recovered when Bow Street located him, swinging from the ceiling of his rented room in Houndsditch. His light lady friend had taken what remained of the money they hadn't squandered or gamed away, and where she'd got to, only her creator knew.

At least the matter had been kept quiet; if his father had known nothing else, he knew the code of the nobility and realized such things must be kept in the family. But since his remaining family consisted of one charming, adorable wife whose pretty head ought not be troubled with money matters, and one young growing son whose shoulders were not yet broad enough to bear the truth, his father had kept the matter to himself and his new man of business.

"I believe the burden hastened his death," the viscount said softly, as his friend nodded, "you remember, Warwick, for at his funeral, Mama said that he had been in a decline in the past months, before the attack that carried him off.

"And then, of course, it was up to Higgins, as his lawyer, to tell Mama, but then, of course, you remember Mama, she was beautiful and gay and utterly lost when serious matters were spoken of. And as Higgins was an old bachelor, and as she could never restrain herself from flirting, God," he said on a reminiscent smile, "she would flirt with the gardeners when they brought in a rose. How was he to know it was just her way? Perhaps it wasn't, maybe she was interested in him at that, he certainly thought so. That's why, he said, he didn't tell her. He didn't want, he said," the viscount said in a louder voice, with a trace of temper coloring his speech, "to coerce her into accepting his suit. That's why I didn't know that the fellow was secretly footing all our bills, keeping me in school, and keeping the estate solvent as he paved the way clear to making her his wife.

"It wasn't charity, I suppose," he said bitterly at last, as his friend looked up at him with a disconcertingly vivid blue stare, "as he was only feathering his own nest, thinking he'd be her next husband. And as to that, I would've been in gravy if he'd become my new father. Higgins was a wealthy man. *Is* a wealthy man," he corrected himself.

"And I wonder," he added, lowering his head so that he could avoid his friend's complete and piercing gaze, "if I'd have protested if when he'd married Mama, he'd continued to keep me in the state I was raised to think was natural. Would I have requested a look at the books any more than I'd have asked it of my father? I never did ask him, you know. Would I have asked any pertinent questions if my pockets were left full and my tailor's bills paid and my club fees in on time? I don't know, Warwick," he said at last, shaking his head so violently that his fair hair rippled in the firelight and obscured his light, suspiciously glittering eyes for a moment. "We were taught to be gentlemen, and nothing else, weren't we?" he asked in an unsteady voice.

After a silence, he raised his head and went on more easily in his usual light and natural tones:

"That's hardly fair, you were always something more, weren't you? But no matter, none of it matters actually. There was that stupid carriage accident, and she was gone before I could get home to say good-bye. That was over a year ago. I was living in London in our town house then, in quite the grand style. And as she was gone before Higgins could finally nerve himself to ask her to be his wife, by the time I got home I discovered that everything had gone with her."

"Nothing is left?" the other man asked into the quiet.

"As usual, Warwick," the viscount sighed, "you are way ahead of me. No, something is left," he said, before he drained his tankard.

"It would be lovely," Warwick said pleasantly, "to be as brilliant as you always credit me. But it's only a matter of simple observation, Julian. If there was nothing at all left, you'd hardly be sitting here tonight, with your coachman's cape drying in the hall. You'd be off and about the world looking for your fortune. You always were intrepid, if not a little headstrong. Something is holding you here beyond your love for the innkeeper's Jamaican punch, I think.''

The viscount's handsome face was distorted for a moment by an expression somewhere between a grimace and a grin. There was no use attempting evasion; Warwick had always understood his mind, from the first moment they'd met at school. He'd been nervous and defensive as always that first day in a new school, because he'd learned his appearance sometimes provoked other boys to test his mettle. And so when he'd come into his newly assigned room and seen a strange gangling youth staring at him, with his head slightly down and forward and held to one side to present one bright eye, in the pose that he'd come to learn was characteristic, he'd demanded at once:

''Is there something amiss with my cravat, sir?''

The boy had continued to gaze at him, seeing things, he realized later, that no one else could see or had ever seen in him, before he'd answered, displaying that strangely winning half-smile he often wore:

''Nothing, my friend, but you needn't get huffy just because I'm amazed. It isn't often that an oil painting walks through my door. It must be most difficult for you. But what a pleasant problem. Now,'' he'd gone on mildly, ''if you'd gaped at me, I wouldn't have bothered to ask. I'd have known it was my cravat.''

He'd not known what to say in reply to such candor and good humor, so he'd only laughed. And that had begun their friendship.

Although to this day, he thought, eyeing the slender man, he didn't know what Warwick Jones derived from it. Even then Warwick had been acknowledged to be brilliant; his tutors would have adored him if they hadn't been so nervous about him. For he was a solitary fellow, not so much alone, as apart from all the others. His comprehension seemed years above his fellows', his humor often soared over their heads, and though his elders appreciated it, it disconcerted them, for it was admitted to be idiosyncratic. That humor, the viscount thought now, was the only sign that Warwick had ever been a boy, for otherwise he seemed to have been a grown man since childhood. It was only his willingness to create his famous complex pranks that had shown his actual age.

His classmates might have envied him his ease with studies, and some might have resented his outspokenness, but few ever tried to physically best him. He'd been an athletic young man and a successful sportsman, taking advantage of that edge that only a keen mind can lend to a trained body. And when he was provoked beyond tolerance, on the rare occasions, when still a boy, that he could be, and lost control of his emotions, he was absolutely terrifying because then it became clear why he kept his anger so tightly leashed, for once unloosed, he lost touch with all else but winning, including the possibility of losing his life. But then when that happened, of course, he never lost.

He came from an old, monied family. He had no title, for as he explained, the canny Joneses from his peculiarly bent branch of the family had always passed up the honors and fame, and knowing the nature of kings, had always kept their heads low to prevent them from being lopped off. When their neighbors were being beggared by the honor of entertaining the queen who'd just elevated them to an earldom, he'd once said, his family had immediately hidden all the silver plate in the backyard and sent a delegation to her, in rags, asking for a loan. That way, he'd explained reasonably, even though she'd refused them, they'd been able to afford to buy their neighbor's estate in the next generation, when that luckless family had run through all their funds carrying on in the style in which they thought they must as noblemen.

But then, the viscount thought, with Warwick, one never knew which of his tales to believe. The most dazzling one, at least, was true. He had one ancestor who defied the family wisdom and came out into the open and courted a king, and so gained fame even as he lost everything. Warwick's great-great-grandfather had supported Charles and when that unhappy monarch lost his head his supporter had been allowed to keep his own, but little else. He'd had his property and funds stripped from him. Then the fellow had turned to a life of elegant crime. He became one of the first famous gentlemen highwaymen to plague and delight the nation by holding up travelers, with exquisite style and grace, as they attempted to travel the deserted heaths leading from London. "Gentleman Jones" had swung for it, from a gibbet improvised on the spot to mark the scene of his greatest triumphs. It had been a sensation. The ladies had wept, the balladeers had sold out all their song sheets, he'd been such a merry fellow that even his victims, they said, had come to his farewell, to drink champagne with him the night before he was turned off. And the greatest joke of all was that though they'd caught the culprit, they never located his ill-gotten gains, although his young son, when grown to manhood, suddenly came up with enough money, from somewhere, to buy back all the family holdings even before Charles's own son had a chance to sit on his restored throne long enough to restore them to him.

It was easy to see that bold ancestor in the lurking humor in Warwick's own dark face, and find the fellow's last jest still shining in those knowing, hooded eyes. Warwick was a fellow who kept to himself, kept his own counsel, and gave out only that which he thought he should. He didn't seem to need anyone, being totally contained and self-sufficient, for though he was offered many, Warwick had few fast friends. But those he had, he held, and kept complete faith with. Why he believed he should be his friend, why he'd ever decided upon it in the first place, the viscount didn't know, had never known, but he was grateful for it. For it was comforting, Julian Dylan thought, watching the gentleman pace from the hearth to the table and back again, contemplating his problem, to speak with a true friend again, even if he was resolved that he'd ask for nothing more than his advice, and accept no more than his concern.

"Then you've not lost the manor, have you?" Warwick asked as though he already knew the answer.

"No, but not only because it's entailed and it would be the devil to get through the courts to the auction block. I've earned enough to keep it," the young man said with some pride, "and keep it going, but barely. I can't live in it, of course," he said on a rough laugh, "but I can keep its grass scythed and its roof intact. I've made arrangements with some pensioners, they live there and take care of the place for little more than a pittance and that intact roof over their heads. That much, at least, a coachman can do."

"Then it should be a simple matter to turn things around again," his friend said with a relieved smile. "You can get enough, putting up the estate as security, to invest handsomely. Then, within a few years you may buy your own coaching company if you're still that keen on the job."

"You expect me to go to the moneylenders with Elmwood Court, and then gamble with it?" the viscount asked in disbelief, sitting bolt upright.

"Not," his friend replied negligently, "to the moneylender . . . me. And I never gamble, I invest."

"I see," the viscount said sadly, settling back in his chair. "Thank you, Warwick, but no. If I'd wanted charity, I could have come to you at once, my friend, and I know it, and I thank you for it. Or, failing that, I could have gone to Higgins. True, the old man married before daffodils could spring up on Mama's grave. It seemed once he'd gotten his mind set on wedded bliss, he didn't let death deter him, he married some other lucky widow months after he'd bid Mama farewell. But he liked me and I imagine he'd have felt guilty enough about it to have been a soft touch, he was a decent chap. But I don't take charity, you see, not from friends."

"And it's difficult enough to get it from foes," the gentleman agreed with some asperity. "Do not insult me, Julian," he went on, his easy manner replaced by cold scorn, "I'm not a fool, and even if I thought you were after a handout, I don't believe you'd have entreated heaven to bring you an ice storm to strand me here with you in this end-of-the-world inn so that you could set me up for one tonight. You were always a favorite of the fates, lad, but that's stretching it too far. No, obviously it was your damnable pride that kept you from seeking my help immediately. And that's a pity. For the definition of help is not charity, and a friend is supposed to help another. Where were you during our English classes, Julian, not to mention chapel?

"I'm an excellent investor, Julian, it is one of my pastimes, actually. That fellow who stopped me in the hall on the way in here tonight, that citified fellow, he's only one of my business partners. You recoil in horror, my dear?" Warwick said with a hint of anger, "but this is 1814, not the good old days when a gentleman could afford to sit back and watch his serfs toil for the good of the king and country, an acre of land, and a healthy cow. Life's expensive these days, and getting dearer. If a gentleman doesn't soil his hands with trade, he may not have anything to trade with in a few decades.

"But then," he said, shrugging, and turning his back to his friend to gaze into the fire again, "perhaps you're right. Why listen to me? I am, after all, not a nobleman. I suppose you can go on driving your coach. Perhaps you can find some wealthy girl to wed. My merchant friend from the city was just inquiring after you, by the by, and he gave me to understand that he has a lovely sister. That might be a good course for you to follow. It's not filthy trade, nor hard work if she's handsome and complacent enough. And certainly a dowry is not charity."

"Warwick," the viscount said, shaking his head and laughing, "oh Warwick, I have missed you," he said, rising and clapping his friend on the shoulder, "for I think I would have planted any other fellow in the world a facer for saying what you just did. But you've always known how to get around me. I'll put Elmwood Court up for security, and I'll give you complete authority to invest whatever it's worth. It makes perfect sense, but I've no head for business. I'd be pleased to go partners with you if you promise not to conceal losses, nor pad winnings."

His friend turned and fixed him with such an outraged stare that the blond gentleman fell to laughing again, even as Warwick said haughtily:

"There is never any need for me to conceal that which never occurs," before he relented, and grinning, said, with a nod, "Done then, Julian, we'll see you out of this tangle entirely in a few years."

But then the viscount sobered.

"That might not be soon enough," he sighed. When his friend looked at him curiously, he added, "There are some things you cannot help me with. You were right, it's not only Elmwood Court that's kept me here. There's a lady, you see, that I cannot bear to leave, and yet can't afford to have just now."

"She's handsome and she seemed content enough. I wouldn't

have thought it would take that much to support a serving wench," his friend said carefully, watching him closely.

"No, not Nan, she's a good girl," the viscount sighed, "but as I said, a diversion merely. There is a lady, though. I met her last year and we were on our way to a firm understanding when the ground fell out from beneath me."

"And she will not wait for you? Then she's hardly worth having, is she?" Warwick said dismissively, though he remained watchful.

"She would wait, I know she'd wait till Judgment Day, and I know she'll be thrilled when I tell her of my new prospects. But it's not her, it's her brother, he's the one who wants her to wed high and wealthily. They've no parents, he has complete control of her future. Even when it seemed I had all, it didn't seem to be enough for him," he said in frustration, his light eyes glowing with suppressed anger. "He's kept her single two full Seasons, although she's had spectacular offers for her hand, I suppose waiting for the most spectacular one of all before he lets her go."

"Come, Julian, with your face and fatal attraction to her sex, don't tell me you can't get her to fly in her brother's face and fly with you?" Warwick smiled.

"No," the viscount said softly, proudly, "for she, you see, is a lady."

"Oh, Julian," his friend laughed outright, "haven't you learned, with all your experience? Real life is not an Arthurian romance. There's not that much difference between ladies and serving wenches as all that. No, even I, who am a gnome to your Adonis, have learned that it's the highest and the lowest who are most willing to kick over their traces and come to a fellow's bed, whatever society says. The highest, because they believe they can do no wrong; the lowest, because they don't care if they do. It's only the poor little ones in the middle, of the bourgeoisie, the kind you're not likely to meet in any event—very like my merchant friend's shy sister, who must ask her brother to ask his friend to ask after a gentleman she fancies—who are afraid. They're the only ones who'll never come ringless to your bed."

As he was chuckling at his own jest, he didn't see the

viscount's expression until he spoke, and then that cut off his laughter abruptly.

"Lady Moredon is not like that," the viscount said angrily, lifting his chin, his nostrils flaring. "She is a lady in every sense of the word. I don't think you should even discuss her, Warwick, for I don't believe you've ever met her like."

"Lady Moredon?" Warwick said immediately, all traces of amusement vanished, ignoring the insult, even if he credited it. "Are you mad? Lady Marianna Moredon? Lord Robert's sister? Good God, what are you thinking of? He's a very bad man. And she's an Incomparable. With twice a fortune, he'd never consent to your suit, he never liked you. Don't you recall? He was four forms above us in school and never tolerated anyone who wouldn't bend to his every idiot whim. He's both greedy and pompous. Actually, I've always thought him very like the pink pig he resembles, and he's as dangerous as a wild boar at that, for he's no sense of humor, or honor, or humanity.

"Yet," he added, calming, "I suppose it's as well that she's caught your interest, for it's a safe-enough passion. But, Julian, not for a hot-blooded fellow like you, since it's bound to be tame as the love for a lady in a picture book. For you'll never get near her, you know."

"But I do and I have," the viscount answered quietly, taking up his friend's abandoned tankard. "She writes to me, and she meets with me when she can. But only that," he said at once, with a warning flash in his eyes, the tankard held steady at his lips, "for, as I said, she is a lady."

"Julian, I'm quite sincere, be careful," his friend said in deadly serious tones, his thin brows lowered over worried eyes.

"But of course," the blond gentleman said, taking a large swallow of punch before adding with a small smile, "I can be little else, can I?"

"Aye, there's that," Warwick replied, the tension of the moment gone. "Now then, since you've stolen my tankard of scent, do you think we can get your, ah, diversion to bring me something decent, like a lovely glass brimming with ginever and lemons? Then we can talk of more pleasant things, and lie a great deal to each other and ourselves and make a delightful night of it, after all.''

The two gentlemen passed the night talking and drinking and toasting each other and all their memories and most of their future plans as the other private dining rooms were abandoned and the patrons of the common taproom began to wander off to their separate rooms or cubbies. They raised a toast to absent friends and present enemies, and laughed a great deal as the inn settled down to stillness, and would have remained there, doing so until the dawn, until they noted the fact that Nan refused to bring them any more tankards of anything but coffee.

"Protecting her interests," Warwick grumbled. "Remind me not to drink with a serving wench's lover again. I only got enough to keep me from freezing to death tonight simply because she wanted to ensure getting enough to keep her warm as well.''

"Alas, poor Warwick," his companion said, causing his friend to grin despite himself at their oldest jest. "My sympathies," he went on as they finally left the parlor to part for the night, "but you've such a hard head, she'd have to serve you for a week before you'd have had enough to notice.''

"Poor lass, how selfish of me, when she was all atwitter to serve you. Good night, my friend," Warwick said, shaking hands as he took the first stair to his room. "I'm bound for London at dawn, so doubtless I'll see you then, if, that is, she allows you to rise for anything but her own purposes.''

And on a laugh, they said good night.

Late as it was, they were not the last to retire. For once the hallway was clear and the inn was quiet, Mr. Charles Logan deemed it safe to lead his sister to her rooms after their long night of discussion and decision. He was tired, but pleased, because after an evening of cajolery and argument she'd consented, at last, to go to London for the season. Although, he thought, once he'd left her to her yawning maid, all that had been for the form of it, solely for the sake of face, because he'd known what her decision would be moments after he'd reentered their parlor much earlier in the night. All discussion had been unnecessary, he thought on a contented chuckle as he entered his own room, from the moment he'd given her his news.

For, yes, he'd reported, the coachman was a true nobleman, and the poor lad was down on his luck through no fault of his own, and being as noble in nature as he'd been in birth, he was attempting to better his fortunes by any sort of work he could turn his hand to. And he wasn't a bit of a snob, for wasn't his best friend, his old school friend, a mere "Mr. Jones"? And wasn't Mr. Warwick Jones her own brother's good friend? And wasn't that gentleman pleased to know of his interest in his unlucky friend, almost as glad as he was to hear that Mr. Logan had a lovely unwed young sister to introduce him to in London? Well, perhaps his news had not actually been the "news," Mr. Logan corrected himself, but what was needful to tell her. And most of all, he decided, as a good businessman should, what was right to tell her. Because, he thought happily as he settled down to sleep, hadn't it made her say yes?

Mr. Warwick Jones was a little concerned as he opened the door to his room, not castaway, nor reeling, for he never got quite that inebriated; he was merely a little blurred and a bit less serious than usual. He didn't feel the chill of the room quite so much when he removed his shirt, and as he approached his bed it might have been that he didn't regret booking a separate room for the young woman he'd brought with him, even though he usually enjoyed having a bit of company in a strange bed in a strange inn. Because, he reasoned, as best he could under the circumstances of several glasses of ginever, after an arduous night the young woman had nevertheless woken him this very morning in the most extraordinary fashion, and enough, he decided prudently, as he removed his breeches, was sufficient.

So he was somewhat less than delighted when he turned back his covers and heard a light giggle.

"I thought you'd never come to bed," she said, reaching up for him. "I was so lonely," she pouted.

"Charlotte, my sweet," he sighed, "you flatter me."

"No," she laughed, "it's Jennie, your sweet. Charlotte

got tired of waiting and went back to her own room. I saw her leave, that's when I came.''

Sitting up, he could just see, in the dimness, that there was a great deal more young woman in his bed than there had been the previous night, and that the hair, on her head at least, was red, not blond.

''Nothing could wake the baron,'' she said piteously, twining her arms about his neck and pulling his head down to her, ''and I got so lonely.''

The baron, he thought a few moments later, must be dead, poor man.

When at last, sometime later, he had persuaded her to go back to the baron's bed, or bier, to the tune of his insincere insistences that she must, to spare poor Charlotte's feelings and the baron's as well, if he still lived, and her fears of a fall from favor softened by the nice cushion of bills he pressed upon her, only as a gift, he claimed, as he knew he was expected to, he lay back and waited for his head to clear, or sleep to come. What he did not expect was another human visitor.

After the door closed as softly as it had opened, he felt a slight weight land on his bed, and a cool hand on his person, and he sighed, but not with the pleasure she'd hoped, and then he laughed, though not from the delight she'd envisioned.

''Charlotte,'' he said, brimming with secret mirth, ''I thank you, sweet, how considerate of you, but you see, I've imbibed so much and it's so late, I'm afraid I simply can't oblige you tonight. Really, my dear, you're as charming and lovely as ever you were last night, but there is a limit.''

Or so he'd thought there was. But then he remembered, when he was able, that she'd said her last steady gentleman patron had been over seventy years of age, and so he supposed it had not so much to do with his prowess as her extraordinary knowledge of anatomy. She might have been a wonderful surgeon, he thought, when he could. But since thinking was never a thing he encouraged in himself at such times, he left off, and as she was remarkably adept, she went on.

It was only after she too had gone, and he was at last alone with his thoughts, that he permitted himself to consider how he'd passed the last of his night. It had been interesting, at the least, different, he rationalized as he settled himself for sleep. The young women had been, for all that he couldn't say he'd known them in any but the biblical sense, very different too. One tasted of cool wine, the other of warm meats, one had the scent of musk about her, the other of gardenias, one had breasts so large he could scarcely encompass one in his hand, the other had scant pointed ones that fit into his palms like the noses of small burrowing animals. One had been quiescent, lying on the bed like a large pillow, only shifting to accommodate him, the other had been an acrobat. One had only moaned and gasped to encourage him, the other kept whispering, murmuring profanities until they were done. And the worst part of it, he thought suddenly, coming half-awake in disquiet, was that even now, only moments later, he couldn't remember precisely which of them had done what.

So the last thought which came to him at the border of consciousness, when dawn slurred the sky with grainy light, had nothing to do with satisfaction and satiation. It had to do instead with a real sorrow and profound distaste for his easily gotten and forgotten pleasures of the night. It nagged at him, burning beneath the pleasant exhaustion he'd worked so hard for. So as always, by training, he doused the discontent quickly, by drowning it entirely in sleep.

The Viscount Hazelton had not been given a room, there was no point in it, for the innkeeper knew that the coachman always took the same one. There was never any profit in it either, since he always shared it with Nan, and she always refused any payment in coin. She asked for little else either, since she was no fool and knew there could be little else between a gentleman such as he, however reduced in circumstance, and such as herself. She only asked for his attentions, and those he was always willing to give her.

She must be tired this night, Julian thought, what with the Swan having been filled to the rafters and the hour being so advanced. But when he came into her bed she came into his arms without hesitation and without a word, so she must have been waiting awake for him despite the hour. She showed him no weariness, and when she smiled at him he saw nothing but eagerness. She'd kept candles burning at the bedside, and as always, when he moved to snuff them before he moved more boldly to her, she said only the once, "No," and reached for him again, saying, "Yes, like that, please."

He shut his eyes at the height of his lovemaking, and so never knew that she always kept hers open wide, with the candles to aid her, for she loved the look of him and had to show herself again and again that it was him, truly him, this beautiful, golden young man, that was with her in reality in her bed, upon her body. It was as well. That knowledge alone of all the things she might have said or done might have kept him from her bed. For he believed their relationship merely a diversion for them both.

When the candles had guttered down to fitful flashes of light and he at last settled down at her side to sleep, his eyes were half-closed as he brushed his lips against her tangled hair and whispered contentedly:

"Ah, you're just the sort of girl I like most, Nan."

"And just what sort is that?" she asked easily, saucily, refusing to give him an idea of how she hoarded up his words.

"Why, the available sort," he said on a warm chuckle.

And since it was a jest and he'd meant it as one, she chuckled too, and feeling her laughter shake her breast beneath his ear, he became interested again and bent his head and put his lips to her again. And thus it might have been that he never noted her fleeting expression of pain at hearing his words, since it so quickly turned into a grimace of pleasure at experiencing his touch, as always.

It was difficult for a great many of the guests at the Swan to sleep that night, no matter how pleasing their accommodations, for not only were many of them otherwise occupied, many more were unused to staying at an inn, or sleeping in any but their accustomed beds. But that wasn't why Miss Susannah Logan lay awake. She couldn't sleep this night because of the sheer excitement of thinking about her tomorrows.

She didn't wish to disturb her maid, snoring gently at her side in a pulled-out trundle bed, so instead of thrashing

and punching her pillow, demanding impossible rest, she sat
bolt upright and waited for the dawn.

She sat in her high chamber, in her white nightdress,
her long fair hair let down to her waist, exactly like the
princess in the tower, and dared at last to dream with her eyes
wide open, of London. Of London, and all the fine gentlemen
and noblemen that she'd so often read and heard about, the
ones she'd been trained up for and then locked away from,
the ones her brother had promised she would now actually
meet. The first of those she'd already seen had decided her on
her future course, and now their names and faces spun in her
mind, keeping her wakeful weaving wonderful stories about
gentlemen such as the beautiful Viscount Hazelton, the elegant Mr. Warwick Jones—all the cultivated gentlemen with
their cultured voices, handsome faces, and high morals and
manners.

4

It was scarcely past true dawn but the courtyard of the Swan was swarming with activity. Curiously, with all the bustle, there was very little chatter. This wasn't due only to the bleary state of most of the guests who spilled, blinking, from the inn into the daylight. It was because most of them found the sight of the bright morning lowering, if not actually embarrassing. The temperature had come up with the new day, and now there wasn't a trace to be seen of the hazardous ice that had caused them to be stranded in the night, not a thing left to show there'd ever been any good or sufficient reason for any courageous person to have halted a journey the previous day.

There remained only a thin glaze covering sodden slush, and that transparent skin crackled underfoot before it joined the rest and rapidly dissolved. But even without spectacular evidence, the guests would have been abashed, for as always when the world returns to normalcy after a disaster, the fears and secret terrors experienced at the height of the emergency seem foolish and overblown in the calm light of a normal day. And it was such an ordinary breezy, early-spring sort of morning that now everyone remembered his place, the coachmen began to take over the world again, and the world shifted back into its real and mundane focus.

Even the elegant gentleman who'd come to the courtyard in his shirtsleeves to see the *Thunder* off had little to say to the golden-haired coachman who sat on his high box and prepared to set the distinctively painted gold-and-yellow coach into motion. He only handed a card up to the fellow, and said, a smile playing on his lips:

"Here is my direction, in case you've forgotten. And if you've forgotten, I believe you'll have to forget our friendship as well. For I expect to see you soon, Julian, if not sooner than that."

"Oh, aye, Warwick," the coachman said, giving one gloved hand down to the gentleman before he said easily, "Now, go back to the inn before you contract a pneumonia, it's not your funeral that I expect to see in London."

But the gentleman disregarded the coachman's orders. He stepped back to watch the *Thunder* fill, seemingly oblivious of the cool wind that snapped at his shirt to send it billowing out from his lean form like a sail and scattering his soft hair into even more casual fashionable disarray than his barber had done.

After the guard loaded the passengers into the coach and made sure all were present and accounted for, he grasped hold of the carriage, preparing to swing himself up to his perch at the back of it. But before he could, he felt a light touch upon his sleeve. The elegant gentleman who had detained him smiled easily and handed him a coin which made his eyes widen, for the fellow wasn't a passenger, and few of them tipped so handsomely anyway. But a calling card with the name and address of one "Warwick Jones" on it went with the coin, and the gentleman inclined his head toward the front of the carriage and said only:

"See he doesn't lose this, will you? There's a good chap."

"Aye," the guard replied slowly, comprehension dawning as he looked the gent up and down, pricing him as he did, "I'll see to it, for 'e's a good chap too, you know."

"Oh, I know," the gentleman said lightly, and still smiling, went back into the inn.

It was only moments later, as the guard began to raise his horn to his lips, preparatory to blowing the first notes signaling departure, the tune of which would blend in with the echoing, fading sound of the *Royal George*'s tin, which had left only moments before, that the fashionably dressed blond young woman stepped into the courtyard and prepared to enter a private coach. She checked, and the stout blond gentleman with her hesitated as well. He turned to see what caused her sudden start and saw the fair coachman on his high box smiling down at her. The older gentleman paused only a second, and then, waving his hand to the fellow, cried merrily:

"Good morning, and a fair trip to London, my lord!"

"Oh, Charlie," the young woman wailed after she reached the privacy of their coach, "how could you?"

"Nothing to it," he chuckled, but then, seeing her flushed face, regretted his impulse and so said with some impatience, "You make too much of it, it's the sort of thing fellows do, Sukey. Why, you ought to get used to it, for you may be meeting up with the fellow again, and soon too. Can't snub a chap and then expect to make his acquaintance with a pleasant how-do-you-do," he grumbled as he tipped his hat over his eyes, not at all sure he was right, but he believed coach rides were for sleeping anyway, so the sooner he got to it and away from her accusing eyes, the better.

She had looked even lovelier in the daylight, the coachman discovered himself thinking as he threaded the reins through his left hand and raised the whip in his right one. She was certainly a spectacularly beautiful young creature, he mused as the guard blew three strident notes and then began to improvise on the theme of an old drinking song to delight the topside passengers and drive the guard on the *Dart*, which waited behind them, to despair, for the fellow couldn't play half so well. Close up, the coachman continued to muse as the *Thunder* edged forward, he'd seen that she had the most amazing brown eyes, and skin that looked like it would be like petals to the touch . . . and then thinking of touching, he remembered to look back to the inn and wave a farewell to an upper window, and grinned as the slightly opened shutters there swung closed with an indignant snap.

As his route took him past the coach the flaxen-haired unknown had just entered, he glanced across to it, and seeing that lovely face at the window, and seeing the sudden surprise in it, he smiled the wider, and for the second time since he had first seen her he sketched a bow, only a briefer one this time, for he didn't wish to give his cattle any wrong notions. And for the second time, she gasped and drew back, and having no door to shut in his face, drew her shade down at once over the sight of his impudence.

Two smiles, he thought on another smile, as the *Thunder* pulled away, and two windows closed on him for them. But his spirits didn't sink, in fact they rose higher with every breath he took of the cool morning air and with each step his horses brought him closer to london. For he wasn't thinking of either of the two females at all now, not the lovely blond girl who'd given him her admiration, nor the obliging brown-haired wench who'd given him all else, for they were negligible, each in her own way only a brief delight briefly noted. Instead he envisioned the cool, lovely countenance of a lady. His true lady, who lay in London and was completely unavailable to him and yet who drew closer to him with each milestone he passed. And soon, thinking on his lady, he delighted the topside gentlemen by raising a sweet tenor to join them, as they accompanied the guardsman in his rendition of "A Lover and His Lass."

Miss Susannah Logan's coach was one of the last to pull out from the courtyard, but if Mr. Warwick Jones noted it at all, he saw only the back of it as he glanced out the window again and drummed his fingers on the tabletop. He only knew that his was going to be the last to do so, and as he'd known it for the last hour, he was in a towering temper as the baron finally seated himself at the table and groaned, clutching his head, wondering if he might be able to make it to the coach. Mr. Jones wished he had some hemlock to give him so that he could be at least carried out, unprotesting, when the landlord obliged with a foaming drink that looked equally noxious, but seemed just the remedy the baron had been seeking.

Mr. Jones, a gentleman to his fingertips, as the two young women agreed as they drove back to London, insisted on giving them and the baron sole use of his coach for the journey. He himself, he claimed, would travel outrider style to see that no highwaymen lurked at Gibbet Hill, despite the fact that he knew very well that none had for over a decade.

Although Mr. Jones was the last to arrive in London, he was one of the first to reach his destination. Not only did he live in the heart of town, once he'd gotten there he'd dropped his passengers off and settled accounts with them with stunning speed and such grace that they didn't know whether to be pleased or dismayed with him until after his dust had died down behind them.

Once ensconced in his favorite chair in his study in a dressing gown so old as to be a friend, he sat back and sighed with relief. A fire mumbled nicely in the grate; he looked about the room to all the curios and books and works of art he'd collected, and felt a great and deep content.

So it was odd that he soon felt restless, and rose from his chair and paced the room, and finally, with a deep sigh, rang for his valet to help him dress again. For the ormolu clock on the mantel insisted on reading only three.

But there was a book he wanted to buy, and he remembered the chore with rising good humor, and after he'd seen to that, a dinner to be had, and then various places to visit in the night: an opera, a play, and a lively possibility that he might find some attractive willing young person to help him pass the rest of it. This time, he mused, a quiet friendly one would be pleasant to have stay with him. Then he paused, and thought of what might actually be nicer, and laughed to himself, alarming his valet, but he was only thinking that not only was he being absurd, he must be getting greedy. He'd already located one real friend, and with any luck at all, would see him again soon.

The Logans reached their destination in London at the same time that Mr. Jones was gratefully sinking into his club chair, even though they'd set out earlier than he had. This wasn't only because Mr. Logan was a cautious man who didn't love speed for its own sake and was no expert judge of horseflesh. He was, above all, an excellent man at business, and however sturdy his horses or well-sprung his carriage, he reasoned that an overworked horse worked for less time in the long run, and a carriage jolted pell-mell over roads needed more repair than one that went at a reasonable clip. So it was a safe, sound two in the afternoon when the Logans' coachman pulled up at number fourteen on a long gray street.

There was complete silence within the coach. Then the gentleman spoke, far too heartily.

"Well, puss," he said jovially, "here we are. Don't look so grim. She's probably the cheeriest body imaginable. She's a bit past her prime, but lively as can be, doubtless that's why she welcomed a visit from a young person and seemed so eager to be back in the social swim again. It don't look too promising here, but it ain't a slum and she does have connections."

"Oh, Charlie," Susannah protested immediately, shamed that he might have seen her disappointment at the sight of the row of unimpressive houses, especially after all her talk of disinterest in the social whirl, "it's enough that she's willing to take me in."

"No, it's not," he replied, taken aback. "What would be the sense of having you come here otherwise? It's shabby here, I grant you, but flash ain't everything with the really old gentry. Respectability, Sukey, that's the ticket. Come, we'll give it a try," he announced before she could resist further. "Faint heart never won fair lady, nor old lady, neither."

He guffawed at his own humor as he handed her out, for a businessman has to have a thousand jests at his command and should always know when to put the light touch to a ticklish situation, and ought to laugh heartily at his own wit as well so that the other fellow doesn't feel stupid or left out and knows it for a jest. But his Susannah never had a head for business, he remembered, when she didn't reply at all but only gazed at him, troubled.

She didn't know this relative her brother had discovered, any more than she knew London, she thought as she reluctantly went up the stair. And respectable or no, she suddenly wondered how Charlie expected some middle-aged lady, however genteel, to see her into the *ton,* or even into proximity of such dashing fellows as the Viscount Hazelton—unless she bought a seat on his coach for her.

She grew even graver when she reached the door and saw a black wreath hung upon the knocker. Her mood did not alter greatly when a wizened maid, dressed in what seemed to be layers of rusty black, opened the door to them. Only then did Susannah's expression change, to one of astonishment, when the old creature squinted at the card she was handed and then snapped:

"Dead. She's dead."

And closed the door in their faces.

They stood there too astonished to say a word, and it was only when Mr. Logan's ears began to grow ruddy that the door was pulled open again.

A female of middle years and height, plump and plain and gray as a field mouse and dressed simply but all in that same hue, stood before them, her distressed round face showing her only color: two high red splotches upon her cheeks.

"I am so sorry," she said at once in a pleasant voice. "Do forgive Agnes, she's old as the hills, and we don't get much company. She went to show me your card, you see, for she cannot read, and was so intent on it that she remembered only that she oughtn't to leave the door standing open, for a cat once got in, and Mrs. Anderson loathed them, and she was scolded . . . I am so sorry," she said suddenly, aghast, as though someone else were talking that she'd just gotten a chance to interrupt, "for there you are, still outside, while I ramble on. Do come in," she pleaded, "and I'll try to explain all."

They were led to a small parlor, and after they'd seated themselves, their distraught hostess began speaking at once.

"Mrs. Anderson passed on a few weeks ago, and more's the pity, for I know she was eagerly awaiting your visit. Of course, she was extremely old, you know. Or perhaps you don't," she said, watching their expressions closely. "But then, she was rather vain, and so I'm not surprised she never admitted it to you. But not in the least infirm, you understand, and as she'd once been very social—oh, yes," she put in, seeing the young woman's eyebrows rise slightly, "her husband was one of the Berkshire Andersons, they were always at court when the old king was in his right mind. Your proposed visit excited her enormously, it would have given her an excuse to renew old acquaintances, or at least discover which of them were still living. She had such a successful funeral, everyone was there, she would have been so gratified . . ." She sighed and then went on more firmly, "But the point is that her heart gave out suddenly, and so a great many plans have had to be changed. I'm a connection of her late husband, and was pleased to be her companion in recent years. But you've arrived just as I've done packing. I'm leaving today. Mrs. Anderson's sister has inherited all, you see, and as she'd married out of their circle, and retired to the country and acquired, ah, a different style of life in the past years, I find I would not suit, and so have given in my notice.''

"But surely her sister will honor her obligations to us," Mr. Logan objected, dismayed and clearly prepared to argue.

"Oh, certainly, decidedly," the woman agreed, getting to her feet immediately. She began to say more, changed her mind, stood hesitant, and then with something very like a shrug said sadly, "Please wait," and left the room.

"Too high in the instep," Charlie said wisely, when she'd gone, "likely that's why she's leaving. Just as well. Maybe Mrs. Anderson was too starched-up for you too. But her sister's a connection of ours as well, remember, so this might even work out better."

But as Susannah didn't look any more convinced of this than he felt, he subsided. Enough time passed so that he was about to admit that the late Mrs. Anderson he'd dug up from family gossip was a very distant relative indeed, a cousin twice removed, and Susannah was about to tell her brother that Tunbridge Wells was not actually the end of the world, as it was on several stagecoach routes, when they both heard voices coming from the hallway that led to the parlor.

They both heard *a* voice, actually; the other accompanying sound was all made up of soft, broken, half-phrased apologetic cautions and only formed a pattering background for the great trumpeting main theme of noise.

"Good Lord," the bass voice complained, "a party can't close her eyes but she's dragged up by the hair by some fools. Tessa, you've got no brains, jingle-brained creature, rousting me from a good rest to see some common . . . Don't shush *me*, my girl," the voice roared, impossibly enough actually able to pick up in volume in anger. "I don't care who hears . . . Damnation!" the voice thundered after a crash was heard. "Who put that table there? Well, well, get on with it, where are they?''

Susannah and her brother were both standing when their relative staggered into the salon, supported by the gray-haired woman who'd greeted them at the door.

"This," that unhappy lady said to them, "is Mrs. Anderson's sister. Mrs. Pruit, here are the Logans."

The massive woman she introduced teetered into a chair, and sank down there, her voice the exact tone as the protesting chair's as she cried, "Well, get me something to drink, idiot. Meeting up with relatives is thirsty work, isn't it?" she added, regarding her visitors at last and giving them a ferocious wink.

She was large in form and frame, and all her considerable person was wrapped in a varicolored day robe that gapped wide in every place a person viewing her wished that it would not. The strong aroma of lily-of-the-valley scent that came from that garment was still not strong enough to overwhelm the odor of alcohol which emanated from her, with the result that the small room soon began to reek as though it were springtime in a distillery.

"Eh, Tessa," she bellowed at the gray-haired woman, "tell that lazy slut in the kitchen, the usual for me. And what's your pleasure?" she asked her visitors good-naturedly.

"Do you possibly have a coaching schedule?" Susannah blurted anxiously.

The Logans waited in their coach and passed their time arguing spiritedly. Then, although Susannah deplored it, as soon as her brother saw the gray-haired woman leave the house, he sprang from the coach to join her on the stair. Susannah saw him tip his hat and talk animatedly, and after a time the gray-haired woman nodded slightly. Then Charlie signaled to the coachman, who went to secure the woman's luggage, and to Susannah's surprise and disquiet, the door to the coach opened and the woman joined her.

"This," Charlie said happily, when he had seated himself again, "is the Contessa Miriam della Casandro, Sukey."

"I'm sorry I neglected to introduce myself earlier," the woman explained softly, inclining her head as a greeting, "but you see, I was in rather a hurry."

"She's graciously consented to be your companion during

your stay in London," Charlie added proudly. "And she ain't doing it for the blunt, neither," he cautioned his sister as she stared at the squabs and looked for a crack in the plump cushions that she could crawl into to die of embarrassment. "No," he gloated, "for she's got her pick of positions. She's doing us a favor."

"Indeed, I was once young too," the contessa said, smiling at Susannah sympathetically, "although never so beautiful, I believe. Still, I had looked forward to your visit as much as Mrs. Anderson did, and am pleased I survived to facilitate it, for though I have no fixed residence at the moment, I too have some social connections. Now," she asked comfortably, "the only question remaining is, where shall we stay for that visit? Mr. Logan?"

"Ah," Charlie said, grinning fiercely, "tonight? At a hotel And tomorrow? Why, that's my little secret," he said, tapping the side of his nose. And Susannah's heart sank, for she'd grown up with Charlie and knew that thin-lipped grin was a sure sign that he was thinking rapidly, and the tapping meant that he was lying most creatively.

As crack coachman of the *Brighton Thunder*, the Viscount Hazelton had arrived in London before either Mr. Jones or the Logans had. But though he arrived first, he was last to reach his destination, having had first to go the round at the stagecoach stop, touching his broad-brimmed hat to his passengers as they got their baggage or waited for transport to their own destination, and then having to stay standing and waiting beside those who'd forgotten to remember that their coachman expected a gratuity for his services.

"Damme," one of the young gentlemen who'd ridden topside with him murmured to a friend, his uncertainty written in plain pink on his beardless young face, "give me a clue, do I give the fellow a tip or no? He's a viscount, I'm only a baron's son, what's to do?"

"Why, young sir," the coachman said on a laugh, having overheard his embarrassed question as he'd been waiting for another fashionable gentleman to dig his coins out of an extremely tight pocket, "the only question that matters is if you enjoyed the ride. For if you did, I hardly think it matters what rank your coachman holds, so long as he holds the reins right enough. I'd tip my barber," he said on a nudge, "if he were a baron."

So amid much laughter, he got his coin, and smiled and raised his hat to the young gentleman for it. But that was the coin he held apart from the others, and that was the one he spent at once, dropping it on the publican's bar as though it were smoldering, when he bought his guard a drink after the passengers had all left.

They talked awhile about roads and conditions and complained about wages and gossiped about other coachmen and guards when they were joined by a few others. But when they'd done drinking and began walking out of the main coaching inn, the viscount looked pale and grew silent, as though his energy had left with his pose of hearty, convivial coachman.

"You'll be laying over for a few days, eh?" the guard remarked as they walked down increasingly narrow and dirty streets.

"Not too long, no," the viscount said softly, stepping aside quickly to avoid a noisome mess that had been flung from an upper window to the pavement, "no one pays me to rest."

"Your friend give me 'is card back at t'Swan," the guard said evenly, "tipped me 'andsome and ast me to see you remembered 'im."

"He gave me one too," the viscount said as he paused before the tavern and lodging house where he had his London room. "The fellow must have had a thousand printed up, no accounting for the way some people throw their money around. Don't worry, I'll remember him."

But that, Julian Dylan thought sadly as he placed his friend's card in a corner of the speckled looking glass in his room, was probably all he would do. For after all, he thought, lying down at last, fully clothed, upon the creaking bed that took up most of his small room, the world looked different on a wild night in a comfortable inn than it did in the cool sane light of a normal afternoon. His decisions to put his home at pawn and invest the proceeds, such a glowingly good idea when he'd been glowing himself with good fellowship and good rum, seemed foolish and dangerous now. The reality of the few coins he'd earned today, the truth of the indignity of standing before his fellowman hat in hand, pretending to a jovial unconcern with the amount they tossed to him, and with the way of his earning it, were all as present and actual as the poor sagging bed he sought repose on. And all the dreams of future wealth and happiness he'd envisioned with his old friend Warwick to guide him seemed about as real as the dreams he began to slowly let himself drift away into now.

His last thought as the afternoon light struggled between buildings to finally find a purchase on his high, narrow windowsill, was that he was lucky to have such a friend as Warwick, and he hoped he'd be forgiven for not seeking him out again, but for once the astute fellow had been wrong. Help might not be charity, and a friend might be expected to help, but he knew no friends who could work miracles. And in his case, only a miracle could help.

When the summons at his door woke him, a long twilight had begun. He'd been sleeping soundly, and the unexpected sleep of the daylight hours was so rare and disorienting that it took him a few moments to remember where he was, for he had several places he called home along his coaching route, and then a few more to recall who he was, for he often thought these days that he no longer knew.

When he groped to the door, he discovered the potboy from the tavern, grinning like a gargoyle, holding out a note to him. There was nothing on the paper but his name and a few lines, but he recognized the shape and scent of it, and snatched it from the boy's grubby hand and scanned those few lines a few times over, not only because he was still groggy but also because it gave him increasing pleasure to do so. Then, grinning almost as widely as the boy did, he reached into his pocket and flipped the boy a coin so large one would think the urchin had just made the Brighton-to-London run in record time and not just skipped up the stairs from the tavern to his room. The boy caught the coin and cried a breathless "Thankee," for he'd run all the way up the stairs, since, though unable to read those few lines, he recognized the paper and the scent when the paper had been handed to him in the tavern, and had some idea of its importance to its recipient.

The viscount read the note, and again and once more, and then took his watch from his vest's fob pocket and checked the time a few more times to be sure. Then he sat holding the watch, which had been heated by his sleeping body so that its smooth metal case glowed warm in his hand as his own heart, and smiled to himself. For, he thought on a rising tide of joy, there was time, while he had life he had time, and if one believed, there was, clearly, still the possibility of miracles.

5

Marbled with age, the looking glass was so small it couldn't hold the whole of the image presented to it. There was no help for it since the room it was in wasn't large enough for the gentleman to step back far enough to accommodate its shortsightedness. The light of the few candles on the table next to it gave the limited image a leaping, flaring, demonic aspect, but even these deficiencies couldn't mar the gentleman's reflected appearance. For he was fair and handsome as an angel, whatever shadows of doubt the glass cast on him.

The Viscount Hazelton had taken great pains with his appearance and so was grateful for the inconstant light because it proved that even after all his trouble, night was exactly what he needed to complete his outfit. The glaring light of day might show his perfectly fitted tight black velvet jacket to have somewhat less nap on its elbows than on the rest of its smooth surface; his shirtfront and high neckcloth gleamed white in candlelight, but after so many washings even the finest linen mellows to a creamier shade which only deeper shade can disguise; his gray pantaloons fitted to perfection, without a crease in them, but their wearer knew it was as well his lady's brother had forbidden his suit, for if he were to get down on his knees in them tonight, it was entirely possible that their increasingly thin fabric might fly apart under such pressure, to leave him standing before his lady bare-legged and shamefaced as a boy.

His boots, at least, were a joy; the good leather had been a sound investment since it ripened with age to take on an easy, admirable shine. And the ease of one's wardrobe, he'd soon found, was of utmost importance to a gentleman who'd had to learn to live without a valet. But some things any man can master. He'd brushed his fair hair until it glowed like another candle in the dim room, and newly washed and shaven, and anointed with the last bit of an expensive cologne he'd once believed he could afford, he was ready, at last, to meet with his lady.

She'd been the one who'd sent him the note; unsigned, he knew her hand, and the fact that she'd remembered his schedule was an extra wonderment to him. The whole glory, the miraculous aspect of it, was that the note had been waiting for him since the previous day, and the assignation she'd arranged was for tonight. And he was so excited about it, he thought as he snuffed the candles with a shaky hand, that it was as well he'd been unaware yesterday, since he might not have slept through the night thinking of it. The fact that he hadn't slept a great deal anyway because of entirely different reasons occurred to him only to be discarded at once. He was a grown man and there were things a man did for his pleasures that never touched his heart. And this lady, ah, this lady, he believed as he took the stairs rapidly, she was his heart.

Those patrons of the Anchor Tavern where he lodged who didn't know him but saw him come down the stair and leave through the taproom, thought he was a gentleman gone slumming. But the tavern wench, two decades his elder and mother to three who were senior to him, nonetheless smiled and remembered a dimple from her youth when he passed her and bent his glowing head in greeting, before he pushed out the doors into the night. He left her dreamy-eyed in the backwash of his lemon-and-sandlewood scent, and he knew it, for he was, he thought ruefully, always a great favorite of tavern wenches.

He was, in fact, he knew, a great favorite of all sorts of females. It was ironic, he thought, that it was only his lady whose sentiments remained in doubt. Her cool, classic features always wore a welcoming smile for him, she always listened with grave patience to his words, and gave him her hand, and sometimes her soft, cool cheek, and once, her lips, to kiss in farewell when he left her. But of all the females he'd ever known well, from the first girl to giggle at him when he was placed on his first pony, to the first one to sigh at him when he placed his body over hers, she was the only one whose affection he'd ever doubted. If he ever wondered if perhaps that was precisely her attraction for him (for he was not, whatever his emotions, a foolish gentleman), he had ample evidence of the world's tribute to her to deny it.

Lady Marianna Moredon was an acclaimed beauty, a famous Incomparable, the object of sonnets and sketches, a female who had birth, beauty, a brain, and a fortune, and unfortunately a brother as well. And Warwick was entirely right in that, he thought as he strode through the streets, because Lord Robert Moredon was all that his friend had said, and possibly worse. He'd always seemed to scowl when he saw him, the viscount remembered. Once, years ago, at school, when his future had looked entirely clear and bright, he'd stopped to talk with a friend of Lord Robert's, and when he'd approached the pair, had seen, that once, for one unguarded moment, the instant recoil, the glimpse of abhorrence and then avoidance in the man's light blue eyes.

Perhaps he'd reminded the fellow of someone, perhaps it had been something he'd said at the time, he'd forgotten. But it was an unusual reaction, since the viscount had found he'd never had any trouble making men friends either. He was, he suspected, an easy fellow to like, since so many people seemed attracted to him; he was, as his friend Warwick had remarked years before, always loved—perhaps that was why he was always so loving. So it was only further irony that he'd never loved anything or anyone as he loved his Lady Marianna.

Because if Lord Robert had disapproved his attentions when he'd been believed to be a wealthy young sprig of fashion, now, of course, being penniless, he was not allowed in her vicinity. He'd been told to stay away only once, in a harsh barking command, and then Lord Robert had turned on his heel, leaving him to the pitying and fascinated stares of all the others at his sister's soiree. Her brother had threatened to disown her if she so much as spoke with him again; she herself had told him so. But though she was a lady, he thought proudly, unconsciously raising his head as he walked and throwing back his shoulders at the thought of her, she had her own mind and knew unfairness when she saw it. So she'd still meet briefly with him, now and again, on certain safe nights when her brother was away, such as tonight. He could only hope her desire to see him was for more than that, but being a lady, she'd never told him more than that, for all he'd laid his devotion at her feet. But when he could honorably do more, he thought, why then, on that glorious day, she might well say more as well. That was his hope, his dream, his reason for continuance.

It was a long journey through wretched streets to reach the Moredon town house, but he was glad of the opportunity to walk. Had the weather been bad, he would have had to hire a coach, taking on that extra expense only so that he wouldn't arrive dripping at her door. He moved swiftly, and went unmolested, though many eyes watched him from the shadows. He looked a gentleman, he looked as though he might have interesting plunder in his pockets. That was precisely why no man came near him, though many who found murder only a means to an end observed him narrowly as he strode past. For they knew no true gentleman would walk these streets so confidently, alone. He was, they reasoned, up to some bad business even as they were, and wild as they were, like the hungry animals they resembled, they weren't fools enough to prey on something they didn't recognize, something that might turn and devour them.

The only ones to accost him were females wishful of selling themselves, because any male was their fair game. He shrugged them off politely. Even if he were a fellow who paid for his sport, he knew enough to never patronize these poor creatures; the very streets they frequented proved they were too debilitated or diseased to find custom in the better districts.

When he neared Lady Marianna's house, when he reached those clean, wide streets, he slowed his pace. He walked as though he belonged here, as he'd once done, he sauntered as though he were a gentleman out for the pleasure of a stroll, because he knew no man with funds ever hurried on foot. No one remarked him, except to note that he was a fine-looking fellow, and he'd returned so far in his thoughts to what he'd been such a little while ago that he discovered himself angry again, and upset once more when he had to turn his steps to the back entrance of the Moredon town house to seek entry as a servant might, and as an unwelcome suitor must. But so she said he'd be safe, and so he waited for her maid to ease open the door and offer him whispered admittance.

It was an indignity to be led, hushed when his footfalls echoed too loudly, past the staff, past the butler, into a small music room to the side of the house, where his lady had asked her chaperon to let her alone so that she could concentrate on a difficult bit of music for her harp. It was embarrassing to have her maid settle wide-eyed in a chair in the corner to oversee the clandestine meeting, as though even his lady wondered about his intentions, though he recognized that as a lady she must hold to all the conventions she could. But all insult was forgotten when he beheld her.

She wore a white gown that showed her youthful slenderness. Her jet hair was pulled back from her serene face, with only a few curls left upon her brow to enhance her camellia-smooth, camellia-cream-tinted complexion. She was not yet twenty, yet her poise was such that she seemed ageless. So Leonardo had painted a Madonna he'd once seen, he remembered, as he raised her slender hand to his lips. But only an English lady could have such a clear gaze, he thought as he looked up from his bow into her calm blue eyes.

They spoke of inconsequential things, as any proper young couple ought, gossip and chatter about the social weather. He told her of her beauty, as he always did, until he could contain himself no longer, and wanting to see something other than cool interest and polite acceptance of his tribute in those lovely eyes, he surprised himself by telling her of his encounter with his old friend Warwick Jones, and of the plans to reinstate his fortune.

"But . . . indulge in *trade*?" she asked with a sudden incredulous inflection in her soft voice.

"Many gentlemen do," he explained nervously, watching her reaction. "Warwick comes from an old family. And I know," he added quickly, "Warwick himself told me, that several other well-known noblemen do too."

When she said nothing further, he went on, as he hadn't meant to do, feeling, ridiculously enough, a bit like a snitch back at boarding school as he did so,

". . . the Duke of Torquay, for example, and the Marquess Bessacarr and Lord Leith, oh, many noblemen have added to their fortunes that way. If it profits me to the point where I can offer for you openly at last, I think I'd trade with the devil himself. But now, at least I have hopes where I'd none before, and really, I don't have to go quite so far."

He said the last with a laugh, to ease her fears. But she only appeared pensive, and when she looked up again, it was to her maid.

"Oh, my lady," that little creature said at once, "the time! I don't know how much longer you can stay here."

"I'm so sorry, Julian," she said, rising and giving him her soft, cool hand again, sighing regretfully. "You must go now. Good luck, and I'll write you again, when I can."

He took her hand as he was supposed to, he bowed and began to leave as a gentleman ought, but then, at the last, because he couldn't restrain himself, he looked back and asked:

"You will continue to wait? You can wait? These rumors I hear of you and the Earl of Alford, they are rumors?"

"As you see, nothing has changed," she said evenly.

It was little enough, he thought as he left the house with the stealth that he'd entered it. But it was enough, he thought, when he reached the pavements again. She was a lady, he an impoverished gentleman, in all propriety there could be no more, as yet. But she'd not forgotten, or given up on him, so neither could he. And so he strode home down all the long streets again, but he wore a slight smile this time, nor did he hurry this time, since all he had waiting for him at the end of his travels was his own narrow bed.

Or so he'd thought. But when he'd almost gotten there, when he was only blocks from his room, his world shattered.

He'd seen nothing, he'd been so intent on his thoughts. So when the blow came it brought him to his knees; the pain and the blinding light felt like a thunderclap on the back of his head, more painful and shocking because it was unlooked-for. But he was a young man, and a fit one; handling teams of spirited horses on the high road gave a man stamina and muscle and sharpened his reflexes, so he was up on his knees and then on his feet again in the space of a breath. He managed to land an immediate satisfactory blow to his opponent, and hearing the man gasp with vengeful gladness, then had no doubt he could best the villain, and waded forward to do so, when he felt other hands grasp him from behind and pin his arms to his sides. As he grappled with this new assailant, his old one recovered enough to deliver a hard blow to his stomach that doubled him over, gagging, but still hanging firmly in that new ungentle embrace.

He struggled to free himself even as he gasped with pain and nausea, and as the next blow landed solidly to his body again, he heard a rough voice behind him say with a curious note of sympathy:

"Eh. Easy, lad. Just take it easy now. It'll soon be over."

It was odd, he thought, above all the frustration and hurt of it, to be beaten senseless by such concerned torturers, for when the pain glazed his eyes so that he could not see whom to snarl at, and when he ceased to struggle, the voice said dispassionately:

"Eh, Fred. It's enough. He's done."

The arms behind loosed him and he dropped to his knees in the street.

"It's just that we'd a message for you, lad," the rough voice said easily, as the man hunkered down so that he could hear him above the thrumming of blood in his ears. "Stay away from the lady, 'e said, and so you can't say you wasn't warned, 'e said as to tell you next time it'd go worse for you. Fair enough? Ah, you'll be better in the morning, lad, but next time we'll do worse, so take a 'int, eh?"

He muttered a curse, and suddenly lurched upright, to kill or be killed if he must, when he was struck in the face with such force that he crashed to the pavement again.

"Filthy scum," a familiar voice growled, and as he tried to place it, and shake the mist from his eyes and rise again, he felt a sharp pain in his head, and then another in his ribs, and another, until he lay still, trying to curl up on himself, unable to think of anything but pain.

" 'Ere m'lord, 'ere, 'old on," the rough voice spoke in

alarm, "you don't want to kill the lad, do you? Eh, well, even if you do, we want no part of it. You said to teach a lesson, m'lord, and that we did, but we'll have no part of murder, no. You're a gent, all you'd get would be a nice scold, but that's the topping cheat for us."

"Not murder, no," the heavy voice said, panting, "I just want to rearrange his pretty face a bit."

Julian looked up through his narrowing frame of vision to see a gentleman's high, shining Hessian boot raising up and coming, as though in impossibly slow and measured movement, directly toward his face. He tried to turn, but found all he could do was to close his eyes against the assault that never came.

For, "No, my lord, I think not," a new voice said, as the other gasped in outrage,

"What are you doing? Let me loose! I paid for this!"

"A lesson is all you paid for and all I'll deliver, not surgery. As it is," the voice said with steel beneath its low, rumbling tones, as it began to fade in and out, "there's more damage here than I bargained for. It's quite enough, my lord."

The other voice began a protest that the viscount never heard the ending of, for suddenly the pain ebbed away, along with all his sense of sight and sound.

"There's a person to see you, sir," the butler said evenly. "He has your card."

It was a simple enough statement, but Mr. Jones pricked up his ears at it, and laid down his fork at once. His eggs were never so interesting as the translation he'd just made of his butler's announcement. It seemed he was being informed that a very inferior fellow had come to call (no other sort of man would be described as a "person") and that though he looked unusual, his business had been deemed important enough that the astute butler had decided it warranted disturbing his master's breakfast.

"You said as to 'ow you were 'is friend," the guard of the *Brighton Thunder* said as he shuffled his big boots in the gentleman's anteroom.

"I was, I am," Mr. Jones answered with a growing sense of dread.

"Then I think you ought to come," the guard said simply, "now."

The gentleman remained silent all during the long ride to the Anchor, but the guard, seated beside him, who was a fellow who'd learned to read faces for his living, saw how his lips imperceptibly tightened the further they drove into the East End, and saw the olive skin grow pale as he was told to stop before the tavern. He didn't see the haste with which the gentleman took the steps up to the viscount's room, for he'd been asked to stay and watch his fine carriage. Nor then did he see those heavily lidded eyes spring wide when there was no answer to his imperious knock upon the scarred door to the high room. And it was as well that he didn't see the quick pain which filled those midnight-blue eyes when he opened the door and stepped into the dim room, for it was mixed with a terrible fear that the gentleman had never allowed any man to see.

The single bed bore a body, its clothes bloodied and torn, and at first, in the dimness, for it was morning and the sun never found this room until the day began to wane, the gentleman only recognized the man by his hair, which, though disarranged and laced with clots of dirt and blood, was a distinctive dark gold. The face was too swollen, the fair skin already darkened with the insult it had received, for him to make sense of all the features at once. Without a word, the gentleman came near the bed, and wincing, reached out one hand to that disordered hair, to push back a lock which had become plastered to the high forehead. At that, one light eye opened and the swollen mouth twitched, and a tired, slurred voice said, shaking with what, incredibly enough, might possibly have been laughter:

"You were right, Warwick. A very bad man."

"His breathing's easy," the physician reported as he drew on his gloves, "so I can be sure the lungs weren't touched. And as several ribs were broken in several places, that was my first concern. But I've taped him up tight and if he remains at rest, his recovery should be certain. However, I should think," he said, casting a wise glance at the gentleman who handed him a glass of brandy, "that would be the most difficult part of his recuperation."

The gentleman smiled, remembering how much trouble the doctor's newest patient had caused, even semiconscious as he'd been, as he'd been carried from his room to the waiting carriage and from there upstairs to the guestroom where he now lay, drugged into unwilling submission at last. The *Thunder*'s guard had been of the opinion that perhaps an extra clip on the chin would have made their chore easier, the butler had wistfully spoken of sleeping drafts, and a struggling footman had paused on the stair after laboring under the burden of the hastily improvised litter to wipe his brow on a sleeve and swear he didn't know how such a slender half-dead fellow could get himself to weigh a ton.

The viscount had been assisted to his room without further difficulty only after his host, after his initial relief at the fact that his friend was alive enough to be so obstructive had faded, then grew annoyed enough with his protests to stop the halting procession and say, coldly and plainly enough for a man at the brink of the grave to understand:

"Get the rocks out of your pockets and your head, Julian. You've been left alive, but not for long if you don't stop being a fool. You are to stay here until you're well enough to get revenge. I promise you that. Now, some cooperation, if you please."

"Of course," the doctor added after a swallow of his drink, "he won't want to show his face for a while if he's a vain chap . . . but no," he said hurriedly, seeing the sudden alarm spring up in the gentleman's eyes, "there should be no permanent damage. It looks bloody awful, but there were no deep cuts, you see, only scratches, nothing broken in the face at all, lucky chap," he mused, "but with that sort of skin, you see, healing will be an unattractive process."

"He will be dissuaded from cotillions," the gentleman agreed. "Thank you, doctor."

When the physician had gone, promising a return in the morning, the gentleman stayed seated in his study for a long time, staring sightless into his fire. His staff knew well enough not to disturb him at such times. It was difficult for the butler to violate his master's privacy, knowing how he disliked it when he retreated to think as he'd done, but the visitor who'd come to call was a gentleman of sorts. And as the butler recalled that he'd come a few times before and had been admitted then, he had no choice, he said with great regret when he disturbed Mr. Jones with the news, but to cut up his peace again.

"Quite right, Mr. Fox," Mr. Jones interrupted his remorseful explanations to say, "and no problem, I've done with my musings and was only waiting for the hour to grow late enough for me to implement them. No matter," he said, with a wry smile for the look of polite incomprehension on his butler's face, "show Mr. Logan in."

"Good afternoon, my friend," Mr. Jones said, extending his hand to the fair heavyset gentleman as he entered, "and what may I do for you today? What have you decided is about to become indispensable to England and provident for us to invest in now? Is it to be copper, cotton, or calico we shall discuss the price of? Have a seat, Mr. Logan, I only jest, but as we met over a matter of ships just last month, I hadn't looked to see you again so soon."

His visitor took a seat opposite to Mr. Jones's desk but didn't speak directly; he appeared to be busy adjusting his large frame in his chair to his comfort. He was, in fact, buying time, for an astute businessman, like a good soldier, never begins an important matter until he's surveyed the terrain for possible dangers. Things didn't look well for his mission, he decided, as he smiled and offered a mindless social pleasantry. Warwick Jones usually displayed a calm, amused face to him. Today, he detected small but rare signs of uneasiness in his host: the way his slender fingers roved restlessly over objects on his desktop, the firm, almost clenched set to his jaw, above all, the unusually distracted look in his darker than normally dark blue eyes. And then too, even as he next reminded his host, he'd completely forgotten the fact that they'd met only a day before and he'd promised to pay him a visit when he got to London.

"But then, I never expected it to be so soon, either," Mr. Logan said at once, letting his chuckling ride over Mr. Jones's immediate frown and apology for his forgetfulness. "And I wouldn't have come to bother you, not so soon, and maybe not ever, if it weren't for the fact that I'm in a bit of a bind, and as I know few gentlemen in London as well as I do you, ah, I thought I perhaps could look you up . . . Ah, damnation, Mr. Jones, you're a solid fellow, might as well spit it out," he sighed, knowing flowers would only make this chap sneeze, honesty would be the only thing to move him. "The fact is that most of the gentlemen I work with aren't willing to let the world know they work with me. You're one of the few I can talk straight to . . . no, maybe the only one. You don't style yourself too far above me to do anything but make money from me," he said on an embarrassed laugh, for being a very good businessman, he was never too comfortable with the absolute truth out on the table.

"Thing is," he went on quickly, "I'm needed at home in Suffolk, my wife's about to present me with another babe. It'll be our second. There was some difficulty the first time so I don't like being away from her now, which accounts for my hurry. But I don't want our Sukey to know of it . . . Lord, listen to me," he sighed, "I can sell you a shipyard with a few good words, but talk of myself and I jabber."

"No, talk of yourself and I'll listen, never fear," Mr. Jones said, relaxing and finally giving his guest his complete attention. "Come, have a drop with me to celebrate that forthcoming event, and take your time, only not too much, if the happy event is quite that imminent," he added with his usual sad, sweet smile, "and then tell me the whole of it. I have nowhere to go until this evening."

After more than a few drops of port, Mr. Logan found he was entirely capable of divulging his story, swiftly and surprisingly coherently. Mr. Jones was a good listener, and it was a brief enough tale. He spoke of his clever, beautiful sister, and her inability, burdened as she was with education, to get a husband from among his cronies, and lumbered as she was with her family background, to land one from the ranks of the gentry she resembled. It took a moment to tell him of his plans for her, and then, because it was most unpleasant, only seconds to tell him about the bibulous Mrs. Pruit they'd met this very day.

"And so how can I leave her there with that sot?" he

asked angrily. "Introduce Sukey to the fancy? Ho," he laughed mirthlessly, "the only titled gentlemen she ever sees are on the labels of all the bottles she empties.

"I can't leave Susannah in a hotel, like a homeless waif," he explained miserably. "I closed up the house we had here in London when I moved the family down to Suffolk for the air. Even if I reopened it, she'd still be alone. We've a small family," he explained. "Maybe that's why I'm so excited about this new one coming.

"And as to that," he said, becoming animated with woe again, "if I tell her about the new babe, why, she'll fly to help me at home, and then I'll never get her back to London. She'd stay, I know her, for she gets on with my good wife like a house afire, and she'd be the best aunt that ever lived, and live with me all her life and never get to be the best mama that ever lived, neither. That's why I keep her away, though I love her. But she's here now, and she should stay and get her chance to get her pick of the best," he exclaimed, bringing his hand down on the arm of his chair, "for she's good and bright as she can hold together and a rare, rare beauty."

Mr. Jones nodded agreement; it was easy enough, for he thought, on an interior smile, breathed there a man who did not have the most beautiful sister in the world?

"So I was wondering," Mr. Logan said then in a smaller voice, because suddenly he didn't feel at all like a businessman but rather like a street beggar with his hat in hand, "if you knew of someone, someone of quality, there'd be no sense finding someone just like me, who could give her house room for a while? For only a little while," he hastened to add, "until the babe arrives and all's well enough for me to come back and see to her permanent disposition."

"Surely not so final?" his host asked easily, and when Mr. Logan didn't smile at his simple jest, his own smile faded and he shook his head, saying slowly, "I'm not terribly social, I'm afraid, Mr. Logan. Indeed, I believe I'm the closest thing you may find to a recluse outside of a forest. Not that I don't get about, but I'm not in the habit of hobnobbing with the 'quality,' as it were. I do have a viscount staying with me now," he said musingly, "but the fellow can't help that.

He's here against his will, actually, as he's quite ill. You saw him at the Swan the other night, my friend from the *Brighton Thunder* that you inquired after, the Viscount Hazelton. No, don't worry, nothing contagious, the poor fellow just had a rather bad accident.''

But from the way Mr. Jones said it, Mr. Logan, who always listened particularly carefully to what was not said, narrowed his eyes.

"Oh yes, the fair-haired fellow with the handsome face. My sister remarked him," Mr. Logan said too casually, so that his host's heavy eyes opened a bit wider. "Accident? With that sort of a phiz I'm not surprised. Bit of a devil, eh?"

"Not in the least," Mr. Jones said coolly. "His face is the only happy accident he's experienced in a long while. As decent a man as you'd wish, but, as I said, unfortunate, in both his present circumstances and his latest ones."

"Ah," Mr. Logan said, his attitude changing slightly, his tone becoming more the way it ordinarily did when he discussed prices and commissions, "I didn't realize you were that close with him. Far more than merely a passing acquaintance then," he said wisely. "So you'd vouch for him, would you?"

"I would, absolutely," Mr. Jones answered negligently, although now watching his guest carefully.

"Decent, honorable . . . and he'd be hardworking too, I expect?"

"Extremely."

"But impoverished?"

"Unfortunately, at the moment, yes, utterly."

"And no family to help him, or interfere with him?"

"None living."

"Well, then," the ruddy gentleman said, leaning forward, "I might have mentioned my sister's interest, but I believe I neglected to mention her dowry," and lowering his voice, he whispered a sum that made Mr. Jones look at him with some interest and then lean back in his chair, but "Indeed?" was all he said.

But as it was said in the same tone of voice he'd used before he'd bid on the opal mines he'd bought a few months past, Mr. Logan, knowing when a man ought not to press too hard, only said:

"Oh yes, and all of it would go to her, or rather, her husband, immediately on their marriage. In cash," he added, when his host did not speak at once.

When he finally did, he said thoughtfully:

"This is a very large house, Mr. Logan. Ten bedrooms in the heart of London, imagine. But then, I inherited it. It gets quite lonely sometimes. I'm very glad my friend's come to visit, but as he'll be recuperating, I imagine things will get very dull for him around here. I cannot sit at his side all day, you know. Your sister has a respectable chaperon, I imagine?"

"Of the first stare," his guest agreed, sitting forward on his chair. "I've engaged the lady Mrs. Anderson had with her. She's no relative of mine, but we could say a 'connection' by marriage. She's of good family and married some frog or such who lost it all in the revolution, so she's a bona fide contessa too."

"Ah," Mr. Jones said thoughtfully.

It wasn't entirely proper, he mused, there'd be a great many who'd wonder at a young woman not related to him staying on in his home, even if she were not as beautiful as her brother believed, even if she were adequately chaperoned. But then, with her breeding, she was scarcely likely to ever sit well, if at all, with them anyway. But she might, he thought, she very well might engage Julian's interest if she were half so bright or pretty as claimed, and then she'd be in a position to do more than merely get him to forget his "lady" for a few hours. She was obviously half in love with Julian already; as ever, his face alone had done that. If he could be brought to exert his considerable charm, even battered as he was, the thing could be accomplished. *If*, he thought restlessly, remembering his friend's obsession.

Or, Mr. Jones thought more deeply, for his, he was pleased to think, was a devious mind, if her staying should eventually be construed as ruinous to her reputation, Julian's noble nature might be prevailed upon to make him do the right thing by her. That dowry would more than make up for the loss of his impossible dream of winning Lady Marianna. At the least he could use the diversion, poor boy, Warwick concluded, and at the most, he could certainly use the money. And as for the girl, as she had no place in society, she'd nothing to risk. In fact, whatever transpired, he thought, she couldn't lose anything but a few months of her time, and might gain a great deal more.

"Mr. Logan," he said after a time in which his guest had scarcely dared to breathe, "do you think your sister would consider staying on at my humble home until matters are settled with you?"

"Why, thank you, Mr. Jones," his guest said as he silently thanked a greater personage besides, "I do believe she would."

When they shook hands good-bye, Mr. Logan, feeling greatly daring with all his great fortune, said lightly:

"You know, Mr. Jones, this is well done, for there was a time when I wanted you to meet my sister very much. I thought she'd suit you right down to the ground."

"Be grateful that I likely wouldn't suit her, not only not half so well as Viscount Hazelton does, but at all," Warwick replied gently, "for I'm an odd, cold sort of fellow, Mr. Logan, and so, if only in the interest of human rights, am not at all in the marriage market myself."

But as this was very close to actually verbalizing an agreement that had been made without a mention that could incriminate him in his sister's eyes if she ever found it out, Mr. Logan only shook his head as he shook his host's hand, and then was shown out, rubbing his hands together over his turn of luck as he hurried back to his hotel.

Charlie Logan wore the broadest grin when Susannah admitted him to her room. And though the contessa looked up from her embroidery with pleased anticipation when she saw him, Susannah's face showed only the deepest foreboding. Her brother, she thought, looked entirely too happy.

"Ladies," he said with great smugness, "I'm pleased to tell you that though I can remain in London only for another day, you'll be staying on until my return with my great good friend Mr. Warwick Jones, *and*," he added smugly, "his great good friend the Viscount Hazelton, who is presently recuperating from an accident at his house. No, nothing serious, else you'd not have been asked to visit," he added hastily, seeing his sister's immediate dismay.

But even thus reassured, she continued to look downcast.

"Charlie," she replied on a sigh as she sat down in despair, "your Mr. Jones is a bachelor. The viscount is a bachelor. Unless I stay on as a housemaid, it will never, ever do. I'm coming home with you now, Charlie, and there's an end to it."

The contessa stirred and gazed at Susannah in mild surprise. "Mr. Jones is, I believe," she said, "related to the Gloucestershire Joneses, quite an old, accepted family."

"It doesn't matter. We're not related," Susannah said sadly.

"But I may be," the contessa replied softly. "I believe my great-grandmother on my father's side is a connection there. It would not at all surprise me. And the Dylans are a very old line. The Hazelton title, though English, may well be the family that my poor late husband was connected to, through the Hapsburgs. No matter, most titled persons claim relationships there. It will do." She nodded. "And when do we go there?" she asked Charlie.

"Oh," Susannah said, abashed, "pardon me, Contessa, I'd no idea you knew them or were related to them."

"I don't, and I'm not sure," the contessa replied patiently, "but it doesn't matter, my dear. It will suffice for a brief visit."

"I see," Susannah said. "Your word is enough for people in society, and they'll believe what you tell them."

"I mean," the contessa said gently, "that persons in society will believe whatever they wish, whatever I tell them. So it scarcely matters if some think I'm related to the Joneses, and others think it's the Hazelton line I claim kinship with. What matters is that it's creditable and can be carried off, and therefore, is acceptable. A great many things can be done if they are done with certitude.

"We can say our visit began as an obligation," the contessa went on thoughtfully, "but as there are so many people involved now, it begins to take on all the earmarks of a house party, and so, less formal rules apply. Yes. It will certainly do for a space. The words are right. If the right words can be put to a thing, it may be considered correct," she explained. "I can be ready at ten, and you, Susannah?" she asked calmly.

And though she doubted she'd ever be ready, Susannah nodded mutely, as her brother, for once speechless, gazed at the contessa with sincere admiration.

Although Warwick Jones was smiling to himself as Mr. Logan left, he soon forgot the incident, he was so busy writing and sending out notes via several footmen in his employ. By the time he'd received some answers, and not received certain others, the afternoon was advanced. Then he went above stairs to check upon his sleeping guest once more, and after standing silently and observing the ruined face turning in troubled sleep upon its pillow, he left and closeted himself with his valet. Then he rang for his butler.

"I'll be going out this evening, Mr. Fox," he said simply. "Have a footman continue to watch the viscount. Mr. Epford has volunteered to attend to him but a valet is scarcely able to run a sickroom alone."

But, the butler thought later, as Mr. Jones descended the stair with the first evening shadows, it looked as though it was his master that the valet was unable to manage alone. For his employer scarcely seemed dressed for an evening out on the town. Although he wore dark breeches and jacket, he wore high top boots, not slippers, so he would hardly be going to a dance or a social evening, and yet he went hatless and his white shirt and neckcloth were covered overall by a dark, voluminous cape of the sort a gentleman might wear out for a visit to the opera.

The butler stared in fascination as Warwick Jones left the town house to slip out of the door and blend in with the shadows of night. He started when Mr. Epford, his master's excellent valet, who moved with the same quiet grace as his employer, said softly at his shoulder:

"A singular costume, yes, I agree. But he said it was a hunting outfit. 'Hunting?' I asked, laughing. 'In the night, sir?' 'Yes,' he said, grinning in the most unsettling way, 'because what I hunt comes out only at night.' Just like the old days when he was a youth. It gave me a turn, it did, Mr. Fox,'' he admitted on a sigh.

The butler closed the door firmly on the night, and said nothing further, for not only was it in poor taste to criticize his master's apparel, it was decidedly unpleasant to think of the wild hunt he was engaged in. And from the expression upon his face as he'd left, distinctly unnerving to consider the fate of his prey.

6

There were places in London that a gentleman might visit if he were bored with his life; the Broken Bucket was where he'd go only if he were careless of it. The gentleman seated at the rear table didn't look as though he'd ever been careless of anything. He was, however, the only breathing being in the pothouse who remotely resembled a gentleman, and so the thin fellow who'd sidled into the room knew immediately that he was the cove he'd been sent to find.

It was late in the evening, so there were few females left in the room. Those few who claimed that beneath their grime they were of that gender who weren't sleeping on the tables or the floor, having also been unsuccessful at finding trade to occupy their whole night, now joined some other ragged creatures of indeterminate sex squabbling over the last of a glass they shared. There were a few rough-looking men whispering in a corner, and a few sullenly drinking themselves into oblivion at their separate table or already half-sprawled upon the floor that would be their bed.

There were no riotous young blades down here slumming as there'd been at The Cock and the Cross or The Bells, nor any roaring young apprentices making merry such as there'd been at the Grapes, nor were there packs of dangerous children here such as frequented The Waltzing Mouse, nor hordes of available females as The Queen's Garter boasted. The gentlemen had visited all these lively places this long evening, gliding from one to another, seeking out certain barkeeps, other select patrons, and asking the same question everywhere. The answers had finally led him to this most abject of places.

It had been a long night because there'd been so much

ground to cover. It was a sprawling district, and even though the poor dwelt in tight huddles, there were so many of them that it made no matter if they'd lived stacked together like firewood, they'd still swallow up a huge share of the city. But not all the places he's visited this evening were so dismal as the area around this decaying taproom where he waited. If poverty were to be compared to a disease, as the reformers would have it, then this would be the terminal stage of it. Only a few streets away there were noisy, colorful striving crowds at almost every hour of the day or night, buying, selling, maneuvering for a little extra room in the sun or moonlight. There, poverty might be a condition of life, but at least it was leavened with hope and laced with laughter. Here, the bankrupt were hopeless, and life itself was too tenuous and brutal to celebrate with anything but oblivion.

The gentleman sat quietly, but his eyes were so alert that the thin man became even more nervous as he approached him and whispered (an unfortunate accident with a knife, or a fortunate escape from one, depending on how one looked at it, had arranged it so that he could speak in no other fashion):

" 'Ere, you the cove what's lookin' for the Lion?''

Warwick Jones fixed him with an appraising stare which made the man shift from foot to foot, before he answered:

"Yes."

It was only one word, but it made the fellow dance in distress.

" 'Ere, well,'' he whispered, "yer t'come wiv me now.''

He said no other word, but only looked about himself anxiously, as though he expected a pack of Bow Street runners to rush from out the greasy corners of the Broken Bucket to nab him, and without waiting to see if the gentleman obliged him, he turned and ducked out of the tavern to evaporate into the night. And Warwick Jones, a gentleman with a reputation of being a very knowing fellow, yet still rose immediately and followed him.

It was precisely because he was knowing that he did so. This was the lowest part of a slum so low that even Bow Street hesitated to enter it; it was such a wretched district that although the gentleman knew that everything and everyone he saw as he followed the little nervous man was for sale, there was no sane man who'd buy any of it. But the gentleman knew what he was about, and so he followed, expecting to find what he'd been looking for at the end of his journey but prepared for anything from attempted murder to random mayhem awaiting him as well. He knew all of the district very well.

Other young men on the town had frequented the general area in their youth as a rite of passage, a coming-of-age ritual. They'd sampled the beverages, the females, had a dust-up or two, and then counted themselves men of the world forever after. Warwick Jones had come down to the area, as he'd put it when he cared to explain himself, to "research the family tree." Whatever his motives had been, he'd been amused and delighted to discover that even as his noble friend's ancestors names' could open the doors to the *ton*, Almack's, and the House of Lords, the notorious "Gentleman Jones" was still a name to be reckoned with in less exalted but no less exclusive society, so was a password to a new and fascinating world for him. He'd been welcomed here, and at that time it had been important for him to have found such a place. He'd not been back for several years, but still he'd known whom to ask his questions of, and more important, how to ask them, and perhaps more important still, how to cope with whatever answer he received, whether it was given in whispers in a thieves' ken or in a back alley with a blade.

They were simple enough questions. He wanted to know who controlled the area now, and who'd hired out bravos to teach a young gentleman a lesson last night. It was, he'd said, without being asked, a matter of some importance to him. And at his voice when he'd said it, the bravest of them shuddered even as they'd accepted his quest, if not his gold, for few would take payment from the great Gentleman Jones's own descendant.

He followed the thin man as he slipped around corners and eeled through narrow alleys, and if in his travels he saw men, women, and children dead or dying, ill or drunken, stealing or fornicating, all in the open and in the plain sight of the Lord who'd seemed to cease to watch over those that lived here, he said nothing, nor did he pause. There were no surprises here for him; those had come earlier in the night when he'd discovered how many persons he'd known when he was young had never reached the age that he was now. Even that hadn't shocked him much after he'd thought on it, and soon he'd accepted it with the same sad resignation with which he took all in his life. Warwick Jones was not an easy gentleman to surprise.

And so he did not blink when—after his guide had led him round about a tenement a treble time to finally climb a stair, and walked about and then hauled down a ladder to scale another height, and then down a hall and thence, after a succession of guard points passed and permitted, to a door that opened after a complex tattoo had been performed upon it—he discovered himself standing in large, airy, well-appointed apartments such as any decent gentleman might be expected to lodge in. It was a well-lit chamber, but even the glow from the handsome chandeliers and lamps didn't betray a muscle that moved in his lean face, except those necessary to open his mouth and form his greeting to his host, as he bowed slightly, and said:

"Good evening, I assume it is the Lion I address?"

The man who took his greeting seemed more amazed than his guest, for few men, evidently, took his measure with such apparent grace. There were others in the room, two dangerous-looking men guarding the door and a few others lounging about, but it was to him that the eye went first, and not only because his physical presence dwarfed all the others. He sat at a deal table, obviously interrupted at playing cards with the only overly ornate bit of decor in the tasteful room, an overpainted young woman.

He was, as Warwick had noted but not allowed himself to so much as widen his eyes at, as tall and broad as a door, and shaped almost exactly like one too. He was dressed well, but it had taken a skillful tailor to cover that barrel chest so neatly, and a deft valet to swathe that bull neck in a fashionable neckcloth. He was not fat in the least, but nothing about him was in the least narrow or lean. Although everything he wore was correct, there was no way such a figure could ever be fashionable, it was far too formidable. And although the broad, genial face above that snowy neckcloth could never be called handsome, being too blunt-featured, the twinkling hazel eyes which assessed his guest from beneath sandy brows were oddly engaging. The mane of coarse sandy hair, of course, accounted for the name, Warwick thought, but when the man spoke, the gleaming white teeth gave him second thoughts about its origin.

"Lion it is," he said in a deep smooth voice, "and this must be Gentleman Jones himself, and not his kin at all, as I was told. It must be him, returned from the grave, because he seems to fear nothing and no one, possibly because he's already met his Maker, and has nothing more to lose," he explained pleasantly to the young woman who sat at his side.

"Do only the dead not fear you?" Warwick asked coolly.

"Why, yes, as a matter of fact," the man answered with great pleasure, "and even some of them do too, since one of my sidelines is the resurrection game. Some of the recently deceased, you understand, don't wish to be disturbed, evicted from their family plots at midnight, and carted off to become toys for eager little surgical students. Sometimes, too," he added ruminatively, "such as now, when there's such a demand, possibly because of exams the eager laddies have coming up, we can't be too picky and have to employ more recently created corpses to our purposes."

When the gentleman didn't betray any emotion, save for a faint cool impatience, evinced by a bored look which he allowed to come into his shadowed eyes, his host grinned the wider and nodded appreciatively.

"Here we have a true gentleman, Sally," he commented to the girl again. "Mark him well, you're not likely to see his like around here again. He won't oblige me with a shudder, not if I threaten him with hot tongs. I wonder what it would take?" he mused. "Well then, how do you do, Mr. Jones?" He smiled. "Yes, I'm Lion himself, there's nothing that goes on in this ken that I don't know about, or profit from, I hope. So what can I do for you tonight?"

"It used to be Bawdy Jack who ran Seven Dials in my time," Warwick said thoughtfully, "but then I understand he took to dancing. He became quite enamored, I believe, of the gallows trot, as did my own ancestor. Then they said it was Billy Bedamned who had the running of the place, until, that is, the night that a runner stopped him for questioning, unhappily enough, forever, and with a pistol. And then they said it was Sam Quirt, until Jimmy Leech decided it was time to take the reins and Sam found himself swimming in the Thames, to his great distress, since he didn't know how to, and could scarcely learn with his arms and legs tied so securely behind him. And now it is you. How pleased I am to meet you then," Warwick said, without a trace of pleasure in his cool voice, as he met his host's now narrowed gaze, "and delighted to find I'm still able to ask you about recent events.

"I'd like to know who paid two ruffians to instruct my friend Viscount Hazelton in courtship methods last night, before they attempted to remove his handsome face entirely. It seemed a rather rigorous lesson. In my day," he added, "such things were accomplished with more grace."

The large man remained silent, studying the slender young gentleman who stood poised before him. Then he threw back his head and roared like his namesake.

"Good God, I like you, Jones," he laughed. "Indeed, I do. No wonder they let you run tame about here, where they have a gentleman for breakfast, and pick their teeth with his bootlaces. Such audacity! I've only seen broadsheets about your ancestor, but you do have the look of him, he must have been such a jolly rogue. Here then, my friend, pleased to know you," he said, leaning forward to extend a hand, "and have a seat, will you?"

"Ah, thank you, but not yet," Warwick replied with some reserve, not moving at all as the man's smile and hand both slowly slipped downward, "for I'd hate to befriend a man that I must then call enemy."

"And how could that happen?" his host asked with such gentleness that the girl seated near him squirmed, and the two guards at the door suddenly straightened.

"Easily enough," Warwick replied steadily, "if you were to say you'd allow such a thing to happen again. For I've learned of the gentleman who engaged you, and plan to take action against him. But I'd like to make it clear that I wouldn't appreciate your running his errands again, before I do. You see, I intend to handle the matter man to man, and I'd hoped to prevail upon you to let it remain a matter between gentlemen, finally settled in that time-honored one-to-one fashion.''

"Gentlemen?'' the other man said bitterly. "I'm very glad then that I'm not of your number, Mr. Jones. If I'd a score to settle, I wouldn't hire two fellows to get my man down and then proceed to try to kick his face in. No, and I, who am about as far from a gentleman as you can get, wouldn't allow it last night, either. I stopped Lord Moredon, because I suppose I wasn't gentlemanly enough to let him get on with it. I'd do almost anything for money, and have done, as a matter of fact, but there's nothing I'd ever do, or permit my people to do, for that 'gentleman' again, for any sum.''

"Then we're speaking the same language,'' Warwick said, putting out his hand, "and it's you that I have to thank for saving my friend's life.''

"Not his life,'' the other man said, grinning again, "only his pretty face, but then, it'd be the same thing, wouldn't it? Jealousy aside, even a fellow with a phiz like mine can understand a man would hate to lose his looks so young, especially when they're so prodigious wonderful.''

"And especially when they're all he's got left,'' Warwick agreed, still holding his hand out. "Thank you, ah, Lion.''

"Stephen Patrick Francis O'Brien,'' the other man said, finally taking his hand in his huge clasp, "and is that all you'll ask of me?''

"All,'' Warwick agreed. "I'll take care of the rest myself.''

"Mr. Jones,'' the other man said, regarding his visitor solemnly, "take very great care. I happened along last night because there was something in the man's manner when he made the arrangement that alerted those he'd struck the bargain with. They're cautious when dealing with the upper classes, and so, wisely, alerted me. It was a good job they did. You didn't see Lord Moredon's eyes last night. I did. There was more than hatred for your handsome friend there, there was perhaps a bit for himself and how he couldn't help feeling about the young Adonis.''

"Ah, thank you,'' Warwick said on a nod. "It's much as I've always suspected. But I scarcely think I have to worry. I am not, in case you hadn't remarked it, precisely a 'young Adonis.' ''

"No, you're more in the style of a Medici prince, aren't you?" the other man remarked on a smile made the wider for the fact that he'd finally surprised his elegant visitor into raising one brow in astonishment. "Ah yes, the dear fathers were kind to an orphan boy, there's an education I had to overcome to get the position here. So I've some learned advice for you. You've successfully bearded me in my den, to state the obvious obviously," he said on a wry grin, "but then, though I don't style myself a gentleman, I'm pleased to think I'm a reasonable man. But do have a care for that particular gentleman, Mr. Jones, he's no manners at all, and you're the amazing pretty viscount's best friend. And I won't be there to help you."

"It won't be necessary, but thank you for your kind thoughts anyway," Warwick said sincerely, "so if I may, a word of caution for you as well? You're too wise for the position, Mr. O'Brien. I heard an explorer speak here in town one day," he went on as the gentleman looked at him curiously. "He'd come from the Ivory Coast to talk about his discoveries. He said that the fiercest creatures in the jungle are not the brave, bighearted ones, like the mighty lion, but rather the small, mindless droves of tiny ants, which together can fell the noblest of beasts. Take care yourself, Mr. O'Brien."

After leaving the giant king of thieves shaking his head in amusement, and the two guards at the door in confused thought, Warwick followed the shifty man who materialized at his side again when he'd left the room. He was led down the stair, out the door, and then left alone again in the night.

Mr. Warwick Jones went directly to his town house, and then straightaway to his bed. He slept soundly, and woke with the dawn. Then he washed and dressed with enough care to gratify his valet, visited with his friend Julian long enough to argue him into taking his medicine, drank only coffee to break his fast, thus nearly breaking his cook's heart, and then left his town house quickly again. He'd done everything with precision. In fact, everything this bright spring morning had gone according to his preconceived plan, and so he'd no way of knowing that an unexpected event was occurring even as he drove away from his door.

For his own light phaeton had driven right past Mr. Logan

and his sister as they approached his house in their carriage, and being so distracted by his own thoughts, he didn't see his business acquaintance frantically trying to wave to direct his attention to them.

"No matter," Mr. Logan said, pulling his head and shoulders back in from the carriage window and sinking back into his seat. "We'll see him when he returns. But, devil take it, Sukey, what sort of thing did they teach you at the Spring academy? You pinched me so hard," he complained, rubbing his arm, "that I don't wonder if Miss Spring didn't get Gentleman Jackson to instruct you girls in self-defense."

"I couldn't have you shouting out the window, Charlie," his sister said unrepentantly. "Bad enough you've landed me on the poor man so soon. If you started screeching my name out the window, we'd both have been embarrassed to death."

"Ah," Mr. Logan said contentedly, gazing at his sister, an eye-filling vision in blond lace this morning, "nothing about you would embarrass any man, Sukey, though it's very likely you'll be the death of several."

Susannah sighed, and made a face she was sure would turn cream, but it only made her brother grin.

It was the life of only one man that interested Warwick Jones at that same moment. It was a subject which engaged his interest entirely all morning, although anyone who might have watched him throughout that morning might never have guessed it. For the young gentleman seemed only to be amusing himself as so many of his contemporaries might do. He rode slowly through Green Park, he visited Manton's shooting gallery, he stopped in at a few clubs, he dropped by Gentleman Jackson's salon to watch a few young men of quality spar with each other under the famous retired prize-fighter's expert instruction. Only someone who knew him well, and that would have been a rare person, would have known how odd his behavior was. For Warwick Jones never did that which all young gentlemen of leisure did, unless he had a reason. It was almost noon when he at last found that reason, in the midst of a clot of other men at Gentleman Jackson's establishment.

Lord Richard Moredon was an impressive gentleman. He

was tall, but seemed taller still from the way he held his square shoulders high, and his proudly carried noble head showed even features and a healthy pink complexion. He and his sister were acknowledged to make a charming pair, for she was dark as his mama had been, and he as fair and light-skinned as their late papa. Lord Moredon was as regular a sight in London in the Season as his beautiful sister was. But he was an adornment at society parties as well as at the Cyprian Ball where no lady ever set slipper, a frequent dance partner to the latest *ton* beauties, as well as a frequent patron of Madame Felice and Mother Carey's less correct but no less popular and exquisite employees. Unwed as yet, he also often had some gaudy creature in his keeping, oftener still, one that many another gentleman envied him for. But he seldom kept any female very long, and though he had a dozen best acquaintances, he was known to have no one friend. He had little patience with his inferiors, and it was apparent that he found their number legion. But then, he was a popular, perfect ornament of society, and so not at all exceptional in any way.

Mr. Warwick Jones, however, stood and gazed so long and hard at the gentleman that it seemed he found him a rare and exotic object. His unblinking stare had such force that some few of the men surrounding Lord Moredon found themselves stepping back from him, as though that unrelenting gaze had heat as well as intensity and they wished to remove themselves from its path to ensure that they weren't the object of that pitiless gaze. At length, even Lord Moredon, who seldom noticed anyone he had not specifically summoned, noted Mr. Jones. He looked up from a tale of an obliging wench he'd been regaling his comrades with, to meet a direct pair of dark blue eyes that he pretended he had difficulty recognizing at first.

"I say, Jones," he laughed after a moment, "what ails you? You look as though you've seen a ghost. Or is there some insect crawling on my vest? Devil take the fellow," he whispered *sotto voce* to some man at his side, "damned insolent the way he keeps staring."

"Oh, no," Mr. Jones said languidly, his voice so at odds with his expression that several gentlemen moved still further away from Lord Moredon, "no, there you're out, Moredon. I may be looking at a phantom, albeit perhaps a few moments prematurely, but I know I'm looking at an insect."

A silence came over the group of gentlemen at that, as each digested the slender young man's words, and then drew in their breath in excitement, not wishing to make a sound or miss a thing, realizing they were witnessing something shocking, and certainly something worth talking about later.

"Are you foxed, man?" Lord Moredon demanded.

"Most certainly not," came the cold reply. "If I were, I might be able to bear the sight of you, thinking it only the sort of horrors one gets after too wild a night."

"Are you mad?" the gentleman asked, amazed.

"Most certainly maddened, enraged that we share the planet, Moredon," Mr. Jones answered with a sneer.

"I will have satisfaction," Lord Moredon said at once, with a sudden smile, "but you may name the instruments and the hour, since you're so mad for execution, of the deed, if not yourself," he joked, looking to his friends and adding, for their benefit: "An odd, peculiar fellow, always was, even at school."

"Yes, I'm all impatience, so let us have it here and now. And with our fists, to have done with it at once," his antagonist said as he began stripping off his tightly fitted jacket.

But Lord Moredon, thinking smugly of his scores at Manton's shooting range, and his skill with sabers and famous eye for other sorts of swordplay, cried scornfully:

"Certainly, Jones, you may back out if you wish, we all have brave moments, later regretted, I'll understand, we'll all understand," he added with glad mockery, sweeping his arm to indicate the large openmouthed audience they'd drawn.

"Really?" Warwick Jones asked, casting his neckcloth aside and beginning to remove his vest. "Are you so anxious for exile, then? I'm not. And I remind you, that's the penalty for the sort of dueling you prefer. Only think, that way even if you win, you lose. Are you eager to leave your lovely sister alone, without your so fond protection, simply for the pleasure of somehow putting a hole someplace vital in me? Or is it rather that you fear taking me on without some deadly instrument to hand? Perhaps it's that you only know how to fight a man when you've got two others to hold him down for you. But I can't think the Gentleman here would approve your usual method.''

Gentleman Jackson himself, who'd been spiritlessly giving pointers to a beardless youth on how to hold up arms that he'd been silently grieved to note had no more muscles than a plate of macaroni, had stopped to listen to the altercation and now hastened to the two gentlemen, murmuring soothing noises intended to calm them. But by then Lord Moredon, his face having grown pale and then bright red with rage, was tearing off his own jacket and shirt, and his pale blue eyes held such a murderous expression that the proprietor of the club turned to Mr. Jones, hoping to find a more reasonable ear. There was nothing but cold, calm reason in the younger man's dark blue eyes, and something in the faint smile he wore caused Gentleman Jackson to stop and appraise the situation more calmly. The opponents were gentry, it would be witnessed, and on the whole, safer to have the argument settled in his establishment than beneath some oak tree at dawn. Then too, whatever fears he might have had about an unequal, unfair match because Lord Moredon was so much larger and more bellicose, vanished when the Gentleman, a man who knew how to take the measure of another by more subtle means than judging the way he spoke or bespoke himself, saw what advantage Lord Moredon stripped down to.

For when the larger man stood, poised, huge fists up and torso bared to the waist, a keen eye could see it was not muscle which rippled at his midsection, nor were the thick arms thickened with sinew. And when Mr. Jones's jacket and shirt were removed, the shape of the man did not go with them, as was the case with so many other men of fashion. The shoulders remained wide, the chest developed, the waist narrow, and while there was no extra flesh, that which was there didn't move as the man moved forward, as his opponent's did, except when the motion of his arms caused the long, strong muscles to slide smoothly beneath the taut olive skin.

The proprietor of the boxing salon stepped back as the opponents in the impromptu match stepped forward. Sudden wagers were placed, with the odds heavily on Lord Moredon, the money going to size and apparent passion. The first two blows that were landed, great slapping punches that sent Mr. Jones's head back, sent the odds flying up further. The next blow, a heavy thump to Mr. Jones's heart, which backed him up a pace, sent the bettors into a frenzy, trying to take sides against the few who'd wagered on the upstart Jones. But those who took a moment to clear their throats before they shouted their bets lost all their chance, though they were soon glad of it. For Mr. Jones, it seemed, had only been taking the measure of his man, and from then on he only went forward, mercilessly forward, patiently and systematically pounding Lord Moredon's face back, and back further.

"For God's sake, Jones," someone shouted after several moments, unable to watch the gory rout any longer, "finish him for mercy's sake and be done with it."

Then, as though the words had caused him to see through the black mist which had narrowed his vision, Warwick saw Lord Moredon shake his dazed head again and again to clear the blood from his eyes, and so, with a sound very like a disgusted sigh, he took the unknown Samaritan's advice and landed a blow to the other man's stomach and another to his jaw, to finally bring him crashing to the floor at his feet.

The room was very still when Warwick Jones knelt by Lord Moredon, and so they all heard what he said to his downed opponent in terse and labored breaths.

"Moredon," he said, "you made two great mistakes. Oh, not just in hiring two men to hold Viscount Hazelton down so that you could kick him into submission. I understand that's your way. But you oughtn't to have left him alive to tell the tale. And you shouldn't have forgotten that though he's lost all else, he still has friends. I am one."

Mr. Jones rose to his feet, and then it could finally be seen that he looked weary unto death. But then he seemed to remember something. He knelt again, and taking Lord Moredon by the hair, he lifted his head and added, coldly and loudly:

"And oh yes, if you hire men to work your revenge in future, I'd advise you to engage two more, permanently, to then watch over you every next moment for the rest of your life."

It was only late afternoon when Warwick Jones returned to his town house, but, his butler thought in alarm, he looked as exhausted as though he'd been out all night. He looked as if he'd been doing a great deal more that his butler ought not to ask about as well, for there were faint bruises darkening on the lean jaw, and after he'd handed his cane and his hat to a footman, it could be seen that he absently held his hand to his chest as though in some humorous imitation of the pose that vile Bonaparte was said to favor. But there was nothing amusing to be seen in the heavy-lidded eyes, which seemed more difficult for him to fully open than ever.

Mr. Jones began to ask after his guest, when his butler interrupted him, a thing he'd never do unless something as momentous as peace being declared or assassination accomplished had occurred in his master's absence. But his news was almost that startling to his employer, and he'd known it would be.

"Sir," the man said with some agitation, "whilst you were out, that Mr. Logan came to call again. This time, however, he came with his sister, and her chaperon, and her maid, and all their luggage. He said that they were to be staying on, here, with us, with your permission. I could scarcely call the man a liar, sir," the butler went on in visible perturbation, "and so could not turn them aside. I let them in," he went on, his voice rising with emotion until it almost reached normal conversational tones, "as I didn't know what else to do."

"Oh, damn," Mr. Jones said, closing his eyes as if in pain, but as his butler began to eagerly say, "Just so, so if you'd like me to show them out—" he cut in to say wearily, "Sorry, Mr. Fox, I am sorry, I'd quite forgotten they were coming. I ought to have told you sooner," he said, though he had to squelch a stab of annoyance at how quickly his sometime business partner had taken him up on his offer of hospitality. He'd never expected the man to come running with his blasted unwed sister so soon, he thought.

But, "Forgive my thoughtlessness," he only went on to say, ensuring his servant's devoted service for another lifetime for his consideration, "and would you please have rooms prepared for them all? And perhaps we ought to speak about hiring on a temporary housekeeper of some sort now that we're not to be a bachelor household for some weeks. But that can be later. For now, I think I'll make my bows, then excuse myself and see to the viscount, there's a thing I have to discuss with him.''

"There's that, too," the butler said, in his excitement sounding like a gossipy commoner hanging over a washline, eager to impart a good bit of tattle to a neighbor, "for she's up there right now. That is to say, she was here when the doctor came and he chatted with her and then he said that with her brother's permission, of course, he thought it would do the viscount a world of good if she came up to chat with him to cheer him up and take his mind off his hurts. And so she's there now, with her brother and her chaperon, the contessa, of course, that much sense they do have, and it has seemed to divert the viscount, he does seem much better than one would expect. . . ."

The butler's voice trailed off in embarrassment as he saw his master incline his head to one side as he listened to him. In the silence that followed, he could hear his own words echo, and realized he'd sounded like a prattling child. But before he could make a recovery, his master asked only:

"She?"

"Miss Susannah, Miss Logan," the butler explained, but by the time the second word was out of his mouth, Mr. Jones had nodded absently and was taking the stairs to the viscount's room.

He'd been so angry and keyed up for so long that when his business with Lord Moredon was done with, he'd felt as physically deflated as if someone had put water in his knees. Then, no matter what the outcome had been, there'd been no question he'd been soundly thumped during the confrontation as well. So when Warwick reached the second landing, his heart beat a bit faster than usual, his breath came with a bit more effort, and when he came to Julian's door, his face was wanner than it was normally, as well.

He saw Julian at once, lying on his bed in a dressing gown, propped up on a quantity of pillows. His face was cruelly discolored and out of shape, but even with the bits of plaster here and there, he could see that his friend wore a crooked smile. A middle-aged woman sat in a chair to one side, nodding at the persons in the room; from her quietude and air of calm, he knew her for the chaperon that had arrived with all the luggage. Mr. Charles Logan perched on the end of a table, grinning like a boy, obviously happy as a man at a wedding feast. And a young woman with an abundance of hair the precise color of the sunlight pouring in the window stood with her back to the door and offered Julian a glass with something cloudy in the bottom of it.

"Careful, Julian," Warwick said softly from the doorway. "That's how the Borgias did it, you know."

He started to smile and went forward to better hear Julian's somewhat slurred greeting and reply, when the young woman turned to face him.

And then, for the first time in his life, between the drawing in of one breath and the letting out of another, he lost a breath somewhere in between, forever, as every life's function he had stopped in that one moment as he gazed at her. He'd been dealt a heavy blow earlier, but this one was the most profound he'd ever received. For she looked exactly as he'd always imagined love itself would look if he ever found it.

But that was only how she looked, so in the space of time he had to begin another breath, he thought on a certain wild hope and despair that she would speak now, and so shatter the illusion forever, for certainly, he thought, her words could never match what his eyes had seen. So he waited for the platitudes, or the polite nonsense, or the stammered foolishness that could release him from this sudden uncomfortable, unsought bondage she'd placed him in.

And she, already too aware of her brother's forwardness, and her own enormous debt to her host, who must surely be this oddly stricken-looking, high-nosed, pale young man who hung in the doorway, watching her as though he'd found her strangling his beautiful friend instead of trying to nurse him, said at once, in her most conciliatory manner:

"Indeed, sir, but I understood that Lucretia did her worst mischief at a dinner table, with the twist of her ring. By the time her victims took to their beds, she was far away, as were they. So I don't think the viscount has much to fear from me, unless, of course, I take to preparing his dinner, instead of only attempting to force upon him this vile sludge the doctor brewed."

Something very much like joy leapt into Warwick Jones's heart at her amusing words, something very like hope sprang up there as well, as delight obviously registered in his eyes.

As Julian tried to make a jest and laughed a painful crooked laugh, she turned to her patient again. It was then that Warwick could see the look of fierce tenderness and the glimpse of something even more profound that she couldn't disguise that glowed in her softened eyes when she but gazed down at his friend again.

And then it was nothing at all like a blow to his heart that Warwick felt, it was rather as if someone had cut into his chest and wrenched that troublesome organ out entirely.

"Why, Julian," Warwick Jones then drawled in his usual cool, dispassionate, ironic tones, accepting the inevitable after only a restored heartbeat's pause, "with all your lumps and bumps and scrapes, my lad, as usual, you're a very lucky boy. Now, won't you introduce me to your lovely lady?"

"Not mine, Warwick," Junian corrected him with a tilted grin. "Miss Logan is ours."

7

Susannah gazed down at the courtyard beneath her high window. Hers was a quietly situated room to the back of the great house and it looked over a tiny but complex garden. Birdsong woke her in the morning, the sun encouraged daffodils and told the afternoon time on a mossy dial in their midst below, and in the nights, the wind stirred the first buds on the few graceful trees and let them gently tap the windowpanes to remind a guest that she was fortunate enough to enjoy one of the best and most unusual sorts of accommodations to be had in the heart of London. But this morning, this particular guest thought on a sigh as she let the curtains slip back into place, that she'd have preferred less exalted lodgings overlooking the busy streets, for then at least there'd be distraction and something to do in her room instead of only having the peace to worry in.

There were a great many things to do beyond her door, of course, but over the three days in which she'd been a guest in Mr. Warwick Jones's house, she'd become more reluctant to leave her room with every morning that dawned. It wasn't because her host treated her rudely or impolitely in any way at all. That sort of behavior actually would have been preferable to her. At least it would be something to complain about, it would be something to take action against, and she could pick up, pack up, and leave without a backward glance and no argument from her brother when he heard of it, either. But it was more than difficult to decide to set out on one's own and take new rooms in London, with only the poor, vague excuse that one felt "uncomfortable" and "uneasy" and "unwanted" in one's host's presence. If only she could find a reason without an 'un' on it, Susannah thought unhappily, why then she could be on her way without a qualm.

But that wasn't true either, she thought with painful honesty, settling at her dressing table and frowning at herself. For she wasn't one to suffer silently, and Charlie wasn't one to care about qualifiers; if she wrote that she was unhappy, he'd let her leave Eden if she wanted to. There was a very good reason she stayed on despite her reservations about her host, and prayed she'd be allowed to stay on even if he took to chasing her about his home with whips or leaping out at her from darkened corners with fistfuls of spiders. And that reason lay in another guest chamber on the other side of the house. For in fact, in many ways she'd never been happier than she'd been in the past three days, and if it were not for Mr. Jones himself, she would have been pleased to stay on in his house until the bronze dial in the garden below rusted away to a heap of fine green dust.

Because the sight of Julian Dylan was as welcome to her as the sight of the sun was each morning. He was admittedly now an invalid, he was undoubtedly, though he constantly denied it, always in pain, it was difficult to watch expressions try to form on his battered face, especially when one knew what glory had been there only days before, but withal, she couldn't remember a time when she'd been happier. No, to be fair, she sighed to herself, it was only that there'd never been a person she'd ever been happier to be with.

She'd thought she'd be so wary of him that she'd never be able to behave with any sense, or naturalness, in his presence, for she'd never before had to actually associate with someone who seemed to be the embodied stuff of all her midnight fancies. Indeed, her first reaction on hearing that he was to be a guest in the same house with her had been one of sheerest terror. It was one thing to fantasize about a man so magnificent he seemed to have stepped out from a book on medieval romance when one was at a safe distance both physically and socially from him, quite another to actually contemplate living under the same roof with his breathing presence. And in fact, that first time, when she'd obeyed the doctor and crept into the sickroom to see him, her heart had been beating so fast she thought she'd soon supply the physician with a new and interesting case to study. For she wondered if he'd ever had a patient who'd literally died of fright. Now she wondered if he knew how to cure such a malady of the heart as she seemed to have contracted from repeated exposure to the gentleman in the sickroom.

The first sight of his injured face had shocked the fear for herself from her. Then when he'd seen her and attempted to arrange those poor aching features into something resembling a smile of welcome, her heart had broken, even as his first stumbling, genuinely warm words of greeting had taken up all those shattered shards and swept them into a heap that would just fit into his breast pocket.

She couldn't be shy of him then, for it was clear he needed her, or someone, to help him ease his pain. She discovered that when there was need of her, there could be no fear in her. Had he been whole, on his feet, and perfect in face and form, she might well have hung back and showed her terror by showing her witlessness. But as it was, she'd responded naturally to him at once, only to find that in trying to give him comfort, she'd given herself to him entirely. It was a thing she hoped he'd never realize, for she'd only lost her heart, not her head.

She was still sane enough to know that for her, at least for now, he was still an unattainable dream. And as no man had ever been more to her as yet, she was still comfortable with that. Yet there was that little sprouting hope now, the thought that someday something more might come of their friendship, and that tiny spark of hope was in its way just as terrifying as it was thrilling to contemplate. So just now she was quite content to wait upon matters, and enjoyed each meeting with him more each day, for as it was, every time she entered his room it was like taking up residence in the pages of her favorite fairy tale.

He'd recognized her from their encounter at the Silver Swan, but had looked so woebegone and contrite when he explained his frivolous behavior, she'd forgiven him at once. That was no difficult chore, she explained, since she'd never really blamed him. But he'd asked for her forgiveness at once, and it didn't surprise her.

Even without his incredible good looks in evidence, the viscount was everything else she'd ever dreamed a nobleman might be: gentle, charming, amusing, and certainly brave. And loyal, as well, she remembered, wrinkling her nose at the thought, for he'd nothing but praises to sing about his cold, cynical friend Warwick Jones. It was undeniably good of Mr. Jones to take his friend in and care for him, she thought, and unquestionably kind of him to oblige another friend and give house room to herself, but there were all those "un's" again that sprang up when he came to mind. And then too, being charitable didn't necessarily make a person likable; if it did, then the minister would be the most popular man in town. And anyway, she thought, feeling guilty about her ingratitude, charity that felt like charity was the coldest comfort in the world.

He *was* cold, that was the thing of it, she decided. For example, she thought, she'd taken great pains with her appearance this morning, and yet after only three days in their company, she could entirely predict the reaction she'd get from both gentlemen she shared the town house with. She stared into the glass and brooded on it. This morning her maid had been in early and had helped her dress her pale hair in high and curling fashion, *à la princesse*, and then helped her on with a soft rose-colored dress cut in the same sort of simple elegant Parisian style. It was high at the waist, long at the sleeves, and low at the neck, and the light wool fell in soft folds to her ankles. Her only adornment was a pair of small coral earbobs. She'd roundly approved her own reflection in the glass, a rare enough occurrence, since though she didn't believe she was a toad, she was seldom precisely comfortable with her image. The problem was that she felt her appearance perfectly matched her place in life—she didn't quite fit in anywhere, in either class or style.

If she had yards of soft, curling ebony hair, the height of style now, she thought with animation, that would be striking, and might suit her form to perfection. A sultry sort of foreign look would complement a female whose family was not considered elevated enough to admit to politest society. Foreigners could get away with quite a lot that a native English persons might not. After all, at school, Lili Berthon, whose mama was an émigré, could be excused any number of transgressions because of her obvious heritage. Of course, those excuses were always in the nature of snide comments about how "she didn't know any better," which was lowering, but on the whole it might be better, Susannah thought, to be thought an ignorant foreigner than an inferior native.

But the only way she could have dark hair would be if she dipped it into a vat of dye, and though she'd once contemplated it, the concoction was rumored to cause baldness, and if Miss Spring were any fair example, it also looked about as natural as two fresh coats of paint would upon one's head. It wasn't that she didn't like her hair; she admitted it was pretty stuff and was rather proud of the way it held a wave. But it didn't suit the rest of her person. If she were fated to be milky-skinned and blond, with a turned-up nose rather than a classic one, then it would have only been fair to have the rest match that delicate fairylike image.

She was not very tall and so found it pleasant to contemplate the fact that she measured just up to the viscount's heart. But though she was slender, some parts of her person were far too ripe to complete the dainty ladylike image she coveted. It would have been fashionable as well as poetic, for example, she mused, to have little champagne-cup breasts of the sort the girls at school had learned from a forbidden French novel that Marie Antoinette herself had had, and been honored by having all such wineglasses exactly modeled on forever after.

But though those two salient points of her own figure were high and well-shaped, a person, she thought on a small disgusted laugh, would get so tipsy he'd have to be carried from the table if he drank from but two glasses modeled after them. Of course, none of her frocks fitted the way they were supposed to because of them, and because of the way her hips insisted on rounding out a saucy bit before they dutifully curved back in at her waist. And she refused to contemplate how unladylike an image she presented from behind; one look over her shoulder at her departing form in the glass was almost enough to make her return to her room at once. A lady, she knew, ought not to have, however small, such a high, definite posterior. In fact, she mourned, a lady ought not to be noticed as having one at all; she ought to look as though it was a wonder she could even sit down.

Such ripe conformations might make the gentlemen sit up and take notice, she couldn't fail to have always noticed that, and it wasn't unpleasant. But it was scarcely fitting either, unless she contemplated a life on the stage. The ladies noticed too, of course, and she couldn't help but feel they scorned her for it. Neither group could guess at how she yearned to be taken for a lady and rued how her looks betrayed her in that, even as her birth had done. The coloring and hair of a princess, but the face of a cheeky street urchin and the body of a peasant—what else might she expect, coming from a family that couldn't trace itself further back than the day her father had sold his first haddock, as a girl from school had once been pleased to remind her? At least one aspect of her hodgepodge heritage that worked in her favor was her eyes: dark-lashed and brown, and not blue as robin's eggs, as everyone expected them to be, she thought defiantly.

But still, whatever her mirror or spiteful schoolmates told her, she knew that this morning Julian Dylan would attempt his lopsided smile and tell her softly that she looked beautiful. He'd approve her hair and face, and being too much the gentleman to remark upon her form, would then nevertheless say her presence alone would speed him to recovery and hasten his leaving his bed. And then she'd laugh and tell him that was no compliment, my lord. And he would color up, and tell her that was never what he meant, and she'd relent and they'd laugh again together . . . and oh, she thought, but that was yesterday.

Before she could discover what today would be like with him, first she'd have to enter the small dining room and encounter her host, Mr. Jones. And he'd look up from his paper or his breakfast plate, and he'd greet her coolly and inquire as to the night she'd passed, and her plans for the day, and if there was anything she needed or wanted, all in that haughty, faintly bored manner of his that made her yearn to stagger him by replying that she'd slept in a tree, planned to walk nude down St. James Street, and needed a quart of ginever, thank you kindly. But all she'd do would be to reply softly and politely, and all the while, he'd never look at her, or if he chanced to, then he'd quickly look away, as though the sight of her offended him.

Perhaps it did, she thought sadly, but she was very hungry, and it was breakfast time, and it might be that today would be her lucky day. Since she'd lingered here as long as she dared, it might be that her host had already broken his fast, and left his house, leaving her to enjoy her breakfast in peace. It was hard to take on a plate of eggs when merely chewing up one's toast made one feel like an interloper. But taking breakfast in her rooms would be rude, and not taking it at all would be painful, for, she thought resignedly as she made her way down the stairs to the small dining room, she had an appetite, at least, to match her background. True ladies might be able to pass up dining, for all she knew, and for all they pretended, they might gather their sustenance from sunbeams. She, however, didn't care to miss her meals.

So it was a truculent expression that she wore as she took her seat at the table and noted that her host had not yet touched his plateful of breakfast meats. After he gave her good-morning and saw that she was served, he immediately began eating with some enthusiasm, and she felt very small when she realized that he'd been waiting for her, not wanting to leave her alone at the table. For he said, between bites:

"I'm afraid the good contessa cannot join us this morning. She has the headache, she suffers from it badly, periodically, I understand, and yet was so anxious to be of use to you that she sat here this morning looking rather like poor Julian around the edges, until I insisted she take to her bed until she felt more the thing."

Susannah bit her lip in distress. She ought to have noticed the poor contessa was absent from the table, she supposed she ought to have asked after her immediately. But truth to tell, although the lady had been omnipresent since Charlie had hired her on right out from under Mrs. Pruit's red nose, she had also been almost invisible as well. The contessa, whom Mrs. Pruit had insisted on calling "Tessa," was such an innocuous person, Susannah realized in some further shame, that even a sober person like herself had difficulty remembering her given name . . . ah, "Miriam," she believed it was.

But it was simpler to call her "the contessa," and indeed, more apt, for running away with a dashing Venetian count in her youth had been the one interesting thing the woman had ever done, for the shock of actually having done it seemed to have quelled her forever after. Perhaps if her impoverished husband hadn't died soon after that thrilling episode, she might have gone on to more adventures. Perhaps if she hadn't had to return home to England with nothing but his title, having to live off better-off relatives or work at companioning for the rest of her life, she might have developed a personality. But the poor lady seemed to have been thoroughly bested by life. And though she was kind and sweet and of tolerable education and far better lineage than her present charge, her present charge found her intolerably dull. Always present, without ever being precisely completely there, Susannah thought she might have been considered the perfect chaperon by a more proper lady. But whatever Miss Logan's background, she did know the proper thing to do.

"Oh dear," she sighed, laying down her fork, "then I suppose I ought to go and see how she's faring."

"Since she said she'd cope by lying in the dark with a wet towel on her head, I don't believe that's too good an idea," Warwick Jones said calmly.

A half-dozen excellent witty, nasty retorts sprang to Susannah's mind, but she only nodded, and looking up from her plate to see him watching her expressionlessly, she ducked her head down again and moved a bit of omelet to the opposite side of her plate so it could get a better view of the mushrooms there.

There might have been compassion in his voice when he said suddenly and softly:

"Are you quite happy here, Miss Logan? I know there's little for you to do as yet, since you know no one in London but the viscount and myself. And he's not in the sort of condition to be vastly entertaining at the moment, and I never was. Good heavens, I just realized that you were dragooned into sickroom duty—does it depress your spirits? Would you rather wait and visit with him when he's a bit better, or at least more seemly-looking? I'm sure he'd understand—"

"But I wouldn't!! Absolutely not!" she burst out, forgetting herself in her consternation. "What sort of paltry creature do you think I am?"

She stopped as she recalled herself, and then bowed her head and mumbled, "So sorry, I didn't wish to be rude, but . . ." just as he was saying, "I'm sorry, I didn't mean to insult you . . ." He smiled at her then, for the first time, she realized, since they had met. A smile was a wonderful cosmetic for most people, but she found it quite transformed Mr. Jones's lean face, entirely banishing haughtiness and arrogance. As it was a knowing half-smile, it lent a certain sad charm to his lofty countenance. She couldn't help but to smile back at him, and he gazed at her, his own smile slipping away. Then he said, in more of his usual dry accents:

"That's very good then, I know he looks forward to your morning visits, and your afternoon ones as well. Actually, I think if the doctor permitted you to go wafting into his rooms at night like a phantom at the stroke of three, he'd quite enjoy that too."

Seeing how she flushed at that, he smiled again, this time a little less humorously, as though at himself, for he shook his head in rue as well, before he proceeded to entertain her better than he'd done since she'd come to his home, by telling her wonderful stories about Julian's school days until breakfast was a memory.

It was when they'd finished with their meal, and were on the threshold to the viscount's room, that her host paused and said pensively:

"No chaperon this morning. Hmmm. This presents a ticklish problem. What do you say, Julian?" he asked, as his valet admitted him to the room, signifying that the gentleman was ready to receive visitors. "The contessa has the headache and here's Miss Logan—dare I leave you two alone?"

"Maht as well, Warach," the viscount answered as best he could, for he found that his jaw still tended to stiffen up in the night and so had some trouble when he first began speaking in the morning. Some of the wilder swelling in his face had begun to go down, the contours of his cheekbones had begun to assert themselves again, and thanks to Mr. Epford's diligent applications of leeches, the black and purple bruises on his face were beginning to turn to a light green tint. But he still moved with difficulty, and so moved only when he had to, and laughter seemed to bring him equal parts of pain with his pleasure. Still, now that his eyes were returning to their normal shape, it could be seen that they were alight with merriment.

"Doubt Ahd be able to compromahse her, but Ahl try if you lahk," he said, with one side of his mouth rising.

"Your head's been rattled more than I thought, Julian," his host replied with a sniff. "In the first place, the question's never about what I'd like, it's what she would, and in the second place, that's far too warm a tone to take with Miss Logan."

"Devil a bit," the viscount replied, wincing for the sake of clarity, "Susannah's not a prig."

" 'Susannah'?" his friend asked thoughtfully. " 'Susannah,' is it now? Have things progressed so far then? And you still in plaster? I had errands to run, you know, but now I think," he said, "that for the sake of my old friend Charles Logan, I had better stay right here."

He sat down in a chair near the window and stared straight ahead, and then, casting a quick glance to Susannah and Julian, waved a careless arm at them, saying:

"Go right on, go ahead with your visit, children, don't mind me. You hesitate. I don't make a satisfactory duenna? Here then," he said casually, and lifting an oval lace runner from the bottom of the viscount's invalid tray, he promptly draped it on his head and then crossed his long legs, and sat back to watch the dumbfounded pair. His elegant attire, his shining Hessian boots, and his high-nosed arrogant face were so at odds with the foolish imitation of a spinster's cap he blithely wore that soon Susannah found she had to bite her lower lip hard to contain herself. When one squeak of a giggle escaped her, he fixed her with a stern stare, the effect quite ruined by the frothy bit of lace that hung down over one eye to half-obscure that dark blue glare, just as he'd intended. Then Susannah couldn't restrain herself any longer and went off into peals of laughter. It seemed he would have been pleased to stay as he was all morning, in a parody of vast displeasure, just to hear her rippling laughter. But he snatched off the bit of lace and rose immediately when he saw the viscount's hands go to his sides and his face contract with something other than his own unrestrained laughter.

"I do have some things to see about this morning," Warwick said then, "and as you've failed the test, Julian, I don't believe I need stay on to chaperon, as yet. But have a care, Miss Logan, it's obvious that he can be killed by kindness just now. Tell him dull stories or read him the *Times*, it's all the same, and I'll see you again at tea this afternoon.

When he'd left, Susannah found herself chatting comfortably with the viscount again, even though she offered to read him the paper, just as her host suggested.

"Mr. Epford can do that," Julian said, giving her a bright glance from one almost clear light eye, "but you can gossip with me, after you apologize for misreading Warwick's character. No sense denying it, you thought him a sad loose screw, didn't you? Your face is a book, Susannah, never try to lie. But he's a splendid chap, isn't he?"

She found herself agreeing, and not just to placate her patient. For now, suddenly, it seemed that her stay in London was getting to be a better bargain every day. She allowed herself to think for a moment (starting a grin that aroused the viscount's curiosity to the point that she had to invent a tale about someone she'd known at school to cover it) that perhaps few other young women would be so ecstatic at being forced to spend their days in the company of a clever but caustic gentleman of leisure and a handsome, noble, impoverished invalid. But she was, she thought as she finally won a chuckle from the viscount. Oh, yes, she was.

But he was an invalid, and so after only an hour she arose and let Mr. Epford in to tend to him and hector him into attempting to nap. Susannah was allowed to leave only after promising that she'd return at teatime, or else, the viscount threatened, as fiercely as he could under the circumstances, he'd refuse to take any of the other, less effective medicines the good doctor had suggested. She left with a smile, and when he was finally left entirely to himself in the half-shuttered, darkened room, the viscount smiled at the thought of her as well.

She was a very good sort of female, he thought drowsily, allowing the doctor's evil draft to have its way, far more clever and much better educated than either her background or her extreme good looks implied. And it was pleasant to have her company while he mended, for he was a gentleman who appreciated women, even if he couldn't at present precisely utilize them as he most enjoyed. Not that he'd ever think of approaching Susannah in that fashion, he thought, fighting up from the fog of sleep in alarm at that dread notion. Lovely as she was, and he was a fair judge of her charms, a gentleman never involved himself with a female from her station in life. Maidservants, shop girls, tavern wenches, complacent wives—all could be dallied with and then left with a kiss and a promise. And he'd done that, he mused sleepily, often enough.

He'd always appreciated females, and they, he was grateful to say, had always reciprocated his interest. His late mama had doted on him, perhaps because he'd been her only child, perhaps because that was her way with any male, but he'd soon found she was not alone in her preference for him. From the governesses he could wheedle out of any sweet he wished, to the serving girls and maids he had similar luck with, with more discreet treats later in his boyhood, he'd always known feminine approval, and always valued it. In fact, he remembered mistily, on a huge contented yawn, he'd enjoyed them all almost equally too, from the farrier's daughter who'd been the first one to show him precisely what wonderful thing he could accomplish with her, to his schoolmaster's housemaid, who educated him on some finer points in that line of endeavor, to Mrs. Pritchard in town, who'd been the first to teach him some fascinating variations . . . He stopped further reminiscence with a sleepy chuckle. Some men, he remembered, counted sheep.

No, for all her charms, he'd never consider Miss Logan in that category. For a leg put over the bed of a bourgeois young woman meant a cap over the windmill. They didn't dally, they married. And when he thought of weddings and promises, and the one face he most wanted to see at his bedside, sick or well, and the only face he'd ever dreamed of seeing at his side at the altar, he thought of his first true love, his only real love, the Lady Marianna, and only then, fell to sleep on a smile.

So it was odd that when Miss Logan came to his door in the late afternoon for her promised tea, she heard him raging within, with such naked grief rising in his uplifted voice that she rushed into the room, thinking he'd taken some sort of turn for the worse.

"Damn you, Warwick!" he was shouting, sitting up, holding one hand on his chest. "How could you do this to me?"

"Stop! What can you be thinking of?" Susannah cried all at once, seeing the viscount's distress, and the way his friend seemed to loom over him. She ran to the bedside and stood there, chin high, glowering up at her host, as though defying Mr. Jones to strike her. Warwick's eyes flickered, but by no other movement did he show how enchanted and enormously entertained he was by her flash of spirit. She'd shown a flare of similar courage earlier when he'd suggested Julian's appearance might have depressed her, and then he'd been beguiled by the discovery that her milk-and-honey coloring disguised a fire-and-brimstone miss. He would have laughed aloud for her fierce expression, caught as he was between complete enchantment with her and the complete ludicrousness of the situation, but her mobile features turned too quickly to abject apology for him to begin.

Because Susannah had noted that both men had grown silent at her interruption, and she paused, now knowing to her profound embarrassment that whatever had happened, no one had done anything aggressive in this room, except for herself. She began to murmur horribly garbled apologies, as Julian attempted to reassure her, when Warwick said calmly:

"You needn't fear that I attacked him, I only made the mistake of telling Viscount Hazelton the truth."

"The truth! If that were all. You've left me nothing, Warwick, damn your eyes," the viscount shouted again, newly enraged, and then growing pale all at once as his loud outcry made him begin to cough.

"Oh, very good," his host replied from where he stood by the bed, his voice as calm as his friend's had been enraged, but the pained look in his eyes stopped Susannah before she could make the error of mistaking their mode of friendship again, as he said coldly:

"Yes, hold your chest, Julian, that should help, for I

understand when there's a hole in the bellows, you have only to hold your finger over it and you can get enough wind up to stoke up the fire again. It doesn't matter if you puncture a lung, so long as you let me know your displeasure. Am I right, Miss Logan? You needn't worry, my dear, Julian's not having a convulsion," he added, seeing her white face, "not precisely. He's only making himself ill telling me how healthy he is."

"No," the viscount sighed, looking a bit shamed at how frightened Susannah seemed to be by his actions, "not healthy, not yet, Warwick, as you well know. But I will be soon," he said more plaintively, his pained grimace giving the lie to his words as he sank back on the pillows, "and you promised me my revenge. *Mine.*"

Warwick began to answer and then, for once seemingly unsure of himself, looked to Susannah and checked.

"It doesn't matter," Julian said weakly, "she lives here with us now, she's close to me now, she may know."

Susannah, who'd been busy attempting to straighten the pillows, but had gone to get a washcloth to put on the viscount's white, perspiration-dotted brow, paused for a moment. At his words, the subtle color left her face, only to return a little brighter; somehow an unforeseen dimple appeared to the side of her softly curving upturned lips, and a look of such translucent joy came into her deep brown eyes that Warwick found himself pausing to watch her in astonished delight. She turned that radiant face to him, not seeing him at all, and then, recollecting herself, composed herself so strictly that when she faced Julian again all that remained of that transcendent moment was her heightened color.

"It wasn't random mohawks that attacked me in the streets, Susannah," Julian said wearily, closing his eyes as she laid the cloth on his forehead. "You may as well know that it was two villains hired by Lord Richard Moredon. But it was Lord Moredon himself who gave me this souvenir of his affection," he went on, tapping his bandaged ribs, "and all because he wishes to make sure I give no more affection to his sister, Lady Marianna."

"Whom you love," Warwick said blandly, staring at Susannah.

"No," his friend said prayerfully, "whom I adore."

"And wish to marry," Warwick added, and though no emotion showed on his face, he winced inwardly at how Susannah's head went almost imperceptibly back at each statement, feeling that once again he was driving someone back and back further, with strong blows, but knowing, once again, that it was necessary. As in any fair fight, she might be hurt, but she'd be better off knowing precisely who her opponent was and what the odds against her winning were. On her own she might have fancied Julian from the beginning, but it might have remained only a gentle dream. He and her brother had placed her into direct competition for him. If she should decide she was still determined to win him, Warwick believed that in all fairness she deserved to make that decision with complete awareness of the situation. That much assistance he owed her, he felt, however painful it might be. Or so he believed, pushing aside the teasing notion that it mightn't be kindness at all, but some lower, more selfish emotion that caused him to enlighten her just now. But she hadn't known about her rival, and that he found intolerable.

"And *will* marry," Julian swore, "and so you should have let me take my revenge, Warwick. *I* should have been the one to batter him to the ground, not you. *I* should have been the one who challenged him and bested him in Gentleman Jackson's, or didn't you think I could?" he asked dangerously, his eyes opening wide and glittering like shards of ice.

"Oh, doubtless you could," Warwick agreed casually, perching on a table's edge, "and likely more quickly than I did. But certainly not just then, nor for a few more weeks. That's why I felt it wiser to wait until today to even tell you of it. But by then, you see, when you were recovered, after all that time had passed, you'd only appear to be a hearty, healthy young man paying off a grudge because the noble Lord Moredon rightly wished to keep you, a highly unsuitable suitor, from his sister. Now, my assault was made immediately after the event, with words as well as fists. And soon I'll allow you to have some gentlemen visitors. When they confirm my allegations as to what happened to you, why then Lord Moredon will find there aren't many left in the *ton* who'll give him the time of day.

"You may kill a man in several interesting ways, my dear," he went on to explain blandly to Susannah, "but it is socially acceptable only if you do it by yourself. It is one of the few arduous things, aside from hunting, horse-racing, and lovemaking—excuse me, my dear, please don't mention my slip to your dear brother—that a man is supposed to do for himself," he mused, "since hiring others to do all one's work is a way of life among the socially pure. Actually, how little a man does shows his condition better than a bank statement. But engaging help in order to knock an enemy senseless will only net him social exile. And that, Julian, is the revenge I took from you.

"The revenge you can bring for yourself," he said, looking at his friend while all the while he watched Susannah from the corner of his eyes, "is that when you're well, and when you're strong, you'll win his sister from him. Either that, or at that time, for by then you may have also recouped some of your fortune, you may snap your fingers in both their faces, take another to wive, and there's a neat revenge, as well."

"A neat living death, you mean," Julian sighed, "for there's no other woman alive I'd want for my wife. But I see. You're right, Warwick, again," he laughed weakly. "Don't you ever grow tired of it? Don't answer, you'll only say something outrageous to make me jar these wretched bones again. I almost finished Moredon's job just then, didn't I? But thank you, and I promise, you may have the first dance with Marianna at my wedding . . . no, with your bizzare charm, let's make that the second one. Do you think me a great fool, Susannah? Ah, I can see the confusion in your eyes, but you're young yet," Julian sighed, as though he were decades older. "Wait until you are in love before you condemn me. No, wait until you see her, *then* you'll understand."

"She's very beautiful?" was all that Susannah asked in a small voice, too glad that he'd mistaken her silence for confusion to say more, too devastated at the look which then came into his eyes to do more than nod and pretend to listen as he began to recite his lady's virtues. But once he began, she was far too busy watching him to pay close attention to what he actually said. For when he mentioned Lady Moredon's midnight-black hair, his clear light eyes shone so brightly she was amazed to see she could make out the small black specks in their gray centers, before, when speaking reverently of her grace, he shuttered them with his blunt fringe of dark gold lashes. She watched more openly when he went on to describe his lady's gentle voice, for he kept his eyes closed then, seeking inspiration to help him convey the charm of it, so she could let her gaze linger, traveling up and around the increasingly defined contours of his classic face. By the time he opened his eyes again to tell her about Lady Marianna's incredible poise, her secret was again safe from him, for by then she was gazing only at the tendril of gold hair which she yearned to brush back, the one that lay so softly to the side of his neck, just beneath his ear.

And Warwick Jones, who stood silent, apparently only listening as well, noted through his half-closed heavy-lidded gaze the way that Susannah's long lashes closed over her great brown eyes as if to keep the tears that threatened there from washing her secrets out. As he watched, he discovered himself wondering of what fragrance her shining, clean pale hair might be, and appreciating the way the waving abundance of it sat on her well-shaped head, and approving her white neck. Then he remembered his roles as host and friend, and tried to keep from staring downward to admire the rest of the curved and supple form that bent over his friend to remove the washcloth from his forehead.

As Julian went on, dreamily relating other details of his lady's perfection, Susannah took the washcloth from his brow. In that one moment, after she straightened from bending so close to the viscount, Warwick saw her eyes clearly. Then, on a silent, indrawn breath, he looked away, not willing to see more, hoping his own face would never show such naked yearning as he'd seen there, such painful, completely hopeless longing, as he was amazed and appalled to suddenly recognize himself suffering, watching her.

8

There was a great deal of laughter coming from the small dining room. The sound was so infectious that Mr. Jones noted his butler's upper lip had the slightest curl to it as he bade his master good morning. Heartened by the evidence of his employee's high hilarity, Mr. Jones himself wore an appreciative grin even before he entered the room. But for all the sounds of merriment, the sight that met his eyes wiped his smile entirely away.

The two fair heads were bent close together, the dark gold one a breath away from the lemon-pale one, and though both pairs of eyes were closed through the force of their laughter, if they should open, the silvery eyes and the dark brown ones would be but a lash's breadth away from each other as well. It was entirely proper, it was morning, they sat at a table laden with breakfast foods, and a chaperon nodded pleasure at their sport not a chair's width from them. But there was nonetheless something in their closeness that had nothing to do with mere physical proximity, something so intimate in the complicity of their humor that their host felt he was watching something entirely private, and it made him feel like intruder, not host. When their laughter died away as they saw him standing, watching them from the doorway, the feeling was so heightened that he lost his appetite, and for one mad moment wondered if he ought to apologize and then simply go away.

But his cold expression made Susannah feel that she'd done something wrong and she looked to Julian at once to see what his reaction would be. Julian knew Warwick well, in all his odd and changing moods. In the few weeks that she'd stayed with him, she'd learned to recognize and appreciate her host's sense of humor, and so the sense of dislike she'd originally felt he'd emanated toward her had faded away. But there were still times, and often, such as now, when his still and watchful air and expressionless face dismayed her and made her feel that she was not only in his bad graces but also in his way.

But Julian knew what to say, he always did.

"Warwick, don't glower. See? We've left you some toast, old man," he said, and as he grinned, so did his host, and the moment passed as though it had never been as Warwick took his seat at the table, inquired after all his guests, and accepted a cup of morning coffee. It was after a few sips of his coffee, and after Julian's laughter-punctuated—and therefore entirely failed—complex explanation of the joke he and Susannah had shared that his friend had missed, that Warwick spoke again.

"Indeed," he said smoothly, in a tone as near to a yawn as was possible, "I suppose one had to be there. But speaking of being there, I understand Charlie Bryant, his crony Harry Fabian, and that young idiot Lord Greyville are coming here to visit your bed of pain this afternoon. You really ought to look more pained, Julian," he added with a raised eyebrow, glancing over to his friend. "At least put a dressing gown over your clothes. Your ribs may still be broken, but everything else has healed so admirably that I doubt their somewhat limited intellectual capacity will be able to take in the fact of your recent incapacity. And they're to be the finishing touches to Lord Moredon's complete shunning by society. They're the last left to persuade to snub him, and they, I believe, are so indiscriminate that if they won't talk to a person, then that person must be either several weeks dead or not English."

Susannah winced at that, looking over to the contessa, who after all was once the wife of someone not at all English and presently several years dead, but that lady only smiled and nodded, proving either that she was amazingly dense, as Julian often held, or that she never listened to what was being said, as Susannah suspected. Seeing nothing but approval in her chaperon's mild eye, Susannah turned to watch Julian's animated response. His host was entirely right. The viscount's evident restored health gave the lie to his recent ordeal. It must be, as he himself often jested, that though he might have the look of a nobleman, he enjoyed the constitution of an ox, for he didn't have the appearance of an invalid in the least any longer. His face had healed without a scar, some slight discoloration was all that remained to show what he'd endured, he walked upright and with only some rigidity due to the continued use of tight bandages about his ribs. It was good, she thought critically, watching him jest with Warwick, that most of the gentlemen of the *ton* had seen him when he'd been bedridden a few weeks ago, although then she'd resented having to be apart from him while he'd entertained them.

But that wasn't only because she'd missed having Julian to talk with during those long afternoons.

Warwick had ruled that chaperoned or not, she'd have been out of her place at his bedside when he was receiving gentlemen friends. She could understand that, since she was neither relation nor fiancée nor even long-standing friend of the family, it would have been awkward explaining her presence. Even if it weren't, she certainly would have felt odd in the midst of all those gentlemen, if only for being the only female in the room, aside from the contessa. But now, as then, she wondered at whether he'd decreed that because he wished to protect her from gossip, as he'd said, or because he wanted to conceal the fact that she was his houseguest entirely, as she was coming to believe. She'd passed three weeks in this house, and in those weeks she'd come to learn a great many things about Mr. Jones and the viscount. But she'd learned nothing about any other facet of life in London. It was true that she'd turned down her host's offer of a tour around the city, laughing that she'd delay that pleasure until Julian could join them, when she'd noted and begged her host to note their bedridden patient looking dejected after hearing the offer, obviously sulking at the thought of being left alone.

She had gone out in the afternoons with the contessa, and had gone to dressmakers and milliners and ribbon shops and shoemakers'. She had, she thought whenever she surveyed the growing booty bought through boredom that was filling her wardrobe, enough finery now to take Tunbridge Wells by storm. And she'd also begun to believe that was the only town that would ever look upon her new splendor by night.

It was true she needed no finery for doing what she most enjoyed, day or night, and sadder but truer still that what she wore would make no difference for it, either. For although Julian always complimented her on her appearance, it was clear the only female appearance he looked to see was that of Lady Marianna. The lady never visited him during his recuperation, but he never blamed her for it, citing her inability to escape her brother. But she was never far from his mind either. So, for all that Susannah couldn't think of anything on earth she'd rather do than keep him company, she was beginning to wonder precisely what she was supposed to be doing here in this palatial town house, and starting to worry again about how her brother had foisted her on Warwick Jones.

Warwick had become a better friend to her in the last weeks, often jesting, often entertaining her wonderfully well whenever they met at breakfast or dinner. But those were coming to be infrequent times, and she wondered now if her presence was making the poor man leave his own home more frequently than he wished. After all, she thought on a sigh, Charlie was the soul of persuasion, and for all his cynicism, she'd found Mr. Jones to be extraordinarily polite. And though she'd looked upon Julian as the embodiment of all she'd ever want in a male, however unattainable he might be, Warwick had come to be all she might have asked for in a host.

"It doesn't matter how I look to them, they'll believe anything I say, Warwick," Julian said cheerfully. "In fact, I hear they're mad as fire because they were out of town when I had better bruises, and so they'll likely invent more hideous ones to talk about just to spite those who thought they saw the worst. They might not be powerfully bright, but they're mighty competitive."

"Likely so," Warwick commented as he pushed his cup away and rose, "and I wish you joy of them. Now I have to get an early start. I'm off to see a man about a horse, Julian, or actually, about two teams of them, just as you requested. And yes, don't fret, I'll tell them you'll take over the job again when you're able. But that won't be until you've knit up again so tightly that a fractious team on the *Thunder* won't wrench your ribs apart again.

"And, oh," he added as he reached the door, tossing the remark back, "since you're so nicely upright now, Julian, old love, what do you think of us taking Susannah to the Swansons' gala ball this Saturday night? They're launching another one of their unfortunate-looking daughters into the social swim, and they've asked my presence, and will be charmed to have yours, no doubt, since I understand *everyone*," he said pointedly, "will likely be there as well."

Susannah held her breath and turned to Julian, but seeing how his eyes widened at Warwick's last comment, and so understanding its other meaning, her heart fell even as her smile rose and she asked, as she was supposed to do, "Oh yes, Julian, if you think you can manage it, please say yes, for it would do you good, and I," she went on to lie, knowing very well that she'd likely finally see the fabled Lady Marianna there, in all her glory, "should love to go."

" 'Course," the guard on the *Thunder* said, pausing on the cobbles in the innyard as he checked the passengers' tickets before showing them to their seats in the coach, "they'll take 'im back soon's 'e's able to get back on the job. 'E's a fair driver, and they likes a pretty face," he confided, moving away from the coach to speak with his visitor alone, "since it means more notice being taken of the line. The competition's fierce these days, twenny coaches at last look flying the Brighton run these days, believe it. Soon, a bloke will 'ave to 'ave all 'is teeth and more curls than a bahlee dancer afore they 'and 'im the ribbons, doncha know?"

He laughed at the notion before he asked more seriously:

"So when's 'e comin' back, sir? Not that I think 'e should, 'e's too good for the game, but if 'e must, 'e must."

Warwick Jones looked down at the stocky man and assessed him coolly before he said, honestly, "I'm hoping never, of course, but we must wait on events. He won't take charity, so I'm hoping to turn his luck for him."

"Which is the same thing," the guard said wisely, "only dressed up diffrunt. Aye, you're 'is friend, all right and tight.

So, I'll tell you, keep 'im off as long as you can. 'E's that desperate for the wages, and when they knows it, they uses it. They give 'im the night runs, where they can give 'im the worst nags, since there's no seeing too good inna dark. It ain't safe, some of the beasts is 'alf-dead and the other 'alf are sick or 'alf-mad themselves. Night runs is the worst, but 'e takes 'em, though there's more chance for folly, and they keep 'im working, like the nags, too long and too often. We all live on the road, but 'e, 'e never gets a chance to breathe. Maybe if 'e did, 'e'd do some clearer thinking.''

"Yes, just so," the gentleman said thoughtfully, and as he began to walk away from the coaching station, his message delivered as promised, the guard called after him:

"And what'll I do wiv 'is 'orse?"

"His horse?" Warwick Jones asked, puzzled. "He didn't mention one.''

"I don't think 'e forgot," the guard said slowly. "No, I reckon 'e thought I'd do for the beast, and so I will then.''

"No, you've done enough, my friend," the gentleman said gently, thinking of the inroads even a daily supply of oats could make on a guard's purse. "I'll take care of the animal. Where is he?"

"At Chapman's stables, not five miles from 'ere, where the company keeps all the coaching beasts, but whatever you do, sir, don't tell 'is nibs I told you, or 'e'll have *my* ribs, cracked and on 'is plate too, 'e's that proud.''

When the gentleman looked at him oddly, the guard paused to add, before he continued his argument with the fat man demanding an inside seat for half-price since the outside was filled up, ''. . . 'Cause a proud man don't want the world to know when 'e's got a poor love.''

There were some five hundred horses at Chapman's, and yet Warwick Jones was deeply shocked when the Viscount Hazelton's was brought out for his inspection. The beast was big and beautiful, black as night and with a fine black and rolling eye, but so high-spirited the stableboy could scarcely hold him on his tether.

"Amazed, I was amazed," Mr. Conway, who oversaw the stables, said as he leaned on the fence and watched Mr. Jones's face. "The man knows horseflesh, and still, he pays for stable space for this one. He saw them trying to team the brute up as a wheeler on the night run, and he jumps down and says, 'No, take him out, and keep him. He's mine.' Handsome, I'll grant, but what could he have been thinking of? A fine-looking bit of horseflesh, but no gentleman, he's wilder than a wild thing because he knows men and hates them, two months in harness and still fighting for freedom. 'Another three months and he'd be broke,' " I says.

" 'Aye, and another three years and he'll be dead,' the viscount says. True, true, they go fast when they're sold into coaching. Bought for a king's ransom, sold to the company for a few guineas, and in a few years, the knackers can pick him up for tuppence, if the dogs haven't had him for dinner already. But handsome is as handsome does, and there's many a gent sells the high-hearted ones into coaching—for revenge, or out of anger because they can't handle such a prideful beast, and damned to the money lost. That's why Lord Moredon sold him to us in the first place, because he couldn't tame him. Who could?"

"Julian Dylan, for a certainty," Mr. Jones replied with a grin, understanding his friend's desire for the animal now, and, handing the man a card, and a sum, added, "I'll send a groom for him, the viscount's staying with me, so his horse will as well. Only not in London, I think. I've a place in the country that will be more to his liking."

But even after his business was done, the gentleman stayed on for a while watching the horses as they came and went, and that was odd, for no one ever looked at job coaching horses, in harness or at their stables. They were like parts of a mighty machine: they did their job and wore out quickly and went unnoticed unless they failed to function properly.

At length, the gentleman bestirred himself and climbed up on his own fine high-perch phaeton to go. But before he did, he gave the stable manager another modest sum, and indicated the other horse he wanted sent to his country home along with the viscount's brute.

"That one?" the man asked, genuinely staggered, convinced that madness was epidemic in the quality. "But, sir, that beast's half-done-for. Look at that back, have you seen the hocks? Why, she's not got enough wind left to blow out a candle.''

"She was once a fine animal," the gentleman said softly, "I remember her when she was for sale at Tattersall's, the bidding went high as her heart then. I suppose the winner that day found her too high-spirited as well?''

"Who knows?'' The manager shrugged, dumbfounded. "That was years ago. Why should you want her now?''

"As you say,'' the gentleman said, taking up the reins and nudging his own fine team forward, "who knows? She breathes, does she not? I remember when she did more, and brushed, she might shine where she still has hide intact. I've a pasture she'll ornament,'' he said. And he thought, as he left the puzzled stable manager behind: She's a cast-off, there's a commonality, I'm in a sentimental mood, and it's a bad world, but a good deed, wherein a gentleman's passing moment of sentiment can save a life, however lowly.

He *was* feeling oddly sentimental as he drove back to London, and he felt marginally better for his foolish gesture, and so it had been worth twice the price to him. It wasn't often that anything lifted his spirits these days. The last moments of pure happiness he'd felt, he realized suddenly, had been on the day when he'd taken Lord Moredon down. And even then, he knew now, it had not been pure, but rather a tainted pleasure he'd experienced.

He still remembered the fierce joy that had overcome him as he'd brought his fists against the larger man, nor could he forget, though he'd rather, that one secret unpleasant moment, that second before some sane man's voice had woken him to reason and caused him to stop. For in that second before he'd put down his fists, in the midst of his revenge it had been possible, and he couldn't deny it, that after a while it hadn't been Lord Moredon he'd been pummeling, but some other large, smug, fair skinned, and red-faced man he'd been about to murder. It might have been, and if it were, then he was shamed for it, as well as for his unusual lapse of control.

Julian and Susannah, Lord Moredon and that other fair-haired man from his past . . . Warwick Jones shook his head in wonder at how many light-haired persons were cutting up his peace as he drove back along the country roads to London. Then he laughed at himself, for he realized it was always the blond persons in this world that had given him grief. He had better never voyage to the Northlands, he grinned to himself, or risk becoming either a mass murderer, or destroying himself just as handily, if more pleasurably, by becoming a complete satyr, for if fair men drove him to one sort of excessive passion, their female counterparts had always driven him to another.

Not always, he corrected himself, growing thoughtful, letting his team set their own pace to carry him home as his thoughts carried him back to an older home. Once he'd been as thrilled and astonished at the appearance of certain fair-haired persons as he'd imagined a Hottentot might be at his first sight of them. For though his mother was a beauty, she was a dark-haired, dark-eyed one, and his father had lived only long enough to leave a fleeting impression of what sometimes appeared in his memory as a mirror image of his own grown face. It was after those first orphaned years, long after influenza had taken his father, that he'd first become particularly aware of fair persons. His mama had decided to give up widowhood, and it was a large blond gentleman who caught her eye, even as he supposed it was her large white mansion and ample dowry that brought him to her notice. For he was a nobleman, and the widowed Mrs. Jones, for all her dark attraction, was a mere "Mrs.," as all the Joneses from his branch of the family had ever been. And, as Warwick Jones reminded himself sadly, with a shake of his head, just as family wisdom always held, it was only when the usually cautious Joneses wished to cut a social dash that they came to grief, and so it was to be again. Only, since his mother had only married into the name, it was naturally, then, he who was to suffer.

He hadn't known that, of course, on the day that the Earl of Camberly married his mama. Nor had he an inkling of it when he'd been introduced to his two new stepbrothers, the marquess and the viscount, and his new stepsister, Lady Caroline. Although, again, it made perfect sense that the widower nobleman would come complete with progeny, since however pressed for funds, a man like the earl would scarcely have wished to sire an heir on a commoner like his mama, however handsome she, or her fortune, might be.

The first months had been very pleasant, Warwick Jones remembered with a wistful smile; perhaps that was why he had at least one particular problem with blond females. For Lady Caroline had been only a year younger than his own seven, and looked up to him wonderfully for that year's advantage of her and because, further, he knew all the nooks and crannies, retreats and hidey-holes in his great house quite well and was pleased to share the knowledge with her. Although Lord John and Lord Avery had been several years older, they had been kind, and he, who'd been lonely as an only child of a single parent, had, in very much the same way that their sister admired himself, lionized them as much for being older as for their offhand kindness.

It was only when the earl, after the honeymoon had shown him his wife was his in every particular (for he'd been pleased to find she was just as pliable and soft-willed as he'd thought), decided to begin to refurbish his own rotting great hall that the trouble began. His wife was happy to leave her home and go with him, that was never the problem. And there were carpenters and stonemasons and architects aplenty, all willing to work, but unfortunately, all waiting to be paid first, as well. It was then, when the earl discovered his credit was in as bad a condition as his ancestral home, that he also discovered that all of the famous Jones fortune was securely tied up. The earl couldn't lodge a penny of it loose, for the first time he tried, distant Jones relatives came out from the woodwork uttering threats of lawsuits, and masses of dignified men-at-law appeared with all sorts of writs in hand.

Because, it transpired, the Jones fortune was well-supervised, well-documented, and entirely secure, and all invested in the one small true heir, who had less than a decade of years to his benefit, although he had more than several hundred thousand pounds, along with securities and properties and annuities, to his name.

The earl's new wife's portion was his, but it was doled out quarterly, and at that, scarcely enough to cover his gambling bills for a year. But the mansion was hers to live in, in comfort, for the rest of her life, with her new family as well if she wished, and poor lady, Warwick Jones sighed, though she didn't wish, she had little choice, since her new husband's home was fit only for mice and deathwatch beetles. So it was as well that the heir to all that the earl coveted was sent off to school when he turned eight, for he was a sensitive child, and better still that the lawyers, after seeing the earl's face when he first heard the news of the disposition of the fortune, mentioned that the boy's legacy would go to a distant uncle if misfortune should ever befall him before he came into his majority.

But if looks couldn't quite kill, Warwick Jones soon discovered they might maim. Because the earl and his sons, chafing under the omnipresent knowledge that they lived on the sufferance of a commoner, and a small, slightly built, sensitive one at that, soon found ways to let their benefactor know how inferior he was to them.

Since nothing could be done for the earl's thwarted hopes but vengeance, that was done in plenty. A state of war was declared, and Warwick, having seen his idols turn from benevolent friends to treacherous foes, learned from an early age that appearances can be deceiving. His mama didn't wish to see discord, and feared her husband's displeasure even more. She was now completely her husband's creature, and so if she ever had regarded the author of all their difficulties as her own son, she never showed it again. His home became a battlefield, but Warwick managed to survive and soon discovered that he had a knack for it. He made certain he became no male version of a Cinderella, in any event; he realized it was they who were quite obviously beautiful, and he who had the wealth, and he was never cut out to be a gentle, placid victim. Thus it was doubly irritating to his tormentors when they came to realize that he was cleverer, as well as richer than they. And even more insufferable when they found he didn't fear pain, and, realizing they couldn't afford to kill him, had learned to bear it long enough to learn to defend himself in physical as well as mental fashion.

So if his stepbrothers mocked his slight, olive-skinned body when he was a boy, and grimaced to each other and complained in loud tones that the "goblin," as they came to call him, had too long a vacation and was getting on their nerves when he came home from school, they learned to grumble instead of shout their displeasure with him when they saw how tall and straight he'd grown and learned how strong he'd trained his body to be when he survived adolescence. Even the earl no longer said the word "goblin" or "commoner" in his hearing—his debts had gone unpaid long enough to make his entry into his club an embarrassment—after his stepson began to handle the family finances himself.

But, in truth, he *was* a goblin compared with their fair splendor, he'd always seen that. He was long-nosed, olive-complexioned, and even the grace notes of his midnight-blue eyes and soft brown hair were as dun compared to their radiant blond good looks. Perhaps that's why they'd come to personify beauty, if nothing else, to him. But they signified a good deal more as well. That might have been why, after he'd been amazed to discover his schoolmate, the similarly handsome, similarly noble Julian Dylan, to be such a good openhearted person, he'd become his fast friend.

And then, of course, there was Lady Caroline, Warwick thought with a reflexive cough, choking on the memory that would never be easy to swallow, not even after nearly a decade. For it was never easy to remember how he'd heard her explain her toleration of his tentative courtship, that day that he'd come cat-footed into the library to surprise his newly grown stepsister with the first daffodil.

For, "Good God, Caro, we like the place, and have been comfortable here for dog's years," the viscount had drawled to his sister, "but it's rather unpleasant to think of you having to bed the goblin to secure it for us."

"But it hasn't gone that far yet," she'd giggled, "and if it does, it will be marriage."

So of course, it wasn't, not after that—not that she'd added another word to the subject, nor even disparaged him, nor ever discovered that he'd heard her. But she'd not defended him. And until that moment, he'd never known how badly he'd wanted that. And after that moment, he'd never forgiven her for showing him his one weakness. Not that she'd ever known that either. For he'd picked an odd method for showing his displeasure. He'd restored their house for them and made them an allowance, and so relieved them of his presence. He seldom saw them again, unless they came to him, gruff and belligerent, needing funds and begging for the money by belittling him, hat in hand. He always gave the money, along with arrogance for arrogance, feeling that he was winning, even as they left feeling they'd cheated him again. But then, he thought, he was undeniably an odd man; they'd always been right about that.

Having been denied love for so long, he never sought it again—now wasn't that odd? he asked himself. He sought women, but that was not the same thing at all. He was basically a solitary man, though he had a few good friends, both male and female. But it wasn't that sort of companionship he constantly wanted. In fact, it was one of the despairs of his life that he had to seek such women out so often, that he was so enslaved by his passions. Because he acknowledged a true goblin trait in himself: the deep and omnipresent need for sensual pleasure, a profound liking for affairs of the flesh. He was, he thought, smiling to himself at the comparison, remembering his studies of Plato, in many ways a driven man, a coachman, very like his friend Julian, but very unlike as well, for he couldn't be half so adept a whipster, since he was always trying to steer his life with two fractious teams linked together: the white horses of sweet reason, and the dark horses of desire. Perhaps that was why, he thought, throwing back his head and laughing, startling a farmer in the fields into thinking it was a drunken gentleman tooling along the high road to London, he kept driving himself around in such peculiar circles.

Well, he amended, smiling to himself, not peculiar so much as improper. He seldom had anything to do with young ladies of the *ton*, knowing very well that two dances and a kiss were equal to a declaration in their society, and he'd sooner, he often thought, find a drab from the streets than a debutante of the *ton* in his marriage bed. Since neither would've had a chance to know him very well before they nipped under his coverlets, both would be there only because of his money, and at least, he reasoned, the tart would be better at what she'd do there. He didn't care for deceit, having had a surfeit of it in his youth, and so he also avoided society's sportive married ladies. And as he'd neither lie nor make promises he'd no intention of fulfilling to fill his bed, this streak of perverse puritanism narrowed the field of potential partners for him alarmingly. But he'd discovered the particular field left for him to cultivate was ever ripe and always held a rich harvest: an obliging female might always be found with whatever color hair, or for that matter, anything else, he fancied, for the right price.

But his life was cluttered with blond persons at the moment, he thought, pleased with himself now that he found his difficulties amusing, and, finding himself amused, decided that what he'd needed all along had been distraction. He reasoned that since such a little bit had worked so well, more would be even better, since, locked up in his house celibate all these weeks with that tempting little Miss Logan, he'd absolutely lost his clear sense of judgment.

He'd come to know her scent the way a fox can sense its dinner wafting on the wind, and he'd felt the ends of his fingers ache every time he'd helped her to her seat at the table or brushed his hand against her skin at some other insignificant moment. She was blond, of course, and supple and sweet-breasted and full of laughter, and he'd been yearning for her like a boy. Even more dangerously, he'd discovered, just as her brother had boasted, she had wit and courage, education and charm. And of course, naturally, she loved Julian to distraction, or thought she did, and who could blame her?

At first he'd avoided her for Julian's sake, and then for his own, for only a fool would seek love where there was such clear infatuation for another, worthier man. Then too, he wasn't precisely seeking ''love'' either, or at least not the sort that was the only kind she could supply, being moral, proper, and conventionally raised. But he'd given up avoiding her when he saw her take note of it, and had seen the quick hurt register in her eyes. Now, of course, the problem was worse. For him, he amended, only for him, for she might still have a chance for happiness with Julian; because of her looks, or her money, or the spite of Lord Moredon, those two beautiful dreamers might yet be joined.

The last tollgate before London came into view, and Warwick gave up his brooding. He'd been uneasy and strangely vexed with himself these past days, for he seldom got caught up in other people's affairs and yet had allowed himself to get completely tangled in Julian and Susannah's lives and hopes. He had never been a romantic dreamer such as Miss Logan so evidently was, and he scarcely knew her well enough to really love her, even if he believed himself still capable of that mythical tender passion. Unlike Julian, he was far too old for infatuation; he believed he always had been. But he was well acquainted with sexual obsession. Too well, he thought on a frown. But at least he knew what he was suffering from, and so knew what cure to take. He might be able to help the others too.

Distraction was what was clearly necessary for them all. They'd all been pent-up for too long to have any perspective. Julian's misfortunes had thrown them too closely together. Their host had already proposed one remedy for them, and was resolved to take another for himself. Miss Logan would soon have a ball to attend, Julian would shortly leave the house again, and for himself, he'd seek out some new female immediately, one who could give him surcease from his impossible desires through satiation of his real ones.

He relaxed as his horses, only two this time, and only real ones, took him through the streets of London toward his home. Everything seemed simpler now. Doing Julian's errand had done him good; he hadn't appreciated, until the weight had dropped from his shoulders, exactly how bedeviled he'd been. But when he'd begun reminiscing about his childhood he'd realized how low his spirits had sunk, and when he'd thought of a resolution to his problems, he'd felt free again. The country air had cleared his head.

He'd lusted after the girl; she fancied Julian. Nothing could be more natural in either case. He needed a woman, Julian needed a fortune, and she . . . Ah well, he thought, familiar desires now ascendant, that was her problem, and not his.

That evening, Mr. Jones bade his two houseguests a good night shortly after dinner, and neither noted that he didn't retire to his rooms, but left the house instead. Nor did either of them note how jauntily he said his farewell, nor how eager he was to be away. For the Viscount Hazelton was himself eager to get to his rooms and pen several messages. The majority of them were various notes to sundry devious people of his acquaintance, all to ensure that the one important message was delivered. And that one was addressed to the Lady Marianna Moredon: asking if she were going to attend the Swansons' gala ball.

Miss Susannah Logan scarcely noted that her host had gone so precipitately, and for once she hardly was aware that Julian had left her side rapidly as well. For she'd only just discovered that very day that for all her lacks, her chaperon had one marvelous asset: she knew fashion as well as she did not know most of the things that happened around her. So there were fashion plates to study, and a dress to be gotten up, one that would make her look splendid, make her look fitting, and most important, make her look as though she belonged at her first fashionable party, the Swansons' gala ball.

Mr. Warwick Jones made his way in leisurely but determined fashion down several twisting streets far from his elegant town house. The house he eventually entered was more expensively gotten up than his own, although far less tastefully. But the young woman he purchased there was tasteful enough to suit his most exacting standards, for she was fair-haired and well-endowed with what he'd been seeking. If she had no conversation, he was content, for he asked for none; it was enough that she smiled a great deal and grimaced at appropriate moments, when she was supposed to. He supposed that to be her training, never realizing that his own early training had made it impossible for him to be less than a superior lover—a man who believed himself to be repellent to women being a man who'd always have to see to their pleasures, even the ones bought only for a night's relief, before his own.

Long after he'd been admitted to the house and the young woman he'd purchased there, he finally made his way, far less jauntily, home again. He'd gotten exactly what he'd paid for, but discovered to his annoyance that temporary satiation had nothing to do with satisfaction. And so he decided that he'd have to take some other route to more permanent gratification, and would likely have to go to the bother of setting up a mistress. He believed, as he lay awake in his own bed again pondering the problem, that for the sake of his own restored serenity that would have to be soon—definitely before he had to escort his disturbing young guest to an evening's festivities, and so certainly before the night of the Swansons' gala ball.

9

Susannah studied herself in the long looking glass for a very long while. It wasn't that she was in love with her image so much as it was that she wanted to memorize the way she looked just now, after her maid and her chaperon had left her to herself. They'd told her again and over again how well she looked, and how perfectly dressed she was for the night. She continued to gaze at her reflection in order to assure herself that she might leave her room confident her appearance was perfectly in order. Then, if anything were said, or if any doubts assailed her after she'd gotten to the ball she was being taken to, she'd know at least that the fault didn't lie in what people could see of her, but rather in what they thought of her actions or personality.

She stared into the glass. A worried-looking, fashionably dressed young woman met her troubled eye. But there was nothing in her gown or hair or form that could be singled out for censure. She saw a deceptively simple, high-waisted grass-green India muslin gown with a series of flounces at the hem of the skirts, the dress tied beneath the breasts with a darker green riband. The puffed sleeves had a myriad of tiny gold and yellow flowers appliquéd upon them, as did the borders of her skirt, so that in all, she thought, the gown reminded her of a spring garden. Her hair was done up with small real flowers, all echoing the gold, yellow, and green theme. The contessa had pronounced Susannah too old to wear classic debutante's white, and yet too young for black, it was too late in the season for brown, and it was too bold for her, as an unknown, to make her appearance in poppy red, thus vetoing all the colors that her charge had selected for herself. It was also too warm for velvet, satin was too overbearing, and silk too sensuous, her chaperon had insisted. And so she wore the simplest gown of the most undemanding hue, and Susannah thought at last, turning from her reflection to draw on her long lime gloves, she supposed it would do.

It did more than that, although she couldn't see it. For all she gazed so long at herself, she never noted the way the color brought out all the subtle tints in her fair complexion, nor did she see how the soft and pliant material draped itself about her shapely limbs so as to accentuate them in the latest fashion, as well as the time-honored fashion of classic sculpture. It was as well that she'd been too busy wondering about color and material to take sharp note of how low the gown was cut, or of how much of her white bosom was bared above it, or of how simple it was to see, in that deceptively simple gown, how her breasts were high and full and buoyant as they rose above her slender waist. And she was so busily inspecting each tiny flower that had been set into her hair, she'd never realized how even the smallest buttercup seemed vulgarly blatant beside the masses of pale curls that had been coaxed to spill like charming froth around the confining riband of her new upswept hairstyle. Nor did she see how her host started when he saw her, for once completely shaken from his urbane pose, because by then she was gazing at the Viscount Hazelton and saying, just as she thought it, that she'd never seen anyone look so splendid, no, not ever.

He wore only standard gentleman's evening wear, and so he told her, laughing at her compliment and turning it back upon herself immediately. But it was true that the dark black jacket and black pantaloons, high white hose and high white neckcloth all set off his athletic form to perfection, even as the stark colors highlighted his golden hair, making it look as though a ray of sun had come out at night solely to illuminate him and pick him out from the common run of men. With his slate eyes and fair skin, the only other color to be seen was in his waistcoat, which was a welter of small golden flowers.

"Warwick lent me his finest feathers." Julian grinned. "Well, at the least, his finest waistcoat, since he insisted on my getting my own new evening wear for tonight, my old jacket having been lost in the wars''—he grimaced, remembering the night he'd worn that jacket last—"so to speak. But here, you'll wound him if you don't butter him up. I haven't seen him dress so fine for ages, and if no one notices the effort at least, he'll sulk.''

When Susannah looked at last upon her host, where he stood smiling lazily, watching her, she noted that he did look very fine, exceptionally so, and if she hadn't been so startled by Julian's transformation, why, she'd have said so at once, and so she said it now. Warwick's evening clothes fitted him to perfection as well, and something in the way he comported himself, something in the set of his wide shoulders above his lean body, and the carriage of his head above his snowy neckcloth, gave him a look of easy command, the look of antique princeliness. His waistcoat, as he begged Susannah to note, suddenly becoming more the fop every moment to amuse her and cut off her stream of compliments, was a medley of silken embroidered blue and green flowers—now, wasn't that superior to Julian's mere golden weeds?

She laughed, as he wished, and never mentioned that the color matched his dark blue eyes, for he was too busy explaining that very fact to her with a great show of wounded feelings because she hadn't commented on it immediately.

"But I was too dazzled to speak at once," she protested. Then she began to compliment him so fulsomely that he took another tack and began to repay her in such flowery phrases that Julian fell to laughing and joined in with him. Soon they were all complimenting each other outrageously, with the words "Venus," "Adonis," "magnificent," and "gorgeous" flying so fast that when the contessa arrived in the hallway to join them, and they began to tell her how well she looked, she could have been pardoned for taking their praise of her new lavender gown and turban for mockery, if she were the sort of woman who ever found mockery in anything. As it was, she took it with a curtsy, as she was supposed to do, and then mentioned the time, and allowed her host to assist her with her wrap. At that Susannah's laughter stilled and she felt her palms grown damp and her heart pick up its beat, and she looked so suddenly stricken that Julian began joking about her competing with the Swansons' lovely daughters to put her at her ease, and Warwick, as he helped her on with her pelisse, said softly, "You cannot fail to enchant them, this will be a joyous evening for you, you'll see."

But she remained very quiet as the coach took them the few streets to the Swansons' town house. As they waited in the long coach line for their chance to be set down in front of the house, she found it difficult to swallow, much less speak. Somewhere out there, she was thinking, somewhere beyond the flare of the footmen's torches, somewhere in that grand and stately house where all the lights were burning bright, somewhere beyond that great and gaping door through which all the elegant people were entering, lay the world she'd only ever dreamed about. The world of gently bred people, the select few, the educated, wealthy, and mannered that her training had prepared her for, and her birth had kept her from. Until now.

As the carriage finally pulled up to the door and stopped in its turn, Warwick and Julian looked down to her white face and then over her bent head and directly into each other's eyes. Each nodded, though no word was spoken.

And so when the butler gave their names to the announcer hired for the evening and he intoned: "The Viscount Hazelton, Mr. Warwick Jones, Miss Susannah Logan," to the company in his best stentorian tones, all the assembled guests looked up. They saw, paused at the top of the stair to the ballroom for their inspection: two elegant gentlemen with one beautiful young woman between them, with one of her gloved hands upon each gentleman's arm. And since it was such a wide and turning staircase, they then could see them walk in just so, three abreast, as though the gentlemen could not, either one of them, bear to part from her.

Conversation picked up again after that, and from the tone of it the gentlemen knew their entrance had made no little stir. Even as they bent over the hand of the latest Swanson debutante (this one, they noted sadly, no better-looking than any of her sisters, and from the tone of her stilted greeting, no wiser either), they could hear the whisper "Who is she?" repeated so many times that Warwick swore later the force of the wind from it disarranged his hair and almost blew his cravat askew.

Punch and orgeat were being served, and as Warwick went to fill his guest's cup, he told Lord Leith that she was his guest—newly come to the city, he assured the Marquess of Bessacarr—and yes, absolutely uncommitted, but only as of yet, he warned the Baron Bly. Thus assured of having at least some few gentlemen he considered worthy of the name with her name on their minds, he delivered a cup of watered wine to Susannah, and stayed by her side as Julian made sure other curious gentlemen heard her name right.

The Swansons always began their dancing late—some wits claimed that this was because they wanted to be absolutely sure the gentlemen were foxed enough to have filled up their daughters' dance cards before they let the music begin. This was unfair; enough gentlemen knew their duty to their hosts, no matter how unfortunate the Swanson girls were in their appearance, to fill up their cards even before they grew tipsy enough not to care whom they danced with. The music was delayed because Lady Swanson knew the most successful soirees ended late, and so, she always vowed, then hers would too. It made little difference to her that her social evenings lasted so long, not because of all the enjoyment the guests couldn't bear to part from, but because they knew they wouldn't be fed until the dancing was done, and they refused to go home hungry.

Thus no one ever came to the Swansons' soirees on time, and as no one wanted to be the first to arrive either, the glittering company continued to assemble, milling and chatting in informal fashion as the night went on. Several gentlemen engaged the viscount and Mr. Jones in conversation, and were dutifully introduced to Susannah, but as they couldn't dance or dine with her as yet, and as she knew none of the guests beyond introductions, she had little to say as she stood and watched the crowd of fashionable persons. She was glad of the babble and distraction, since she was so awed by all the magnificent-looking people she doubted she could have managed a coherent word to them, much less a full conversation. All the words she'd been tossing about in jest with Julian and Warwick earlier seemed applicable to these elegant persons. Seeing them in the flattering glow of candlelight, burnished by her daydreams, and glorified by the fact that she was actually among them at last, they were all of them, indeed, gorgeous and magnificent, to her.

Glancing down to her, seeing her brown eyes wide with wonder, the faint rose in her cheek accentuated by the excitement, her attention wandering with her gaze all about the vast ballroom, Warwick and Julian again exchanged nods and bemused smiles over her head. She would do, this would do, and as soon as the Swansons' allowed the music to begin, they were sure she'd take her first little step into society, and eventually achieve her dream.

But as Julian's own attention soon wandered again, and he could be seen to be studying the crowd and watching the door and practically jumping with anticipation each time the name of a new arrival was pronounced, Warwick doubted that Miss Logan would soon achieve her brother's secret dream. Julian had become her good friend—that couldn't be doubted. But still the idiot continued to treat her like a sister, Warwick thought in some exasperation, as he saw his friend restlessly searching the crowd for a glimpse of the Lady Marianna. He knew that was Julian's quarry as well as if his friend had called her name aloud as clearly as he was so obviously hoping he'd soon hear it announced. But at least Susannah didn't seem to notice this, she was so busy drinking in all that lay before her.

It was when Warwick realized with dismay that he had been gazing at her as nakedly and avidly as she surveyed the crowd that he determined it was almost time for him to go. There were few sights more lovely that watching her soft lips part in wonder, there was little in the room as pleasant to look upon as the awe in her bright eyes, and few visions as riveting as watching her white bosom rise and fall with every excited breath she drew. But he couldn't continue to stare, with every passing moment making him wishful of doing far more in homage to her beauty. And since there was nothing and no one else in the entire room to interest him tonight, he decided he'd leave her to Julian's care as soon as he made sure Lord Moredon was not in attendance. For he himself had, if not better, then at least more fulfilling things to do this night.

By the time the first fiddler scraped a tentative bow across his strings, the company was entirely assembled. As neither of the noble Moredons was in attendance, Warwick had a rueful smile for his friend Julian's brave front in the face of defeat. Then he had a few private words with him, took Miss Logan's hand and kissed it in farewell, bid the contessa good night, and after pleading his abject apologies at having to leave such a paradisiacal place so soon due to a previous commitment, took himself off gratefully into the night. The Swansons were momentarily grieved to see him go—he was youthful, of good family, and enormously wealthy. But then they contended themselves by reasoning he was an odd fellow and too antisocial for their Elizabeth, too old for little Sarah and Laurel, too tall for Helena, and far too clever for poor Cecile, whose come-out it was.

Susannah had her first dance with Julian, and as she stepped across the ballroom floor in the patterns of the set in time to the stately music, she wished that living moments could be captured, like pictures, on some sort of canvas or book, so that they could be taken out and lived through again. If there were one moment in which she wished to pass the rest of her life, it would be this one. All the graceful couples turned and spun around her, yet she was one with them as she touched hands with Julian now, and then again. She exchanged smiles with him and saw the approval in his light eyes as she stepped around him; surely this, she thought, was not only as wonderful as, it was even better than it had ever been in all her fancies.

But no joy was eternal save that in one's creator, or so she'd been taught. And so it was, for when the music ended, Julian looked up to the stair and she swore she could see his breath stop. She looked up as well and understood on a sigh of acceptance, as the graceful young woman continued to descend the stair, that a fool's paradise had been no place to expect to set up residence. Lady Marianna Moredon was every bit as lovely as Julian's rapt face clearly, though mutely, said she was.

Her silken gown was blue as gentians or her own calm eyes, her midnight hair was parted simply in the middle and drawn back to form two ebony wings to either side of her pale and lovely face. She held her white neck like a swan as she breasted the crowd and her tall slender form moved to its own stately music. No wonder, Susannah thought, as Julian took an unconscious step forward, entirely forgetting whatever he'd been in the midst of speaking, no wonder at all, she thought sadly, recognizing defeat, and finding it bitter for all she knew it to be just.

Julian and Warwick had told her she looked beautiful tonight, Susannah thought bleakly, and she wasn't blind and had seen admiration in other men's eyes. But so they might enjoy ogling a barmaid, she thought in despair, for one glance at Lady Marianna reminded her that there was the true beauty of a true lady, of the sort that nature had seen to it that she could never aspire to. It was that which plagued Susannah even as it defined the other as a lady in her eyes equally as much as her name at birth had done. For Lady Marianna was tall and straight and slim—when she descended a stair, Susannah decided mournfully, she obviously never had to worry about things moving in the front of her frock in an unseemly fashion, and clearly she'd never have to fret for a moment that she'd ever leave viewers with a distasteful wobble to remember as she left them behind. Nature, and not just training, Susannah grieved, had seen to it that the lady could glide.

The Honorable Miss Merriman might be a raven-haired beauty too, but even she accepted defeat when the assembled company's attention flew to the new arrival. Miss Merriman had also been named an Incomparable, but as they both were dark beauties, as was the current rage, they shared the Season's laurels. However, Lady Moredon's title was higher and her name older. So there was an instant stir among the chaperons and mamas at her entrance, and even the dashing widowed Countess of Keswick seemed dismayed. But there was no one to hold a candle to her, or so Susannah thought, for not only was there the evidence of her own eyes, so her escort obviously believed as well.

The musicians, having been quiet for so long, were eager to earn their wages and had begun the opening bars of a new set, a country dance, when Julian looked down to Susannah and said, although his gaze went past her to his lady:

"I can't dance with you two times in a row, Susannah. It

isn't done, you know. But here's Lord Leith coming, he's a very good chap, and you promised him a dance. I'll see you after. Have no fear,'' he said, joy suddenly ascendant in his handsome face, "you'll do very well. And I'll be here."

Lord Leith was an extremely good-looking gentleman, tall and dark, and charming to boot. He danced with grace and Susannah enjoyed herself, the better perhaps because she couldn't hear the whispering about her beginning on the sidelines. This was natural enough considering that the mamas, chaperons, and wallflowers had little else to do but gossip, and the object of their attention was an extraordinarily lovely young woman who'd come to the ball with two amazingly attractive gentlemen, and now was dancing with one of the Season's greatest catches. Any one of these details would have made her an object of speculation. The fact that she was an unknown as well made her even more delectable to discuss than she was to see.

"Julian's nowhere in sight," her partner said when the dance was done, as he looked down at her with a gentle smile. "I'll deliver you to your chaperon then, Miss Logan, for I see Warwick's eloped as well. The fellows must have gone stony blind," he murmured as he led her to the contessa, "leaving you alone."

He stayed at her side and joked with her awhile, and when the next set struck up, left her, with a smile and bow, never to return to her side. This wasn't because of the increasingly cruel tone of the gossip on the sidelines of the great ballroom, nor was it because he found her unattractive. But the gentleman was presently bedeviled by another miss he'd met, so Susannah could have been the embodiment of Venus herself and he'd not have been able to oblige her with his attentions.

The heat in the ballroom was increasing with the company. The press of people augmented the warmth given off by the tiers of hanging candles and blazing lamps and gaslights. But the Swansons kept the windows tightly latched, for they'd hopes of the Regent honoring them with a visit and knew how he detested drafts. The ladies scarcely minded; not only did they have gauzy gowns and fans, but they'd no choice if they wished to meet the gentlemen. But the gentlemen began to wilt in their high collars and tight jackets, and those without escorts or pressing interests in the party began to plan escape into the cool spring night. Thus, both the Marquess of Bessacarr and the Baron Bly, although noting Miss Logan's charms, decided they could do without furthering their acquaintance with her this night since they had more interest in survival than in sociability. And since neither was remotely inclined to contemplate marriage at the moment, they also reasoned, as many other reckless single gentlemen did that night, that however charming she might be, they could find more obliging female companionship in a cooler place, such as a tavern or even the streets. In any case, they believed they'd be fools to remain in the Swansons' stifling ballroom, and whatever else they were, they certainly were not that. So despite the interest they'd shown their friend Mr. Jones, they left as soon as they were able, without ever requesting a dance from the gloriously lovely young woman he'd pointed out to them.

Susannah scarcely noticed the damp pervasive warmth; actually she began to feel a sudden chill, for the dancing went on, the night went on, and not only did no other gentleman approach her, no other stranger of any gender did. She became painfully aware that she was entirely among strangers. She stood and talked with the contessa until she realized that she was speaking foolishness for the sake of appearing to be conversing, and then she subsided, hoping that her face was as impassive as her emotions were not. It seemed to her that everyone else was talking animatedly, and every other female present was laughing and gossiping and making merry, except for herself. This was true. Even the most insignificant debutante was in full spate, even little Miss Protherow, whose idea of a conversation was a review of the weather. This was also understandable, because all of them knew each other, had known each other from childhood upward, and would continue to associate with each other unless one of them died or made a dreadful misalliance by running off with a commoner, which would amount to the same thing. This was one circumstance that Susannah's two usually astute benefactors had forgotten.

The other was that someone might know who she was.

For the whispers from the sidelines soon had to do with the dread words "trade" and "cit" and "commoner." It scarcely mattered whether the informant was some young woman who'd been at school with Miss Logan and resented the way her beau was eyeing the fair young woman, or whether it had been some papa who'd recognized the name and didn't wish for anyone to talk to the beautiful girl long enough to discover that he did business with her family, or whether it had only been Miss Merriman, who'd heard a snippet of something and blew it into something larger with her trilling laughter, once she'd noticed the unknown was taking attention away from her. It was enough.

Susannah was left entirely alone. She felt embarrassment increase to shame and then turn to persecution, because although it had been hard enough to ignore being ignored, now she seemed to think every overheard bit of laughter was directed toward her, and believed every smile she saw was one of mockery. But she couldn't leave. Because, as the contessa pointed out uneasily, Mr. Jones had already gone, and though she doubted the viscount had deserted them as well, he was nowhere in sight and they could scarcely leave without him.

The Viscount Hazelton was nowhere in plain sight, and he was overjoyed because of it. His lady had actually led him out of the ballroom, into the hall, and then through a side door to the back garden. In the sudden natural darkness he could barely see her before him, and could scarcely credit his good luck that she was there.

"I must be brief," she said softly. "We don't have much time—if we're discovered, we must say you took me here to enjoy the cool of the garden because I felt faint."

She breathed the words so quietly he leaned closer to her, delighted that her soft voice gave him the excuse to draw so near he could almost touch her with his own lips.

"You told me you'd be here tonight, and so I came too. But who is that girl you are with?" she asked curiously, and it took a moment before he remembered Miss Logan and replied, quickly so as to turn the subject so that they could talk about themselves as he wished:

"No one, that is to say, a friend and a guest of my friend Warwick Jones. A very good sort of girl, actually," he mused.

"Oh?" she replied. "She's very beautiful."

"Is she?" he asked with a smile she could hear in his voice, pleased that she'd noticed, thoroughly enchanted that she'd seemed a trifle piqued by it, and his answer made her emit a tiny satisfied chuckle before she said more seriously:

"My brother's still not well," and at that Julian was glad she couldn't see his face, before she added, "Imagine—being set upon by thieves, poor fellow, shortly after you were. The city is becoming a jungle. But he'll recover, though he must rest now. He let me come here tonight with Bridie, my chaperon, and she's let me have some moments to myself, for she's a good soul and willing to listen to good reason." She paused, and decided not to mention that Miss Bridie listened especially to the jingle of good coins, and then said hurriedly, "But you asked if you might see me here tonight, and I said yes, and, Julian, it is of utmost importance that Robert doesn't discover I've seen you, for he's still adamant that I should not, but . . . Oh dear," she whispered so close that he could feel each soft sigh against his cheek, "it's so dark, so it would be no lie if I said I had not, for I can scarcely see you here, can I?"

"Can you now?" he whispered, and greatly daring, impelled by the darkness and her closeness and his longing, he took her into his arms and took her soft cool lips. He kissed her gently at first, and then, dazed by his good fortune, he drew her closer and opened his lips against hers and moved against her as though she were his lover, not his ideal. He realized his mistake soon enough when she pulled away from him, catching her breath in a shocked gasp.

"I'm so sorry," he swore, almost stammering in his fury at himself and his clumsiness. "Forgive me, Marianna, I forgot myself, it's only that I've wanted you for so long. Oh, my love," he said in dismay when she didn't answer, "I wish the time would pass so that I didn't have to meet you like this to steal embraces. It's the desperation of it that made me so crude, forgive me."

"You mustn't say that," she said at once, and before his white smile could grow enough for her to see it in the dimness, she explained, killing it at its source, "because I'm not your love, and cannot be, since my brother has forbidden it.

"Now I really must get back to the ballroom," she said curtly, and when he didn't reply, she placed her lips against his cheek and gave him a soft, cool, chaste kiss as she breathed regretfully, "I shall dance with the Earl of Alford, Robert believes me to be permitting his courtship. But though I'm in his arms, believe that my eyes shall be seeking yours. More than that," she said quickly, "I cannot say, don't ask it of me."

He did not. He only led her back to the ball, and stood to the side, by a potted palm, by himself, where she asked him to remain so that she could see him, and he kept his eyes only upon her as she danced by with Earl of Alford and then a dozen other gentlemen. He noted, with the only joy he felt for the rest of the evening, that she kept to her promise, and whenever she danced, in whosoever's arms she floated past him, her eyes frequently sought him out where he stood alone and longing for her. It was only when dinner was served at long last and she went off on the earl's arm that he again allowed himself to feel such mundane things as hunger for food, and the excessive warmth of the room, and the lateness of the hour, and then at last he remembered Susannah Logan.

Warwick Jones had also forgotten the unexpected warmth of the evening. But then, he was in a far less crowded chamber and had a great many other things to do to keep his mind off the weather. Nettie Fletcher had a pleasant, airy set of rooms, and knew that if she wanted to move further up the ladder of success she'd already climbed from out of obscurity, entertaining gentlemen like Warwick Jones in those rooms was most important. It was Nettie's business to know what was important to her career, for her career was the business of pleasing wealthy gentlemen.

She was anxious to please, and at first that gratified Warwick. He'd met her at a soiree of a far less socially elevated sort than the one he'd lately left to keep his appointment with her, and this evening they'd arranged was the first one he'd passed entirely alone in her company. It was, both knew, though neither said, in the nature of a test, to see if they'd suit. Meaning: to see if the gentleman was willing to pay Nettie's way in life for the next several months, or years, or days, or for whatever time he deemed possible and found her pleasurable, or she found profitable. For she too had some say in the matter; she wasn't common street-ware, being young, newly arrived in town, almost educated, friend to Harriet Wilson and some other famous courtesans, and suddenly in fashion, and so she still had some choice in such matters. She wasn't precisely beautiful; though she had a quantity of curly brown hair and a dimpled countenance, she was too ample and blunt-featured for such a designation, but she had a lively, if somewhat raucous wit, and that was more treasured in certain sets than mere beauty.

Although Warwick had always disliked the idea of setting up housekeeping, if only light, occasional night housekeeping, with any person, and could not quite forget he'd be paying for the privilege, still he knew that now he needed more distraction than he could get from chance-met, chance-taken females. She would be, he thought, even as she began removing her dressing gown at his touch, a person who would come to know and perhaps care for him, his needs, and his personality, and not just the demands of the body she was now urging him to uncover to her.

She had, he noted with growing pleasure, a body as full as her laughter, and as pliant as her morals.

"Oh, very nice," she said, in her turn, eyeing him with pleased interest as he disrobed to join her in her wide bed, and he took it for false coin and paused, before he took her in an embrace, to tell her on a small laugh that it wasn't necessary. But she'd told nothing but the truth as she saw it. She knew full well there were others in society she could have taken up with who were far more prominent in the *ton* she wished to make her mark upon. But she was young, and suddenly in demand, and so she'd reasoned she had time enough to indulge herself this once, instead of only her career. She'd chosen this unusual gentleman because she thought he had more than the killing wit she deeply appreciated: he had a thrillingly different, sensual sort of face, and a clean, well-coordinated body, and as she discovered so soon that she had no time to tell him any of this, he had a way about him, a way of making a female, even a professional one, forget what she was about to tell him, whether he would have thought it merely flatter or not.

But Warwick Jones, to his chagrin, discovered that he couldn't stop thinking about how he was purchasing the right to what he was doing, no matter how he tried to transcend the moment and enjoy it only for its own sake, as he was used to do before he began to desire things he could not have.

Sometime later in the evening, when Miss Nettie began to wonder why the gentleman had not yet committed himself to her for even a short term, even after his obvious appreciation of her, she decided to rouse herself from her deep content to ensure that he would. She'd discovered, for all the reasons she'd originally imagined, as well as for several new ones that she couldn't know had been caused by him trying to forget why he'd come to her, that he was precisely what she wanted, tonight and for the foreseeable future.

He was amused at her diligence, and being human as well as polite, cooperated beyond what he'd thought his desire to be. But at length, some of the doggedness in her effort communicated itself to him, and he left off stroking the nape of her neck and touched her lightly on the shoulder.

"You need not do this, you know," he said softly.

"I know," she said smugly, before she returned to her labors, "but I'm very good at it, aren't I?"

He smiled wryly at that, and then, taking her by the shoulders, raised her up to end her persistence, which he now couldn't help but feel was more akin to salesmanship than sensuality.

"You flatter me," he said, and then added a little roughly, "Now let's see if you overestimate me."

Laughing, she desisted, accepting that, and him. And if he found he wished, no, yearned, midst all his pleasure, for a lover who could offer him more than expertise, he never mentioned it, not then, not later.

But much later, as he drove back to his town house, he thought she'd looked a little saddened at his leaving, even though he'd left her a great deal more money that she'd expected, for he hadn't proposed another meeting. He might yet return to her, he sighed, because she'd been very welcoming, and tonight at least, at last he felt numbed and weary, surfeited and content, entirely free of the compulsion that had sent him into the night seeking surcease. Still, he thought on a shrug, remembering her disappointed, subdued farewell, as he gave his coat to a yawning footman before chiding him for being up so late and dismissing him for the night, what else could he expect, she'd been a very good actress, such women always were.

It was while he was thinking of vagaries of womankind that he heard the slight sound, and following it to its source through his darkened hallway, he came to his own library. He wondered who might be ransacking his shelves at such an advanced hour of the night—no, he realized, at such an early hour of the morning. Only one lamp was lit, and as he edged the door open, he saw his guest, Miss Susannah Logan, crumpled in one of his great leather library chairs, weeping into the arm of it as though it were a wide brown comforting leather breast she'd cast herself upon.

She still wore the finery she'd worn earlier, only now, of course, the green muslin was crumpled and limp, and her hair had come down from its high riband, and the small flowers that had bloomed in the glory there were shriveled and half cast-off, with only a few still hanging loosely from their fair moorings. He found he could walk, all unnoticed, almost up to the chair, before she noted his presence. But then when he said, "Odd, I always thought Ophelia should be drenched in that final scene, but not with tears, precisely," she started, leapt up, and stood before him, her tender skin blotched, pink-faced and red-eyed, and yet still, he thought, thoroughly lovely.

"Oh dear," she sniffed, "I'm sorry."

"For what?" he asked curiously, reaching out a finger to catch one teardrop that spilled out from her glistening eye to trail down her cheek. "For weeping? But why? Nothing dreadful has happened, has it?" he asked, suddenly abandoning his playful, thoughtful air, alarmed, wondering anxiously if perhaps Moredon or some others had revenged themselves on Julian again, or, he thought wildly, taking in all of her disheveled appearance, on her, while he had been at his low pleasures.

"Oh no," she said, speaking a little thickly because her voice was so glutted with tears, "I'm just being f-foolish. It's only because I was so unhap . . . unhappy tonight at the Swansons' ball," she said, her lip quivering with misery.

He grinned at her then, he couldn't help it, she looked so absurdly sad and so very young. And she, seeing that fellow feeling in his tilted grin, drew a sobbing breath and then came into his open, comforting arms, just as he'd intended. Once there, she wept freely again, and midst sniffles and new freshets of tears, stammered out her woe: how they had all ignored her, how everyone had let her alone, how she couldn't find Julian all night, and how no one had spoken to her, how she had to pretend it hadn't mattered.

"Hab you eber . . . ?" she began, only to stop in watery laughter as he pointed out how nasal she sounded, by mimicking, "No, I neber . . ." before he urged her to use his proffered handkerchief. She did, and then immediately went on, more clearly:

"Have you ever had to stand and pretend it made not the slightest difference that everyone ignored you in a roomful of chattering people for hours? Oh, Warwick," she moaned, sinking into tears again, "I didn't let on to Julian when I came home here, I was so brave! I didn't want him to feel bad, but I couldn't find him anywhere until it was time to leave. And then I came down here because I couldn't sleep or stop weeping once I started. I was so alone. It was awful, *bloody* awful, as Charlie would say, and just die if he heard me say it . . . yes, *bloody* awful," she repeated, before she began weeping and laughing at the same time.

He held her close and comforted her with foolish little half-words and sounds until she subsided entirely, only lying in his arms and heaving little broken half-sobs at the end, as a tired child would do. His chest was hard where she laid her head upon it at last, but it was comfortable to be held thus against a muscular frame, with strong arms around her, and a deep voice she could hear at its source murmuring comfort. His jacket was softest velvet and his scent was a cool and pleasant blend of spice and fern. She rested peacefully against him, and he never wanted her to move from him again, until, looking down at the crown of her pale hair at his lips and finally scenting its honeysuckle fragrance, he realized that once her sorrow stopped, he'd become aware at last of the exact shape of each contour of the form pressed so closely, if innocently, to him. Then he stepped fractionally away from her, and as if his distancing had woken her from her reverie, she looked up at him at that.

He was gazing at her as though mesmerized. Despite all his best efforts, he was helpless again in the grip of the desire he felt for her. It hadn't diminished, nothing he'd done this evening had even blunted it. Because, he distantly realized, it was of a different order entirely from the lust he'd slaked tonight and so hadn't been so much as touched by anything he'd done.

"But you're not alone now, Susannah," he said then, very softly, and then hesitantly, almost against his will, added, "For if Julian's not, I'm here now. Won't I do?"

And looking down at her hurt brown eyes beneath their long tear-beaded lashes, and seeing her swollen lips, he found the impulse irresistible at last, and never taking his dark blue gaze from her puzzled eyes, he moved closer and only looked to her mouth at the last as he slowly brought his own lips to hers. But then her eyes widened as she became aware he was about to do something she was unprepared for, and startled, she stepped back quickly, exclaiming:

"Ah, no!"

She hardly had to, for though he'd no awareness of drawing back again, he'd done so too in that moment, before she'd ever spoken. For he'd been jolted back by a sudden thought before his lips had even grazed against hers. He'd not remembered his manners, or that he was her host, or any proper thing he was supposed to. Instead, all that he'd done all through the night had come back to him in brilliantly clear obscene images and full force. Then he'd withdrawn instantly, as if even unthinkingly he hadn't wanted to sully her with his lips, with his hands, not this lovely trusting girl, not now after all that he'd so lately done. Only after he'd pulled his head back did he hear her exclamation of horror. Then he stood stiffly still, after drawing in his breath as though she'd stabbed him, and watched her with opaque eyes.

She said nothing more at first, but stared at him as if seeing him for the first time. After a few silent seconds she recovered herself and tried to explain her cry, appalled to recognize it as insult, but he, after that moment, said gently, in a quiet, consoling voice:

"It's very late. Odd things happen at this hour. Things will look better in the morning, or so my nurse always said, though personally I always found they just looked clearer, perhaps because of all the light. You're very weary, so am I, go to sleep now and we'll talk it over, all of us, then."

She said nothing more than good night to him, and went directly up the stair to her room, as he'd asked. He saw her safely there and then went slowly to his own rooms. Then he sank to his bed, his head in his hands, and congratulated himself bitterly, remembering the shock in her eyes when he'd drawn close. "Well done, Goblin," he muttered. In the midst of his self-loathing he realized that naturally he'd found relief tonight where he'd sought it, but obviously, no surcease where it was needful, for he could never be allowed that, of course.

And after she'd closed her door, Susannah closed her eyes in embarrassment, as she finally realized what she ought to have noticed despite her own preferences, or his own kindnesses. Now, too late, she was aware at last that whatever else her host was, he was, of course, what she'd entirely forgotten or ignored: a man.

10

It rained in the early morning after the Swansons' ball, and the next day dawned cool and gusty. No one who'd been there was surprised, fewer still were disappointed, and a great many people never noticed it at all. The warm heavy dampness resolving itself into cleansing rain lifted spirits rather than depressing them, the servants who had to clean up after the affair were just as glad that it wasn't a balmy spring day they were missing, and most of the noble guests poked their noses out of their covers, and feeling the chill in the air, decided to sleep the rest of the day away.

But Warwick Jones was in his small dining room taking coffee with his newspaper at his usual hour just as though he'd been to bed as early as a deacon, although his guest thought his heavy eyelids drooped a bit lower and his usually olive complexion was a shade lighter. She didn't have an opportunity to study him long, for almost as soon as she set a silent foot into the salon, he looked up at her. She hadn't the time to read the expression in those dark blue eyes before she dropped her own gaze and made her way to her seat, murmuring her good morning as stiltedly and awkwardly as though, she thought in disgust, when she'd heard herself, she'd just dropped a pitcher of milk in his lap and not a curtsy in his direction.

But there was no one else at breakfast as yet, and so as soon as the butler had left the room and the footman bearing a pitcher of cream had gone to refill it, she spoke.

"I have to explain and apologize to you," she began hurriedly, speaking even faster when she saw his surprise, registered by an uplifted brow and his coffee cup suspended in air. "I never meant to insult you, indeed, I'm very grateful to you for comforting me when I was so wretchedly unhappy last night, and you never actually, ah, *did* anything, ah, to me, so I believe I was only extra sensitive and being absurd and foolish and—"

"What a lot of rubbish," her host commented pleasantly, putting his cup down in its saucer at last, and cutting across her hasty speech in laconic but clearly audible tones. "I believe I'll stop it now, although I'll admit I'm curious to hear what other abuse you can heap upon yourself, 'absurd' and 'foolish' being, I perceive, only an introduction to a more comprehensive list of your faults, but Mr. Fox is fleet-footed and I'm positive he'll return before you're done, and I do want to have my say before my toast grows cold. But no, my dear, there was nothing irregular in your behavior at all. I may not have "done" anything precisely, but you're entirely right in what you imagined I planned to do, and so entirely correct in your refusal to be party to it. Some religious persons hold that the thought is equal to the deed, only it's not half so much fun, I'd say. In fact"—he paused and seemed to ponder, his head tilted in thought, before he went on—"if I thought that were the case, I believe I'd go ahead and do everything I thought straightaway, since it would eventually be weighted equally in the eyes of the Creator. I suppose," he mused, "that's just what I've been doing all my life anyway. But I digress," he said calmly, looking at her expression of incredulity with amusement,

"And I apologize to you, Miss Logan, for a gentleman ought not to force his attentions on an unwilling female of any sort, not to mention one that is his guest, as well as a friend he's supposedly comforting. I hope I don't presume in that as well—saying that we are friends," he prompted, seeing her confusion, "and I do hope we shall be able to remain friends. And I promise not to repeat the episode."

"But of course we're friends, at least I'd be proud to think that we are," Susannah said at once, "and I still think I was being missish and you don't have to make any such promise, or any promises at all, really, because I know it was late, and you were only trying to comfort me."

"And I was foxed and you were mistaken and I was so weary I only wanted to rest my lips against yours and it was merely a trick of the light and a thousand other polite lies, yes," he said with infinite weariness, "yes, I see, but thank you," he added with something like amusement in his voice, "for refusing my promise of future good behavior. It lifts my spirits—there's nothing like having something naughty to look forward to for cheering a fellow up . . . Ah, good morning, Julian, Contessa, you come in perfect time to prevent Susannah from straying from the paths of righteousness. The marmalade must have been left to ferment too long, she's making all sorts of rash statements this morning."

"I'm the one who strayed, Warwick," Julian said as he slid into his chair, and sighing, added, "and you can't know how sorry I am, forgive me, Susannah," looking at her with such contrition in his clear light eyes that she would have forgiven him anything, even the fact that he'd deserted her the previous night, as he now asked her to do.

"It never occurred to me," he explained to Warwick, as soon as she'd protested there was nothing to forgive, "that she'd be left alone, how was I to know everyone would behave like such a pack of dunces? She was clearly the prettiest one there," he went on, as Susannah thought: Ah yes, but your lady was the loveliest one, wasn't she?—"and I expected her to be surrounded by admirers. But Bly and Bessacarr left early, and Leith was in a snit over something some chit said to him, and cut out as soon as he could too. In fact, a great many other fellows made a run for it as the ballroom heated up. Swanson must have been trying to hatch eggs as well as get his filly popped off."

"It was certainly a tropical atmosphere," the contessa put in, as she steadily spooned her eggs, "and a great many gentlemen did leave because of it. But I believe the difficulty lay in what was said within the ballroom by those who remained, and not in what was not said by those who left it early."

"Indeed?" Warwick said with great interest, looking at the contessa with sudden interest just as his two guests were, but not displaying shock at her sudden loquaciousness as they were.

"Yes," the contessa continued, meeting his gaze with equanimity, "so I believe, because it's the lot as well as the duty of a chaperon to listen to what's being said along the sidelines. Unfortunately," she said, with something very like real unhappiness fleeting across her usually pleasant round face, "there was a great deal of talk about Miss Logan's circumstances, actually about her family, you understand. That talk was couched in such derisive terms that it would've been a very brave gentleman who asked her to dance, for had he done so after having heard it, he would've felt he looked like a fortune hunter, or so I believe."

"I see," Warwick said thoughtfully, as Julian, leaning forward, asked quietly, if a bit bitterly:

"And I suppose, having come in with her, and my financial state being well-known, I was looked upon as one of those fortune hunters?"

The contessa dropped her mild gaze to her plate again. "It was not Miss Logan whose name was linked with yours, my lord," she replied with great care, avoiding a direct answer to his direct question.

"Oh well," the viscount said with great false humor, shaking his golden head in rue, "then it's only Lady Marianna's fortune they think I'm after. I should be pleased—half a rogue is better than one, I suppose."

"Interesting," Warwick said, refusing to so much as smile at his friend's pun. "And I?"

The contessa didn't attempt to misunderstand him, since it seemed to the others that the lady found it easier to speak with him than to anyone else in the household. Although Julian always jested with her, it might have been the combination of his title and radiant good looks that accounted for her continued self-consciousness in his presence. Her formality with Susannah may have been caused by her outsize sense of duty, for she evidently took her responsibilities very seriously and so took great care with what she said to her charge, despite all of Susannah's efforts to get her to be more natural with her. It might have been that Warwick had an undeniable way with people, as Julian claimed, but it was actually because he'd sought her out when she'd first come to his house and spoken with her at length then, to learn what he could of her and put her at her ease. Neither Julian nor Susannah knew this, but Julian at least, knowing his friend for so long, wouldn't have been surprised to learn it. If he had, he'd have said it was precisely Warwick's way, since Warwick always swore he found people even more fascinating than books, while he also always vowed there was little in life as interesting as books.

"You, Mr. Jones," the contessa said, a rare real smile gathering on her lips as she spoke, "are acknowledged to be a mischievous gentleman. And so little that you do is held to be remarkable."

"Wonderful," Warwick said comfortably, contemplating a biscuit he was slathering with preserves. "Now I may go out and commit mass murder and not cause any chatter. But," he added over all their laughter, as he noted the footman's hand shaking more than his tightly compressed lips were while he poured a crooked stream of coffee into his cup, "I'd rather they didn't say anything about any of you either. It's interesting that I, who don't give a damn—excuse me, Contessa (no, I won't apologize to you, Susannah, you've given me leave to do wickedness)," he said blithely, before he went on, "I, who don't care what they say of me, am free of censure, while Susannah, who's blameless, and Julian, whose only sin is temporary insolvency, are so maligned. Interesting, interesting, but wrong. I think we ought to set about righting it, don't you?"

The first thing to do, they decided, once the cups and plates were cleared from the table and they sat around it like generals plotting tactics against Napoleon, rather than three young persons and a chaperon plotting the overthrow of the social code, was to be sure they were most in sight. After all, as the contessa agreed, it is easier to gossip about persons one does not see that about persons one runs into all the time. Absence made tongues wag faster, she commented ruefully, causing the company to recall that having eloped with a foreigner, she had in her time been the object of a great deal more gossip than they could imagine, since it was easier to say dreadful things about persons one didn't expect to have to face again the following day. Or, as Warwick put it succinctly, as Susannah giggled and Julian winced, "In society, obviously, familiarity breeds content."

If they weren't going to be invited to *ton* parties, Warwick decreed, they'd go to the theaters, the operas, the dog shows, or wherever else polite society went, in order to keep themselves clearly before the *ton*'s wide watchful eye. And, as Julian said with a grin, he and Warwick could certainly go to other sorts of entertainments in low society as well, where they might see the gentlemen of high society. When Susannah looked put out at that, and said pettishly that not only was that unfair, it was likely immoral, Warwick replied, "Boxing matches immoral?" in the loftiest tones, even as Julian looked insulted and said that cockfights might not be humane but they were scarcely immoral. Then when Susannah flushed so rosily that she looked sunstruck, both gentlemen began laughing and Warwick said he thought it was very generous of them to sacrifice their fair bodies in her cause, and Julian added that it was positively brave as well, before the contessa shushed them, if not for the sake of propriety, for the sake of her charge's complexion, which was growing more brightly red by the second.

"Eventually," Warwick said, when order had been restored, "our very accessibility will do the trick, and if you are seen everywhere, doubtless you will be invited everywhere as well. I can't promise you Almack's, child," he told Susannah gently, "because I don't work miracles, only possibles, but it's possible to be accepted into society even without admission to that august and overrated social club, as any number of good people can tell you. One of my friends who is no less than a duke, and pious to the point of boredom now that he's married and given up his youthful indiscretions, is still not admitted there. Or so, at least, I think he isn't, because being an intelligent fellow, the Duke of Torquay would, I think, rather have his foot surgically removed from his leg entirely than set it over their threshold even now."

"But, Warwick," Julian said slowly, "although I don't doubt that eventually a viscount turned coachman might come to be considered amusing rather than scandalous, and a young woman of beauty and wealth might be admitted to their ranks because it seemed she'd already been, don't forget that Lord

Moredon's a fixture in society and will be best pleased if we're not. He'll try to throw trouble in our path."

"I understand Lord Moredon is about as popular now as a recurrence of the Black Death, wouldn't you say, Contessa?" Warwick asked.

"No, actually, a little less so, sir," the lady replied thoughtfully.

As Warwick grinned and rose, saying that they all should be in readiness to go to the theater that night, Susannah also stood, but she sprang from her chair and then spoke up abruptly. She'd kept to a brooding silence for a long time, or at least for longer than she usually did, and was obviously very grieved.

"No, I think I'd rather not," she blurted, and when they all stopped to stare at her, she explained, "Everyone's been wonderful to me. Everyone here, that is," she said at once, "but although I know it's meant as kindness, I see that this is coming to be foolishness itself. Oh, I'll admit I once had certain dreams, but this is reality and I believe I've had enough of it. And if I have, why then, why should you all put yourselves out so much and open yourselves to insult, and all for the sake of thrusting someone into a society that doesn't want her? Especially when she doesn't want them, no, really, not anymore."

Warwick began to reply, with great reasonableness, that it was because he had nothing better to do, when Julian stood and took both of Susannah's hands in his.

"Believe me, I only wish I were that noble," he said sincerely as he gazed down into her troubled eyes, "but it isn't all for you, you know. I have very good reasons for wanting to be acceptable too, since the one I want so much is so much a part of that world that I couldn't ask her to leave it even if I should ever succeed with my wildest dreams. My helping you will help me as well, and I thought that you wanted to help me too."

Warwick found Susannah's expression so painfully stripped of artifice that he had to look away, but Julian was pleased her face was so transparent a key to her emotions, thinking he'd convinced her and that all the pain and sorrow he saw were sympathy and concern for himself and his plight.

"Of course," she said, glad to be the object of his search-ing gaze even if it seemed he never actually saw her, even though this rare moment of having his complete attention turned her hands to ice, then caused them to burn, and made her breath quicken. "Of course," she said, "I'm not so selfish. I'd only forgotten," and then, to his mildly aston-ished expression, she explained, "I was so wrapped up in myself, you see."

They parted then, and while Susannah went to cool her cheeks and hide her confusion in a book, Julian went off whistling, pleased that he'd been the one to convince her to persevere for her own sake, as well as his. Then he set out to discover if there were a way he might compound his luck this day and lure his lady to the theater this night as well. And Warwick, although knowing that his box at Drury Lane was free for the night, still said he was going to see about tickets, for he needed to get clear of his house to clear his head. Because even though all his suggestions had been taken and all his plans adopted, he was strangely subdued.

His butler noted it, but handed his master his hat and helped him on with his greatcoat without a word of inquiry about it. Not only would the query have been presumptuous (for it was not his place to ask such, even after seven years of service with his master), but having known Mr. Jones ever since he'd set up his bachelor establishment, he reasoned that since his employer often wore a melancholic expression, it was often difficult to say if he were lost in thought or sincerely troubled.

He was more than troubled. He was remembering what he'd jested at the last, and thinking with a certain amount of sudden incredulous shock that he'd only stated a cold fact. For he'd realized with complete dismay that in truth, he had nothing better to do. Nothing at all.

As he strode down the streets, he discovered himself defen-sively documenting his usual pastimes, and becoming in-creasingly depressed as the exact meaning of the word "pastime" was borne in upon him. He had no steady occupa-tion, even his many investments and business dealings sel-dom took up a great deal of his time. Being a city dweller, he left his estates to capable managers; although he went over accounts every few months and implemented changes, the handling of his properties could scarcely be considered even a preoccupation of his. Those endeavors were his political concerns. But for all his interest, he realized suddenly that his actual labor usually amounted to no more than supporting those with good ideas, and writing strong objections for various other politically active men to use against those he disagreed with. He'd done some diplomatic work for his country in the past when he'd been abroad, he did some planning and investigation on its behalf now, for though there now was peace, he wasn't the only one who worried about its permanence. But even there, for all it was important, it seldom amounted to more than a few days and nights out of his busy life.

And it *was* busy, he argued with himself. He collected manuscripts, invested in art, supported charities, fenced and sparred, read voluminously, patronized the theater and a quantity of light females who otherwise, he finally thought, in a wry admission, might have to find employment standing up. But he'd been well pleased with his life before Julian and Susannah had descended upon him to change it altogether. Or at least, he'd never fretted if he hadn't been.

Odd, he brooded, as he walked faster, as though to escape the unpleasantness of the thought, how paltry, petty, and unworthy a man's diversions seemed if he had to document them, hang them out singly in all their naked inconsequence, and defend them, if only to himself. Could a man who conventionally wed, bred, and raised the requisite family claim he did more, he wondered, or was it only that he never felt he had to claim anything? But then, he remembered, with a cynical grin, that he was never a conventional man, so for all his astuteness it would remain an unanswerable question for him, since it had never arisen, and likely never would.

Mr. Jones held the lease on a box full of seats that jutted out high over the orchestra, and though it was located to the right side of the theater, and had the best sight lines for both seeing and being seen, and was usually occupied when there was a good program being performed, it was seldom stared at for any length of time by other members of the audience. Warwick Jones was a peculiar fellow, everyone knew that:

rich as Croesus, secretive as a clam, and though oddly attractive to many in the *ton*, oddly inaccessible to them as well. Of course, he was obviously seldom inaccessible to the parade of lovely ladybirds that could generally be seen clinging to his arm or sitting by his side in that box when he decided to grace it, but though invariably polite, and incredibly charming when he put his mind to it, socially correct persons generally received only the most correct of acknowledgments of their existence from him. But tonight he bowed and waved and saluted the more social of his fellow theatergoers as if he found their presence more gratifying than Kean's own. That wasn't the only reason his box was ogled so much this night.

For "that smashing yaller-haired chit" was there again, as Lord Greyville burbled to his cronies, and "that simply exquisite Viscount Hazelton" was there as well, as the Honorable Miss Lancaster simpered to her frowning mama, while Lord Bigelow had to suffer hearing his adored Miss Turnbell tittering about the fellow's resemblance to a Greek statue. And when he replied spitefully that Hazelton had about as much in his pockets as one of those stone boys did too, she replied that Adonis did very well without pockets, and turned her back on him and kept her eyes on the box for the rest of the night too, to prove it.

But then, people in society seldom went to the theater to see the performances, except for those of Kean and Mrs. Siddons, and even there they went only to say they'd been, Warwick explained when Susannah whispered a complaint at how she could hardly hear the singer's performance. As Warwick began to tell her how lucky she was, for actually he could hear it very well, Julian leaned close and explained further about the way the *ton* went out of an evening and found more entertainment in keeping tabs on each other than in what was happening onstage. But when Julian leaned so close, she became very still and then realized she was no better than anyone else in the audience, for not only did she not hear anything happening onstage then, she scarcely heard what he was saying, since she found herself listening only to the soft cadence of his voice and never to his words at all. Thus she never asked him about all the gentlemen she'd noticed who could scarcely take their eyes from the stage when the ballet began. And so she spared her escorts the pleasure of informing her that such behavior had to do with other sorts of hungers than that for culture. For those enraptured gentlemen knew no more about ballet than the fact that a great many shapely legs were needful to create it. Their attention was focused on the dancers, not the dance, as they busily selected their evening's future treats from that lively menu, since most were hopeful of hiring on those same young females after the performance for other sorts of performances of a more private nature.

This sort of information would have amused and titillated her, but when Julian sat so close and spoke so softly into her ear, she had no desire to know more, although she was glad of the dimness when she discovered a great desire to do more than listen to him. She was so staggered by the sudden notion that came to her that it was as well that Julian thought she was embarrassed at the way the dowager in an adjacent box was staring at them, and continued to try to divert her with lively gossip. Because all this while, as he'd been recuperating, she'd sat by his bed and been content to chatter with him, and when he'd gotten more mobile, she had been pleased to become his confidante, even if the plans he made for his future with another female had caused her some pain. But even that had been a pleasurable pain, since he was her first and only experience with infatuation and she'd never felt such a way about a male before, and until circumstances changed she'd expected and hoped for nothing more than the sweet bitterness of the excitement and pleasure in his company.

But suddenly now, tonight, she sat by him, so close she could scent the bay rum upon his newly shaved cheek and feel the warmth emanating from his vibrant body beside her through the thin material of her gown. He was so near that she could sometimes feel the whisper of a strand of his golden hair brushing against her cheek when he bent to whisper to her, and though they didn't touch, she was acutely aware of his hard thigh close by her own body. This alone made her giddy. But then, as he smiled at something to do with some lady he was talking about, she found herself staring at his perfectly chiseled lips and suddenly wishing to have more than words from them. For the first time she realized he was not just some picture-book hero, but a breathing male, and that she wanted his lips as close to her own as his friend Warwick's had been last night, and then closer still.

She was one-and-twenty and she'd been kissed before. But only that, and never for very long, and never very excitingly. Young men her brother had introduced had courted her and she'd been curious about what a man's lips might do, for she'd read a great many novels that had passed among the other girls, under her covers at night at school. After a few of those hasty embraces she'd decided that physical pleasure was not for her, and in all, she'd been relieved. Because in the past there had been certain longings, certain thrilling sensations in unmentionable parts of her body when certain subjects were discussed or forbidden illustrations pertaining to them were seen, and she'd feared that was only more proof of her common background and nature, only more reason that she wasn't a true lady, aside from the accident of her birth.

She'd been taught, just as she was told by those at school who were entitled to the name, that a lady never felt such things. A lady loved her husband, and lay down on her wedding night in obedience to him, and suffered the mysteries of that marriage bed in order to bear his heirs and give him his strange joys. For gentlemen always took great pleasure from such things, it was the way nature had formed them, they couldn't help it—that much, at least, she knew. But that sort of intimacy ought not to stir a lady, that ordeal ought not produce the sort of secret inner tremors and tinglings she'd experienced at some of her more secret thoughts on the matter. No, that was for common women, that was never for the princess in the tower. So she'd been pleased that her suitors' embraces had won only her slight distaste or embarrassment, and that the idea of love itself continued to give her the greatest pure pleasure. Because romance was for true ladies, and sexual pleasure for sluts.

But last night Warwick had come very close to her, and something in his very proximity, or something in his eyes, or something in his intent, had woken something in her, and it had been fear of that which had made her cry out. Now, looking at Julian and feeling him so near, she was amazed again to discover that yearning, and now she recognized from all her readings that it could be nothing else but that other hallmark of her common state, for it could be nothing other than rising physical desire. Always in the past, she'd yearned for his attention, his admiration, and his devotion. Now for the first time she saw him as more than just amazingly handsome, now she wondered just what those astonishing lips would actually feel like upon her own, and what that strong perfectly proportioned body would feel like upon . . . She raised her head with a jolt, deeply shocked at the direction of her thoughts.

Julian thought she'd reacted to his wit and smiled at her, and went on with his commentary. But she gazed about the box frantically, searching the theater for something to take her mind out the abyss she'd wallowed in. Her glance fell upon her host, and she discovered that he'd been sitting at the rail of the box, his chair turned round so as to better see the stage, but that he'd been looking steadily at her. In that moment something in his sympathetic aspect, something in the tilt to his head and his rueful smile convinced her that incredibly, somehow, he'd read her thoughts, and understood her so thoroughly that he was amused with her, and yet he grieved with her as well.

But Susannah was a reasonable creature, and in a moment she recovered herself. She realized that Warwick often wore a sardonic expression, and that what was in one's head, even in this modern age of miracles and scientific discovery, was still one's own private property. Her amusement at her own fear of having her thoughts pirated saved her, as did the lights which were lit and then flared up to announce an intermission. The darkness bred secrets, not the least of which were secretive sensual thoughts, which was why, she thought, turning a composed and amused face to Julian at last, she'd been taught that gentlemen sought most of their odd pleasures after nightfall. Remembering the girl who'd told her that all those years ago, the one who'd vowed never to visit with a gentleman except in sunlight, she smiled, restored by humor and common sense, and looked forward to discussing the forthcoming play with Julian sensibly now.

But he was up and on his feet and staring across the theater to an opposite box. And from the exultant look he wore, she knew immediately who it was he'd seen there as soon as the lights had come up.

Who could blame him, Susannah thought miserably, as Julian squeezed her hand and whispered a hurried good-bye as he sprang from out of his seat to hurry down the hallway at the interval, for Lady Moredon looked exquisite in red. She'd wanted to wear red herself, she brooded, childishly, but although the contessa had agreed that it was only fitting to dress more theatrically for the theater since everyone did, almost as though they felt they had to take advantage of the dramatic lighting and compete with the painted females on the stage, theatrical was not the same as blatant. She'd probably been too kind, Susannah now thought sadly, to mention that it was the dark-haired beauties who glowed in red like graceful poppies, while whey-faced light-haired creatures such as herself would disappear from view entirely in such a vital color, until they looked like gowns perambulating on their own, without a person inhabiting them. No, she breathed in a tiny sigh, blue it was for her, dark and clear blue, almost the color of the gentleman's eyes who then interrupted the thoughts which were becoming the hue of her gown, by rising and saying cheerily:

"Now we must parade along the corridors to give everyone a chance to see how well our unknown lady looks in blue. Lovely shade," he said softly, taking her hand and placing it on his arm as he led her through the curtains and out from their box, "my favorite color actually, or is it green that I prefer? Odd, that," he said gently. "My partiality changes every time I see you in one of your new frocks."

She had the grace to blush, and then the courage to look up at him although she was again as close to him as she'd been the night before, only now midst a crowd of people, and now with his promise of propriety between them, and she said only "Thank you." But she said it with such heartbreaking sincerity that his lean face grew grave, and he discovered and hated himself for patting that hand that lay upon his sleeve just as an aged, indulgent uncle might.

"His ribs are almost completely mended," he mused as they strolled out into the crowded hallway, and she didn't pretend to have to ask whom he spoke of. "One hopes the rapid beating of his heart doesn't shatter them again. It's an infatuation," he said, as he nodded to a staring gentleman as matter-of-factly as if he were discussing the price of coal, rather than the state of her own wildly beating heart, "and infatuations are transient. Not to worry, he'll need someone to pick him up when she falls from her pedestal. Ah," he said then with great pleasure, glancing at her, "much better, nicely pink-cheeked now, embarrassment is the best cosmetic for young innocent girls, it's only when you can't summon up a blush anymore that we'll have to resort to the rabbit's foot and rouge, but then, we'll also know you've succeeded with him and precisely what you two have been up to, won't we? *Very* nice!" he said admiringly. "Now let's introduce you to everyone before that alarmingly attractive flush and our opportunity fade away."

While Susannah curtsied and nodded and smiled at an amazing array of gentlemen and ladies who had only whispered about her the night before, Julian stood just outside the curtains of another box on the opposite side of the theater. He waited there so long, turning his back and pretending he was engrossed in a program whenever anyone came along, that he feared the interval would be over and the deserted corridor would be flooded with returning theatergoers before he achieved his aims. But just before he decided to give up and seek his own seat again, the curtains stirred and a tall, thin, frowning woman pushed her way out through them. His wide smile of greeting was not returned, but then Miss Bridie knew no handsome young gentleman ever smiled so widely for her, but for what she came to tell him.

"She says," the woman whispered harshly, "she can't come out, and can't speak to you now. But she says she's glad to see you, and that she came so she could. And that's the sum of it." The woman sneered, and then, never forgetting that, importunate or not, impoverished or no, he was a gentleman, she added, with difficulty, "So good night, my lord."

It was very little, he thought as he made his way back to Warwick's box, but it was enough. Enough to know that she thought of him, enough to believe, as he gazed across to where she was sitting with her chaperon and the Earl of Alford, that she was nevertheless as acutely and exhilaratingly aware of him at this moment, even if she never looked to him, as he was of her. And it *was* exhilarating, he thought, as the lights dimmed and the stage lights came up, this game of now you catch me, now you can't, for it was a game he'd never played before. She was the first female to have ever refused him anything, and even so, he thought, gazing at her instead of the ranting Macbeth below him, he had every expectation, no matter the obstacles, that it wouldn't be long before she granted him all he desired, which was only all of herself, for all time.

He was completely in charity with the world then, for all that the world hadn't treated him very well of late. But he had his health again, he thought, for he'd only occasional twinges in his chest when he exerted himself, and he had his dreams, and his investment in the future, which Warwick had only this day assured him was already so well in hand that at the very least he'd never have to take up the reins on the Brighton coach again if he didn't wish to, but most of all, he thought, he had his friends. His best friend, Warwick, and his new friend, who was daily becoming more like the sister he'd never had—the charming and gentle and lovely Susannah.

And so he told her, when they were seated in the carriage again on their way home, for by then he was completely filled with goodwill and wanted to share it with everyone. Her sigh, he thought, was one of content, but the mockery in Warwick's voice gave him pause.

"How enchanting," his friend commented from his corner of the coach, "just what every beautiful young woman wishes to be told by a handsome young gentleman: 'You are like the sister I never had.' Oh, charming. Doubtless almost as enjoyable as you'd find it to be told you were the brother some young lovely never had. What a happy family we are indeed."

Julian tried to get a glimpse of Susannah's face when he handed her down from the coach, but she'd turned her head away from the gentle glow of the streetlamp's light. As he attempted to see whether it was laughter or tears she was near as Warwick paused on the pavement to tell her to hurry along before Julian decided she was getting to be more like a mother to him every day, he lost sight of her face as the first blow fell upon his shoulder, spinning him halfway around.

And then as he automatically crouched, fists coming up, thinking wildly that it was dreams that were supposed to recur, not nightmares, he saw the three ragged men with clubs wading into their midst, and heard Warwick shout, above all the confusion:

"Julian, to Susannah! At once! I'll handle the rest!"

11

There were three things that Susannah desperately wanted to do when it was over. She wanted to hide, she wanted to weep, and she wanted to seek comforting. She did none of these. Instead, she acted without thought and soon found that her instincts had been right, and everything she'd read, or been told, or thought a lady should do in such circumstances would have been entirely wrong, at least for her to do, at least then.

So although her hand trembled badly as she held the handkerchief to Warwick's streaming cheek, she kept it there, and even though her knees shook just as badly as she knelt on the pavement beside him, she stayed there until reason returned to his eyes and he shook his head and attempted to rise. And after he'd been helped into the house and seated, she stayed near to him, and insisted on holding the cloth to his cheek, even though he grimaced and told her he was getting blood all over her, and she ought to let him be, since the doctor had been summoned and was on his way. But she'd noted that the bleeding slowed when she kept pressure on it and so she ignored him, and in fact became bold enough to raise her shaking fingers to brush his hair back from his face to keep strands of it from being trapped beneath the cloth and getting into the wound, although when she did he glanced at her and frowned. But then he only put his head back against the chair as the contessa advised, and closed his eyes.

Julian returned to the room after a few moments, reporting that the physician was on his way, and frowning himself, he propped himself up against a wall as though he was still too keyed-up to sit, and stared at Warwick. Susannah glanced to him, and he smiled briefly, reassuringly, and though his hand continued to absently massage his side, she believed that he was as well as he'd claimed to be. It had been Warwick who'd been hurt in the foray, although he hadn't acknowledged it until the last of their attackers had turned and run away, and only then he'd allowed himself to slump to his knees. Then Susannah had broken from her immobility and left the shadow of the coach to run to his side as he knelt on the pavement, the blood streaming from the long cut along the side of his face.

At first she'd been horrified into absolute stillness. She'd never seen violence done before, not of this sort, nor of this nature and magnitude. A horse being whipped, a child being slapped by an impatient mother, those had been the only acts of human rage she'd ever seen committed. But the reality of the three men marching forward, swinging clubs and being met by Warwick and Julian and their coachman's fists, had shocked her to a complete stand. Then when she'd heard the sickening sound of the club landing on Warwick's shoulder, she'd broken from that trance, and hadn't known she'd lunged forward until she'd felt Julian thrust her back behind him again, and felt the contessa hold her firmly there, saying in a shaking voice, "Stay still, he'll be killed protecting you if you don't."

She hadn't realized that the sound of violence was as horrific as the sight of it, for men gasped and grunted loudly when they fought, and she never would have believed that she'd have been too terrified for Julian's welfare, when he dodged a descending cudgel to duck under his foe's arm and land a blow, to worry for herself. No, and she hadn't known she could feel such blinding rage as she did when she looked to see where the other two men were grouped around Warwick and saw the knife flash in one of their hands, nor did she realize she could feel such grief when she did, for it was so profound she scarcely rejoiced when the door to the house swung open and footmen came rushing out to aid them. When the last of the three attackers fled limping into the darkness, she'd known only such a surge of impotent fury because they'd gotten free and not been killed in retribution that she'd wanted to run into the night after them and deal out justice herself. And only then had she felt sickened and weak-kneed and shaken.

But those reactions didn't come to her until she had time to indulge them, when silence had fallen over the room where they all waited for the doctor to arrive. Then Susannah realized that she'd wanted to be alone after the attack, that she'd wanted to run to her room and hide beneath the covers, and that she could have gotten away with being fragile and calling for salts or help or sinking gracefully into a swoon. But she'd done none of these acceptable things; instead she sat next to Warwick and kept a blood-sopped handkerchief pressed to his face as she stroked back his hair, forgetting her place, her manners, and all her pretensions to being a lady in the process.

But the doctor approved her actions, and he told her so as he peeled back the handkerchief to study the wound. He brought a lamp closer so he could get a better look at it, so that when Warwick then opened his eyes and saw her face, he went a shade paler himself.

"Good grief, Susannah," he said weakly, "don't look at the thing. Contessa, see her to her room, this is no sight for a young girl."

Before Susannah could object, the doctor did, misinterpreting the delicacy of feeling Warwick was implying for Susannah as being his diagnosis of the extent of the damage.

"It's not half so bad as it looks," he muttered as he began to clean the wound, "nor half so deep, lucky chap, though it's true you've bled like a stuck pig, and would've bled yourself out if it weren't for this lady's quick thinking. Aye," he said, as his patient winced at something he anointed the wound with, "and because she's kept it pressed together, I believe we can get away with not stitching it up too, for if I did, no matter what my craftsmanship, then you'd have your face decorated with a jagged track for the rest of your life. Believe it or not, you've cause to be pleased the villain had a nicely sharpened knife in hand, because he's left a nice clean cut behind him. So I think if I seal up the ends neatly now, and keep them together with the salve and the bandage, we can have you healed without a lifetime souvenir of the night."

"It scarcely matters," Warwick laughed softly, and then added in a thready voice that was far from his normal tone, "I'm not the Mona Lisa, my friend, so my defacement wouldn't be a crime, even if it were noticed."

But if he had no illusions about his beauty, he was still, after all, a young man, and so found himself relaxing, vastly relieved that he wouldn't be transformed into some sort of a monster from his night's adventures, and so he began to say, until the doctor hushed him, saying it was delicate work he was doing and his patient had to oblige him by keeping his mouth closed and his face still for it.

When he was done, the doctor nodded with satisfaction and then asked the ladies to leave, since he wanted his patient to remove his jacket so he could get on with the examination of other hurts.

"Sometimes the shock of such bloodletting conceals something even more vital," the doctor mused.

But as Susannah and the contessa nodded mutely and began to leave the room, they heard Warwick disagree, and turning, saw him rising from his chair, although it was clear he had to grasp onto the back of it to do so.

"No, doctor," he said in a strained monotone as he came to an unsteady stand, "see to my friend now, please, for I've unfinished business to see to tonight. I assure you I've no other hurts, or at least none that can't wait until morning."

The doctor scowled and stepped close to his patient, peering into his wide-open glazed eyes.

"Aye, shock setting in, as I thought. You're one of the most reasonable men I've ever met, Mr. Jones, when you're in your right mind, which I believe you're not at present. I don't think it's from a blow on the head, I think it's a passing thing, from the loss of blood and the surprise of it. But if you go now, you'll wind up dead, if not from finding what you're looking for, then from going to find it. And you'll open up that wound again."

"I really have to leave now," Warwick said, beginning to make his way across the room.

"Warwick!" Julian cried sharply, striding to his side. "You must not."

"Indeed, you mustn't," Susannah said, surprising herself

as much as she did Warwick, for he paused and frowned down at her as she came up to him and laid a hand on his sleeve, "for I don't wish to come with you, but I must if you go, if only to see that all my work didn't go in vain. I'll have to stand by you, bandages at the ready, and I'm really very sleepy now, but I don't wish you to be scarred, you see," she said cajolingly, further amazed to find that he was standing still attending to her just as though it weren't nonsense she was spouting in an attempt to get him to stay.

"Exactly," Julian said in the same spirit, though his eyes were troubled, knowing that if his friend were in his right senses he would laugh them out of his way, "and I do ache a bit, Warwick, and don't fancy going trailing after you tonight either. Come on, old man, let's get you into bed, with a hot brick at your feet, and we'll pursue it further tomorrow. For my sake," he added, as Warwick wavered, his eyes growing blanker with the effort of his thoughts, "and if not for me, then most certainly for Susannah.

"And," he added to Susannah and the contessa later, as he came to report promptly on Warwick's condition after he'd helped get him to bed, hurrying down the stairs still buttoning his shirt after the doctor had seen to him as well, "I promise you, if he hadn't taken a hot brick at his feet, I would have dropped it on his head to keep him home tonight. And thank you, Susannah"—he smiled then—"for helping to get him still, and for your quick thinking. Remind me to call on you next time we're attacked."

"And you?" she asked at once, her great brown eyes so concerned that he checked for a moment, gazing down at her, before he said lightly:

"Ah well, I didn't do my ribs any great harm, but I didn't do them much good either. That fiend of a physician taped me so tight this time that I thought he was planning to bury me in Egypt. No," he laughed, "I'm fine, really. Now, you get to sleep yourself," he said, flicking a finger against her upraised chin, "before I send the doctor to check you out too, and he's in such a fit of healing, he'll brew you an evil-tasting posset before you can explain there's nothing the matter with you."

But there was, she thought as she ducked her head and

agreed and went to climb the stair to her room. Although, she thought sadly, as she allowed the result of fatigue and fear to take their toll at last, there was nothing any doctor could give her for it.

In the morning, Susannah was amazed to find that her limbs ached as though she'd been mountain-climbing the previous night, instead of only watching as an attempt was made to murder her two closest friends in the world. The contessa nodded when she came into Susannah's room and heard her complaining in wonder over it, as she sat at the edge of her bed with her knee bent and her leg in her hands, attempting to massage the stiffness from out of her calves.

"A hot bath will put you right," the older woman advised. "It's only that your body, you see, was ready to do all the things that you've been trained not to do. A lady mustn't face violence of feeling with violence of action as the gentlemen do, but I'm afraid her body doesn't know that, and so it gets all knotted up tightly and ready for battle no matter what she's been taught. And then, having done nothing to release all the waiting energy, it frequently sets that way. It's the price," the contessa said a bit sadly, "for being a female in this world, I believe. Or, at least, a well-behaved one. For if you'd actually been fighting," she said thoughtfully, "which, of course, you could not, I believe you'd not be in such a condition now. In fact," she added, after she'd requested that Susannah's maid bring her a steaming bath instead of her usual tepid morning pitcher of water, "I too had to have a nice hot soak, but knowing the state of my emotions, I took it last night. I didn't think to advise it for you, my dear, for I believed you needed sleep more then. And yes," she said, before she left Susannah to her bath, "no need to hurry, I've been up for hours and asked and Mr. Jones is sleeping peacefully, oh dear, that sounds more dire than I intended," she went on apologetically, "I only mean he's doing very well so you can soak for as long as you wish."

Susannah relished the idea of sinking into the warm water for hours, but before she did she had another question to ask, and so waited for the lady to be done with her rambling speech. She'd gotten used to her chaperon's way of expressing herself, believing it to be the result, as the lady herself once said during one of her longer soliloquies, of having spent too much time with Mrs. Anderson, who'd never listened to her at all, much less replied. So she waited until the lady was done, and then asked:

"And the viscount?"

"The viscount?" the contessa answered with a puzzled look—"why he's fine, and downstairs having his breakfast."

So Susannah didn't linger in her bath long, after all.

But two gentlemen were seated at the breakfast table when Susannah finally arrived there. Both had already done with their breakfast, but only one arose at her entrance. Warwick remained seated, but he said at once:

"Forgive my not rising, Susannah. Not only do I fear that Julian will sit on me if I do, there's also the matter of the fact that I'm not properly dressed, due to my invalidish condition. Now, while I do believe this to be the most beautiful gentleman's dressing gown in existence, I don't believe I ought to be flaunting it in front of a well-brought-up young female. But they won't let me get dressed, and I won't remain in my bed. So if you do what all well-brought-up females are so excellent at, which is pretending they don't see what is right under their noses, and haven't a clue as to what the gentlemen are doing, we'll manage to scrape through this embarrassing moment with our reputations and our sensibilities intact."

"I see only that I don't have to ask: obviously you're feeling quite yourself again this morning," Susannah replied coolly, with only a hint of laughter coloring her voice as she took her seat at the table.

"Estimable creature," Warwick said admiringly. "Yes, thank you, I am."

"And I see it is a lovely shade of blue, and green," she said, lowering her head to conceal her rising giggles.

"Just so," he answered appreciatively, looking down to the long silken dressing gown he wore. "I'm particularly pleased with how many flowers there are per inch, and with how beautifully executed the occasional bee is, but then, Eastern weavers are quite accomplished."

"Flowers?" she asked with a great show of amazement. "Bees? Why, whatever are you talking about?"

And while Warwick looked at her oddly, she went on quickly, before she could burst into laughter, "Why, I was discussing your eye, sir, and not your robe. Although, I'll grant, I forgot to mention the purple, which is causing perhaps the greatest and most interesting color contrast to the rest of your face."

Warwick grinned ruefully, acknowledging the gibe, touching the skin on his unbandaged cheek beneath his swollen, discolored eye as Julian and Susannah began to laugh together, but there was an enormous amount of appreciation to be seen glinting in his other, undamaged eye, as he said:

"Saucy creature. Well, what can you expect from a girl who breakfasts with gentlemen in their nightclothes?"

They all laughed at that, and Susannah got on with her breakfast, as the two gentlemen grew more serious and went on with the discussion that her entrance had obviously interrupted, which was about the last night's events.

Susannah was still smiling to herself, enormously pleased with the success of her jest, and delighted to find that it grew easier with every passing day to joke with her host, and he seemed to like that very well. But so did she, for the longer she knew him, the easier she became in his company. She was congratulating herself on this newfound facility when she chanced to glance up at him again, and what she saw killed her laughter in her throat. For when he wasn't exerting himself to be charming, or smiling, which he wasn't while talking seriously with Julian, she could more easily see the extent of the damages he'd sustained.

He might not believe that he had a pleasing countenance, but it was, Susannah thought, or rather, it had been. Although his were not the sort of looks which astounded the eye instantly, as Julian's were, he had a strong and strongly attractive face. But now a patch of white bandage obscured his right cheek entirely, and his left eye was, just as she'd mentioned, swollen to a profusion of bruised colors. His dark complexion was off color, and there were dark smudges beneath his eyes, as though his sleep, though sound, had not been a healthy one. The contrast between the two gentlemen couldn't be more acute than it was this morning, for though Julian seemed equally concerned as he listened to what Warwick was saying, his golden hair and fair skin gave his handsome face the glow of youth and health, while Warwick looked worn and weary and very troubled.

But Susannah was too, when she began at last to listen to what they were saying. Warwick chanced to look to her, as she sat, fork arrested in air, halfway to her lips. Then he smiled again.

"We've been rude, Julian. No, worse, we've been thoughtless, because rudeness can be amusing, and what we've done to Susannah isn't amusing in the least. She's heard half, poor girl, and half overheard is worse than all listened to, because, look at her face, she's built on that half and come up with something far worse than there is."

"I don't know what can be worse," Susannah admitted, putting down her fork, her appetite entirely gone. "You think that this Lord Moredon was behind that attack. Because he hates you both and because he wants to keep his sister from Julian, and he's rich and influential and may have the support of this . . . ruthless king of the underworld, this Lion you mentioned. How can anything be worse? How can either of you ever set foot out the front door again, knowing this?"

"You're right, Warwick," Julian said on a smile, "far worse. Susannah," he said, "it's not half so bad as that. Yes, it's Lord Moredon that's responsible, or so we think, because we haven't that many enemies, and it certainly wasn't coincidence. Those men weren't set on robbing us, only maiming us. But with all his money, Sir Robert's not so influential any longer, and the point is that Warwick has some . . . connections, and one of them may be this Lion fellow, so we can find out just who is responsible. Then we can put a stop to it. It's when you don't know who's at fault that you have trouble, so don't worry, we've got everything in hand."

"Everything in hand?" Susannah said, aghast, and then angry; and then, suddenly far too angry to be aware or shocked or even care that she could speak up so to Julian, and dare to confront Warwick as well, she gasped:

"In hand? It seems to me," she went on furiously, "that you've gotten everything in ribs, and eyes, and faces up to now, but I don't recall the doctor patching up any hands lately. Perhaps that will be next time, eh? All you have to do is to let Lady Moredon alone, and you can live without pain. All you have to do is continue to see her, and soon, likely, we'll all have everything in hand, and face and heart too, no doubt, aye!'' she said, too wound up to care that Julian was staring at her gravely, or to notice that Warwick was watching her with something very like delight.

The silence that greeted her when she was done was sharper than a rebuke. She colored up and dropped her gaze, unwilling now to look at the hurt she could at last recognize in Julian's open face. She kept her eyes on her breakfast plate, and so could only hear him say softly, gently, and entirely reasonably:

''Ah, Susannah. You may not agree with my taste in ladyloves, and you don't have to, but I promise you, I wouldn't pursue where no lead was given. And I'm trying to erase those objections of her brother's. In fact, so soon as these ribs you mentioned are knit up tightly enough, I think I'll be getting back on the *Thunder*, and so will bring no danger down upon anyone here any longer. I'll do anything to restore my fortunes faster, anyway, for that's the problem as I see it. Lord Robert doesn't want a beggar to carry off his sister, and for all he's not a good man, who can blame him? But more,'' he said in so imperative a tone that she looked up and so was as caught in his clear knowing gaze as if he'd shone a light upon her, ''he's gone beyond objecting to my suit, he's interfered with my life . . . our lives. And what sort of a man would I be if I allowed my liberty to be taken away because of another man's whim? Whether I loved the lady or not, I'd not be much of a man then, would I?''

''And as I certainly don't love the lady,'' Warwick put in softly, ''it's clear the issue is more about the state of our freedom than of Julian's heart.''

''If it's your safety that's worrying you,'' Julian said at once, ''don't worry, that's what I'm off to see about today, and if there's any real danger to you, we'll certainly make sure that you're well out of it before we go any further.''

''Ah, not too well put, my boy,'' Warwick said, smiling at Susannah's outraged expression, ''since right now she looks—in hair, coloring, and certainly in emotion—like a direct descendant of one of those fierce ladies who rode in a chariot, spear at the ready, protecting her menfolk from those nasty Roman chaps when they threatened them. And anyway, Julian, my dear friend,'' he added, turning his attention to the blond gentleman, ''you're in error. *You* are not going anywhere, I'm sending out various summonses today, and tomorrow, as soon as the doctor peeks under his dressing and pronounces me fit to scowl and shout again, I shall be going. Not you. They'll eat you alive where I'm bound.''

''Oh yes,'' Julian said angrily, wheeling about to face his host, ''I only drove the coach from Brighton and back past midnight and across the heath for a month of Sundays, so I'm clearly far too delicate a flower to do what the great Mr. Jones can do. They'll eat me up alive,'' he mocked. ''Oh, I'm terrified, can you point out a bed I can hide under, Mr. Jones?''

''I know the lay of the land,'' Warwick said icily, looking down his long nose at his friend, an effect that would have been coldly aristocratic but was somewhat ruined by the battering his face had taken, ''and however virile you undoubtedly are, you look much the gent, my dear.''

''And you, I suppose,'' Julian said with some heat, ''look far more able to defend yourself, swathed in bandages like Ramses the First.''

''Why don't you go together?'' Susannah asked softly, as Warwick replied:

''Bandaged or not, Julian, I know those low streets, I know how to deal with the king of the dunghill, and you do not,'' as Julian snapped:

''Yes, and they'll deal with you promptly enough, they won't even need a knife this time, I believe they can use a feather—'' and Susannah said again, more sharply:

''Why don't you go together?''

The annoyance in her voice, as well as the tone of it, stopped them abruptly. They gazed at each other, and then at her, and they both began to laugh.

''Thank you, Mama,'' Warwick said contritely when he was able. ''And will you come with me tomorrow, as Nurse asks, Julian?''

''I'd be pleased to, Warwick,'' Julian said, on a grin. ''And thank you, Susannah.''

She smiled to herself, and was thinking up a suitably cool reply to cover the amazingly good feeling their restored good feeling evoked in her, when Julian commented approvingly on the civilizing influence of females, and then Warwick agreed, and began to mention such famous feminine peacemakers as Eve, Medea, Joan of Arc, Helen of Troy, Mary, Queen of Scots . . . until Susannah pretended outrage, and they all fell to laughing again.

Watching the two gentlemen so in concert with each other again, Susannah, oddly enough, felt her own merriment fade. There was a flash of awareness in that moment for her. For it seemed to her then that the two gentlemen, one dark, one light, were part of each other, and parcel of her happiness, and yet since the one she wanted could never want her, so she would always be doomed to doing just what she did now, which was to only look on and watch their happiness and try to take what comfort she could from that.

They took her sudden silence for concern for them, and then began to assure her of their safety, and of her own. But she'd never for a moment worried about herself, since she felt more secure when with the two of them than she ever had in her life, and thought that no hostility, physical or verbal, from either acts of desperate ragged men in the streets, or words of silk-clad aristocrats at a ball, could touch her, or harm her, so long as they were there with her.

But they were gone all day the next day, and it was dreary for Susannah, and there was no mistaking the fact that she was nervous and uncomfortable with herself as she wandered the house wondering what was happening to them. Warwick had been pronounced fit enough to go out if he were a madman, as the doctor had said, and as he'd replied that was fair enough, it hadn't been long until he and Julian had left to search for the man they called the Lion, who might have knowledge of those who'd been hired to assault them. Not for the first time, Susannah regretted the circumstance of her gender, for it didn't seem fair that she could only pace and wait for word of them, while they might go out and meet their difficulties head-on. She remembered the contessa's explanation for her aching body the day after the attack as she continued to prowl the lower portions of Warwick's town house, and wondered if her body were again refusing to admit to the rules society forced upon it, for there was no way she could be comfortable sitting down, or lying down, or even standing still this day, not until she knew what had become of her two gentlemen.

There wasn't even anyone for her to talk with as she wandered and waited. Since the contessa had different training, or at the least, more experience with it, and also because she wasn't so personally involved, she'd gone to her room for an afternoon nap that threatened to slide into evening and become a night's sleep. Susannah was bored and anxious and edgy when the butler went to answer a summons at the door in the late afternoon.

And so that was why she completely forgot her role as guest and ran to the door to hear if it were news of Warwick and Julian. And, of course, that was why she then completely forgot her role as lady, and despite all of the astute butler's hints—raised eyebrows and discreet coughs, telling of his hesitancy to comply with her wishes—insisted on inviting the strange gentleman in, and interviewing him herself, by herself, in the drawing room.

They'd taken Warwick's light curricle into a district where hired hackney coaches would not go. Although Julian had wondered if they weren't making too much of a splash, as he noted the crafty, hard, and sullen faces observing them as their blooded high-stepping team picked gracefully through the filthy, teeming streets, Warwick assured him that his clothes, face, and voice were enough to alert the entire district, so there was no need to try to dissemble by walking where they might drive. And anyway, he'd said, with the fleeting ghost of a smile behind his bandage, the way news traveled in such a place, they were probably remarked the moment they set out from his town house.

His friend was amazed at how well Warwick knew the area, how easily he steered his team, threading it through narrow streets and down darkened alleyways, seeking out one low house after another. He was further astonished at how well Warwick predicted the people he met—for every starveling brat he picked as postboy did his job perfectly, so that not a scratch was ever found on the curricle when they emerged, blinking, from out of some stygian tavern, or when they came down from some hovel in one of the tenements high above the rank streets. And he was no little disturbed at how Warwick remained impassive as he interviewed opium eaters and drunkards, filthy bawds and pickpockets, procurers and their bizarre living merchandise of every sex, and received just as much respect from them in turn, however grudgingly given, as if he were the King of Thieves himself, while reacting to it as casually as if he dealt with them every day.

"But I did once, my friend," Warwick explained as they drove to what they hoped would be their last stop for the day, for evening was drawing on, and even Warwick seemed uneager to spend the night in the area. "Or almost every day, in my youth. And please don't imagine I've got onto some unhealthy new scheme for increasing my riches. I receive such devotion here because of my wild youth, and I got that only because of my name. Yes, my ancestor Gentleman Jones may have ended rotting on a gibbet, but his great-great-grandson is rated aristocracy here because of that ill-famed life, and even more for his ill-fated end. It's the nose, I think, that cinches it," he said lightly, running a finger along the length of that high and narrow feature as he did, "that was handed down in the family with the ill-gotten goods, or so all the portraits and broadsheet caricatures insist. It's the only good thing about it, I believe," he mused, "except for the fact that I'd likely last longer underwater than such a pretty lad as you, if only because my standing on tiptoe would save the day for me," he commented, as he drew his horses up under a half-legible sign which declared that they'd finally arrived at the Lost Sheep Inn.

Once within the dark and foul-smelling place that had only a few wretches sleeping, or dead, in the sawdust on the floor, they were eyed by two reasonably healthy-looking young men, and then told that they were expected upstairs. As they climbed those narrow, circling steps, Warwick recognized the place as being the Lion's den, and so he paused, and so he told Julian. But at Julian's look of relief, for he was growing weary with the search, since everyone had been glad enough to talk with his friend, but they'd all grown silent as the grave at the mention of the Lion he was seeking, Warwick only chuckled.

"It's the same place, and so it's his lodgings of course, but of course he isn't here, and won't be anymore."

Before Julian could challenge him, he said softly, as he continued following his escorts up the stairs, "Of course he's not, because they've directed us here and let us see where it is."

It was the same apartment Warwick remembered, the same guards seemed posted at the doors, and the same bright-haired overdecorated young woman sat at the table. But this time, she was alone.

She was young, though there was that in her small face which had never been young, and beneath her bright red hair it was entirely possible that her bright face might have been as beautiful as she'd painted it. Her figure was attractive as well, and displayed to advantage in her almost fashionable gown, and Warwick suppressed a smile as she rose and walked, swaying provocatively, toward her visitors, for he knew she'd never have approached them so if her protector were anywhere in sight or within leagues of hearing what she said.

"He's not here," she said, while all the while she looked at Julian, studying him until he, although used to a female's scrutiny, looked away, discomfited by her blunt appraisal.

"Obviously," Warwick answered, "but you'd hardly have allowed us to be led here again if there weren't some message, or reason, from him."

"Oh, too true," she said, giving up her examination of Julian in order to study Warwick's battered face, only not so closely, and from a further step away. "It wasn't him what got you, I was to say."

"And that's all?" Warwick asked.

"Aye," she said, although she seemed amused now.

"And he won't be back here?"

"Who's to say?" She shrugged.

"I thought you might," Warwick said, smiling sadly.

"I thought so too," she said on a sudden laugh, "but the runners are onto him now. Someone's set the cat to the pigeons."

"It wasn't us," Warwick said thoughtfully.

"Oh, I know." She grinned widely at that, looking far younger than she had. "You're breathing, ain't you?"

"And no other message for us?" he asked, smiling back at her, though Julian seemed stunned.

"Naw, not right now, not yet, not here, leastways," she answered, seeming to grow more amused by the minute.

"Tell him I honor my debts, all of them," Warwick said, suddenly very serious, suddenly in great haste to be gone.

He said very little to Julian after they'd left the Lost Sheep, and only replied in curt monosyllables as he sprang his team as best he could out of the slum district and then through the increasingly congested London evening traffic. Julian followed him as he hurried up the stairs to his town house after he'd thrown his reins to a footman, and was on his heels when he came walking rapidly into his entry hall.

"You have a visitor—" the butler began, as his master snapped, "I know, has he left?"

But he didn't wait for a reply as he went to the drawing room and threw the door open wide.

Susannah stood and smiled a greeting to them, her smile slipping and becoming more tremulous when she saw Warwick's face. But standing in back of Warwick, Julian couldn't see the expression that had alarmed her, he could only see the enormous, broad-shouldered square of a man who lazily rose from a chair at their entrance, as a grin of greeting spread over his wide and craggy face.

"This is Mr. Sean Jonathan Ryan, Warwick, Julian. Mr. Ryan, may I present Mr. Jones, the Viscount Hazelton," Susannah said correctly, introducing them.

But though Julian took a step forward with his hand outstretched, Warwick moved to block him, and did not himself put out a hand, or incline his head or his body into the least semblance of a bow. Instead he stood erect and said coldly:

"Otherwise known as Stephen Patrick Francis O'Brien."

"Possibly, but," said Susannah, looking very surprised at the rudeness her host was showing to his guest, "also, of course, as the Lion."

12

The fair, lovely young woman stood quite still as the two gentlemen paused in the doorway to the drawing room. They remained where they were standing, arrested, as the large gentleman they'd just been introduced to shrugged and dropped his ignored outstretched hand to his side again.

"The penalty, I might inform you," the wide-shouldered man then said on a smile, "for murder, is the rope. But then, I need hardly remind you of that, Mr. Jones, need I?"

Warwick unbent enough to smile, though he never took his eyes from Susannah as he replied absently:

"No, but I doubt I worry you a great deal Mr. O'Brien . . . ah, Mr. Ryan."

" 'Lion' will do," the man rumbled comfortably, sitting down again and crossing his legs, "but I cautioned you because it's the young lady I was worried about, not myself. You shouldn't blame her, she couldn't help it, you know, not really. Not that I held a gun to her head, mind, for my dear old mam taught me good manners, but I've a silver tongue, you know, which was the only other thing the poor old soul left to me."

"No," Susannah said at once, "there's no need to defend me, Mr. Ryan, I was not in the least beguiled, I was curious. You said you knew something that would be to Julian and Warwick's advantage, and so I decided to admit you. It was entirely my own decision, for I couldn't see what harm it could do."

"Aside from the fact that your visitor might have had you in seventeen pieces in less time than it takes to talk about,"

191

Warwick said easily, though his fists remained knotted and his eyes blazed, "that is, if he didn't decide to have you in less spectacular but more usual ways, why, none at all."

As Susannah's face grew very pale, the large gentleman chuckled and said softly:

"Now, now, Mr. Jones, it's true she's lovelier than anything I've seen in many a long day, but I've had a long day myself, and then too, you've seen my own little sweetheart, dear Sally, again only just this afternoon. She's an engaging little creature, isn't she? And demanding too. I'm a talented fellow but I have some limitations, and only so much stamina." He grinned before he added slyly, "And today, at least, to misquote wildly from a nobler gent, I came to bury enmity between us, not to praise the lady"—he glanced at Susannah in such a way as he had not all the time he'd passed alone chatting with her, causing her to grow even whiter as she realized for the first time that Warwick was absolutely right and she ought never to have done as she did—"praiseworthy as she most certainly is."

"Then I think we ought to talk," Warwick said, relenting, realizing no harm had been done, and from Susannah's transparent distress, that the lesson had been taken. He turned his attention to his visitor. "No doubt you know we've been searching for you all day? Your dear little Sally was too amused at our call for it to be coincidence to find you here waiting for us."

"Of course," his guest replied, obviously approving his host's logic, "and I would've been glad to give you a chance to have at me with swords, or fists, or words, whatever your pleasure, gentlemen, if I had the leisure. But I had my own business to attend to, as I said. Someone peached on me, and though I generally find I can pay enough to turn official interest elsewhere, this time someone with entrée to higher, wealthier authorities made it difficult for me to remain where I was. Now I'm moved, now all's secure, so now, before I go to ground, I thought I would oblige you. Now I'm at your disposal."

And so saying, he folded his hands in his lap, and looking very amused, sat back and waited for the two gentlemen staring at him to make their move.

Julian had remained silent all the while. When Warwick had called Susannah to task, his own heart had seemed to stop as he became aware of the danger she'd put herself in with her attempts to help them. He recognized the man he saw before him, the one she'd entertained alone, as a dangerous one, not only because of his size and shape. This Lion's obvious intelligence, purring speech, and easy humor made him all the more formidable. There was something about the man he almost recognized, but more that he was instantly wary of, and the way that he'd looked at Susannah had chilled him, so he said, before more could be said:

"I think Susannah ought to leave now, don't you agree, Warwick?"

"*I* most certainly do not!" Susannah cried before Warwick could answer, her color having gone from white to a fiery blush. "It's hardly fair! I sat and waited for you all day. I sat and spoke with Mr. Ryan too, and for all he pleases himself by leering like a jack o'lantern now, he was the soul of decency with me when we . . . were alone," she said more quietly, realizing as she did that she ought not to have mentioned that again. So she went on quickly:

"And if I have to suffer with you when you are hurt, and worry for you when you're in danger, it's not right that I should be asked to leave just when explanations for it are discussed. I'm not a child, and . . . and . . . being female doesn't mean being senseless and blind and deaf too. If you want me to leave," she said, realizing that they were all staring at her now in some wonder, and becoming slightly terrified by the unexpected force of her own emotions herself, she concluded, raising her chin so her voice wouldn't lower, "why, then, I shall. But I'll leave this house too, forever, and at once."

The first one to break the silence was the large sandy-haired gentleman, who said, in some wonderment:

"I congratulate you."

But as he said this to Warwick and Julian, and not to her, Susannah was not best pleased, but she knew she'd gone very far and so didn't say a word even when he added:

"Whose is she, may I ask?"

"Her own," Warwick said in some amusement, the tension in the room suddenly gone with the smile he wore, which was answered by the one Julian displayed as well, "and I'm very sorry, Julian, but I don't think I'm brave enough to oust her just now. Well, I'm still in bandages. Do you want a go at it? You're almost mended. Or shall I ask the Lion here to do the honors?"

And as the Lion quickly uttered his disclaimers with great mock apprehension, and Julian denied his willingness with equally outsize horror, they all began to laugh together. It was being accustomed to just that sort of masculine camaraderie, Susannah thought, that easy familiarity that these diverse gentlemen could show to each other now, even though two were true gentlemen and one was a professed thief and worse, that had seduced her into declaring her true feelings in the first place. Constant association with her two gentleman had changed her, she realized. She'd never have believed she could be so nonchalant in speech with gentlemen, as free with them as she'd been with her own brothers, as easy with them as she'd been with her bosom friends at school, nor had she realized how quickly she'd lose all the airs and graces she'd been trained up to at that school. Surely, she thought, as she took the chair Julian indicated she should, near to him, surely a lady would not act as she had. But, she thought, hugging the thought to herself as Julian smiled reassurance at her and she settled to hear the men speak, then surely she would not have so much pleasure as she did now.

"I came to say, as I told the pretty lady," Lion said, "that I had nothing to do with the attack on you last night. I see you've gotten yourself some trophies from it, Mr. Jones, but as there were three of them armed and ready against your unpreparedness, I believe you came off best in the match. Oh, I know the details, though I didn't arrange it or know of it until after. There's nothing that goes on that's wrong that I don't know of, eventually. But I promise you, if I'd arranged it, it would've been done better. Aside from the fact that I believed we had an understanding, if I'd a grievance with you and wanted it finally settled the other night, Mr. Jones, trust me that our little chat would've been quite impossible to hold today."

He paused to let the import of his words register before he

added, simply, "And because I believed we had that under-standing, I came today as a matter of pride. My boyos wouldn't have made such sloppy work of it, but then, my cullies won't take coin from Lord Moredon neither, nor will any I've control over. And that's a great many. But hunger drives out fear, and there are too many in London town starving to care whether it's me or hunger that gets to them first. There are wretches who'll sell their mothers, their children, and their souls if the devil didn't already have them, in order to eat, or drink. Those are the sort he hired this time, because those, the rogue ones that no one else wants, except for anatomy lessons, are the only ones he can get."

The Lion's voice became sober as he said very seriously:

"You shamed him in the world's eyes, Mr. Jones—even in my quarter the tale of his thrashing at Gentleman Jackson's is famous. You continue to court his sister, Viscount Hazelton, despite all his threats. Oh yes, we on the dark side of town know exactly what's happening in the light. Footmen have eyes, and scullery maids have ears. So the gentleman is understandably frustrated. And the gentleman, I believe, though I'm no physician, is more than a little mad, and not just in an eccentric fashion. I saw his eyes that night he hired my lads and then attempted to remodel your face himself, Viscount, and though living where I do I'm well used to rats and mad dogs, they were not something I'd choose to see again."

"You!" Susannah breathed in shock. She was amazed. Because almost all else he'd said, he'd told her before the other two had returned home, but this news—the incredible fact that he'd been responsible for, as well as present at the attack on Julian—she'd not known, or guessed.

"Yes," Julian said slowly. "That voice, I knew it, but not from where, but now I remember. No, Susannah," he cried, half-laughing, half-horrified as he jumped to his feet to wrap his arms around the girl, who'd risen to her feet, visibly trembling, to stand looming threateningly over the man called Lion's chair. He drew her close, and held her so close he could feel her slender body vibrating against his from the force of her suppressed tension. Then, holding her securely, his own frame a buffer between her and the Lion, he said slowly and clearly:

"Whatever you're thinking, Susannah, unthink it. He helped me. He actually did, whatever he originally contracted to do. It was Moredon who was set on killing me once I was down, and as I remember it now, it was this gentleman who prevented him. A belated thanks," he said to the Lion, now speaking over Susannah's bent head as he continued to hold her close, and she at last rested limply against his chest, worn out by the sudden cessation of her unspent rage.

The Lion nodded as he watched the blond young woman breathe an almost imperceptible sigh as she settled into the blond young gentleman's embrace, he noted the brotherly pats the fair young nobleman gave to her quivering shoulder, and then, glancing to where Mr. Jones sat on the edge of his chair, saw the sudden look flash in those pained dark blue eyes before they were promptly shuttered by their heavy lids again. Then the large man nodded once again as though to himself, before he said casually:

"No thanks are necessary, it was my own good, or bad, name I was saving as well as your remarkable face, my lord. At any rate, you've just repaid me. Because I begin to see it wasn't Miss Logan who was in any danger before you two arrived, it was me. Luckily, you were both here when she discovered I'd been in on the attack on her . . . friend."

"Indeed, fiercely loyal is our Miss Logan," Warwick drawled.

"Indeed I am, and what of it?" Susannah exclaimed in a tremulous voice, emerging at once from Julian's embrace, finding it too pleasurable, too public, and too casual all at once, to bear another second. However difficult it might be for her, she quickly decided it was better to talk to them now and try to make sense, and hope that they'd all take her trembling limbs and voice and heightened color for the rage which had already been replaced by her own secret confusion.

"I cannot understand how you can all sit and speak as friends when one of you was paid to injure the other. I cannot," she complained distractedly.

"It was only a matter of business," the Lion began to explain patiently, but the fierce look she gave him silenced him temporarily. Warwick spoke up at once and she listened gravely to him, while the Lion listened as well, watching her incredulous face bemusedly.

"It *was* business, Susannah, that's the point. Our visitor is in trade, but of a different sort than you're accustomed to. He provides that which his customers can find nowhere else. He deals in pain, pleasure, and commodities that are not usually available. But whether it is to be pleasure or pain, it's not a question of any sort of passion, anger, cruelty, or revenge with him. It's a matter of business, solely of money paid for service rendered."

"Just so," the man called Lion commented generously, "and very well said. I believe I should hire you to advertise for me, Mr. Jones. In fact, I wasn't even the one who contracted for the lesson to be given to the viscount, it was a job of work taken on by two associates of mine. Not that I would have refused it, mind. It was a straightforward-enough task. He was simply to have been given a bit of discomfort, never enough to inconvenience him for more than a few days, enough time to think over the message they were paid to deliver. It was Lord Moredon who took things too far—"

"Yes," Julian agreed, "and it was, as I said, the Lion who stopped that. So I don't harbor a grudge, although I'll admit," he said, grinning at the larger man, "that I wouldn't mind having a few names from you, my friend, so that when I'm able, I can arrange to have a few words with the two fellows who waylaid me, one at a time this time, that is."

"Terribly sorry to disoblige you, my lord," the Lion said loftily, "but that's quite against company rules."

At that, all the men began laughing, as Susannah stood and stared at them with such apparent dismay and growing annoyance that they laughed the louder when they noted it.

"I'm afraid a lady such as Miss Logan can't understand such commerce," the Lion said then, wiping his eyes, and sighing. "Females, ladies or not, I have found, do not usually understand such cold-blooded dealings. Oh, they'll do mayhem and murder with the best of men, but they tend to do it through passion, and personally. They take a much more personal view of life entirely in all things," he mused, "for if you've noticed, they don't seem able to take their pleasures as casually as we do either, there's never really been a booming market in males for sale for the night or by the hour such as there is . . . Oh, I beg pardon, I do, Miss Logan,'' he interrupted himself before anyone else could, to go on in the most patently artificial manner Susannah had ever heard, "forgive me, my tongue ran away with me, I forgot myself entirely. My dear mother would be appalled at me, a thousand pardons. You gentlemen aren't going to call me out for my lapse, are you?"

But as this was said with great amusement and no little eagerness, Susannah realized that their visitor was, for all his joviality, a man who never allowed anyone to forget the potential menace he represented. She moved to lighten the moment, for in one nervous glance she'd noted that Warwick had narrowed his eyes, and Julian's face and entire body had stiffened.

"Mr. Ryan," she said coolly, "I make no doubt that you gentlemen thrive on such meetings and are positively enraptured by the thought of letting blood again, but I remind you that it is the ladies who have to do the nursing and the mopping up after you. If you don't mind, I've had quite enough of that, even if they have not. So I'd ask you, as a favor to me, not to invite these two gentlemen to any more such sport, at least not while I'm staying on with them. And as for insult to me, why, I didn't mind what you said in the least, sir, though I didn't find it edifying, it being far too obvious."

The large gentleman checked, and after an appreciative smile and nod, commented only, "Indeed, it's as my dear mother herself used to say: if women had the running of the world, what a better place it would be."

"What a lot she had to say," Warwick said reflectively. "The good fathers that raised you must have let her have a room nearby."

"Just so," the large gentleman agreed, and then, rising, he went on, "But now I have to go, however pleasant this visit has been, since I find myself in great official demand, and have considerable interest in keeping that demand unmet. So although it won't be impossible, I fear it will be a bit difficult for you to contact me again—for a short while only, I hope. I'll leave you with a bit of advice, my friends. Lord Moredon is a very bitter man. He's revenging himself on various people, various ways. He's made it difficult for me, for instance, since he has access to high places. But even without me—I might say, *especially* without me on the scene—he has access to low places too. So I'd suggest, since Miss Logan deplores bloodshed no matter how we enjoy it, that you leave town for a while.

"Until, at least," he added, "things sort themselves out to our satisfaction. As he's a lord, it's not easy for me to pay him back. I'm not mad enough to forget that a lord of the realm has certain powers that even I don't. But there are always ways . . ." He paused, and the brief silence in which he meditated was a chilling one. Then he smiled charmingly again and shrugged and said:

"Ah well, later days. For now, I wouldn't think it cowardly to leave the scene. I am doing so, in my own way, as well. I wouldn't think of it as exile if I were you, neither, for I hear," he said lightly, looking at Julian, "that Lord Moredon himself is sending his own lovely sister out of town for a spell. To cooler climes. To Brighton, in fact. There's quite a social whirl there too now that the Regent's there, I hear."

This time when the large gentleman extended his hand, he found it taken, eagerly, and then shaken by Julian. And Warwick gave him his hand too, as he went with him to the door.

"Yes, Brighton's a lovely place this time of year," the Lion said reflectively, "far from the turf of evil men such as myself, even further from the danger of the sort of easily hired violence town offers. And I understand, Mr. Jones, that you have a country home close to the Devil's Dyke, near there too. How convenient for you."

"Is there nothing you do not understand?" Warwick asked curiously.

"No, nothing. Am I any less than you?" the other man asked as he prepared to leave. But then in a lower voice he added, "It would be for the best, you know, for all of you. For the pretty fellow so he can have another try at the lady he adores, without her brother to interfere; for Miss Logan, so she can be safer; for you, sir, so you can have time and opportunity to show her what she's missed seeing as she's been so busy looking elsewhere."

Warwick paused. It seemed he grew a bit white about the mouth. Then he said, with great casualness:

"Ah yes, I don't believe she's ever seen Brighton, or the seaside there."

"Just so," the large gentleman agreed, considerably amused, before he glanced down the street both ways and then quickly left.

It wasn't until he felt the sun upon his upturned face and the wind blowing his hair back that he fully realized how much he'd missed the life he'd thought he was so eager to give up. But the speed, the motion, the sound of the horses' exhalations and their steady hoofbeats, the sway of the coach, the scent of newly blooming things in all the hedgerows that lined the road he drove down were like balm to Julian, better for him, just as he'd sworn they would be when he'd begged Warwick to let him have the reins again, than all the potions, than all the beds and rest and doctors in creation.

He'd stooped to begging, and he hadn't cared. For it was just as he'd told Warwick. He was feeling sounder, the horses were well-bred, amiable fellows, not like some of the mad, desperate things he'd harnessed and driven for the company, and the coach was so well-oiled and maintained that he could drive them all the way down to Brighton without pain even if he'd a rib wedged in each lung and one through his heart. That heart had been pierced, but it had only been by love, and since he was coming closer to Brighton every moment, even that wounded organ felt lighter by the moment.

It was a rare, warm sunny spring day, Julian had the reins in his hand and hope in his heart, and he vowed he'd never felt better. But even as this was England, and so he knew rain clouds always gathered even as the sun shone, he knew that no joy was unalloyed. Warwick had spoken of new investments, annuities and returns he'd made for him, but still he hadn't enough money in hand to take his future firmly in hand, or to take his lady's hand in lawful matrimony. He supposed he might soon have to go back to the *Thunder* after all, back to a life on the road, back to bone-shaking, bone-breaking journeys through heat and rain, back to shambling for tips like a performing bear and swallowing down the indignity of it even as his fist swallowed up the coins. But on such a bright and hopeful day, when he thought of that life on the road, he remembered its advantages the most: the savor of beautiful days . . . and then he recalled the better nights, enhanced by the likes of Nan at the Silver Swan, and Mary at the Crown, and Mrs. Bower in Cucksfield . . . and then he found that he was grinning widely to himself.

He enjoyed them all very well, as he'd always enjoyed women, and as they'd all always insisted they enjoyed him. Physical pleasure was an uncomplicated thing, not like love. What transpired between himself and all those willing females had to do with pleasure, nothing to do with love or what he felt for Marianna. He never felt as though he were betraying her when he sampled other females, simply because he never thought of her in such terms. She would one day, he hoped, be mother to his children, she would one day, he prayed, find joy in his arms, but if he thought about it deeply, and he seldom did, he believed she'd never find quite the sort of pleasure there the others did. Nor would she expect to. She was, after all, a lady, and one of the highest kind, so her love had little to do with the sort of writhings and releases gentlemen found in such sport. If he were wrong, he'd be delighted, but when he pictured her in his mind's eye, it was in his home as hostess, wife, and mother, and never in his bed as temptress and lover.

A fellow had to be careful to differentiate, he thought, frowning so now that Warwick's regular coachman, riding alongside him on the high hard driver's seat, looked at him with some distress, wondering if the young gentleman hadn't some pains in his ribs after all. The other day, Julian thought, with some unhappiness clouding his otherwise shining day, when he'd taken Susannah into his arms to comfort her and prevent her from attempting to slay the Lion, between his laughter and his dismay, he'd also became aware of two things. Well, more than just those two, he thought to himself, his irrepressible spirits rising momentarily. But that was just the point, he thought more soberly.

He'd become aware that she was a delicious armful, fragrant and curving, and whether she fully knew it or not, willing. He was appreciative enough of her sex to judge her eminently desirable, and enough of an expert on it to realize that she had a real response to him as a man. He couldn't think to do anything but release her at once. Because she was a friend, and even if, strictly speaking, she wasn't a lady, she'd been raised as one. Even so, with her glorious shining hair and lovely face and yielding, excitingly, unexpectedly lush body, he might just have decided to oblige her anyway. She was young and inexperienced; but it would have been pleasant to instruct her, she was a friend; but pleasure between friends was even more pleasurable; she was trusting; but then, he thought, he'd never hurt her, only enjoy her and teach her enjoyment. But, overriding all else, he knew she was, however, wealthy and wise, sprung from a family of newly arrived, prosperous cits. She was a bourgeoise. As Warwick had once jested, a female of that sober middling class—unlike a fashionable lady who stoops to sport, or a common girl who sports for the sheer joy of it—was untouchable, except in marriage. And though he could give her a great many other things and would very much like to, that, he could and would never offer her.

But it was a shining day, an easy day, a day for simple solutions, easily implemented. He would remain friends with Susannah, indeed, he liked her very well, more each day, in fact. She was very bright, and amusing, and as goodhearted as any man he'd ever known. But she was undeniably beautiful, so he'd stay away from her physically, for what a man could touch, he thought with a rueful grin, often changed what a man thought to do.

All his problems settled by the rushing wind, the sun, and the fresh spring air, Julian lifted his head and gazed out at the scenery about him. Then he bit his lip, frowned, and raising up the whip he held in his right hand, gave the reins a sharp crack with his left and sprang his cattle until they began to race down the road. But they didn't travel fast enough to carry away the cry that arose from within the coach.

"Here, Julian," Warwick shouted from his open window, "slow them, stop them, no more of this. Julian! At once!

"The charming idiot," Warwick explained as the coach slowed to a stop on the country road, "was trying to spare my feelings, I think."

The contessa looked up at him, as Susannah grinned. She didn't know what sort of jest he was about to make, but he'd been amusing her so effectively, they'd laughed so much together since they'd gotten into the coach this morning, that her lips had been curved in a constant smile and his smallest statement brought anticipation of more merriment.

When they'd pulled away from the town house with the lumbering luggage-laden coach behind them filled with those servants who were making the remove to his country home, she'd become unexpectedly anxious. She'd written to Charles to tell him where she was bound, but she'd never been at a gentleman's country estate before, and though she knew the change was for the best, she couldn't help thinking that if she'd been shunned and ignored in London, which teemed with fashionable persons, why then, she'd be completely a hermit when they were at Greenwood Hall, Warwick's home. Of course, she could easily leave then, she'd have the excuse of being out of London to make Charlie swallow it, but then, she'd be leaving everything that she'd gained in the past weeks: her friendship with Julian and Warwick, and the small matter of all her hopes for the future. For withal that she'd become such fast friends with both of them, it was an odd sort of alliance, founded by her being landed on Warwick and cemented by the troubles that had beset them all. Whatever it was, however, she wasn't foolish enough to expect that they'd either of them ever contact her again if she left. So she couldn't leave, she thought, not if it transpired that no one in Brighton spoke to her or uttered her name, except for calling birds.

It might have been because Warwick saw how downcast she was, or it might have been because he was as glad to be leaving town as he claimed to be, but he'd soon cheered her out of her sullens and into high good spirits. She'd known he was amusing and had often felt the edge of his quick wit, but she hadn't known how cleverly he could draw other people out. Not only did he have the contessa telling them all about Venice by the time they'd passed the first tollgate, but as he'd been there once, he had them all laughing at his experiences immediately after they'd been subdued by the tale of the contessa's daring but disappointingly brief marriage. Then he'd had Susannah tell him, without ever meaning to, about all the places she'd ever dreamed of visiting. After that, they played a delightful game he invented, imagining what places they might want to visit if they could travel through time as well as range the world, and then they imagined what it would be like to actually visit with some famous people from history or literature, and by the time the contessa closed her eyes to pass her journey as she always did, in sleep, Warwick had Susannah doubled over with laughter as he acted out all the parts of the dinner party he'd give for Cleopatra, Queen Elizabeth, and Casanova.

So after the coach finally rolled to a halt, and Warwick swung open the door to have a word with Julian, she was still smiling widely as she watched them having a conference in the road. She greeted him with a quizzical grin when he came back in again, and Julian, returned to the driver's seat, started the coach once more, only at a more moderate pace this time.

"He wanted to spare me the sight of the Gentleman's Oak, he planned to make the horses fly so that I'd not notice we were passing it," he said as he seated himself again. "The clunch," he said, with a little smile, "I pass it every time I go home, and never turn a hair. In fact," he said on a skewed smile, "I'm so callous a lout that I'd likely charge tuppence a look if he were still hanging there in chains. It's an enormous old oak, you'll see it to our right in a moment. And it is quite famous in certain circles, being," he explained gently to her polite look of inquiry, "the tree they hanged my highwayman ancestor, Gentleman Jones, upon. Actually," he said, lowering his voice so as not to waken the contessa again, "it's a sufficiently gruesome story to merit its fame. For it happens he was every bit as decorative as they'd wished, so they coated him with tar afterward, to keep the birds from spoiling sport, and put him in a gibbet so that he might adorn the old oak until Christmas Day in the morning. And it was only April then.

"They were overly optimistic. Someone cut him down one dark and windy night and spirited him away, so they never found a hint of him or of their money again. Good heavens, Susannah, don't look at me like that! You make me want to bawl. I've seen merrier faces at funerals. My dear," he said gently, looking at her woeful face, "he was my ancestor but I didn't know the chap. Don't know that I'd much like him, either, though he had the most excellent attributes, being said to be as much like me as he looked like me, which was, by all old accounts, considerably, poor fellow."

Susannah remained very silent as the coach went past the ancient oak. It was too early in the season for it to be in full leaf, and too full an old tree for her to imagine which particular broad limb had borne that terrible burden. But she saw Warwick's reflection interposed on the window glass she looked out at the oak from, and in that moment she could swear she could also see his doomed ancestor as he approached the great tree and his last hour.

Though Warwick wore the sober hues of his generation, and his ancestor would have been attired in gaudier patterns and colors, there would have been a commonality, for Warwick wore his tailored clothes as though they were velvets and satins, and his ancestor would have been sedate in all his lace and finery. The Gentleman would have worn his soft brown hair back in a queue, not in the fashionable, if overlong, Corinthian style his descendant affected, and he wouldn't have had a white bandage across one thin dark cheek, of course, unless Cromwell's men had toyed with him before his sentence was carried out. But he too would have been lean and cool and arrogant, she was sure, even on that final march. She knew he would have quipped as well, and looked down his high nose at the rabble breathlessly awaiting his last breath, and his dark blue eyes would have blazed contempt even as he'd stepped off into eternity.

But there would have been, she was equally sure, well-concealed tremors coursing up that long back and across those wide shoulders, if not for his untimely end, then for the thought of how the body he'd soon leave behind would be treated—mocked and left to swing in the wind, becoming disfigured and disgusting to be seen. For that long-ago gentleman had great dignity too, she'd swear to it, and that desecration, she suddenly knew as surely as she'd begun to know his descendant, would have been what horrified his fastidious soul the most. Because with all his reserve, she knew that he would be vulnerable, and her lower lip quivered with foolish sorrow when she thought of that painful ending, that long-past suffering, as the coach slowly passed the old tree.

She swung around suddenly to see if Warwick was indeed as immune to the specter of his ancestor's misery as he claimed to be, and in that moment she saw all that same vulnerability in his living face, with all that sorrow and despair, but also, to her confusion, saw that he'd not been looking at the old oak at all, but had been instead staring directly at her.

"I suppose," he said then, turning quickly to the window, willing to admit to any shameful thing but what he was sure she'd seen, "that I overestimated my coolheadedness. For it's rather like *Hamlet*, isn't it? One can see it several dozen times and still be moved."

And then he began to tell her a tale of another highwayman, but this one a fumbling one, that had her laughing so merrily within minutes that he had to shush her so she wouldn't wake her chaperon with her unrestrained mirth. When he made her laugh, he found he could look at her without her knowing it, and since he took such pleasure in seeing her so close, so joyous and so free, he took great care to keep her laughing. When they stopped for a luncheon and a change of horses at a wayside inn, she stopped him by placing her hand lightly upon his sleeve as he was about to leave the coach.

"Thank you," she said sincerely, looking at him directly, her slightly tilted wide brown eyes warm and friendly as the tone of her voice. "You are very kind, Warwick, thank you."

And that simple statement kept his spirits so high he had Julian and Susannah and the contessa rocking with mirth all through their stopover, until Julian complained that he'd really like something to eat, so he'd be pleased if his friend would kindly go visit his humor on another table, since it was very difficult to swallow when one was laughing. But it made things no easier for him when Warwick nodded and promptly rose and found an old man dozing at another table and proceeded to chat him up with such animation that soon they were all groaning with the pain from their guffaws. He kept them all merry, in fact, until it was time for the final leg of their journey and Susannah convinced Julian to give up the reins and rest within the coach.

Then he grew quieter and sat back, disposed to watch Susannah intent upon Julian as he sat opposite her and told her a dozen stories about his coaching days, suitably edited, and yet sufficiently thrilling to keep her watching the storyteller with her eyes on his lips and her heart in her eyes, all the way to Warwick's country home.

Then no story, no tale of highwaymen or coachmen could distract her from gazing at Warwick's home.

"It is . . . oh, insufficient to say, I know, but it is . . ." But she couldn't find the words at last to express what she thought of his home. "Magnificent," she thought, was far too stately a word for a home of such warmth and charm, yet "charming" would signify a cottage or a thatched house, and Greenwood Hall was large enough to accommodate a dozen cottages within it. It was a long and rambling house, built before the infamous Gentleman Jones had drawn his first breath, improved upon by the funds he'd doubtless stolen for it, and gently nutured ever since. Of golden stone and brick, it took some form from every Jones that had thought to improve upon it, and so was as eccentric and delightful as the gentleman who owned it. And so at last Susannah dared to say, when it seemed she must say something to her host as he watched her remove her gloves in his front hall and waited for her to voice her judgment of his home. Although "eccentric and delightful" might not be the description most gentlemen would like to hear given about their homes, he seemed as genuinely pleased as the contessa was disapproving of her charge's candid appraisal.

The contessa's hasty claims of Greenwood Hall's being "elegant, graceful, imposing," were cut off by the sound of a whoop of unrestrained joy. Julian had been handed a message along with a curtsy when he'd been given an introduction to the housekeeper on his arrival. Having been told it had waited for him since morning, he'd taken it and read it instantly. Now he turned and stared at Warwick, Susannah, and the contessa as they all stopped and looked back at him. His smooth fair face bore an expression of almost incandescent joy; it now appeared to be lit from within as brilliantly as his coloring and fair hair illuminated it from without.

"She's here!" he whooped, advancing on Susannah and picking her up and lifting her high in the air. "And she wants to see me," he laughed exultantly as he swung her about, "and at her friend's house, and at a picnic, and at a ball!" And after he threw his head back in laughter, he put Susannah down again and lowered his golden head to give her a sound and hearty kiss.

But something on her lips slowed it, or something of the taste of her slowed him, and so something unexpected in the moment turned a kiss of good fellowship to a thing only a heartbeat more languorous. But when he raised his head that extra second later, he paused, a bit disconcerted, to look down into Susannah's dazed eyes.

"Sorry," he murmured then, embarrassed and angry with himself, "sorry, Sukey, I was carried away."

"No, that's wrong," she stammered, aghast at herself, at how she'd stayed so quiescent in his clasp, willing him to stay a second longer, in her desire to find what might have been discovered there, and desperate to make a recovery, she was grateful for the easy jest that flew to her mind and then to her traitorous lips as well: "*I* was . . . and carried far too high, Julian. I hope no one's around but the Lion next time you get a pleasing message. I'd like to see you fling him to the ceiling."

"And kiss him soundly," Warwick offered with dry humor, from where he'd been watching, although as he continued to observe Susannah's heightened color and downcast eyes, there was nothing remotely humorous in his dark face.

13

The little man was very nervous. It was not so much the tic in his cheek which showed it, for he always had that, and at any rate his face was so grimy that not many people cared to study it long enough to note that the thin cheek pulsed and twitched with clocklike regularity. Nor was it the fact that his sharp light eyes darting this way and that, never resting too long on any object, as though he mistrusted everything in his environment, gave his feelings away. For in his environment he'd be a fool not to cultivate distrust. No, none of these outward signs was necessary to convey his unease. He could, instead, be taken at his word. He said it the once, then he repeated it to be sure it was understood:

"Not me, sir, no. I'm too nervous is wot I am. I wouldn't do it, no, and I couldn't neither. Not me."

"But your friend?" his inquisitor asked smoothly.

"Ho. My friend is even scairter. No, he's not bright, nothing like, wee Georgie isn't. But he's got brain enough to be scairt. No, not him neither, sir."

The little man sat on the edge of his chair as though he sat on tacks. It took a great deal of bravery for him to be explaining this to his questioner, and so he'd said it, and so it was. But the gentleman he spoke with didn't seem grateful or impressed. This frightened the little man even more. He was, he knew, caught between two grinding stones, and could only hope that, as usual, he was small enough and quick enough to slide out from the middle before he was crushed by either one of them.

They sat at a cracked table in the corner of a low tavern in

one of the meaner sections of London. The floor was slick
with filth, despite the sawdust over it, the windows evenly
grimed except for occasional ragged circles that random sleeves
had made now and again in their history so the curious could
peep out from them, even though all that would be seen was a
cluttered alleyway. The drinking glasses were as opaque with
dirt as the windows were, and had almost as many jagged
edges as the chairs did, but still, it was a far better sort of
place than the little man usually frequented. It was, however,
entirely obvious—terrifyingly obvious—to the little man that
it was the lowest tavern his visitor had ever entered, much
less sat himself within.

He didn't belong there any more than the little man did,
though their business had caused one to sink lower and the
other to rise higher so that they might meet in the middle to
discuss it. For if the little man would never even be allowed
to linger on the sidewalk outside the sort of place his visitor
usually frequented, his visitor would not even step outside his
carriage to enter the sort of hostelry the little man passed
most of his time in. Even so, it was plain that the higher
classes had less mobility than the lower, if only because there
were fewer of them, for though the little man was profoundly
ill-at-ease, where he sat, he did not look especially out of
place. The gentleman who sat opposite him was so wildly
mismatched with his surroundings that all conversation had
ceased the moment he'd ducked his head down to walk in
through the low door.

Still, they had privacy. The little man's business was too
well known, even here, for sane men to care to overhear what
he was up to. The gentleman was too rare a sight to be a
healthy one, and he had too dangerous a look to him, anyway, to even tempt a fellow to try to cadge a penny piece
from him. The loiterers in the tavern might not be able to
read, but they'd learned to read their fellowmen right early
on, or else they wouldn't have been able to survive to adulthood. And they could easily see that not only was the gent
too tall and broad and well-set-up for one man to take on
alone, but it would be wiser altogether to avoid a bloke with
that sort of cold edge to his voice, that forbidding look in his

wide, fair face, and that something they saw glittering now and again in those blue eyes that was far too cold for sanity.

That look sparkled in his light blue eyes now, and the little man shivered, but then, he often did, but then he said a thing he almost never did, for it was the truth, and it had been frightened out of him at last:

"Sir," he said anxiously, "I can't do nuffink for you. No, and I mean that. It ain't the job, for that's my bread an' butter. Snuffing a cove's easy. Nuffink simpler. Be he high or low, if the price is right, Jimmy Spiv's yer man, they told you right in that, all right. There's not many who'd say it, fewer still who'd do it—takin' on a highborn gent, for fear of their necks. But mine's not worth much, an' I know it. Aye, I'd dance on a rope if they caught me, but for what you'd gimme 'twould be a dance of joy, 'cause I'd die richer than I ever lived. But I can't."

"And why not?" the gentleman asked.

Jimmy Spiv kept his hand in his ragged jacket, and fingered the sharpest knife he had concealed there over his wildly beating heart, but for once it didn't comfort him, no, not when he had to look back into those quietly cold eyes.

"Because of t' Lion," he said at last, and swore and then cursed himself for a fool, for as soon as the word was out he knew his mistake and knew he'd have to leave this tavern and then London itself for saying what he had.

"Ah, Lion, yes," the gentleman said thoughtfully, "I know the man. But if you don't fear the rope, Jimmy, why fear the Lion? Death's death, when all's said."

"No, it ain't," the little man said, rising, beginning to dance away from the table sidewise, in a crabbed scuttle. "Lion's worse'n death, sir. Bank on it. Good day to you, sir, good day."

And hopping away from the table, he backed off, and moving quickly backward, left the tavern, leaving the gentleman alone at his table.

It was not the first time this day, nor even this week, that he'd been left so. But oddly, now here, where there was no one he knew, or cared to know, to watch him suffer the indignity, he was even angrier than he'd been before. Last week, at Watier's, he'd been discouraged; the day before, at Madame Felice's, he'd been displeased; this morning, at his club, he'd been disbelieving; but now he was beyond all that, he was enraged. Lord Moredon had never known defeat; though he'd suffered it before, as all men do, he'd always been able to disguise it for himself. Now he found there was no way to circumvent the thing. It was simplicity itself, that was why it was impossible to get around. He wanted revenge upon Julian Dylan, Viscount Hazelton, he needed revenge upon Mr. Warwick Jones. He could get neither, he could get none. Nor could he forget it.

He'd tried for revenge, he'd attempted obliviousness. So far he'd had no success with either.

He couldn't get the incident at Gentleman Jackson's out of his mind. Neither wine, nor women, nor sleep, his usual retreats, could get the sight of that dark, avenging, implacable face from his mind's eye, or take the shock he'd felt as he'd found himself unable to defend himself from his memory, or take the taste of the shame of defeat from his mouth, and that taste has been more bitter than the blood he'd tasted there. It was Warwick Jones's blood he wanted now. Nothing else would mend the insult. But Warwick Jones, who ought to have been the easiest target for retribution, had turned out to be the most impervious to it.

The first step to destroying a man, if it were to be done well, and done entirely, was to take his good name away. Warwick Jones lived alone, he wasn't an ornament of society, but was part of it by birth, and known to be odd, unusual, and reclusive. That being the case, that being famous in fact, who would have believed, Lord Moredon thought, staring down at the bare table he sat at, that the man would be so well-defended?

For he'd gone to Watier's not four nights past, so soon as his face had healed enough for the sight of it not to cause talk, and he'd gambled for such high stakes at that gilded gaming house that he'd attracted attention to himself for it, and that was what he'd been after. He was annoyed to discover himself realizing it was wildly extravagant, dimly recalling the exigencies his man-at-business had lately been plaguing him about. But he'd needed one scandal to over-shadow the other, believing it better to be discussed for being reckless with money than to be spoken of as having been defeated by a man younger, leaner, and altogether less sizable than himself. Then, as all had gone according to plan, when he'd had wine with a group of influential gentleman after, he'd dropped the name, so cleverly working it into the conversation that he believed it looked as though the drubbing had slipped his mind, and that if he recalled it at all, it was only as the merest jest.

Then at that table with the other bored gentlemen—an earl, a duke, a famous poet, and a confidant of the Prince among their number—he dropped the hint. He'd mentioned that though he wasn't best pleased with losing the blunt tonight, he certainly wouldn't set about repairing his purse the way some supposed gentlemen did. And when no one inquired further, he began to speak of rumors he'd heard of certain persons who trafficked in certain secrets for their money. And then he'd mentioned such names as Napoleon, and Joseph Bonaparte, and Warwick Jones.

He'd offered to say more. They'd left. At once, en masse, silently, and immediately.

It transpired that they all admired Jones. Some of them had been to school with him, some knew him through various businesses he involved himself with. Warwick Jones might ignore society, but society never ignored him. Lord Moredon hadn't known that then, but found it out later that night, from a drunken fop too castaway to care what he said, much less care that it was no longer considered correct to be speaking with him.

He hadn't wanted a girl from Madame Felice's the next night, but he'd known that there would be other influential men gathered in the grand salon of that ornate bawdy house. And so, as he'd gossiped and bought wine for several gentlemen and prostitutes there, as he'd circled his own choice's breast with one hand and his wineglass with the other, he'd laughed and mentioned that it was too bad he couldn't meet Mr. Warwick Jones or his pretty friend Viscount Hazelton there as well, but then, everyone knew those two were such good, intimate friends that they had no need of the sort of sport Madame Felice could provide them. The silence that met that remark had been so profound that others in the huge and gaudy room had turned to see what had caused it, as surely as if they'd heard a scream ring out instead of the sudden, utterly complete hush that fell over that quarter of the room. He'd had to pay Madame Felice extra that night for the damage he did later in his fury at how all of the gentlemen had left him alone at the table with the whore, but it was worth it, since Madame Felice then swore the girl would never talk about what had been done to her.

This morning at his club he'd been shocked to find that the few men he'd managed to collar had drifted away from him, making feeble excuses at best, or at worst, providing none. He'd never been treated so. Although he had no one close friend, he'd thought he had many, for he'd always been a popular man, at school, in society, in his world. He could scarcely believe it, he knew it was all Warwick Jones's fault. He couldn't see the expression on his face when he so much as mentioned Warwick Jones's name now, nor could he hear the tone in his own voice when he did so, thus he'd no idea of how he terrified some of his listeners and disgusted others.

Those weeks lying in bed, not receiving visitors so as not to feed the rumors about what had happened to him, lying alone with himself day after day for the first time in his life, after his first real defeat, after his great public shame, with little to do but remember the indignity, had helped him plot his revenge but had also changed him. He soon forgot all else as the injustices the dark and the light young gentlemen had visited upon him grew clearer, grew larger. Thoughts of revenge ripened as well, becoming so much sweeter that soon even remembrance of the shameful incidents that made it necessary became delicious to think on. Of course, it changed him. But the change was so subtle that he himself couldn't see it, for it was only an intensification, bringing out all that which he'd hidden for so long from the world, and more, from himself.

He'd been to gambling hells, he'd visited houses of pleasure—he'd been shunned there. He'd been ignored at his club, and then he had found no cards of invitation to select parties and teas and routs and ridottos and balls waiting for him when he'd returned home. Those cards had always begged his attendance at those affairs which occupied most of his life, and were usually stacked so high each day that he had to pick and choose from among them in order to winnow out the best each night. They came no longer. He'd sent his sister away to keep her clear, in name and person, from his doings. Now there was no one to speak with, there was no other recourse.

He'd have to see to the death of Warwick Jones, whether he could disgrace him first or not.

And as for the beggar viscount, the boy he'd remembered from school, the lad with the unearthly beautiful face and body, the one his sister thought to taunt him with, he, Lord Moredon thought, trembling with the force of his frustration, he'd find death preferable to what was planned for him. But that, he discovered to his relief whenever he allowed himself to think about it, could not be thought about, it would have to come second. First, he must bring down the viscount's devoted friend, Warwick Jones.

Yet he discovered that even here in the slums, among creatures who scarcely qualified to be called human, he was refused. Now, because of a man named Lion. There were a great many terrible things Lord Moredon was, especially in his altered condition, but he was not a physical coward.

He rose from the table and strode to the sagging wooden bar. The barkeep looked at him in some apprehension. The tall fair gentleman spoke in loud, carrying accents, addressing the room: some huddled sots, the few dozing petty thieves, the failed procurers and cutpurses who frequented the tavern.

"I seek," he announced, "the Lion. I want him to know this. I'll pay a reward, a handsome reward to anyone who helps me in this. I want the Lion to know that I shall count him afraid of me if he avoids me. I want to speak with him. Now. Today. I'll wait here. I shall await his pleasure."

The alleyway twisted so many times that Lord Moredon gave up trying to memorize it in order to learn his exit. If he'd come this far, it was too late to turn back, even if he'd wanted to. It was obvious he didn't want to, for it was that very look of eagerness, barely restrained, that his host first noticed when Lord Moredon was ushered into his parlor. The next thing he noted about his noble guest, to his great interest, was the fact that the gentleman was obviously having difficulty veiling that excitement, as well as other emotions which raced across his face. As this was a gentleman placed high in the *ton*, this was exceptional, since it was the style of such men always to display cool impassivity, especially to their social inferiors. And, as this was also a gentleman who clearly didn't realize he suffered from this handicap, it was disturbing as well. But although he was no gentleman, only a King of Thieves, the Lion's own face revealed none of these ruminations as he arose and offered his hand to Lord Moredon when the nobleman was shown into his presence.

Lord Moredon took the proffered hand, shook it, and with an expression of great affability, immediately ruined by the fleeting impression of secret self-congratulation that flickered upon his fair face, said heartily:

"Well, Lion, we meet again. I'll admit I wasn't best pleased with you when we last parted. But, indeed, I've heard so many good things about you since, I find I cannot hold a grudge. Thank you for giving me an audience," he said on a laugh of such falseness that the Lion looked at him sharply as he offered him a chair. But since the gentleman took the chair, crossed his legs, and seemed entirely at his ease, it was apparent to his host that he'd no idea of mockery, or rather, had not the smallest notion of how transparently he concealed the mockery he meant.

"I heard you were seeking me, my lord," the Lion answered calmly, seating himself as well. "It was clever of you to offer a reward for getting the message to me, prudent of you to wait in the tavern for so many hours for my reply, brave of you to follow my man here, but foolish, very foolish, I'm afraid, to frame your request to see me as a challenge."

There was a moment of silence as Lord Moredon looked at his host. The two men sat in a plain but well-furnished parlor in a ramshackle building. The interior of the house was as acceptable in cleanliness and taste as the exterior was not. In fact, if it weren't for the pair of brutal-looking guards at the door, it would seem a commonplace social call between gentlemen. The two men were of a height, both were fair-skinned, both had fashionable hairstyles, though one had thin light hair and the other a springy ginger crop. Both were clad in proper gentlemen's attire. But there their resemblance ended. For the Lion was twice as broad about the chest and neck, his features were as hewn from rock, and about as mobile as one too. But, after hearing his host's statement, the other man's refined features showed hasty anger, cupidity, and only after a brief struggle resolved themselves into the icy calm of a gentleman's polite expression again. Only then did the Lion frown, and seeing that alarming change, Lord Moredon spoke.

"Brave? Hardly. And foolish? I don't know. I knew you for a man of business, and so I believed you'd think any tactic that got us together for mutual profit would be acceptable. I'm certainly not mad enough to challenge *you*, sir," he added, and for once, there seemed to be some honesty in his speech, for his face didn't belie his words. But then, the Lion noted, it seemed that the gentleman, upon achieving his end, which was this interview, was rapidly settling down to normalcy again.

"You wouldn't call laying evidence against me with Bow Street a challenge?" the Lion mused in a low rumble. "You don't consider complaining about my activities to certain parties in the prime minister's entourage, in Liverpool's own circle, who'd made it very difficult for Bow Street to ignore me, a forthright challenge? My dear Lord Moredon, pray, what would you consider a challenge to me then?"

"A glove in the face," he replied haughtily. "I'm direct, sir. As to the other unfortunate occurrences, why, I believe what has been said might be unsaid. Bow Street is none too eager to press forward without a push from behind. That pressure might be removed, with a word . . . or two."

"Ah, and all this through your goodwill?" the Lion asked innocently.

"Alas," Lord Moredon said, now so deeply into whatever game he was playing that only his lips moved in his serene face, "I'm a man of goodwill, but I'd require a little more than that to move me to such effort. But only a little more, only a trifle. You need do nothing, sir—in fact, you need *only* to do nothing."

Lord Moredon laughed gaily at his play on words, but

there was that in his laughter which caused the two men at the door to glance at him with sudden attention.

"Mmmm?" the Lion murmured in a low hum of interest.

"I require something done," Lord Moredon said with great pleasure, that pleasure now showing in his eyes, "but I hear it can't be done without your approval. Very well, plainly said, give me your approval, and there's an end to it."

"An end to what?"

"An end to Warwick Jones," Lord Moredon said, and his face as he said it was suddenly so naked in its desire that the Lion, who had seen many worse things than desire, nevertheless looked away to his fingertips as he replied:

"Ah, no. I'm sorry, my lord. That I can't do. That I won't permit. The gentleman is a friend of mine. No, not strictly true, say 'an acquaintance.' But we've an understanding. You'll recall the matter concerning the Viscount Hazelton? Ah, yes, but how could you forget? That's where we first met, as I was preventing you from kicking the young gentleman's face in. Then I took action without knowing the fellow, only because I didn't wish to see a work of art defaced. In a most literal sense," he added, smiling to himself at his inadvertent pun.

But seeing his visitor's own blank white face so filled with suppressed emotion that it was obvious he was in no mood for humor, he went on smoothly:

"Now I have the pleasure of knowing both gentlemen. And I'll say only that if I wished them harm, I'd do it myself. I wouldn't take hire to do it, nor, I believe, should any man of honor."

"Man of honor!" Lord Moredon breathed, his eyes wide, so enraged that a vein pulsed noticeably in the center of his forehead. "Honor among thieves, more likely. Do you protect him because of his gallows-ripe ancestor? But that was centuries ago. I tell you I have a grievance against the man, and you've no right to thwart me!"

Lord Moredon sprang to his feet even as his host rose slowly to his and the two men at the door stepped forward. The Lion casually waved them back, and stepping forward himself until he was almost nose-to-nose with his furious guest, he said in such a sweetly reasonable voice that it was chilling:

"I do not thwart you, my lord. If you want him . . . get him . . . but without my help."

"I don't know what he's given you for protection, but I'll double it!" Lord Moredon shouted.

"I doubt you can equal it, much less double it. It's simply a matter of taste, my lord, and I've no taste for your business. And that business—taking a man's life because you've taken a beating from him in a fair fight—it's a trifle . . . excessive, is it not? Especially since, as I understand it, your quarrel originally was nothing to do with him at all, but only with his friend, and his honoring that friendship."

"Friendship?" Lord Moredon sneered. "If that's what it's called now. But yes, that's how it began. They were always friends, back in school, before that pauper began to court my sister, before he dared to try to lay his hands on her. It was always remarked how they stayed together, and mocked other people, and laughed together, as if no one else in the school or the world mattered except themselves. They needed a set-down then. And now?" Lord Moredon raged, "See how they still defy me? If you try to hurt the one, you must deal with the other. So," he said, calming and casting a brilliant smile to his host, "it is simple: to deal with the one, you must hurt the other."

"No," the Lion said, "*you* must hurt the other—I will not. And I suspect you won't either, though not from want of trying. And why should you? Come, my lord," he said in a conciliatory tone, his voice purring so warmly and soothingly it was almost as if he'd actually laid a hand on the other man's shoulder as he spoke, although he made no movement at all, "after all, what have they done except to be friends, the sort of friends you or I would be glad of? And what has the handsome viscount done, after all, except to fall in love, as either you or I might have done?"

"He's been forbidden to go near my sister," the other man said coldly. "He's defied me."

"But what of your sister?" the Lion asked reasonably. "She could discourage him, could she not?"

"How can she?" Lord Moredon said rapidly, dropping his

voice to a fervent whisper, his face working as he strove to conceal whatever it was that struggled to be out. "Who could? I myself had not forgotten him, or anything about him, and I'd not clapped eyes on him for years before he met up with my dear sister. But he is beauty itself, he is beauty incarnate, his face, his form: manly perfection. He haunts her dreams, she dreams of his touch, of those mocking lips, not mocking, but touching, of his body, and of touching it, she cannot resist him, she can't forget him, though she's tried, don't you see?"

"Ah," the Lion breathed, seeing the white tense face of Lord Moredon, and taking a step back, as though he didn't want even the other man's breath to touch him now, "yes, my lord, I do see. But can't you? Killing that which you desire doesn't kill the yearning for it. You must kill the desire for it first."

Lord Moredon blinked. It was possible he had heard and understood what was said, but then, if he had, he should have been hotly denying it, or been enraged to the point of battle. Instead, his expression became crafty as he said, brightly, as if he'd heard nothing but what had been discussed earlier:

"But you don't have to help me. There are many ways to kill a man. If you cannot get him, why then, you can get at those who matter to him. I've endless resources. I'm not done. But I've wasted my time here, and there's little time to waste. Good day."

He turned abruptly, and although the Lion gave the nod, a look at the gentleman's face might have been enough to cause the two guards to let him pass by them anyway. Then it seemed as though he didn't notice them at all, his own expression became so bent in upon itself.

"Aye," the Lion sighed softly to himself as he watched the gentleman rush off, already walking less erectly than he had when he'd come, already moving with a certain jerky, erratic gait, "make haste, my lord, you're right, there's little time left. All eternity wouldn't be enough for you, poor fool, since a man can never run fast enough if it's himself he's running from."

Lord Moredon hurried to his own town house. Once there, he shut himself up in his library for hours, and paced and thought, and made notes, laughing to himself at times, only to stop laughing to look up and around the room in puzzlement at who had been laughing at other times, before he fell to feverish planning and pacing again. At nightfall, he let his valet change his garments, and then he went to his club for dinner, and ate it in silence, never seeming to care that not a few gentlemen nervously noted his lips moving as though he spoke to someone, although no one had greeted him, much less joined him at his table.

Then he took a hackney coach to an address on Curzon Street, and still murmuring to himself, rapidly took the stairs and let himself into a small house there. The girl who had been resting on the recamier in the small salon had been thumbing through a book of fashion plates, but when she looked up to see the gentleman who'd entered her lodgings standing in the doorway staring at her, she gave a glad cry and rushed to meet him.

She was genuinely glad to see them. For she knew she was young, entirely too young for the position he'd hired her to fill, and was grateful for the employment. Although she had an attractive face and a quantity of pale hair, she'd been underfed for too many years, and had too few of those years to her credit to have attracted a protector before she'd been raised up from the streets by this tall fair gentleman. He'd taken her in a doorway, and then, instead of merely paying her her shilling, he'd established her in these rooms, the most sumptuous she'd ever seen or imagined in all her brief life. If the gentleman brought her nowhere else, she expected no more; if he visited certain painful indignities upon her person, she expected no less; she was, after all, only fourteen, she had, after all, no other way to earn her keep. He provided her with food and clothing, and so she was beholden to him enough to allow him anything he wished in the month since he'd installed her here.

He said nothing to her, but then, he seldom did, unless it was to order her to do something for him or to him during his play. This time, he frowned as he removed his clothing, so her own hands shook as she undid hers, and her thin body trembled when she saw he was ready but that he remained only standing and frowning down at her as she awaited his pleasure tonight.

Her body was still as slender and straight as a boy's, her attitude just as abject as he'd wish, there was nothing about her that was feminine in the least except for the absence of one salient feature, and the presence of that profusion of billowing waist-length, thin, light hair that had first attracted him. He turned suddenly from contemplating her and marched into the bedchamber, and she followed, shivering, and watched as he rifled through the chest of drawers until he found what he was seeking. When he strode toward her then, she did not quake at the sight of the obvious evidence of his arousal as she often did and always tried to conceal doing, but she put her hands up before her face and whimpered as he approached her with the shears. But before she could gasp more than "Oh no, sir, oh pity," he'd grasped her by her hair, and pulling her head back, he brought the shears to her throat.

She trembled with relief when he cast the scissors aside after having only sheared all her hair off where he'd clasped it, at the nape of her neck. She didn't even mind that he'd left her head cropped closer than his when she saw him gazing at her with desire, and she was so incredibly relieved at his loss of anger and renewed interest that she stepped right over the discarded pale puddle of her hair without a regret as she sought to enter his arms. But then when he spun her around with hard hands and laughed, she began to know that she'd no reason to be glad. None at all.

He'd saved her from starvation, taken her from plying her trade in doorways, and given her food and safety from the streets filled with those who'd preyed on her since she'd been old enough to run. She had thought herself lucky, whatever his demands had been. Where she'd been bred, without protectors, girls starved, if they were lucky. She wasn't a fool or she wouldn't have reached her age, and she'd known that a little pain was fair payment for all that he gave her.

But as soon as he'd at last fallen into an exhausted sleep, and as soon as she'd realized that tonight he slept like a dog, so that all his moans and twitching wouldn't wake him, she dragged herself up and painfully dressed herself. Then she put all she could into an improvised sack and stealthily let herself out into the night. She crouched on the doorstep for a scant second to look up to the house where she'd been so pleased to be allowed to live. There were a great many dangers awaiting her this night in London and she knew it. But young and uneducated as she was, she had survived much, and so she knew, as she crept off down the dark street, that there was far worse waiting for her in that beautifully furnished bedchamber she'd just left forever.

Susannah fled the garden, laughing. Julian had threatened to put a daddy-long-legs down her neck, and she'd gathered up her skirts and run, her rippling laughter floating behind her, all the way through the entry hall, all the way to the morning salon. There she stood, sheltering behind a small writing desk, catching her breath and reviewing her defense, as she waited for her tormentor to approach dangling the unfortunate insect between two fingers, as he'd done in the rose garden.

"It's the poor bug I'm worried about, honestly," she cried at once, cowering away as he entered the room, "for though it wouldn't be pleasant for me, it would be hideous for him, poor thing, and . . ." And then she saw that he'd nothing in his hand but a letter and he'd forgotten their play entirely, he was so absorbed in it. Then he looked up from it to her with such a look of luminous joy that her heart sank, and she knew at once, of course, what it was about without even seeing it.

They'd been at Greenwood Hall for a week, although to Susannah it was more like being in Eden for twice as long. She loved the countryside far more than the city, and Warwick's home was as comfortable and welcoming in actuality as it had been in appearance. In the days she'd rested here, there had been so much laughter that she'd had no time to wonder if she should stay, or question why she, who was supposed to be being introduced to society, should be remaining in the sole company of her chaperon and two bachelor gentlemen. For they passed the days exploring the grounds, and the nights singing and laughing and talking and playing at cards or charades, and day or night, there was nothing but pleasure in her visit. Warwick was an excellent host; he always made her laugh and kept her company whenever

Julian was not at her side. But Julian often was there as well, telling her stories, twitting her, and accepting her as a friend. Unless, of course, he thought of Lady Moredon, and then he took her for his confidante and poured all his hopes and dreams into her ears. She was pleased to listen, if only so that she could watch him as he spoke. Now, from the softened look in his light eyes, she knew whom he was about to speak of, so she sighed and sat down at the desk.

"It's another invitation, Sukey," he said with some excitement, "to a picnic, and I think I'll go, but where the devil is Eaton Hall?" he asked, going to a drawer of the desk and rummaging impatiently through it before he found what he was seeking. Spreading the map out upon the desk, he ran his finger down it, saying:

"Thank heaven for this map Warwick's always guiding me to. I'm an excellent coachman, but I must know where I'm heading . . . yes, here it is, Eaton, Eaton Hall . . . Hove, it's to be a picnic in Hove, fine."

She looked up from the map and laughed at him.

"Oh, Julian, if it were to be a picnic on the Moon, you'd say 'fine,' so long as you knew she'd be there."

And if there'd been a little sorrow in her voice, she'd learned to laugh to cover it, and so he joined her. It was the sound of their merriment which drew the observer to the door of the salon. He'd been in the library reading, or trying to, since he'd determined that he should leave them alone together when he could. That, after all, had been the whole point of inviting her to his home in the first place, as he reminded himself time and again. And she, after all, noticed no one else when Julian was with her anyway, as he never had to remind himself. But the laughter had drawn him to its source, as surely as a man left in darkness is drawn to the light.

Now, seeing Susannah all in white, her shining flaxen hair bound with a white riband, beside Julian in his white shirtsleeves, his golden crop glinting in the sunlit room, a man, Warwick thought, could go blind from the glare given off by the pair of them, if not deaf from the noise they created. And so he said as they stopped laughing when they noticed him watching them. He didn't mention that a man might also be so dazzled by the joy he saw in their faces that he might do anything to warm himself at even a small part of it.

But as they began to interrupt each other in their eagerness to tell him what they'd been doing, he remembered that in that odd instant he'd also seemed to see all three of them as if from afar, the two bright persons as well as himself—the intruder who'd caused their laughter to die. But he'd seen this as if from some odd vantage point outside of himself. Then to his own eyes it was as if he saw an envious goblin, as green with envy as he was olive-skinned, standing at a half-open door, peering through the darkness to watch two of the fair folk at their joyous and incomprehensible, eternally private play.

"Julian's been invited to a picnic in Hove," Susannah explained, "so we were looking over the map to find where it was."

"It's not at all far. I might even be able to walk there if you intend to be mean about a carriage," Julian put in easily.

"My dear," Warwick said, settling himself in a chair, "according to the good doctor, you could vault there, stopping off every half-mile to lift a heifer in the air or loft a mill-stone across the road."

"That's jealousy speaking," Julian said knowingly, nodding to Susannah, "for he knows I've got lumpy ribs now, the doctor even said so, if I weren't a gentleman I'd show you, or tell you to run your fingers across them to feel the ridges there, they quite ruin my symmetry, you know," he complained archly, "but though all he's been left with is that spider's thread of a line across his cheek, he's been spiteful to me since the bandages came off. Very vain is our Warwick, don't you know."

"On the contrary," Warwick said loftily, running a finger along the thin red line left on his cheek, "I rather like it, and hope it doesn't fade. A tiny flaw suits me. Perfection being so boring, you understand."

The two gentlemen grinned at each other. Although it was obvious spoofing, it was the sort of raillery Susannah seldom joined in. For when they mocked each other, though they never took offense at what was said, she often thought they came too close to the edge of civility, too near to real insult, for her to dare to participate. As if in answer to her thoughts, Warwick added:

"Doubtless then, Julian, my pretty, you'll have your shirt whipped off in a trice at whatever tea you've been asked to grace, and will be soliciting eager little fingers to discover your wounds."

"Jealousy speaks again," Julian confided loudly to Susannah, "since he knows that because of their location, searching for my injuries will make for far more interesting sport than seeking out his."

"Too warm, Julian, my pet," Warwick said lazily. "You forget our innocent guest. But so far as that goes, there might be a great many females who'd find the examination of my face far more interesting than letting their fingers roam over your entire corpus."

"Oh yes," Julian laughed, "but taking into account the size of your nose, my friend, they'd have to be blind ones. And blind one's you'd lied to, at that. For if they found that great prominence interesting, I'd wager you'd have told them that it was your, ah, corpus they were examining, and not your face at all."

"Far too warm!" Warwick frowned, sitting up sharply. "Susannah, forgive us, you're so much of a friend that we sometimes forget you're a lady."

"But she isn't," Julian protested on a laugh, and then, hearing no other laughter, but seeing Warwick glower and Susannah staring down at her hands suddenly, he took up those two hands in his, and looking down upon her bent head, said gently:

"Sukey, my little friend, is he right? Do I have to offer a thousand apologies for one warm jest, or beg forgiveness for a thoughtless comment? I didn't think I'd have to put on a hair shirt for the joke, and never imagined I'd offend you with that last comment that's got Warwick scowling at me so. You know very well what I meant by that at least, or you ought. I only meant you're not a *titled* lady, and that's all to the good.

"Because," he said, smiling tenderly at her, "I'm very glad you are what you are, because I never have to watch my tongue when I'm with you. That's not to say you're not well-bred, or well-versed, or the most well-tempered little soul I've ever found wearing skirts. I'll swear I'm so comfortable with you I forget you're just as female as any 'lady.' No, thats not true either, you're nothing like a gentleman friend. You're unique and that's why I love you, but if I have to apologize every time I forget to stand on ceremony, why then—''

'' 'Standing on ceremony' is a bit different from making the sort of jokes she can't join in,'' Warwick snapped, cutting off his friend, diverting his attention from the suddenly pale girl whose hands he still held. ''Only think, aside from the propriety of it, if she laughs at such jests, she looks underbred, and if she doesn't, she seems priggish. What a position you put her in!''

And if she doesn't understand, then she's embarrassed to admit it, and if she does, she knows very well that she oughtn't, he thought to himself with some amusement. But then he frowned because he knew it wasn't any of this that had made her lose her faint color or caused her to bite her lip. It was the fact that Julian still held her hands, and had called her his ''love,'' yet had vowed nothing like the love that could be so clearly read in her transparent face as she raised it to him. That look fled as she turned from Julian to smile at Warwick and say with such strained merriness that he winced:

''There's no need for apology. I didn't find the conversation 'warm,' Warwick, for I didn't understand a word of it. So would you please explain it to me?''

As Julian gave a shout of delight, and a grudging but admiring glint appeared in Warwick's eye, he gravely explained that he hadn't understood Julian either, but from knowing the fellow for so long, had expected the worst. Then, before a triumphant Julian could ruin the temporary peace with another jest, Warwick mentioned that he too had gotten an invitation to the picnic, and told her that he expected, of course, that she'd come along with him as his guest. She hesitated just long enough for him to nod in satisfaction and say, ''Very good, I knew I could count on you to keep me company.''

They made light chatter about the people who might be at

the picnic, decided it would probably be rained out three times before it was actually held, and when Susannah was given the first opportunity, she pleaded letters she must write and escaped the room. Julian watched her graceful figure go, and smiled. But the smile slipped from his face as quickly as she'd exited from the room when he heard his friend say harshly, in low, angry tones:

"Damme, Hazelton, if you aren't an idiot!"

14

The two young gentlemen were alone in the room but the fair-haired one spun around on his heel and gaped at his host with as much shocked surprise as if he expected it was some other person who had spoken to him. For if there had been none of his friend's customary underlying humor in the rough exclamation he'd just heard, there wasn't a trace of it to be seen in the shadowed, brooding face either. Warwick's dark visage had a dozen eloquent ways of expressing sorrow, real and counterfeit, and more than that many more to show haughtiness, amusement, and pleasure. But anger, real anger, was unusual for it. Now his blue eyes blazed and his thin brows drew together over that high arched nose his friend had so recently jested about.

"Good God, Julian," he said in exasperation, rising from his chair in one fluid motion to stand and face the blond gentleman, "have you no eyes? Ears? Soul?"

The two young men were both cleanly made, agile and fit. And though Warwick was leaner and the taller by a few inches, as they stood there toe-to-toe and confronted each other, they were, in a fashion, like reversed mirror images: the dark and light reflection of each other's temperament and passion, for one was fair as an angel in his innocent puzzlement, and the other, glowering and in his brooding humor, lowering as his elongated cast shadow.

"You're serious? Yes, by heaven, you're serious!" Julian breathed in astonishment.

"And you ought to be more so," Warwick said furiously, struggling for control of the emotion he always rode so hard, but failing this once because of the very incredulity he read in the other man's eyes. Malice he could have contended with, but this ignorant, blithe cruelty was too much for him. And so he spoke before there was any help for it, and added, the further words torn from him before he could prevent it, in response to that maddening continuing look of offended incomprehension:

"Don't you see the girl adores you?"

Only then, hearing his own words, did he wheel around and stare at the window, reining in all his rage so that he could speak the things he knew he must with the proper detachment, with the correct cool humor that he always used, with the distance he especially must when it was, as it was so rarely, as it was now, his own heart involved.

For it seemed he'd forgotten he had one, he realized as he slowed his breathing. Until she'd come, he thought, as, finally, familiar sorrow banished dangerous fury.

"Admires me? Yes, of course. But it will pass, she's very young," Julian said on a half-laugh, which failed when his friend replied in his more usual caustic tones:

"Oh yes. Extremely. A veritable infant. I take it then that you've conceived of a passion for infants? She's two years older than Lady Moredon, I believe. And who knows how much senior to that poor drab you pleased yourself with at the inn where we met."

Julian stiffened in insult. His light eyes grew hard as glinting ice and his white face set as chill as his voice as he said:

"At the inn where we met when I was driving a coach for my daily bread. Add that bit, Warwick, for I'll swear it isn't far from your mind. And now," he went on, amazing his host again with how cruel and glacial that graceful smiling face could become in an instant, as he always had on those rare past occasions when he'd lost his temper, "read me the rules I must hew to if I'm to be allowed to stay on with you and take your food and lodging for a day longer. Talk to me about ingratitude, Warwick, lecture me on my duty to my savior. Come, remind me of my obligations . . . does 'found in the gutter' come next? Or will 'battening on your good nature' follow? Is 'parasite' a word you're looking for? No matter, if you can't speak it, write it, and I'll eventually get it. I am grateful for your consideration, Warwick, or I'd say far more. But in gratitude, my exit line will be more unexceptionable. Thank you, but good-bye, Mr. Jones," he said, turning on his heel.

"Very well done," Warwick said with equal coolness, but his arm swung out and he clasped the other man hard on the shoulder. As Julian wheeled about, his hands closing to fists and his expression grim, his host went on coldly, "Before we come to blows, listen. I'm impressed by your righteous wrath. But believe me, I don't give two damns about whom you've been sleeping with, nor do I care what lady, or trull, you've plans to oblige in future. Nor do I give one small damn about gratitude, and I'll finish your lady's charming brother's work for him if you so much as dare to hint at it to me again. I'll swear I deserve better, and not because of my pains with you recently, because I know you'd do the same for me if matters were reversed, but for the sake of all those years when we both only gave friendship to each other, and took only friendship from each other, as well.

"But I do care when I see someone in over her head and drowning. The girl is besotted with you, Julian, and as her brother's friend, if not as her friend, I have to ask what you mean to do by her, whatever our friendship is or has been. Julian," he said then, amazement in his expression and words, "have you never looked into her eyes to see anything but whether or not your lustrous hair needed combing?"

"I knew she liked me very well . . ." Julian said hesitantly, taken aback, his anger vanished, to be replaced by sudden unease, as he said as shamefacedly as a boy, ". . . I suppose I knew, Warwick, but I suppose I didn't care. You're right," he admitted, entirely deflated, offering his friend a self-mocking smile, "I'm a lout and insensitive, but, oh well, it's rather pleasant, being admired, you know . . . and . . ."

"And rather commonplace for you too, isn't it, poor lad?" Warwick said on a sad answering smile. He took his hand from his friend's shoulder then, and ruffled his hair as though he were the boy he'd been when he'd last seen him looking so abjectedly contrite.

"How you pretty chaps ever grow a conscience is a mystery to me," Warwick sighed, as his friend grinned at the old gesture of friendship and Warwick made his hand into a fist and thumped his shoulder gently for emphasis. "That you've acquired one at all is a minor miracle at that, and is your one saving grace, my lovely lordship. All your life you've but to smile at some poor susceptible creature—and if she wasn't susceptible before she met you, she becomes so, and instantly dotes upon you . . . my God, Julian, you might have become a monster, you know."

"I believe my friends kept me from that," the viscount answered soberly.

"Don't believe that for a minute," Warwick replied just as seriously. "Friends are only drawn to what already is to be found in a man."

" 'Show me a man's friends and I'll show you what he is'? Not like you to be so clichéd, Warwick," Julian said wryly.

"No, show me a man's friends and I'll only be able to show you what they like to be associated with," Warwick corrected him. "Show me a man's enemies and I'll show you what he is. But we're not talking philosophy now, we're speaking about a young girl who just happens to dote on you. Entirely and transparently. You've given her encouragement, that's what's alarming me."

"But I've told her about Marianna time and again," Julian protested.

"Oh yes, I've noticed that, in along with all the gossip and conversation and jesting you've entertained her with, along with all the smiles and fond pats bestowed upon her in all those hours you've passed in her company. Although, I'll admit," he said, lowering his eyes as he said it, as if to attend to straightening his shirt cuff, "if there was to be something tangible for her at the end of it, more than a broken heart or a spirited lesson in lovemaking, that is, I wouldn't care. Something permanent as well as legal, since her brother, after all, had something of that sort in mind when he left her in my care. Make no mistake, she may not be titled or highly bred, but she's very well-off, Julian. Dowered as handsomely by her family as she's been by nature, in fact."

"Whoof," Julian said, sitting down suddenly on the arm of a chair and gazing at his friend wide-eyed, "there's plain speaking! All right, my friend, I can match you. I didn't mean to encourage her, or if I did, it was a thoughtlessness, not a deliberate enticement. Plain speech for plain speaking: she's a great deal of fun to be with, bright as a sunny morning, good and kind, and so far as attractiveness goes, I can think of few more enchanting things than engaging her in that spirited lesson in lovemaking you mentioned. But I know that's not possible, since I happen to be burdened with being a gentleman, albeit, yes, a thoughtless one. And I'm glad she's well-off, but not for my sake—she deserves no less. Yet with all her wit and character and beauty and wealth and the pleasure I find in her company, I don't love her. So I'll leave her, thanks. But don't worry, without a broken heart, for I'll be kind, but increasingly, and very obviously, very brotherly toward her. Now why do you look so puzzled?''

"I was only wondering . . ." Warwick answered, and it may have been that it was one of the rare moments when he was being absolutely candid as well, his friend thought, since his dark blue eyes were troubled and seemingly innocent as a child's now: "If all that you mentioned is not love, Julian, then what is?"

"What I feel for Marianna," Julian answered at once, his voice softening at the mention of her name. "A sort of worship, Warwick, that's what it is. An awe, more than appreciation, a kind of wonder. It comes from knowing she's better than any other female, far better than I, in fact. And . . . it's hard to explain, damme, Warwick, I'm no poet, you're the one that always has the words, but I'd have to say it's knowing that I aspire to her, even when I'm with her."

"Ah," his friend said thoughtfully after a pause, "I see. And you don't feel that toward our Susannah."

"Lord, no," Julian laughed, "Sukey's a friend."

"You intend to make that clear?" Warwick asked, his head to the side as he awaited an answer.

"Yes, Grandfather," Julian said merrily. "I promise."

But after Julian had left, pleased that his friend understood him and that all was well between them again, he couldn't have imagined that his friend would remain standing lost in troubled thought because he understood, he thought, all too well. For if Julian didn't as yet know the difference between a dream of love and what love itself was, he did—to his sorrow, he thought, he did. And if Julian was determined to pass up a chance at such a love, then he himself would not—to his consternation, he vowed that he could not.

When Susannah had been very young, before her father had decided his money should buy her all the accouterments of a lady, she'd gone on many picnics with him and her brothers and they'd been the delights of her life. She wasn't an amazingly sloppy little girl, but she was a little girl of means, and so usually lived under stricter rules of behavior than did other children she observed. So she'd especially loved the informality of picnics, primarily because when she went on one no one minded when her clothes were ruined by outdoor calamities, like grass stains or bird droppings or pollen smears or the muddy residue from sudden rainstorms. She was never scolded for such disorder, because she'd always made sure to put on her oldest frocks, the ones ready for the rag basket, or spirited out from it as soon as the picnic basket was packed up, so that such destruction wouldn't matter either to her clothes or to her governess.

Thus when the morning of the picnic dawned bright and warm, Susannah took her breakfast in her room and then put on an old faded flowered muslin dress that had been outgrown at the ankle and let down to conceal that deficiency, only to have its previously hidden hem revealed to be so brightly colored in comparison to the rest of the frock that it showed the rate of her growth as clearly as any yardstick might, only in tiny pink flowers instead of linear inches. It was also too tight at the bosom and had an interesting asymmetry, since the pink ribands that tied one sleeve high on the arm were missing on the other. But Susannah's maid, country-bred as she herself had been, only helped her mistress with the last of the mismatched reluctant buttons at her back and sighed when she was done:

"There. Now you're ready for anything."

What she was not ready for was the contessa's shrill shriek of horror when she came to collect her.

And "Never!" and "Oh, my!" and "You mustn't even think of it!" were the only coherent words Susannah could get from her for the first few minutes. Then, since an argument raged for the next ten minutes, and some sulking of a high order was indulged in, in turn, by both of them for another ten, and then it took yet another half-hour until her chaperon pronounced her suitably attired to be able to leave her room, Susannah was obliged to be late for the picnic. That was not the only reason she wore a truculent expression to go with her violet draped gauze gown, with matching parasol and slippers.

"Forgive Julian," her host said as he helped her into his open carriage for the short ride to Hove, where Lord Fowler's daughter was having her picnic, "he was on fire to go, and so left before us. . . . Well then, if you won't forgive Julian," he mused, staring down at what he could see of the obstinate face beneath the floppy violet-strewn brim of her straw Florentine hat, "forgive me. You're right, I ought to have sat on him until you came down."

"Oh no," she cried, looking up from her abstraction into his bemused eyes, "it's not that."

"I clash with your slippers, then," he said mournfully.

She giggled.

"No," she said, smiling up at him at last, and though her face was half in the gridwork of shadows cast by her hat, he could see her full curving mouth well enough, too well for his own comfort as she leaned closer to say, with a glance to her chaperon, who was politely and properly ignoring them and looking out at the hedgerows they passed, "it's only that I'm being rude and childish. I wanted to dress for a picnic, you see, and the contessa swears that one dresses for the opera for a picnic here."

He found, as she went on to detail what she'd been originally wearing for the picnic in increasingly lurid terms as she herself began to see the humor in it, as she always did, that he was beginning to forget the stunning fact of her beauty as she entertained him, as he always did. He came close to ignoring how her eyes sparkled as she spoke, and nearly didn't dwell on her matte white complexion and softly waving sunstruck hair, all but neglected to take his usual imaginary nibble at the tip of her foolish little nose, and almost forgot to torment himself with how the low neck of her gown showed the top of smooth white breasts as they rose and fell with each breath she drew. Her narrative was so amusing, in fact, that soon the contessa had to pretend to coughing to pretend to be ignoring her continuing description of the ragged finery she'd had to take off before she'd been allowed to leave her room.

"So of course, now if a bull becomes enamored of me—as who would not, in my elegance?" she went on happily, watching her coughing chaperon out of the corner of her eye, "or I have to escape a hornet's nest, or I slide to my knees into the water when skipping a stone, I'll be able to ruin several guineas' worth of fabric and fashion, which is, I suppose, the entire point. I assume it's all because I'm supposed to be making a point of my wealth?" she asked defiantly, chasing all laughter from her two listeners' minds, "so that I'm considered acceptable here as I was not in London? So be it. I'll play. See? I'm all rigged out. But I intend to have a good time at the picnic anyway," she said on a sniff, "and will go berry-picking and hunt up flowers and loll on the grass to my heart's content like everyone else, anyway."

She could understand why her two companions seemed shocked, for she'd said an aggressive thing. But she failed to understand why they then glanced at each other, with the contessa holding a gloved hand over her mouth, and Warwick grinning, before they met each other's eyes directly, and both fell to laughing uproariously, even though this time she hadn't intended to say an amusing thing.

She understood when the carriage drove through the gates of Lord Fowler's estate and then was directed to a clearing in the midst of the home wood. She knew why they'd been laughing then, she sighed, with a rueful grin at Warwick, but not, she confided before they stepped down to the grass, why their hosts called it a "picnic" at all.

Several long damask-covered oaken tables had been carried out to the clearing, a wide bland meadow that had been created in the ruthlessly cleared heart of a tall oak and rowan forest. A long white canopy, held aloft by poles placed at periodic intervals, stirred slightly in the slight breeze above the tables that stood exactly in the middle of the sun-drenched meadow. A legion of perspiring footmen scurried every which way, adding finishing touches of flowers and candles to the tables, and a trio of red-faced musicians seated in the sun made music for the guests to talk by as they stood in little clots and waited to be called to the table. And that company, Susannah saw, was indeed dressed for the opera or the theater, in laces and silks, jewels and satins, their only concession to the outdoors being the parasols and bonnets the ladies wore, the high beaver hats and high Hessian boots the gentlemen affected.

"It's a picnic because it's held out-of-doors, ignorant wretch," Warwick said in a low voice as he took her arm and strolled forward into the company, "and so should you like to ask that lady to go skipping stones with you? No? Then perhaps it's because you're shy. Speak up, now. Do you want me to ask that gentleman to go berrying with you, then?"

She tried desperately not to giggle, because they were passing the lady and gentleman he'd mentioned. The lady was enveloped in so many tiers of intricate lace that Susannah doubted the poor girl could move without rippling like a pond surface disturbed by a stone herself, and the gentleman, a young fop with quizzing glass in one hand and snuffbox in the other, looked as thought he'd die of shock if anyone suggested he walk anywhere that might get a drop of dew on the surface of his gleaming boots.

But she kept her countenance and looked about with interest as Warwick strolled with her. There were over fifty gentlepersons on the neatly scythed grass, and far more of the common sort to wait upon them. Susannah was looking for one particular glowing head in the throng, but though she saw many fair persons, she was a bit surprised that she didn't see Julian anywhere. She was equally as surprised at something else she did see.

She'd accompanied Warwick to the theater and a ball, but always with Julian by her side as well. And since Julian always took up her attention, in public or private, she'd never actually observed Warwick in polite society before. He was, she'd been told, reclusive. He was, she knew, scathingly clever and impatient with fashionable fools. What she hadn't guessed was how much in demand he'd be, what she hadn't anticipated was how many females would gaze at him.

They didn't stare at him in fascination or awe as they did at Julian. This was something, she soon realized as they promenaded toward their hosts, of an entirely different order. It was so discreet that it was no wonder, she thought, that she'd missed seeing it before, when she'd had so much to distract her. For the ladies looked at him sidewise, and then looked away, but not too quickly, with fluttering lashes and pretty blushes when he returned their interest. Although no one of them ever stared in open admiration, they posed for him, she noted, they preened for him, she saw, and they all but, she thought cynically, rang little silver bells and peeped through veils at him like Arabian dancers when he came by.

Miss Fowler, a plain-faced young girl all in debutante's white, curtsied when Warwick took her hand, and gazed pointedly at that little white hand while it was still held in his, as though to make a point of how delicate it looked by contrast, swallowed up in his large tanned grip. Then she laughed at something he said, and showed all her little even white teeth, and tossed her curly brown hair for good measure when she put her head down to blush at his compliment of her good looks. Her hostess, Susannah thought sourly, as Miss Fowler looked her up once, and then down, before she ignored her entirely in order to smile at Warwick again, was making the most of every good feature she had. She almost warned Warwick to take care, because if the girl believed she had attractive thighs she'd find some way to show them to him as well, before she became aghast at what she'd nearly said out loud. Warwick took her silence for hurt feelings when they walked away from Miss Fowler, and to reassure her, quickly said:

"She's too confused at her party to take especial care with strangers, she meant no insult."

"I know she didn't," Susannah said easily, while she thought guiltily: But I did.

She gazed at him thoughtfully as he went on to describe some of the other guests before he brought her to them for an introduction. He looked very well, she suddenly noticed, and it wasn't only because of his gray pantaloons and dark blue jacket, or any other particular of his correct attire. She could see that he stood out even among all these other fashionable persons. Although he was undeniably tall and moved with a certain graceful elegance, it wasn't because of his personal beauty, as it was with Julian, for his was not a beautiful face, not in that sense. But it was a fascinating one, a blend of strength and intelligence, and humor, she realized, as she saw him smiling at her.

There was something other than humor in his eyes in that moment, after he'd caught her studying him, something amused and sad as well, and he gazed down at her thoughtfully. She braced herself for some acute and probably deservedly embarrassing comment, but he said nothing. He only smiled, and taking her arm again, walked her into the company in order to introduce her to everyone.

They were all monstrously polite, she decided. For they all smiled, and bowed or curtsied and said, "Ah, yes," and "Lovely day, isn't it?" and "How charming," but they were so pointedly polite that by the time she'd met most of them she felt as though she were wearing a placard reading "IMPOSTOR" on one side and "FISHMONGER'S DAUGHTER" on the other. And so she was delighted to see a familiar dark gold crop of hair glowing in the sunlight as Julian stepped toward her through the company. Now, she thought contentedly, now they might all do as they would, for she'd have her two gentlemen with her, one on either side, to protect her. She was smiling widely as he approached, so pleased that it took a moment for her to realize that he had the most beautiful young woman in the *ton*, if not the wide world, at his side as well.

Lady Marianna Moredon's cool and lovely face showed serene and total pleasure when she was introduced to Miss Logan and Mr. Jones. She bent like a reed in the wind as she curtsied to them, and when she arose from that graceful maneuver, her thin black brows etched a question over her wide blue eyes as they met Susannah's.

"Are you related to the Logans of Newton Abbot, Miss Logan? I met Sir Henry Logan some time ago," she offered.

"No," Susannah said quietly, as Julian quickly said, "I don't believe so," when his lady then wondered aloud if Susannah might be related to the Logans of Wilde Manor.

"I know!" Lady Moredon said pleasantly. "It must be the

Logans of Hampstead you're connected with, you have the look of Lady Cecily Logan, especially about the mouth . . ."

"No, my lady," Susannah said very quietly, "I'm afraid I can't claim kinship with any exalted Logans. No, I'm not afraid to, precisely," she said on a shrug as the dark-haired young woman gazed at her with interest, "I'm only unable to. My family, you see, has no such connections. We are simply 'Logans,' and we are in trade."

Seeing those beautiful azure eyes widen in surprise and dismay, Susannah, with the remembered insults of many school years to spur her on, decided, in both a sort of celebration of self-denigration and a try at self-esteem, that she wanted to see even more dismay reflected there, and knowing the only way she could inflict it, blurted perversely:

"We're in fish, actually."

"Not 'in' fish precisely," Warwick said smoothly, to fill the deep silence that followed her words. "I'm sure Miss Logan didn't mean to imply that her family actually stands about in fish up to their armpits. They made their way in the world via fishing interests, one might say."

"Precisely," Susannah snapped, not daring to meet Julian's eyes and bracing herself for the horror his lady would display at this revelation.

But there was no distress or unpleasantness to be seen upon that lovely countenance.

"I see," Lady Moredon said calmly before she turned to breathe her joy at meeting the viscount's famous friend Mr. Jones at last. Then they stood and chatted about the picnic and the warmth of the day and sundry country matters until Susannah let her breath out in a long sad sigh. She understood then that Lady Moredon was all that Julian claimed her to be and more, for she was a true Lady. She also realized that she'd never see any unpleasant reaction to her inferior state registered on that exquisite face. Because as she came to see long before they were finally called to table, Lady Moredon had simply decided that Miss Logan no longer existed. This Miss Logan she'd met, Susannah understood when Lady Moredon took Julian's arm on her right, and captured Warwick's on her left, had simply been registered as a non-person in the lady's mind, like all the other nonexistent persons that had surrounded her for all her privileged life: footmen, maid-servants, gardeners, coachmen, shop clerks, street and chimney sweeps. One more common miss, met at an acceptable social affair or not, was precisely the same sort of living, but invisible, unreal being to her.

Or so Susannah grieved to herself as she hesitated before following the others to the table. Or so she continued to think when she didn't see Lady Moredon glance back to her for a second, and so entirely missed the brief look that flickered in the cool beautiful depths of those famously limpid eyes as they registered every detail of Miss Logan's face, figure, and mood. There had been more than polite disinterest in that look, there'd been, instead, in that fleeting moment, simple amused triumph clearly registered there.

It was certainly a delightful picnic, Susannah thought as she cut her lettuce leaf into tatters. She sat at Julian's side, but as Lady Marianna sat on his left, and Warwick on the lady's other side, she had only young Lord Beccles to converse with. And as Lord Beccles, a perspiring fattish young lordlet, found her entirely lovely, but had a mama who glowered at him from a distant region of the table if he so much as bent his head of thinning hair in the lovely young commoner's direction, he had to pass all his time chatting up Miss Protherow, who was on his right. And Miss Protherow, he knew, was not only a bluestocking, she hated him, and besides, she wasn't a patch on the stunning blond thing sitting so silently on his left. But lust ran a poor second to fear of his mama, so Lord Beccles made halting conversation with Miss Protherow and, as always in such situations, entertained himself by thinking up some truly monumentally lascivious fantasies about the female he couldn't talk to, much less have.

Although Susannah had no one to speak with, she was frustrated in trying to eavesdrop on the three to her left, since the babble of the company was so loud and there was no hope of hearing anything said out-of-doors unless one watched the speaker's lips. She could scarcely watch Julian's lips, she thought sadly, when all she could see of him was, however entrancing a sight it might be, the sidewise tilt of his broad shoulders in their snug-fitting brown wool jacket, and the tendrils of curls at the back of his golden head.

She comforted herself with the thought that it was just as well that she couldn't get a better look at him. Whenever she'd chanced to gaze at him when he'd been with his lady before they'd sat down, he'd looked at Lady Marianna with such pride and with so much tender, wondering joy patent upon his fair face that she could scarcely bear it. But she had borne it, again and again, finding the need to observe them together exactly like the compulsion to dart a tongue into a sore tooth, since every brief glimpse caused her such intense pain it bordered on some sort of exquisitely addictive perverse pleasure. She could scarcely miss that, or at least, shouldn't miss it, she decided, and as for his conversation, why, since it usually centered on Lady Marianna anyway, she didn't miss it at all.

Instead, she found herself growing peeved because she couldn't at least have Warwick's intelligent conversation to see her through the meal, or have his laughter to leaven the hurt of it, or his wry and sympathetic eye upon her to keep her from brooding, as it always did, or share the foolishness of it all with him, as she always did. But even he, she remembered, had given the lady his warmest smile, and unbelievably, but certainly, she was sure she'd glimpsed a certain voluptuous appreciative gleam in his heavily lidded eyes. Even now, though she couldn't see him, now and again she could hear the distinctive sound of his laughter joining Julian's and Lady Marianna's.

The only thing Susannah had cause to be grateful for was the one deference to informality that having a picnic signified to her hosts. Instead of the courses being served by one remove after another, as they would be in their great dining hall, all the dishes were put out at once. The luncheon itself was not planned to take very long, and took considerably less time than that since so many of the females present claimed to be ladies and so toyed with their food, wishing to show that they had delicate appetites, in the middle of the day, at least. Since the gentlemen couldn't sit and stuff themselves all afternoon as the ladies looked on, it wasn't long before the assembled company rose and began to chat, discussing all the things they might do if they weren't so beautifully dressed, to while away the rest of the glorious afternoon.

Most of the invited guests stood and mingled with each other. Since this gathering was mostly for unwed young persons for the purpose of changing that circumstance for them, it was an approved way to pass the time. Some of the more daring couples left the meadow to stroll to nearby leafy glades, seeking shadows to hide from the sun, chaperons, and mamas within. Since wise chaperons knew such encounters sometimes produced similarly desirable, and perhaps even faster results than the picnic itself, many of them developed cinders in their eyes or pebbles in their shoes. Certainly no one paid much notice, then, when Miss Logan set out determinedly for the depths of the wood, for she was No One. Even her chaperon shrugged and went back to her knitting, for she was also obviously alone.

But not for very long. She'd only enough time to blunder deep into the wood to discover a nicely bubbling brook to cover the sound of her sobs, and find a huge lovely mossy boulder to perch on while sorrowing for herself, and hadn't the opportunity to settle herself comfortably enough to drop one lonely tear before she heard a familiar voice recite:

" 'By the waters of the Babylon, there we sat down, yea, we wept, when we remembered . . . *Julian?'* No," Warwick went on, in great mock puzzlement, as he leaned up against a tree to watch her, "I'm sure that's not how it goes. But is that how it goes with you? I don't see your harp hanging on any willow tree, so I expect you simply were looking for some shade. I'm the one who ought to be chanting about desertion, anyway. Why the devil did you desert me?" he complained.

"I didn't," she said, stung, as he raised his shoulders from the tree and came to her side on the rock, and knelt there effortlessly, balancing himself on one knee with his elbow resting on the other, bent one.

"Indeed you did," he argued, looking from her face into the sparkling water. "I looked around," he went on as he gathered up a twig and tossed it down to watch it ride the bubbling currents, "and you were hidden on Julian's other side. There was no way I could snag you without a scene, since the Incomparable Lady Moredon had already wrestled me down at her side. Not nice, Susannah," he said seriously, "nor polite. I believe," he went on wonderingly, gazing up at the latticework of leaves above them, "that you've insulted me."

"I didn't mean to," she said defensively, all thought of tears vanishing as she looked at him, for he did look terribly wounded, and she'd never meant to hurt him. "It happened so fast. One moment I was near you, the next, she was between you two. Anyway," she said, gazing into his sad face suspiciously, "you seemed to be having a fine enough time. I never saw so much smiling and laughing, and leering. Yes," she said, sniffling in indignation, "leering. And who could blame you?" she went on, accusation turning to despair again. "She *is* divine, as graceful as a swan, just as he says."

"She has about as much conversation as one, at any rate," he agreed.

When she looked at him in amazement, he added, "She doesn't speak much, you see, unless it's about who's where, and who did what to whom, although she does agree a great deal," he mused. "I missed you," he said simply.

"Because I talk so much," she sighed.

"Precisely. You," he explained, "talk constantly, and quite entertainingly. If we are to extend watery metaphors, since you claim to be so used to living among fish, I prefer the company of a lively brook, like this one, to a pool of stagnant water, no matter how limpid."

She giggled.

"Better," he said approvingly, "although you looked quite dismal, and nicely poetic, perched here staring into the water."

She had looked more than poetic, he thought, as she turned to smile at him. He'd seen her sitting in the dappled sunlight, motes of light glancing around her, thin shifting rays that had slipped through the trees to touch her hair, bright bits that reflected up from the dancing water to caress her face, glowing light that had lit her from behind to clearly delineate, through the sheer gauze of her frock, every curving, tempting, swelling, uplifted line of her slender body. He'd been so entranced that he could only hope that his voice would be cool as he'd spoken to her, and now, gazing down at her, he still fought to conceal the emotion that threatened to give the lie to his hard-won calm. He found this so difficult he had to look down at the plain gray worsted fabric stretched tight over his knee, where it touched the smooth stone he knelt upon at her side.

"Warwick," she said softly, sadly, so quietly, he looked up at once, "this is all very foolish. Of course they looked beautiful together, they're birds of a feather. They suit. All of them do. But I don't. I don't belong here, you know. *She* does, Julian does, you do, but I don't."

"*Very* foolish," he concurred, smiling gently, reaching out to lay his hand alongside her cheek. "You belong wherever you wish to be."

They were very close, and she discovered herself looking deeply into his sad dark blue eyes. It seemed to her then that she'd never actually seen him as clearly before as she saw him now, even in the dappled, changeable moving shade they rested in. He was, she realized, still a very young man, a thing she often forgot because of his poise and his calm, dignified demeanor. But there were no lines on his lean face, and she noted that his skin was fine-grained and pure, except for the spidery thin red line fading on his cheek. His thick hair shone a silvery brown in the leaping light, and his lips, she noted as his head bent lower to hers, were unsuspectedly full, and shapely and very near.

His lips touched hers and she was surprised at the lightness of that touch as well as the warmth of it and the odd shivery tingling the contact produced. In a moment, a very brief moment, he lifted his head and shook it ruefully, murmuring:

"*This* is foolishness itself, awkward, dangerous, and unsatisfactory, isn't it?"

He rose swiftly to his feet and gave her his hand and drew her to a stand beside him. She looked up at him, not knowing quite what to say.

"Yes," he said as he lifted her down from the rock they'd perched on so that she stood on the firm bracken-strewn ground with him, "much safer," he said as he kept one hand upon her waist to pull her tightly to him as he used the other to cradle the back of her head and guide her mouth to his again, "much better this way," he breathed before he covered her lips with his again.

15

The wood was deep and cool and filled with the earthy scents of fern and the compost of last year's fallen leaves as well as the green odors of moss and crushed bracken and the warm summer-sweet breath of trees. But Susannah noted none of it, being too involved with the man who held her so close, the man who blocked out all sensations further from her than her own skin. For the scent of him was that of good soap and some indefinable masculine blend of spice and cedarwood, and that alone was what she breathed in as he held her, his mouth to the side of her neck, his heart—or was it hers?—beating so loudly that she could hear only it, and not the sound of the rushing brook or the leaves whispering above them.

When she could think, she thought vaguely that she ought to say something, and so, it seemed, did he. But when he pulled his head back and looked down at her, he only murmured something indistinct and drew her close once more. Then his lips begged hers to open and as she tried to reply, they did, and he kissed her more deeply and banished coherent thought for her again.

Her mouth was warm and soft as he'd believed it would be, and far more innocent than he'd imagined, and yet it soon grew more accomplished than he could have hoped, for it seemed with each moment that she followed him further, as though she caught fire from him. When her lips opened beneath his, he tried to bring her closer to him. But finding that that was no longer possible, he found himself trying to invade her with his tongue, taking advantage of the admittance he was offered, and discover her with his hands, seeking to appreciate more fully the curving line of her hips and then the awakened tight buds on her breasts that he'd felt rising against his chest through the thin material of both their garments, while all the while he tried, impossible as it was, to bring her closer still.

It was when he opened his eyes again to see all that he was feeling that he saw his own hand where it was caught in the glorious tangle of her pale hair, and that, more than any of the other warning voices which were whispering to him, stopped him. He shuddered, as much with the effort of finding control as with the image that instantly came to him when he saw that large, thin, dark hand locked tight in all the light fine glory of her hair. It was the goblin he saw again then, despoiling the fair lady, yet for once he was glad for the unsought, punishing image. It gave him the spur he needed to end what he'd begun.

She didn't try to stop him, for she was entirely lost. Nothing in her experience had prepared her for that kiss, or for the embraces which followed. Nothing in the storybooks hinted at it, nothing in her school friends' giggling gossip had anticipated it. And although she'd abandoned all higher reasonings when his mouth touched hers, still she'd been dimly aware with each new sensation his touch evoked that it was entirely too delicious to be right, but she didn't know if she would have stopped him, or if she could have done so. It had been so entrancingly new and thrilling; he was, after all, her friend, she trusted him entirely. Since she'd ceded all control to him, she was unprepared when she felt his body tighten and his mouth grow still and his whole strong lean frame tremble as though he struggled with some enormous effort, as he wrenched his lips away. Then he quickly stepped away from her as well. Only then did her thoughts come streaming back. Only then, when she opened her eyes at last and saw Warwick Jones standing and staring down at her in amazement, did she begin to know a real disgust with herself and feel deeply shamed.

He gazed at her with wonder, and shook his head again. He could scarcely believe that a man of his wide experience would become so aroused at having taken what were, for him, only the simplest, most basic first steps to seduction, and more staggering still, that he would have taken them at all when his only aim had been to begin a gentle courtship.

"You didn't cry, 'No, don't!' in time this time," he said, on an unsteady laugh, still fighting so hard for control of his face and body that he didn't notice how white-faced she'd become. "See how far I can go with that sort of wild encouragement to spur me on?"

When she didn't answer with so much as a weak smile, his heart sank. He found himself wondering if he'd disgusted her beyond her ability to conceal, and had reason to be glad, at least, that she'd kept her wide dazed eyes upon his face as he composed himself. Yet with the remembrance of the enthusiasm of her embrace, he found it difficult to believe he'd shocked all her sensibilities. He might well understand her being angry, but she didn't appear to be enraged. Whatever her emotions, he wanted to know of them, for he felt very vulnerable now and was confused at her continued silence. It was unlike her.

"Oh, Warwick," she cried then, looking stricken, and yet still so enticing with all her hair down about her face and her gown in some disorder that he had to clench his fists to keep from comforting her again, and thus distressing her again, "I'm so sorry. I don't know what came over me. Can we still be friends?"

He checked. And then looked at her with his head to one side, but he could hear no mockery in her voice, nor see anything but real despair in her eyes.

"Ah, but that's what I'm supposed to say," he said carefully. "I believe you've got the text the wrong way round."

"But what must you think of me!" she cried, sinking to sit down on the rock, looking to her hands where they wrung her skirt in her anxiety.

"I think only that I owe you an apology, for I was only joking, you really didn't encourage me, if that's what's disturbing you. But after all, in self-defense, remember you rejected my promise not to try that again. Even if you had accepted it, I might have gotten round that, for you'll admit circumstances are very different this time: it isn't night now, for one thing, this isn't my house, and I wasn't comforting you. In fact, as I felt you'd just insulted me rather badly, I believed I deserved some comforting myself.

"Susannah, at least look at me," he said a little desperately when she didn't answer, not at all the cool gentleman he normally was, his face so earnest that it would scarcely have been recognizable to her had she dared to look up at him. "I'm still Warwick Jones, gentleman eccentric, you know. Has what I've done sunk me forever?"

"Warwick," she said, raising her head then, misery so plain on her face that he winced, "I told you and I told you—"

"I know," he answered with suppressed anger at himself, "I ought to have listened. I am very sorry, Susannah, I am—"

"—but you didn't believe me," she sighed, being so intent on what she had to say that she disregarded his words entirely, "but now you should understand why I don't fit in here, you see why it's no use, I'm simply not a lady."

"Susannah," he said patiently after a puzzled pause, "whatever are you talking about? I just pressed my attentions, in the most literal sense imaginable, upon you. Although that makes me something society doesn't permit me to pronounce in front of you, it makes you no less of a lady."

"But you're my friend," she said softly, lowering her gaze to her lap.

"Precisely," he sighed.

"And I'm not in love with you," she said very quietly.

"Very true," he agreed, wishing she'd struck him instead.

"And yet I didn't stop you," she whispered very low.

"What a very good friend you are, indeed," he complimented her sourly, as he sought diversion by dusting off the knees of his breeches.

"Because I didn't want to," she confessed, and then he stopped and stared at her.

"It was very . . . pleasant," she said in such a soft voice that he drew closer. "I found it exciting. A lady wouldn't."

"Because I'm only a friend?" he asked curiously. "But such things happen," he said quickly, realizing that she was too inexperienced to understand all the ramifications of sexual desire, and too well-bred to understand, as he and so many gentlemen did, that what the body experienced was often, or indeed, sometimes sadly, always, at odds with what the heart felt. He was wondering how to couch this simple biological fact in sufficiently proper terms so that he could tell her of it, when she replied:

"Because a lady doesn't feel such things at all. Oh, it's just another reminder of how I don't belong here, Warwick. I do believe I should go home."

"Yes, to get your head carefully examined. What are you talking about?" he asked angrily.

And so, looking away so that he wouldn't see her face, in very much the same manner, she thought in disgust at her cowardice, that she'd read that Australian ostriches hid from their enemies, she explained, although she wondered why she had to, about how she'd always believed that ladies never acknowledged such feelings, because they didn't suffer from them. It was an odd thing to discuss with a gentleman who'd just been making improper advances, but since those advances had been so enthusiastically accepted, she felt it was a thing he already knew. She also discovered that she'd rather think and speak about that part of her response to him, no matter how embarrassing it was, than cope just now with some other aspects of what she'd felt and done a few moments ago. She was badly confused and so her most pressing need was to have things back the way they'd been before that disturbing embrace had begun. She badly wanted her good friend Warwick back again, and he'd certainly been one of her best friends. But she began to doubt that when she'd done, for all he did was to stand and stare and say:

"Rot! Absolute rot," he said, as annoyed as if she'd said a cruel thing about him. "I know some idiots of both genders who subscribe to that notion, but I promise you, Susannah, it is not true. There are females who earn their livings at such doings who find no pleasure in them, and great ladies who are trollops because they enjoy them so much."

But here he paused, because he didn't know very much about great ladies, having avoided them assiduously all his life. He did know human nature, though, and so continued confidently:

"It is very individual. Some gentlemen prefer to play cards

rather than, ah, play at other things, and some very proper ladies prefer it above all things. Well, it's an appetite like any other. I like olives, after all, and I note you always roll them to the edge of your plate and would hide them under your napery if you dared. You, on the other hand, adore custards, which I believe only condemned prisioners ought to be forced to eat. Does that make either of us less a lady or a gentleman?''

"Only an appetite?" she asked disbelievingly.

"It is part of life," he said quickly. "Lust, of course, changes it to a craving, style can convert it to an art, and love, of course, transforms it to something altogether ethereal. Or so they say. It's also, I assure you, entirely possible to enjoy with someone you do not love," he said on a twisted grin, "just as it's possible to dine when one is not hungry. Yes, that's a poor comparison, it's very intimate, of course. So intimate, in any event, that proper young females are not expected to indulge outside of marriage," he added, feeling uncomfortably priggish for doing so, "and so, my humblest apologies for forgetting that. But I fear I'm one of those who might be compared to a glutton. Seat me at a lavish table," he said on a sidewise grin, "and I can't help picking up my cutlery. Oh, sorry. You see? There's no hope for me, I will forget my manners," he said airily, feeling much better for it.

But then he noted her complete unsmiling attention focused on him, and sighing, said:

"Quite seriously, my dear, I believe there's no sane man who'd think your enjoying his attentions made you less the lady. No," he added, "most men I know would be delighted."

He hadn't said "Julian," but from her expression of relief, he thought he might as well have done. For she rose to her feet and began to arrange her hair again, and asked, in a sprightlier manner, if he didn't think they ought to be getting back to the others.

He hesitated.

"There is one other thing, since we are speaking of matters of propriety with such impropriety," he said slowly. She thought he looked more uncomfortable than she'd ever seen him as he bent his head in thought, and then raised it and gazed at her with no expression she could read upon his solemn face. She stopped with a hairpin poised halfway to the neat coil she'd made of her hair, to listen closely to him.

"In some circles," he said, choosing his words with great care, "in our circles actually, what I've done is tantamount to a declaration. That is to say, many people would expect me to offer for you now, considering that I'd compromised you. I . . ." He paused, and then, thinking that there was a look of something very like horror on her face as she lowered her arms and gaped at him, he went on quickly, "I do so offer now, Susannah. Or at least, I want you to know that I'm prepared to do the correct thing. And I assure you," he said on a small uneasy laugh, "I wouldn't find it any hardship. In fact, I think I . . ." He hesitated again, feeling awkward as a boy, trying to gauge her mood, trying to select the precise words.

But after he gazed steadily at her, his attitude changed abruptly. What he saw in her eyes caused him to bring his head up high, and then, with far more ease and brightness than he had before, since he'd already read her answer in her expressive face, he drawled:

"I do believe we could make the most of a bad bargain, don't you my dear?"

"Yes, of course we could, but no . . . no," she stammered, brought close to tears by his gesture of friendship, and distraught, after an already profoundly confusing day, by this further evidence of his gentlemanly consideration.

"Oh no, but thank you, Warwick," she said, so embarrassed by his infinite kindness to her that she wanted to sink into the ground. "It's not necessary. No one need ever know. But thank you for asking."

"You're entirely welcome," he said with a sad smile.

He watched in silence as she resumed arranging her hair and finished putting herself in order. Then he offered her his arm. But before they left the wood he looked down at her curiously.

"Then I'm forgiven?" he asked.

"It is all forgotten," she said on a smile, and nodded.

"Oh, but I didn't ask for that," he said gently.

* * *

Lady Marianna Moredon was telling the Viscount Hazelton about her trip into Brighton and what she'd seen there. There were a great many interesting things to talk about, from the glimpse she'd gotten of the Prince's new carriage to the hat she'd purchased there. They'd found a patch of shade under an oak, and he'd gotten chairs for them, and he sat and held her fan and listened, but all at once she had the uncanny notion that he'd stopped listening and was somehow much further from her than her side.

He was, and it troubled him. Today he'd been privileged to have his lady with him for several hours, longer than he'd ever been able to get her to himself since he'd begun courting her. It was true that most of the time was passed in plain sight of a throng of people, still he'd never been able to keep in her company for so long before. But now something had happened to take his attention from that delightful fact. Susannah was missing.

He couldn't call her absence to anyone's attention for fear of ruining her reputation. Some young women had wandered off with their beaux; he, after all, had himself had the glory of having Marianna entirely to himself for several long, delightful moments before the picnic. He'd gotten her alone in a thicket of trees, he'd been granted a few gentle kisses, and if he'd wanted more, he'd understood when she'd taken alarm and pushed him away. He'd have been surprised, in fact, if she had not. But now Susannah had been gone for over a half-hour, and he'd not a clue to where she was or whom she'd gone off with.

The only comfort he had was that Warwick had obviously noticed the same thing, and since he was also nowhere to be seen, was likely searching for her. But since he too had been gone for a very long while, Julian wondered not only if he'd found her, but if he had, if they mightn't have gotten into some sort of difficulty together. Warwick, he was sure, could handle himself against any of the gentlemen here at the picnic, but what if they'd stumbled upon a crew of thieving itinerants, or a band of Gypsies, or even, he thought, glancing at his lady in some alarm, another collection of villains sent by her brother?

"Yes," Lady Marianna said with a silvery laugh, "it was

absurd, you're quite right to look so alarmed, just think—a chip straw bonnet with black ribbons on it! 'Is it for mourning?' I asked. 'Oh no, my lady,' the little clerk said, ' 'tis for afternoon'!''

She laughed a great deal at that, and it was unusual for she seldom laughed so openly, or so loudly. This was because she didn't believe a lady ought to show her teeth. But the richness of her own jest was too much for her, and she laughed immoderately, holding her hand over her mouth as she did so. A great many people at the picnic looked over to them then, and nodded, and commented to each other, as they always did, about what a handsome couple they were, and then, in softer voices, about his finances and her brother.

When Marianna's mirth subsided, she went on to detail the more important moments involved with the selection of her new hat, and Julian's attention drifted again. He would've given a great deal to be able to tell her what was worrying him, a good deal more to make her notice that he was worrying, and, he suddenly realized to his considerable confusion, much more to have been able to simply stand up and bow and say good-bye and leave to seek his friends.

"Julian," she finally said, in answer to one of his unspoken wishes, but as she said it rather flatly, in the letter but not the spirit of it, he realized it was best to be specific even in one's wishes, "that is the third time you've consulted your watch."

She added nothing to the comment, neither question nor admonition, but she didn't have to, he knew his manners.

"So it is," he said easily. "Possibly it's because I can't believe my good luck. All this uninterrupted time in your company!"

She gazed at him. It was impossible for that smoothly beautiful face to give away her thoughts, she'd trained it too well for too many years. Emotion destroyed beauty; she'd be lovely into her dotage, and her face would never show more than serenity, because in truth, she seldom felt more than that. Now she was conscious of a slight stirring of displeasure. Julian was amazingly handsome. He was entertaining, charming, she could scarcely think of a better accessory for her own spectacular appearance than he was, and he was entirely devoted to her. He had been, she corrected herself, entirely devoted to her. Lady Marianna Moredon might not notice, or care to note a great deal that went on around her, but on the subject of herself and all those things which centered on that fascinating subject, she was expert. Only three things had the power to distress her; all three had to do with things which threatened to destroy her image: age, illness, and a human rival to her beauty.

She'd immediately seen that Miss Susannah Logan was uncommonly lovely, as striking in her way as she was in her own. It was, Marianna knew, never a question of one being more beautiful than the other; choosing between the two of them would simply be a matter of taste. Mr. Jones, after all, who would have been a very amusing flirt, had no eyes for her own dark beauty, she saw he'd been taken up by the fair charms of Miss Logan. And now, though she could swear he was constant, Julian kept sneaking little glimpses into the wood and running his gaze over the crowd. Inattention was the one thing she was not used to seeing in his face. It was vexing.

Miss Logan hadn't been seen for over a half-hour; Marianna knew that very well, for wherever she sat or stood, she always noted who watched her, and so like the sunflower that tracked the progress of its chiefest influence as it crossed the afternoon sky, she always felt a rival's pulling power and knew precisely where she was. She alone was the cynosure of all male eyes now. Miss Logan, then, was still absent.

"Perhaps," Marianna said in exactly the same tones she used to describe her charming bonnet, "she's gone off with Lord Beccles. He is not precisely a catch, but away from his mama he might be more forthcoming. Then too, one may not be able to say a great deal about him, but," she said, so pleased with her turn of words that she twirled her parasol, "whatever one does say, at least it must be said with a 'Lord' before it when one does."

It took a few seconds before Julian fully understood her. It hadn't been only the slumberous afternoon and his concern about his friends that had dulled his wits. Her tone of voice hadn't changed and she'd been droning on about her bonnet when he'd caught the tail end of what she'd said and then had to reconstruct the sentences he'd heard but not listened to. Then too, he had the sudden disturbing realization that he'd not been attending to her for some time to contend with, as well. In all, it was a few seconds before he completely understood, and then he was so annoyed with himself that his voice was sharper than usual when he replied.

"I doubt she's run off with Beccles, his title wouldn't matter to her."

"I didn't say 'run off,' Julian," she said calmly, watching him closely, "for how should I know how far they've gone?"

She stopped to smile at that play on words—it was mildly naughty and very amusing, really; she felt she was in rare form today. Then she almost frowned when she realized that Julian was not appreciative of her humor. There was, then, she felt, one more thing to be said.

"Miss Logan not interested in a title? But she admits her family is in trade, or as she put it, 'in fish.' I'm sure she'd find Lord Beccles a fair catch."

And then she really had to laugh again. And then she actually frowned, for Julian was obviously not at all amused.

"I doubt," he said quietly, "that Susannah would be interested. She's too honorable a girl to be after a man for his title."

"Indeed?" Lady Marianna said.

But she was as shocked as if he'd slapped her, for she couldn't remember him ever contradicting her before, or not appreciating her humor. And though the word "honorable" was an unusual sort of word to use to praise a female, it was still a compliment, and moreover, one that he'd never applied to herself. Most telling of all, she'd not said a word to him now for several seconds and he'd not noticed.

But he was bedeviled by the fact that he'd never noticed how cruel Marianna's humor could be at times. He quickly excused her, remembering that, after all, such acid wit was the highest form of cleverness in society. He looked into her calm and beautiful eyes and smiled at her then, in apology for himself, as apology for her. And it was such a winsome smile, and he was so extraordinarily decorative, she thought on a repressed sigh, that she decided to be bountiful and forgive, for she had definite plans for this golden, amusing, charming young man. Although, she mused as she saw the admiration for her on his handsome face slip away, to be replaced by outsize relief when he spied his friend Mr. Jones strolling up the lawn with Miss Logan on his arm, she certainly had no intention of forgetting.

Julian excused himself and went striding across the grass to greet his friends, an expression of such warm welcome on his face that Susannah felt her heart leap up. She raised her face to bask in the approval he bent down upon her, but his smile turned to a scowl as he asked his first question.

"Where the devil have you been? People were beginning to talk. Warwick, was there any difficulty?"

He asked the last in sudden concern, for it seemed his questions made Susannah color up and drop her gaze, and his friend Warwick wore such an innocent expression it was immediately suspect. If he hadn't known Susannah and Warwick both better, Julian thought at once, he knew what he might have imagined they'd been up to, but the thought that had come to him unbidden was so patently impossible that he wondered if they had, indeed, met up with some misfortune.

"Susannah," he asked again, "where were you? And whom were you with?"

"Nowhere," she spoke at once, guiltily, "with no one."

"Thank you," Warwick said sweetly.

"Oh, but that's never what I meant," she said, wheeling about to stare at Warwick, one hand over her mouth.

Warwick gave her such a warm and tender smile in return, and she colored up so then, that Julian's eyes widened and then he grew a troubled frown at his next thought. But he had no chance to say another word on the matter, for Marianna joined them then, and asked Susannah very politely where Lord Beccles was. And then Julian shot such a cold, affronted glance at Marianna that she scarcely heard Susannah's confused reply, she was so busily observing him, as was Warwick. In all, there was no one regretful in the least when the contessa approached to end the conversation and remind them that the other guests were beginning to leave.

As Lady Moredon was staying the weekend with the Fowlers, Julian took her up in his curricle to deliver her to the great circular drive in front of the country house, in order to save her the walk and say farewell to her there. For the sake of propriety, Warwick then took up her chaperon in his own carriage and followed them. By the time both carriages had reached the house, Julian and his lady seemed in better accord, and by the time Warwick had helped the ladies down so that they all might say a proper farewell, they all seemed in perfect charity with each other again.

Indeed, they made a handsome sight as they stood and chatted and said their good-byes on the wide and rolling green lawn. The two young couples were becomingly dressed and perfectly balanced: the golden-haired young gentleman smiling so sweetly at the famous dark beauty, the elegant Mr. Jones gazing down with something perhaps even beyond fondness at the unknown flaxen-haired girl at his side. But that was a thing that only a very closely observant viewer might perceive. Still, the man who was observing them very closely did see that, and a great deal more besides, even from where he stood at the window of the drawing room where his hosts had told him he might wait for his sister's return. He missed nothing. He stood and watched, his hands locked together behind his back, and he rocked back and forth from heel to toe as he did. And Lord Moredon smiled and smiled at what he saw.

16

The thick cream-colored card fluttered down and landed upside down on the desk. Before the gentleman could turn it over to read it, it was snatched up again.

"Oh no, get your own, envious Warwick," Julian said merrily as he held the card up and out at arm's length and read it off in rolling, plummy tones:

"Lord and Lady Hoyt request the pleasure of the company of Lord Julian Dylan, Viscount Hazelton, at a Midsummer's Night Ball in honor of their daughter, Miss Lillian Mary Cornelia Hoyt, on Tuesday evening, the twenty-first of June, at eight o'clock, at their home, Broadoak Court."

"Behold me ill with desire," Warwick said on a yawn, pushing himself away from the desk and looking up at his bright-eyed friend. "What has you in such alt? The lovely Lillian? As I recall, she was the plump little party at the picnic who dissolved into shrill giggles every time you looked her way, which, fortunately for our ears, and your reputation as a man of some taste, was not very often."

"Sweet Lillian can dissolve into a puddle for all I care," Julian replied blithely. "Marianna will be there, that's all I know. She's staying with them now, but since it's a very exclusive do, I never expected to be able to go. After all, I wasn't invited when I should have been, when everyone else was, weeks ago. I was in London then, and so they can explain the thing away that way to save face, even though it's clear I wouldn't have been asked then even if I'd lived next door. They're trying to get little Lillian popped off, you see, and wouldn't want any impoverished viscount-coachmen who made her giggle around her. Maybe they were afraid I could spirit her off faster, since I had a coach to do it with," he said on a suddenly bitter laugh, "but," he added, his face brightening again, "now I have been asked. And I understand, from the note which accompanied this perfectly proper and valid and indisputably correct ticket of admittance to the festivities, that it was all due to Marianna's efforts."

"I hate to deflate you, Cinderella," Warwick sighed, "but it can't be that exclusive a soiree, since I was asked weeks ago, and sent my regrets long since."

"Ah, but you," Julian said, interrupting him, "are a hermit, so you're sent invitations whether they want you or not, since no one expects you ever to come anyway."

"True, but lately I have been in evidence at a great many tedious affairs, since, if you'll recall, my entire reason for being here is to get Susannah safely into the social swim. Unfortunately," he said softly, "that's a singularly apt choice of words, since in the last week I've been made to suffer quite needlessly—at picnics, simple suppers, and musicales— only to be reminded each time that our Susannah may never be allowed to swim freely in such waters, simply because of how her father took his money from more tangible seas."

"Yes," Julian said seriously, his smile vanishing, "that's true . . . damnably true. But this ball, I'll be there, and perhaps I can get Marianna to put in a word or two . . ."

"The only words the lady ever addresses to her are 'Good evening, Miss Logan,' and even if she did say more, when Lady Marianna is there, for all intents and purposes, so far as Susannah is concerned, you might as well not be."

"That's not true," Julian said angrily, his eyes becoming lighter as his voice grew colder.

He couldn't defend his lady's treatment of Susannah, for it did appear that she wasn't fond of her. So he seized on a thing he could hotly deny.

"I've spent a great deal of time with Sukey, even when Marianna's present," he said.

"Yes," Warwick answered calmly, his lids drooping to cover the expression in his eyes, "but only when you've deemed it unwise to start gossip by taking up too much of your lady's time, and even though you'd said you had no plans for the girl and so wouldn't continue to encourage her.''

"Chatting with her, joking with her, commiserating with her—do you call that encouraging her?'' Julian demanded.

"Yes,'' Warwick said quietly, "since it's so apparent you take such enjoyment in it.''

"Oh?'' Julian asked after a pause. "What do you suggest I do then, Warwick, snub her as the rest of them do?''

When there was no reply, but his friend only looked up at him, arrested, his startled silence conceding the point, Julian went on:

"You chat with her too, and take similar pleasure from it. And why not? She's a delightful baggage, is our Sukey. But do I lecture you about enticing her? Really, Warwick, what am I supposed to do? I'm getting tired of having you read sermons at me for being a friend to her,'' he said gruffly.

He also felt slightly guilty because he admitted to himself that he might well have passed too many merry hours with Susannah even after he'd decided not to any longer, and even after he'd not intended to. So he added, half-thinking the ludicrousness of the statement would end the discussion, half-uneasy that it might not:

"Is it that you resent the competition, Warwick? If so, I'll step aside and never give Miss Logan so much as a 'good-morning' again, I promise you. Sukey's a rare delight. But only a friend, and though I'd miss her, it's simply not that important to me now that I've my Marianna.''

His friend looked up with something very like shock registered in his dark blue eyes. Then the shock became a parody of itself as he recovered himself and said haughtily:

"What, resent your competition, Julian? Do you think I'm ready for Bedlam? *I*, resent your competition? Why, my good fellow, you may look like Apollo, have the tongue of an angel, and have to hire sweepers to clear your path of fainting females every time you go out into society, but do you honestly believe, for even a minute, that you might be able to compete with *me?*''

Warwick's avowal of his beauty and charm being one of their oldest jokes, tension faded and they laughed together.

"So, do you change your mind and take Susannah to the

ball,'' Julian asked, when they'd done, "or shall I escort her there?''

"Neither, I think," Warwick said sadly. "I believe she's had enough for a week."

"Enough?" Julian asked incredulously. "One paltry picnic and a few tame evenings out? That's hardly enough amusement for anyone."

"Enough insult, I meant," Warwick said, rising, "or don't you remember the reception she was given at each of those outings? Ah, I see you do. And there's nothing we can say or do, since it's all so politely done. It's never the cut direct, nor is an insulting word ever to be plainly heard. But their eyes slide over her, they brush past her as though . . ." He shook his head.

"But," Julian said, "if I go, and you stay home with her, it will look very bad."

"Indeed?" his friend asked with great interest. "Are you still casting me in the role of chief competitor, or is it vile seducer you now have in mind? Speaking of which, have you seen my bottle of laudanum? I'd thought to put a great deal in the contessa's wine tonight," he confided, "and will need only a drop or two to render Susannah senseless enough to work my wicked ways on her once her chaperon is insensible, she's so much more slender, and drug dosages go by body weight, you know," he explained reasonably.

"No, and if you ask where your whips and chains are," Julian laughed, seeing his friend's sparkling eye and anticipating his next outrageous claim, "I'll leave. It's only that I thought Susannah's likely to be more offended at being kept away from the ball than she'd ever be by being insulted there. At least I'll dance with her, and you will, and we two might start a trend. Those other affairs were small and stilted ones, run by the dowagers. A ball's another matter, and a merrier one. Brighton's not London and Broadoak Court isn't even precisely Brighton, it's far from being Prinny's set. A dance isn't a commitment, everyone knows her by now, and she's lovely enough to tempt any gentleman to fly in the face of convention."

"Julian, my friend," Warwick said slowly, and with some apparent amazement, "I do believe you've acquired some sensibility. Good heavens, is our little boy growing up? But you're absolutely right. I'm a fool for not having seen it. She's courageous, and if I saw her staying away tonight as a way of avoiding unnecessary pain, she'd see it as cowardice . . . which I supose it would be.

"Do you know," he asked slowly, incredulously, as if to himself, "there's absolutely nothing to being brave when you've only yourself to consider? But it's very easy to be a coward when it comes to protecting the feelings of someone you care for, when all your instincts call for you to save her from pain at any cost. It seems having a Susannah to take care of is changing us both, or is it just that it's ennobling to look after anyone besides oneself? In any event, yes, we'll all go. But never fear, we'll not step on your toes. We'll go separately, I'll see that you're left plenty of room to do your courtship dance, my peacock. For I wish you luck with your lady, Julian, I really do, you know, I don't believe you know how much I do, in fact."

His friend grinned, pocketing his invitation, and then Warwick spoke again.

"But, Julian," he began, and then paused and said seriously, "I hesitate to say this . . ."

"Old friends shouldn't hesitate to say anything to each other," Julian commented simply.

"Ah, but sometimes new loves interrupt the flow of old friendships, as they should, I suppose, as they should," Warwick sighed. "But still, you're right in that as well. This seems to be your day, entirely. So indulge me in this and don't answer, with either fists or words, before you've thought it through. . . . Are you entirely sure, my friend, that it is Lady Marianna that you want? Or is it only that she's the only woman you've ever known that you seem unable to have?"

Julian didn't answer at once, and when he did, he asked, with the smallest smile:

"Warwick, have you never been in love?"

His friend gazed back at him, and smiled as well, a crooked sorrowful smile of the sort that came so easily to his lean face. And that smile was his only reply.

It wasn't until after they'd parted, in charity, but in silence,

that Julian realized to his discomfort that Warwick had replied to him with laugher and smiles, but that he'd never
really answered his questions about the state of his own heart,
no, not any of them.

It was a ball given in honor of Miss Lillian Mary Cornelia
Hoyt and it was given because she'd sunk without a trace
when she'd tried London's deeper waters earlier in the Season, so her mother was very pleased when the Viscount
Hazelton finally finished making his bows to her and moved
off down the reception line. It was bad enough that several
young misses present were so attractive that they made poor
Lillian look no-account, it was worse that the handsome
young man that took her hand cast her into the shadows as
well. He was so tall, blond, graceful, and radiant, Lady Hoyt
was near to tears by the time he left the entry hall, for not
only had he taken all the attention, he'd taken every shred of
her awkward daughter's countenance with him as well.

But then, nothing had gone right for the Hoyts this Season.
They'd given house room to Lady Marianna in the hopes that
some of her rejected suitors would settle for Lillian, but it
seemed that lady never cut line from any of her admirers,
preferring to keep them all on various lengths of string for her
amusement. Still, Lady Hoyt thought as she automatically
greeted her next guests, there was only one week left to the
lady's visit before she returned to London. If they were good
hosts, it still might be that the Incomparable Marianna would
donate some new acquaintances or used suitors to poor Lillian
in gratitude, as a parting gift. So long as none of them were
romantic-looking young pauper viscounts, they'd count themselves repaid. Craning her neck to see the expression on that
viscount's face as he greeted Lady Marianna in the ballroom,
Lady Hoyt sighed with relief and relaxed enough to pinch her
daughter to remind her to stop slouching. For the first and last
time in her life, she was actually pleased that Lillian was not
more attractive. For the handsome viscount had everything a
mother would want for her daughter, except for a full purse,
and the emptiness of that article, of course, outweighed all
else.

Then that social-climbing *nouveau riche* Miss Logan came

along the reception line, and in her buttercup-yellow gown with her fair hair done up in a coronet of curls and flowers, she cast Lillian so much in the shade that it even took her own mother a few seconds to see where she was standing and gaping openmouthed at her new guest. Lady Hoyt couldn't even celebrate the fact that her invitation had lured the wealthy reclusive Mr. Jones to her ball, she was so busily despising Miss Logan and thinking of all the criticisms she'd have for her daughter the moment they were left alone. Fortunately for the graceless Miss Hoyt, that wouldn't be for some time, for the ball was well-attended and had only just begun.

Lord Hoyt opened the ball by dancing with his daughter, and though some parents and chaperons cooed their approval at how pleasant a scene it was, every other eye was on a more spectacular couple. The Viscount Hazelton danced with Miss Logan, and the fair-haired pair were so dazzlingly lovely they attracted the eye like sunlight glancing off a windowpane. As one gentleman hastily explained to his annoyed partner, it was not so much that one wanted to watch them as it was that one simply couldn't help doing so. All the other dancers glanced over to them often, even the darkly beautiful Lady Moredon, in the arms of a perfectly pleasant young gentleman, even Warwick Jones, as he honored a wallflower by stepping into the dance with her.

Then there was a waltz, and Mr. Jones relieved the viscount of his fair partner, and then there were the country dances, and more waltzes and minuets and reels, and so soon the couples mixed and scattered and separated and came together once more in more ways than one, for no unwed, unengaged couple could dance together more than twice and keep to society's dictates.

Julian had two waltzes with his lady, and that was all he could have. Usually, when he was at a ball that she graced, he then repaired to the sidelines, content to watch her for the rest of the evening. He was well used to languishing at the side of the room, communicating with her chiefly with his eyes throughout the long night. She'd spin past with a smile for him alone, he'd watch and wait so that she could always see him wherever she danced. But tonight he also danced with Susannah twice, and neither time did he look away from her to exchange so much as a wink with Marianna.

When he'd done dancing, he stayed to the side, as ever, but this night he didn't pine, but rather wore a smile as he watched Susannah when she was swept off by Mr. Jones, and then Mr. White and Mr. Hughes, and Lord Beccles and a half-dozen more gentlemen, even including Lord Hoyt himself, the unlucky gentleman enjoying himself hugely, never knowing what his lady-wife had in store for him later.

Tonight Lady Moredon wore white, and although there were a dozen other girls in white, since it was a debutante's color, it was pure and suited her dark beauty, and so it was as easy for Julian to single her out from all the others as it was for her to outshine them all in it. But Susannah's yellow frock was like a shout of laughter, and exactly suited her radiant fairness, so it was equally simple for him to pick her out from the mass of dancers. Warwick came to his side and they grinned at each other as they saw her whirling about the room in a lively country dance. Julian was so engrossed with their protégée's success that he entirely failed to see the particularly winsome sidewise smiles Marianna gave him over her partner's shoulder as she danced by him.

It was an odd night for the viscount. He actually found himself fidgeting, instead of envying his lady's partner as he stood and watched the dancers sail past during the waltz. He was pained by his foot falling asleep, instead of his heart sinking down, when other gentlemen claimed two dances from Marianna. By the time supper was announced, he realized he was actually quite hungry, and took a full plate to his table, instead of the usual meager rations he toyed with when he was forced to watch some other, more fortunate fellow take Marianna in to dine. And yet, as he shared that table with Warwick and Susannah, he passed more time laughing than eating, no matter how hungry he'd gotten.

For, "Well," he'd asked Susannah at once, when they sat down together, the three of them alone at last, the contessa having joined the other chaperons, "how do you feel, Miss Social Success?"

"Dizzy," Susannah replied thoughtfully, "and my feet hurt, for many of the gentlemen are more enthusiastic than accurate dancers, although you two," she said quickly, "are perfection. And," she added, stirring her aspic round her plate and watching it melt as though she were reading omens in its gelatinous depths, "afraid, I think, of going to the ladies' withdrawing room by myself, because I don't think some of the other ladies are exactly thrilled by my success. Oh dear, I oughtn't to have mentioned that, should I have?" she asked innocently, knowing very well she should not, but delighted that she had, when her two companions threw back their heads and roared with laughter at her face, as well as her words.

"No," Warwick said, vastly pleased, looking down at her fondly, "but thank you for it. She quite enlivens a party, don't you agree, Julian?"

"Oh yes," the viscount agreed, bending a softened smile upon her as well. "I don't know how we got along before without her, in fact."

There were a great many other persons watching their table, like vultures, Warwick complained, and so when the musicians began to tune up again, he announced that he'd take unfair advantage and immediately claim his second dance with Susannah. Julian, having had his two with her, and two with Marianna, and desiring no more with anyone else, wandered to the edge of the dance floor again. As he watched his elegant friend smiling warmly as he led Susannah to the floor, he realized there were few gentlemen here he'd care to call friend save for Warwick, and as his evening was ostensibly done, all he had left to hope for was that country hours would close a country ball down earlier than one held in town.

But before he could decide where to station himself for the rest of the night, however long it might be, he felt a light touch upon his hand. He looked up to see Miss Bridie, Marianna's dour chaperon, standing beside him. For an odd moment he couldn't place her; she and her mistress had been, for once, far from his mind.

"She wants to see you," that tight-lipped female hissed.

"And I, her," he replied amiably. "Only tell me when, and where."

Since this was the common way Marianna let him know

when she might next meet him in private, he was already pondering when she was planning to schedule a visit with him, when his breath was taken away by the unexpected reply.

"Now. And here," Miss Bridie said in a fierce whisper. "Or at least, outside of here, out those French doors and down the path to the right. And she asks you go casually, your lordship," she added coldly, "and by slow degree when the dancing's most active, so no one notices you've gone."

There were dozens of couples wheeling about the floor in a spirited reel when the viscount backed off to blend in with the shadows and slowly exit the room by the side door. He did it so cleanly he believed no one noticed. But, he thought, if Warwick saw him leave (and it would be remarkable if he missed anything), it wouldn't matter. It might actually be to the good. Warwick was knowing and could make plausible excuses, if necessary, for his absence. If a footman noticed him depart, it made no matter. The evening was getting on, there were always some young people getting on with other things in various clandestine fashions, and footmen were only human. They'd alert their employers only if such activity involved young persons of their house. They were sympathetic, for they were, after all, young too, even if they were invisible. The only advantage they'd take might be the amusing conversation they'd make of it at the servants' table as they finished the leftover cold meats of the party with a tasty relish of odd bits of juicy gossip.

It was a warm night, and a light one; the half-twilight would last until past midnight on this short magical night of the longest day of the year. The shrubs and trees stood out against the hazy dim night sky as clearly as if it were first dawn and not last light, and Julian felt the enchantment of the soft night rising with his own excitement at this unexpected turn of events. Marianna had never been so bold in her preference for him, he'd never had her to himself in such a romantic setting, although he'd often dreamed of it.

Thus when he turned a corner of the narrow crushed-shell walk and saw his Marianna standing alone waiting for him, he didn't wait. He was as bold as she'd been as he came up to her and took her in his arms and kissed her. And she let him.

Only after a long moment did she put her hands against his chest and hold him away. Then he sighed and obediently stepped back from her, for he'd expected no less, but however brief it had been, it had been lovely to feel her cool mouth against his, her long slender form quiescent in his arms. Then she surprised him again.

"Not here, Julian," she said. "Come with me."

She hadn't said, "No, I cannot," or "You must not" or "Oh please, Julian, you should not," as she always did. So he was bemused as she hurried him down the path, and then beckoned him through a gap in a yew wall, only to stoop and pull back a long quavering branch of hemlock to lead him along another narrow walkway through an alley of towering, fragrant evergreens. He followed her, expectant, enchanted, feeling more and more a character from a summer masque celebrating an ancient night of wonder. He wanted to share it, to tell her on a laugh that he felt like Bottom, poor, unworthy, ensorcelled, donkey-eared Bottom the Weaver, blindly pursuing his love, Titania the Fairy Queen. But when he began to speak, she turned and held a finger to her lips. He fell silent and followed her deeper into the remarkable night.

They crossed a swaying rustic bridge that creaked louder than the frogs did in the small ornamental pond it took them over. He scented honeysuckle as they skirted the margins of the little pool, whose waters were gray and still as slate in the half-light. And then, set a few steps into a birch wood, they came at last to a child's summer playhouse, a charming thing made of rough-hewn logs, with long windows that held no glass but made do with strands of ivy and night-blooming vines instead, to keep out the summer breezes. He had to bend his head as he entered it, and couldn't stand at full height when he did, but Marianna seemed calmer there, and she leaned against the half-scale table that, along with a pair of miniature chairs, was the only furnishing in the room.

"Now," she sighed, her hand to her heart, sounding slightly winded, "now we can talk freely."

"Indeed, this is charming—" he began, but she hushed him at once, whispering, "Softly, Julian, you must speak more quietly."

"But you said we could speak freely," he protested, as she

whispered, "Yes, so I think. No one can see us here, but there are no windows, and who knows who's abroad tonight? Lillian said no one knew of the place but herself, for it was hers when she was a child, but we can't be too careful."

"Well, then," Julian said on a smile, moving closer, seeing her face as a pale blur in the dim light in the little room, her dress glowing with the strange luminescence white takes on in shadowy light, "since we can't be seen, here's a thing that can't be heard," and he gathered her in his arms and kissed her again.

He'd meant it as a poetic gesture. It was a romantic night, a daring encounter for her to have arranged for them, it was the least he could do in tribute to her cleverness and thoughtfulness. He was only surprised when he found it was entirely possible to do more. For though she did no more than lie still in his arms, she did remain so, and never pushed him away, or protested, or demurred, even when, at length, his hands stroked her, moving up along her waist, touching the cool skin at her breast. It was he that was suddenly shamed when he realized that he was only half-attending to what he did, because he was waiting for an order to stop that never came. Then, precisely because of her unusual cooperativeness, he became aware of her complete stillness: her soft but totally unmoving mouth, her hands hanging limp at her sides.

He released her, apologizing, puzzled because he'd never gone so far, never having been allowed to, and yet once having achieved more than he'd dared, he was amazed to discover that he'd no wish to do more. For he couldn't forget that she was a lady, and he, no despoiler.

"I understand," she said softly, brushing aside his apologies, "I do, that's why I arranged to meet you here tonight. But, Julian, things can't go on as they are. My brother has come."

At that, he stopped mulling over his reasons for his unease at her accepting his embrace. He stood very still, and could only ask:

"Where is he?"

"I don't know where he is now," she sighed. "He's gone, thank heaven, but he stayed all yesterday and we brangled far into the night. There's no hope for it, Julian, he's determined. I'm to marry Alford, in the autumn, as he wishes."

"Marianna!" Julian cried, forgetting to lower his voice in his distress. "You can't!"

But then he could say no more, for she stepped forward and laid her hand across his lips.

"Of course I can," she said with a bit of annoyance, "and since I must, I shall."

He took her hand in his and pressed his lips to her palm and then said in a lower, calmer voice, although he felt not at all reasonable:

"You mustn't, Marianna. I can repair my fortunes within a year. Only a year. There must be some way you can wait out that year. Marriage is forever, surely it's worth the wait of a year. It's no pipe dream, my love, I'll have the funds by then for us to live comfortably by any standards, with what Warwick has invested, with what I can add, it won't be long, and if you think you can't wait, then," he said desperately, "we can run away. There'd be no shame to it. Only you mustn't buckle under, not now, not when it will all be resolved so soon."

"Julian," she said sternly, cutting him off, "I won't be buckling under to Robert. It's time to be perfectly honest, and utterly sane. I've no intention of running away with you. We've had a lovely association. I do enjoy your company. But I'm already past nineteen. It's time for me to wed, and I've"—she paused and took in her breath— "always intended to have Alford anyway. There it is. I'm sorry, but there it is.

"I put it off as long as I could, because I enjoyed my single state very well, but my brother tells me he's having some difficulty now, some misunderstanding with important persons. When I return to town he says I might not have the same entrée into society as I had before. So I might as well settle the matter with Alford. He and I have had an understanding forever."

He didn't answer. He couldn't. He only looked down at her, and at his complete silence she grew a bit uneasy, and trailing her hand along the little table and avoiding his eye, she said defensively:

"Our parents decided it, actually, donkey's years ago. Our

lands match, they march together on the western border, it's a thing we've always known. Everyone's always known it, Julian, you ought to have.''

"You never mentioned it," he said stiffly.

"Why mention the day is light?" she said with flippancy, and then went on testily, "It wasn't any secret."

"You don't love him," he said flatly.

"Of course not," she replied, turning to face him. "I never have, that's the point. He doesn't love me, either."

"But you encouraged me—" he began, as she interrupted him to say:

"Just so. I still do. Oh, Julian," she said fretfully, "you're being so difficult. So provincial. You can still be my gallant. That's precisely what I want," she said eagerly, "for ours is to be a modern marriage. Alford will be a complacent husband, I'll be an understanding wife. So long as his heirs are his, we agree to grant each other freedom. Oh," she said pettishly, sitting down on the little table in an attitude of dejection, "I thought you were a man of the world. Half society lives that way. My own parents did. Would you rather," she asked angrily, raising her head when he didn't reply, "have me run away with you, scandalize myself, anger Alford, his family, my brother, and all for 'love' ''—she sneered at the word before she went on—"when we can have that love and all the rest as well?"

He froze, shocked, and yet thinking deeply. She was right in that there were dozens of such marriages in the *ton*, perhaps more of that sort than any other. And it was further true, he realized, that she'd never promised him anything in so many words. But, he thought, gazing at the upturned face he could scarcely read in the dim light, she was so very young, had lived her life among so many superficial people, how could she fully understand the sort of loveless, cold, hypocritical life she was about to commit herself to?

She saw him standing immobile, his entire frame stiff with insult, and she sighed. He was entirely handsome and noble, and though she was vexed with him, she was also delighted with his refusal to accept the loss of her. She'd worried this evening, she'd wondered tonight, when she'd seen him with Miss Logan, the beautiful, wealthy Miss Logan, if she mightn't have already lost him. That would be painful. Because Alford was dull, and not at all attractive, and scarcely caused a stir wherever he went. But Julian was a perfect foil for her, and never boring, and she wanted him at her side. Only Robert disliked him, really; even Alford agreed that he was an excellent escort for her. She was resolved to keep him, even though it meant making certain disagreeable sacrifices.

"Julian," she said then, rising and taking the one step to his side, "Julian," she whispered, laying her hand alongside his cheek and resting her head against his chest, "Julian," she said huskily, "must I show you how much you do mean to me? How much we can still have together? Should you like to make love to me?"

Oh yes, he thought then, his spirits soaring, his white teeth showing in a grin even in the half-light, he was right. She was very young, and it was precisely that youth that he'd use to show her how foolish her plans were. He lowered his lips to hers as a reply, and kissed her for a very long while and held her unprotesting form close.

Her scent was of cool violets, and her skin was as fine and pure and powdered as a moth's wing, and her mouth compliant, but only that. He was a gentleman of vast and varied experience, and nothing in her response led him on but the lack of protest in it, and the knowledge that he held the one woman he'd ever loved. That, and the fact that he knew he must show her that physical love was no small, easy thing, and that physical joy was more than she'd ever imagined. Thus he might win her, so he could convince her, then he could claim her and carry her off with him as his wife.

So he was infinitely patient. He dragged the top of her gown down by slow and light-kiss-measured degrees, he let his hands drift lightly along the contours of her body, barely touching, yet all the while drawing her closer, his fingers gathering up the folds of her skirt as carefully as though it were made of spiderweb, as gently as though the material itself were some sensitive living thing. Still, she remained passive and he found himself growing anxious instead of aroused, until he heard her whisper urgently:

"Oh, Julian, hurry."

That did surprise him. He was no amateur, and he'd had no

evidence of her desire. He stared down at her, but her face was in shadow. Still, her skin was cool and dry, her breathing calm and even, her heartbeat slow and measured against his chest. He frowned.

"The table," she said rapidly, as though she'd read his thoughts. "It's being pressed against the back of my legs. Give me your jacket," she said, and mutely, confused but obedient, he let her help him off with his tight-fitting velvet evening jacket. She tossed it to the wooden floor, and then, still holding his hand, she lowered herself to sit upon it with as much ease and graceful aplomb as though he were helping her to a seat on a cushion at a picnic, instead of watching her, her clothes in disarray, as she dropped to the floor of an abandoned cabin in the dark of night. She tugged at his hand to urge him to follow her.

"Come to me, Julian," she whispered, "now, hurry."

But he hesitated. The night was becoming too complex for him. He'd wanted to seduce her only so that he might carry her away, but nothing in her reaction spoke of abandon, except for her words. He thought dazedly that she was acting unlike herself, and so she was. But then a startling thought came to him so suddenly that he had to pause to think it over, even as he stood poised above her. Because they'd never had much time together, scarcely any of it alone, and all of it had been spent discussing his plans, her appearance, and polite gossip. And so he could hardly say he really knew her at all, or even half so well as he knew Susannah. But that thought stopped him entirely. Then it was as if he could see himself where he stood and felt profoundly foolish, looking down at a half-undressed lady sitting on the floor on his best jacket, as composed as though she were at a tea, as he loomed above her in a child's playhouse.

"Julian," she demanded in exasperation, "come to me. We haven't much time left. I can't stay out all night. Don't you want me?"

He did, of course; he did not, of course—he scarcely knew what to say as he sank to his knees to approach her on her own level. She smiled, that he could see, and then she slowly lay back. Then he was truly speechless, as she dragged at his hand and begged him to come to her. Obediently, unthinkingly, he lay down beside her, one hand going to her smooth hair to stroke it, the other to tentatively touch her mouth. He traced his finger over those perfect lips and was about to tell her that they'd gone far enough, that he couldn't compromise her after all, no matter how he loved her, for he was, after all, a gentleman, and she a lady, and it was enough for him that she wanted him.

"Julian," she complained, "can't you be quicker about it?"

Then, forgetting she was a lady in his perturbation, he asked, astonished:

"But, are you ready?"

"Of course," she said complacently, and wriggling as she adjusted herself further, she whispered, "Can't you see?"

He saw only that which made him doubt his eyes. For the Lady Marianna Moredon lay next to him, with all the portions of herself that ought to be covered, exposed, and all that was blameless, covered over. Her breasts shone white, their dark nipples like empty eyes staring into the dimness, her body beneath them swathed in billows of bunched white fabric, until one saw her flat white abdomen, the black of her pubic patch making another inky blot at the juncture of her long white legs. It was absurd, and shocking, in fact so bizarre that Julian, though confused and dismayed, was suddenly stirred by the very perversity of it.

"Julian," she pouted, "why do you delay? Oh," she laughed, her small pointed breasts bobbing, "is it that you don't have one of Colonel Cundum's machines with you? No matter, if you leave before you have come, as they say," she said gaily, "it will make no matter."

He sat back and rose to his knees. He wanted nothing more than to be gone, but now there was dignity, his as well as hers, to think of. There was no worse way a man could insult a woman, he knew, than to refuse her favors. But at the moment he could think of nothing worse than obliging her, for surely one of them had run mad. All arousal gone, he only managed to whisper something about not wishing to despoil her before her wedding.

"Think of Alford," he said, finally.

"I have," she said impatiently, "so you should not. He

was the first, that's all he cares about. And, Julian," she said softly, tenderness in her voice for the first time in their mad encounter, "you deserve some pleasure. I've been very bad to you. I want to make you happy, please let me, Julian."

He liked females very well, he'd loved her, and once he heard that plea, it was impossible to refuse her. He allowed her to help him undo the buttons on the fall of his pantaloons. Then, trying to forget whose female body he gazed at, and seeking oblivion in his senses from his reasoning, he sought to bring this anonymous partner to some sort of readiness. But she hurried him on with her words and her hands. Before he had time to regret it, he'd entered her. And because he'd been celibate for so long a time for him, he soon found himself rocking to some sort of relief, touched as it was already with the small chill of despair.

"Oh no, Julian," she cried, returning him to himself at the height of his moment, in just the same voice that she'd always spurned his chaste kisses, but then it was too late to obey her. Still, she was surprisingly strong and entirely uninvolved, so she managed to topple him so that he reached completion by himself, doubled over and gasping at her side, totally shamed and vulnerable, pouring out what he'd thought would be his love onto her crumpled muslin skirts.

While he lay back trying to regain his breathing and his senses, she sprang up and began to straighten her clothes. She avoided looking at him. She was embarrassed for him. It was a constant wonder to her how gentlemen could take their pleasure in such unpleasant fashion, and how the handsomest of them could look so determinedly witless while they were at it, and she was continually amazed how enfeebled they were after. But, of course, she knew it was necessary to them. Once it was done, of course, she was always vastly relieved.

"That was lovely," she said brightly, to make him feel better, as she twitched her bodice into place.

He'd raised himself to a seated position when she begged his handkerchief, and then, announcing merrily that it was lucky they were so close to water, she told him to wait while she freshened up, too polite to mention the blot he'd left on her gown. Then she left the little playhouse.

Soon he rose to his feet and adjusted his clothing, and

then, leaning against the wall of the house, he looked through the long windows of air and saw his lady in the moonlight, white and cool as some virgin goddess, busily cleaning the last traces of his touch from the hem of her skirts. He ran his fingers through his hair, shook out his jacket, and struggled into it again. When she returned to him, he was Julian Dylan, Viscount Hazelton, completely again, just as she was once more the Lady Marianna Moredon that he'd never known.

They strolled back to the ball slowly. She slipped a bit of columbine from off its tall spike and breathed in its scent. He took it from her fingers and placed it in her dark hair as she smiled at him, as though they were two gentlepersons back from an evening stroll. He was back from far more, and finding himself again, was as facile and clever and sure with her as he'd always wished to be. Now he wanted to be free of her easily as much as he'd ever wanted to have her. But he knew how great she considered her gift to him to have been. However well he knew now that she'd detested giving it, he was never cruel, and as a considerate lover he was determined to bring her to joy, however belatedly. If she was never to find that pleasure in the actual act, at least he knew, at last, how to satisfy her.

For when she began to speak of their future, of more secret meetings and clandestine plans, he stopped and took her hands in his and gazed into her eyes tenderly.

"Marianna," he breathed, "it cannot be."

"I don't understand," she said. "Wasn't it lovely? Don't you have everything you wanted now?"

"Yes, precisely," he said. "You've given me all I've ever wanted. This was, perhaps, the most perfect night of my life. I can't hope to equal it. I can only break my heart trying. Tonight was mine alone, and I'll never forget it. I must let you go now. Seeing you again, I would have to touch you. Touching you, I would ruin the memory of what we had. The perfection of that memory is what is most important. But I thank you for it, Marianna, and respect you completely."

She'd wanted to keep him as an escort and adornment, even if it meant having to keep him as a lover. But he'd just given her far more, and she'd have to give far less for it. To be enshrined as a gentleman's perfect vision of love was all she'd ever wanted. She was disappointed. But she was content.

He kissed her cheek, and then left her by the door to the ballroom, with happy tears in her eyes. He was, she thought, for all he could not help being a man, a gallant, gentle one. And he, striding toward the stables to collect his horse, felt as though he'd wallowed in mud, and yearned for some cleanliness. He'd loved many women, and never felt so filthy at it before as he had with his one true love. He'd bespeak a tub, he thought, when he got back to Greenwood Hall, and he'd scrub until his skin ached. And then he'd sit and talk with his friends.

And at the thought of one particular friend, who'd been as transparent in her devotion to him as he'd once been to another, he felt a strong surge of protectiveness. As he rode back to Greenwood Hall, his spirits lifted, and he began, at last, to think about the nature of true love.

"Now," Warwick said as he delivered Susannah to his house again, "now you know what it feels like to be the belle of the ball."

"So I do." She smiled up into his eyes. "Thank you."

"Now I suppose," he said lightly, plucking up a flower that was about to tumble from her hair, "there'll be no keeping you at home."

"Now," she said firmly, "there'll be no keeping me awake tonight, but that's all. And thank you, Warwick," she said, and rising on her toes, she planted a swift kiss upon his lean cheek before she grinned and went up the stair.

He watched her out of sight, and then, with a belated crooked reciprocal smile, remembering that she'd known very well that Julian had gone off with his lady and yet never seemed to care, he relented, and at last admitted that stranger, hope, into his heart.

17

The rain came down in torrents, a damp wind briskly shepherded fresh black clouds in to replace the gray ones that had worn themselves out with thundering, even ducks huddled at the sides of their overflowing ponds. It was a perfect day for a day after a party.

Susannah could have stayed in bed, pillows behind her head, sipping chocolate and nibbling pastries for sustenance, holding her coverlets to her neck, pointing her toes toward the hearth and hugging her memories to herself for warmth, and no one would have blamed her. She'd been such a success the night before that she'd have been forgiven for idle gloating the morning after. But luxurious smugness was for those who were used to triumph. Susannah needed to be certain it all had actually happened. She could use some reassurance, but after what seemed to be a lifetime of it, she certainly didn't need any more introspection. She wanted to share her glory.

If she also needed to escape from herself, she didn't mention that as she detailed all her other reasons for her early appearance downstairs to her host. But perhaps he knew it, she thought as she looked up from the chessboard into his amused eyes. He certainly seemed to know and understand all else. Which might be, she thought, as she frowned and pretended it was all for the fate of her pawn, precisely why she had such mixed feelings about him now. This morning he was a perfect host, keeping her company during the dull time after their riotous breakfast, where he'd served her compliments with her coffee, celebrating her success as wittily and easily as he'd helped to create it for her last night. Last night he'd been more than a social catalyst, he'd been a marvelous partner, laughing her through her nervousness, bolstering her courage, and supporting her every anxious step of her way into society. A few days before, in the wood, he'd been something quite different, although equally as marvelous and supportive a partner. But then, for all she knew he hadn't meant to, he'd frightened her.

Or perhaps she'd frightened herself. It had been a staggering experience, whoever had caused it. She'd been kissed before, of course, if never so thoroughly. She'd had previous suitors, and for all they'd been proper young men, she'd been curious, and though she'd been taught a kiss was no simple thing, even her family didn't believe a girl should go entirely untasted before her marriage vows. A stolen kiss or two was quite unexceptionable in her brothers' circles. But all those experimental kisses had been given only after much thought, and taken very seriously by their recipients. Then too, she realized, none of her suitors had been society gentlemen, for whom nothing was serious and to whom an embrace was evidently as lightly given as a smile.

Nothing had prepared her for her experience in the wood. She'd never realized that the merest meeting of lips could cause such tumult in every other portion of her body, or such a shameless desire for the meeting of far more. And all that sensation had been caused by Warwick Jones, a good friend and an attractive gentleman, but never the man she'd dreamed about at all. It was wholly startling that it had been so entirely thrilling. For if she'd been taught that ladies didn't care for that sort of thing even after marriage, even with gentlemen they adored, she knew that certainly they did nothing of the sort before, with anyone. And being a lady was, after all, all she'd ever been after.

But she was aware that she was in the midst of a great process of change, and if she was afraid that she'd never again be precisely what she was before she'd come to live with Warwick Jones, she was even more afraid of what she might become. So it was a thing she preferred not to dwell upon, having decided immediately after the incident that too many new things were happening in her life now for her to stop to ponder them all. She reasoned that she was, after all, truly out in the world for the first time, living among fascinating people, going rapidly from experience to new experience. If some of these things confused her, she'd have to set them aside to contemplate later when she had the time, since she didn't doubt that none of this could last: the fishmonger's daughter's life would eventually return to normal. But for now, even with the occasional snub and disappointment, she'd never had so much pure excitement. Last night she'd even tasted triumph. She was determined to go on without self-doubt or else she might end up just like the cat she'd once seen caught halfway up a tree—afraid to go further up, terrified of dropping down, and all because it had stopped to look to see how far it had come.

This habit of living an unexamined life was, however, not an easy thing for a thoughtful girl to cultivate. So if she felt a frisson of fear now, sitting opposite her host, she forced herself to endure and discount it. And if she couldn't help but note now that his face was far more than interesting, having discovered that it had its own aloof beauty, or if she remembered, unbidden, exactly how those curling lips had felt against her own and precisely how those slender hands could evoke glorious confusion, she quickly looked aside, suppressing those memories firmly. A little fear was, after all, a small price to pay for such a rich friendship.

She never doubted that he was her friend. She couldn't be angry at his actions in the wood, because he'd caused her no hurt, and meant none, and being a blasé gentleman, had probably meant it as flattery, as well. He'd seen to it that she couldn't be embarrassed with him, or with others. Not only would he protect her from idle chatter, he'd discussed the incident with her as coolly as if it had happened to someone else. That had helped. But then, she expected no less from him, for as friends, she knew that they could always, in any circumstances, reason together. And so even if he might want to repeat the episode (for she'd come to see that he was a rather hot-blooded gentleman), she trusted him and somehow knew that he'd allow her complete control over when, or even if, they'd ever have further adventures of that sort: the sort that kept returning to her mind, to trouble her. It would be entirely her decision. But having experienced what she had in his arms, the thought of what her decision might be was what truly terrified her now.

"Don't worry, I'm not that good a tactician," Warwick commented dryly, studying his opponent's face, "and even if I won, we never wagered on the outcome. No need to contemplate suicide, Susannah.

"Or," he asked as she looked up guiltily from thoughts that were far from their game, "is it 'Sukey'? You haven't given me permission to call you that, but I've noted your brother and Julian do, and I wondered if you preferred it. I'd hate to think you always think 'Stuffy old Warwick' every time I call you Susannah."

"Oh, that," she said, feeling easier with a new thought to distract her. "It was a childhood name my father called me. But my school friends didn't, though one brother does, and the other doesn't . . ." She laughed. "It really makes no matter, because though 'Sukey' sounds too countrified for some, 'Susannah' certainly isn't sophisticated either. I like both, or rather"— she frowned—"I don't like both."

"Something sophisticated is what you're after?"

"When I was younger, yes. I tried to get everyone to call me 'Celeste.' I thought that was a name fit for Versailles and a king's company. Or 'Cynthia.' I once fancied 'Saralinda.' " She sighed. "I guess the whispery sound of my own name pleased me, or I was used to it, but I was desperate for something far more exotic."

" 'Harry,' " he said mournfully, turning his head and gazing longingly into space, "or 'Tom.' 'Fred' or even 'John,' I remember, was my dream. Well, you'll admit," he said, smiling into her curious eyes, " 'Jones' is well enough, but when you're burdened with something like 'Warwick,' which is fine for a castle or a history lesson, but less so for a child, you might naturally tend to yearn for something commonplace, if only so you could put your fists down for a moment when you were a boy. But you weren't," he sighed, "so I doubt you'd understand."

Soon their game was all but forgotten, as Susannah, when she was done giggling, asked him about his youth. And he, sitting back, pleased at an excuse to continue looking into her wide brown eyes, or because she was a very good listener, or even perhaps because he'd been searching for a way to show her himself in another, less threatening light, found himself telling her a great deal about that youth. And in so doing, told her even more than he'd intended to.

"I wonder you let Julian and me into your house now," she couldn't help exclaiming when he was done, for she'd found it a pathetic, unhappy history, for all he dressed it with wit and told it charmingly. "If I were you, I'd have developed an outsize dislike for fair persons. Imagine," she said with some heat, "those awful people calling you a 'troll'! I think you must have been a very taking little boy," she sniffed in indignation.

"Ah, that was a 'goblin,' actually," he corrected her gently.

"Oh," she gasped, "I just said something far worse then, didn't I?"

"Ah, but then, you are a blond person," he sighed.

She looked to him in consternation, and then saw his lips half-lifted in a smile. They laughed together until she saw something else in his face as he watched her, something that was there in an instant and gone in another but that had been so clear and keen and painful in its intensity that it caused her to take in her breath, even though she wasn't quite sure of what it was, having never seen it in a man's face before. At least, not when he looked at her.

He cursed himself silently and savagely as he looked down at the chessboard, and sacrificed a blameless bishop to his anger at how transparent he'd been in his desire for her. Might as well, he thought, furious with himself, leap over the table, tear at her dress, and embrace her while you're at it, idiot, for you've startled her just as much with your leering. But as he stared at the game board, he reined in his rage, realizing he must learn to live and cope better with his longings. For what he'd come to feel for her had obviously grown so profound as to make him as maladroit as a boy, though he was a man who liked to pride himself on his cool diplomacy.

She was lovely this morning in a rose-pink gown that made her bright beauty into something rare and porcelain, but he'd seen every tint in the prism flatter her. Initially it had been her beauty that had snared him. But he knew his weaknesses. If anything, he deeply distrusted his reaction to females with pale hair and complexions like the smooth inner lips of seashells, and so he tested them more harshly, and so they always failed him. Then he'd been enchanted by her wit and charm. Still, having schooled himself against illusion, he wasn't a susceptible man. But as he'd lived with her and grown to know her, he'd become more entangled. After all, her courage, compassion, and kindness were things he might not have discovered from merely looking at her or dancing with her. And the streak of passion he'd unearthed in her had delighted him, for he was honest enough with himself to admit it was important for a man of his tastes and leanings to find a female he could share that pleasure with, so that he'd not be forced to continually satisfy his desires alone, outside of love. Because now he had to accept that she'd become much more than a friend, although she'd become one of his best ones. Now he loved her entirely.

She wasn't his perfect vision of love; being a reasonable man, he no more sought perfection in his lady than he did in himself. No, and a perfect female wouldn't have such a sly, cutting sense of humor either, or love gossip half so much, or be so headstrong or so damnably vulnerable, he thought. Or be so romantic. So romantic, in fact, that she'd fallen in love with another man from the moment she'd seen his beautiful face.

But he didn't think her unattainable; that never lent her additional glamour in his eyes. Though he was far from beautiful, he believed that through friendship he might yet win her. Especially now that Julian firmly disavowed interest in her and seemed to have a chance to win his own dream lady. Susannah Logan was no dream lady. No indeed, Warwick thought, smiling to himself, watching her frown at the chessboard, very perturbed, distrusting his bad move so badly she was about to misjudge it as a clever one and so ruin her game, and he knew how she hated losing. No, she wasn't perfect in the least. But reality seldom was. And she was very real. Unfortunately, her fear of his attentions, he thought as he sighed heavily, causing her to decide she was making the right move even as she destroyed her chances, was just as real.

It was as real as his present protracted state of complete celibacy. It wasn't just because he was in the countryside now. London wasn't that far, and as he'd cause to remember, certain endeavors were as available, if a shade less obviously accessible, in rural areas for enterprising gentlemen. But she'd ended all possibility of such diversion for him, if not the yearning for it. Since he'd come to fully know his mind, the thought of holding any other female to his heart was repugnant, the idea of purchasing one for his bed entirely squalid. He'd always had an investigative bent and wished he could be pleased to have discovered at last that whether he was ever able to offer it or not, at least he possessed a heart, and it was a faithful, constant one, at that.

If he sorrowed because he had to court his love as if he stalked some wild thing, steadily and patiently, never letting her see his true intention lest he frighten her into flying from him, he had to conceal that from her too. And he'd have to continue to, and do it far better, as well, he thought ruefully. When Julian finally defected and left to take up with his lady, then he'd have to be patient as he comforted her, and if he were subtle and clever enough, then he might woo her, and only then it might be that he'd win her. For they were good friends and she did like him very well, and there was a beginning. But he didn't deceive himself any more than he'd try to fool her on that score. He was, after all, he knew, a poor substitute for a fair dreaming prince. But he'd be no elfin changeling, either. Even if she could never come to love him as he loved her, he would, he vowed, at least make sure that she never regretted him.

She looked up expectantly from the disastrous move his inadvertent sigh had encouraged her to make. Then it was with real sorrow that he said, for he knew she'd feel losing the game as keenly as he'd miss playing it with her:

"Checkmate."

In the next moment they were both very quiet, Susannah sulking, even though she grew furious with herself for the childishness of it, and Warwick hiding his smiles at the sight of her peevishness, yet regretting he'd altered her mood.

They were both glad to see Julian when he strolled into the room a second later, but Susannah's greeting went beyond mere gladness.

She swung around in her chair, turning from Warwick to greet him, her face clearing as she gave him an unclouded, warm, and loving welcome.

As Julian dragged a small chair to the table and bestrode it backward, locking his hands over the back of it and resting his chin on his hands to study their chessboard, Warwick took out his watch. He glanced to it, and drawled:

"Almost noon. My, you're getting fashionable. How soon before you begin to haul out a snuffbox when the conversation lags, or begin to affect a lisp, I wonder."

"As soon as you stop taking advantage of Susannah. I saw her defeat in her face as I came in. But this game has all the earmarks of a rout! How did you get her to make such a disastrous move so soon?"

"Drugs," Warwick said lightly.

"Chicanery of some sort, no doubt," Julian agreed. "A poor way to congratulate her the morning after a stunning success. Come, you take the white, Sukey, forget this evil fellow, I'll be the black prince this time."

But she was heartily sick of chess at the moment, and was about to tell him so, when she caught a clear look at him. Then she paused and stared at her would-be opponent. He seemed chastened, his customary fires banked, even in his appearance. His golden hair was darkened by the rain-dimmed half-light admitted by the study's windows, his fair face was shadowed with exhaustion, and his fragile skin showed blue smudges beneath the softened, gentled gray eyes she met.

". . . something the cat dragged in," Warwick murmured. "Julian, did you ever get into a bed last night?"

But then a light rose glow appeared high on the viscount's pale cheek, though he only mumbled, "Late, Warick, quite late."

He might be running a fever, Susannah thought, alarmed, but Warwick only narrowed his eyes and then told him that they'd taken their breakfast at a decent, reasonable hour, but that, of course, he'd be glad to throw his cook into a frenzy and his kitchens into a turmoil to whip up something for his dear fashionable friend.

At that, Julian recovered himself, replying in much the same tones that there was no need, for he'd already strolled by the kitchens and seduced the good women there into feeding him bountifully. Then he turned to Susannah and began to tell her an anecdote about the ball, and as she responded, began to pry her reactions from her as well. Soon she was discussing all she had with Warwick before, but with even more ease and delight, for Julian was attending to her every word with interest, smiling at her all the while, his whole aspect brightening as he did. She was enchanted. It wasn't as though he'd ever been cold to her, but he was usually more casual.

This morning he looked at her with new interest, as though he'd never really seen her before. He hung on her every word and kept watching her animated face almost as if he'd just met her and was impressed with what he saw. She reveled in the altered quality of his attention, taking it as one more proof of how acceptable she'd become since her popularity of the night before. Now even Julian was taking new stock of her.

They discussed the ball until there was little of it except for the footmen's buttons that they hadn't examined and laughed over. The contessa came down at a truly fashionable hour and smiled at their enthusiasm, but it wasn't until the butler brought Warwick a message and interrupted their chatter that Susannah realized their host hadn't contributed anything to their conversation, but had only sat back watching them expressionlessly.

Now, however, his expression darkened as he read the note he'd been handed. At once their attention was all on him, and the room fell silent, for he looked profoundly discomfited, and his face as he raised it to them was troubled, and oddly youthful in his transparent distress.

"My uncle," he said distractedly, "it appears he's ailing again. Odd, I'd thought he was well on the way to recovery. Or at least as well as a fellow of his age could be. He's the one I was visiting a few days before I met you at the Swan, Julian. A peculiar old gent, reclusive, yes," he added with a self-mocking grin, "like all the rest of his family—you needn't say it. But it's true. He's quite old, and never married. And so I, who am actually a nephew a few times removed, and who have always been his distant relative in every sense of the word to his—and, I suppose, my own—satisfaction, am his sole male survivor. He does have a younger sister, but she never wed either. Ours is such a discriminating family that it seems we shrink, rather than grow, with each generation," he sighed, nodding his head as if in sad recognition of that truth.

"It appears," he went on, "that as his heir, if nothing else, they want me at his bedside now. But I hadn't thought to leave now," he murmured. "I don't really care to continue that particular family tradition, so this isn't a time when I want to go, or be anyplace but here with . . ." He seemed to suddenly hear what he was saying and stopped abruptly, his eyes widened in alarm as he looked at his guests, as if remembering their presence and wondering what they'd made of his rambling.

"I'm not making a great deal of sense, am I?" he asked, raising a thin winged brow at his own question. "But I'm somewhat distraught at having to leave . . . at hearing this news, I suppose."

He looked far more than that, Susannah thought, he looked wretched, nothing like his usual calm self. She thought he must be fonder of the old man than he'd admitted.

"I'm sure he'll recover," she said stoutly. "Is there anything we can do?"

"What?" he asked. "Oh no, nothing, thank you. I'll have Mr. Epford pack a bag, and I'll take a horse and have some others sent on ahead for me so that I change them the faster on the way home," he said, making his plans as if he spoke to himself. "A carriage is comfortable, but much slower, but since I'm going to Gloucestershire, this way I'll be able to take side roads cross-country for extra speed as well. I won't be gone long," he said then, as if promising himself that, and rising from his chair added, "but I must make ready to leave at once."

He strode to the door of the study, clearly still busily thinking. Then he paused and swung around.

"If he's better, I'll return immediately; if he goes, it will be a simple interment, and I'll be back soon too. If he lingers, I'll . . . Julian,'' he said, raising his head and meeting his friend's eye, ''I know you'll be passing a great deal of your time with Marianna, and I'm glad for you for it, but I'll have to ask you to sometimes include Susannah with her in your plans, so that she doesn't grow too lonely, or at least so that,'' he said more pointedly, ''you always are aware of just where she is.''

''I'm sorry, Warwick, I'll be happy to look after Sukey in your absence, very happy to, in fact,'' Julian said on a quirked grin that it seemed he couldn't suppress as he gazed at Susannah, before he looked back at his friend with more solemnity, ''but as for that last bit, I'm afraid I can't oblige. You see, the Lady Marianna Moredon is plighted. That is to say, she's going to be wed, in the autumn, to the Earl of Alford. So I'll not be seeing her again.''

Susannah stared at Julian. He seemed not at all downcast making a statement that ought to have had him near tears. But in fact, he held his golden head high and looked at Warwick with private wry amusement, and something very like pride.

''But be sure, I plan to care for Susannah,'' Julian said carefully, ''in just the way you want me to, Warwick. In just the way,'' he added significantly, ''that you always wanted me to, in fact.''

But at that Warwick's face became still, and very pale, and his eyes opened to a look of incredulous dismay. He seemed to waver where he stood in the doorway, and then shook his head as a man will after a blow. Then he nodded, and looking as though he'd already heard that his uncle had passed away, he turned and left without another word to them.

It was shortly before teatime that Mr. Epford summoned Julian from the salon where he was sitting with Susannah and the contessa. Warwick was checking the straps on his portmanteau when Julian appeared in the doorway to his bedchamber. Julian stopped for a moment to marvel at the huge old canopied bed with its myriad carvings and hangings, and then glanced around at the few other pieces of heavily ornamented furniture that stood upon the Turkey rugs. He would have whistled his approval at the way the high-ceilinged room was otherwise kept rather stark, so that the spareness of it highlighted the excellence of the few beautiful ornate old pieces, but from a look to his friend's grim face he realized it was no time to be chatting about interior decoration.

"I didn't know you were so fond of the old chap," he said simply, placing his hand on Warwick's shoulder.

"Uncle?" Warwick said with a frown, tugging the straps tight on his traveling case. "I'm not. Not that he isn't a good-enough fellow, but he's been ill for ages and is as old as the hills, and about as communicative as one too. No," he said, fixing Julian with an all-encompassing stare, "it's that I don't like leaving now. There's too much unsettled, too much in the air. I'm not being Delphic, Julian, but I cannot like it."

"You still worry about Moredon?" Julian said, amazed. "But I've broken it off with Marianna, there's nothing left to fear."

"He was insulted," Warwick said, lifting his case and striding to the door to his chamber. "A man like Moredon never forgets. Did you break it off with her, or she with you?" he asked suddenly, pausing and looking hard at his friend.

"I with her," Julian said simply, evading his eye, for he could swear that Warwick always saw too much when he looked at a person as he did now. From the quick nod his friend then gave, he also had the uncanny feeling that before he'd hastily looked away, Warwick had seen every embarrassing thing that had transpired in that absurd playhouse last night in his eyes. He was a gentleman, and as such had a code of honor, but even a gentleman might share certain confidences with his best friend, if he knew he could trust him. And he would trust Warwick, had trusted Warwick, he recalled, with far more, he'd entrusted his life to him. Perhaps one day he might tell him the story of what had happened with a certain lady one strange night. But he'd rather keep to himself just now while it was still so new and raw an insult to his intelligence. It had been, he remembered uncomfortably, Warwick, after all, who had joked with him all those weeks ago about how similar the morals of society ladies and poor wenches were. Then he recalled the one class of female his friend had sworn were innocents. There was another, happier confidence he could share with him. He smiled widely.

"But never mind. Never doubt I'll take care of Sukey."

Warwick stood absolutely still, and such was his distraction today, Julian thought, that for a facile fellow, he seemed to be struggling to frame a reply. When he spoke at last, he amazed his friend.

"You'll be alone with her, to all intents and purposes, once I'm gone," Warwick finally said stiffly. "One bachelor in one house with or without a chaperon is an entirely different matter from the arrangement we had before. Are you sure you want to stay? Perhaps you'd prefer to come with me, or stay at an inn until I return?"

"Warwick, you astound me! How gothic," Julian laughed. "I thought you wanted her protected, and now it seems you want to protect her from me. So it will be different, and that's all to the good. I won't compromise her, or if I do, be sure it will be with her complete cooperation, and I'll speedily do the right thing. I want to do that anyhow. Yes, I've seen the light, old friend, and it *is* fairer than the dark," he chuckled.

"What a slowtop you must take me for, what a fool I've been," Julian confessed, "looking so far afield, when it was all just as you said: Sukey is absolutely right for me, bedamned to the money, it's only a bonus, she's bright, beautiful, virtuous"—he paused as he said "virtuous," as though savoring the word, before we went on—"and thank God, I believe it's very much as you said: I can have her. Or, at least," he said on a small deprecating smile, "I can try. The other? She was just an illusion I invented because I couldn't have her, and it was the trying for her, I think, that I most enjoyed. Don't look so worried," he laughed, looking to his friend. "It will all work out, and it is, after all, what you've said you've always wanted, isn't it?"

"Yes," Warwick said softly, "it is what I said."

Susannah and the contessa bade Warwick a farewell at the front door. The only private word he had for Susannah, just before he left, was cold and stilted.

"Mr. Epford has my direction should you need to reach me. I'll be back as soon as I can. Keep well."

But then he halted at the door as though he'd thought of

something important, and turned round to her again, some consternation on his face. But after a moment, "Remember, I'll be back soon," was all he repeated, and then, frowning, as though annoyed with himself, he walked out into the rain.

They all watched him as his mount took him down the long drive, and they waved until he disappeared from sight.

When he reached the main road, a thunderclap caused him some difficulty with his horse and then the skies opened and the rain plummeted down on him.

"Yes, thank you. It only needed that," he muttered, looking up to the drenching clouds, pulling up his collar. Then, something like humor returning to him, however grim it was, he kneed his horse to a brisk canter as he hurried into the growing evening alone, as he began to fear he always would.

Dinner that night at Greenwood Hall was an awkward affair. No one seemed to be reacting normally to anyone else, Susannah thought. The contessa looked distracted, and spoke very little, looking as though she were wondering if the situation were correct through every mouthful of her dinner.

Julian was charming and warm and considerate, but Susannah felt wrong laughing loudly at his jests when she knew their host might be grieving. And although she'd believed she could sit and stare at that particular bright face for hours in content, tonight she felt oddly disloyal doing so, as though there were the reflection of some other countenance, a familiar, sad, lean one, imprinted on the dark streaming windows, looking in from the night and the rain at them, in all their warmth.

Perhaps Julian felt the same, she thought. Because after dinner, the most intimate time, he made only random conversation and then, as early as was decently possible, he begged exhaustion and went to his rooms. As he'd looked uncommonly weary since morning, Susannah took no offense, though she was yearning to know more about Lady Marianna and had been trying to think of a clever, casual way to work her name into conversation. Whatever had happened, he certainly didn't seem to be pining for the lady, she thought as she brushed out her hair that night. And then, as she curled into her own bed for an early evening, she thought of how she'd have the whole day with him tomorrow. But it was both her gentlemen she thought of as she prepared for sleep.

Odd, she thought, that though Julian was her dream of perfection, she wasn't at all afraid at the prospect of being alone with him, as she now was with Warwick, because she found she wasn't a bit confused or nervous about him or his behavior, or her own. She was only a little shy of him now, she supposed, because he was suddenly treating her with such courtesy and deference. That would take some getting used to, she thought on a smile, as she began to drift off to sleep. She quite looked forward to it.

But in the morning, it was Julian's turn to appear perturbed and anxious.

"Take a look. You see," he said on a deep sigh, "it's specific. I hardly know what to make of it. But it's clear the owners of the *Thunder* want a word with me, and now, and they say it's to my advantage. With the way things have changed, I don't plan ever to have to drive the Brighton coach again, but I'd mentioned to Warwick that I'd like a chance to invest in the entire coaching line, not only for the money but also as a gesture, I suppose, of independence. You understand, Sukey," he said, smiling at last, and smiling so warmly that she'd begun to nod before she even heard what it was he wanted her to agree to, "if there's going to be gossip about my past, I want to be able to shout it out, instead of cowering and trying to hide it. Very like"—he paused to grin—"loudly announcing to society that one's family is in fish, for example.

"So for all I know, Warwick's already had a word with someone. I can't ignore this, at any rate. And I'll leave you well-guarded—"

"Guarded?" she asked in amazement. "Do you think I'm about to be carried off by Gypsies, or is it that you're afraid I'll run off with them?"

He looked down at her. Her hands were on her hips, her expressive face both petulant and defiant, and he couldn't resist dropping a small kiss on the end of her nose. Once so close to her, he found himself tempted to do more, but was forestalled by the contessa fidgeting in the background, wondering, he imagined, if the tip of the nose were a private-enough portion of a young lady's person to be considered inviolate. Not for the first time that morning he wished he could simply tear up the note he'd been delivered and stay on with Susannah, especially now, since with the opportunity to be alone he'd be able to resolve his future more quickly with her. But the note was direct. "To your advantage," it said, "the twenty-fourth of June," it stated, and that was tomorrow, and "Portsmouth" was written large and plainly on the company stationery.

He looked back when he reached the end of the drive, but this was a sunstruck day and Susannah stood on the gravel and waved her good-bye, so Warwick's edgy, eerie premonition of danger seemed foolish and further away than it had been in the night. Still, he rode quickly because something in the thought bothered him, and he wanted to be away from it. She was safe, he swore to himself as he pounded toward Portsmouth, she was in a gentleman's country home, surrounded by servants. But he wanted to get back to her as soon as he could.

The house seemed completely empty when Julian had gone, and as Susannah wandered back into the salon where the contessa alone awaited her, she began to feel foolish. With the two gentlemen gone, her position was awkward, she looked like a stranger lingering on at a gentleman's estate after the party was over, for no reason and to no purpose. But then she remembered those gentlemen, and sighed, and knew she'd wait here, alone if she had to, until their return, no matter how odd it looked to the world. For they were, she suddenly realized, her only world.

Warwick Jones returned to Sussex late on Saturday, near to twilight. He'd ridden hard, all the way from Gloucestershire, stopping only to ease himself or his horses, down some refreshment, or pay tolls at the turnpikes. Now, having reached the long road that led to his home, he at last eased his speed. Now that he was a few miles from home, he could admit how foolish his mad ride had been.

If she'd indeed chosen Julian while he'd been gone, his absence these past three days was not the reason for it. And for all that he'd tormented himself, twisting his sheets in the sleepless nights as he wrestled with the tormenting vision of those two golden creatures entwined in each other's arms, he realized now that if it were fated, then so it would happen, whether he were in Gloucestershire or in the next room to them. Now that he saw familiar trees, and trotted down a dusty, familiar lane filled with evening birdsong, the other unspecified dangers he'd worried over seemed to be only extensions of the dismay he'd felt on leaving her, perhaps to lose her, if not in any of the vague violent ways he'd feared, then certainly just as surely to another man's arms.

But for all that he could now see how vain all his fears had been, he slowed his horse as he rode home, not at all sure he wanted to see what had transpired in his absence. As he turned a bend, he saw a familar sight as the other rider turned his guinea-gold head to see who rode behind him. Then he spurred his horse.

"Julian," he cried, "give you good day. What are you doing riding out alone? Had a spat with our Susannah, have you?"

But as he came alongside his friend, he saw how dust-covered his high boots were, and how travel-stained his clothing.

"Where have you been " he demanded then, too anxious to mind his words or his tone.

"Portsmouth, since the day after you left," Julian replied, sounding as bone-weary as he felt. "I rode like a madman to get back by this evening. What news of your uncle, Warwick?"

"He lasted only until I got there, poor fellow," Warwick said, shrugging off condolences, brushing aside all mention of his inheritance as he quickly asked, "Portsmouth?"

"Aye, and what time I wasted. There was indeed an opening for another partner in the stagecoach line, my negotiations were successful, I think. But getting any information took forever, I had to drag it out of them through sheer tenacity, since no one of them would admit responsibility for summoning me in the first place. But when there's a falling-out among partners, I suppose that's to be expected. At any rate," he said defensively, seeing Warwick's confusion change to sudden pallor, "that's why I rode down a horse and had to lame another before I bought this nag, to get here before nightfall.''

They stayed a moment in silence, then looked at each other. And then without a word they urged their horses forward to race toward Greenwood Hall together.

Warwick threw his reins to a stableboy and reached his entry hall by long, striding steps. Julian followed closely, and when they entered the cool confines of the great marble hall, it seemed to them both that their footsteps echoed too loudly.

"Where is she?" Warwick asked at once, when his butler and Mr. Epford appeared in the hall.

"The contessa was summoned away the day after the Viscount Hazelton left," the butler explained nervously.

"Indeed, I urged her not to go," Mr. Epford said with great grievance, "but she was too excited by the letter from the law firm in Edinburgh claiming to have news of her husband's estates being restored, and she wouldn't listen to reason, she—"

"Be damned to the contessa," Warwick shouted. "Where is she?"

"Gone, sir," the butler sighed.

"To London, to see her brother," his valet put in soothingly. "She received a summons from him this very morning, asking her to meet him there. Indeed, it was all in order, Mr. Jones, he even sent a coach to collect her, here is the note she left to you, it was all correctly done."

The note was simple and exactly as his valet had said, and after Warwick had scanned it, assuring himself that she promised to communicate with him as soon as she found what dear Charlie wanted with her so urgently, he sighed and handed it to Julian. Then as he stripped off his gloves, his butler presented him with another message.

"It came an hour ago," he said calmly, seeing that calm was being restored to the hall, "and was addressed, as you can see, to either you, sir, or Miss Logan. But as she was already gone, it hasn't yet been read . . ."

Warwick Jones grew ashen as he scanned the note. The thin red line left from his battle with attackers in London stood out in bold relief against his cheek, and it could be seen that all the muscles in his jaw were knotted. His eyes held a terrible, naked fear for one moment, but in the next, his butler shivered to see that it mightn't be fable that the gentleman's ancestor had been a murderer as well as a thief.

"Warwick?" Julian asked quietly, fearfully, his light eyes already growing bleak.

"It is from her brother Charles," Warwick answered woodenly. "It joyously announces the birth of her nephew last night. It comes from his country home in Dedham. Of course, of course, he is not in London."

18

The coach was not half so luxurious as any Susannah was used to, but she reasoned that Charlie had settled for whatever was available when he sent for her so quickly. She worried about the reasons for that hasty summons, praying nothing had gone wrong with her sister-in-law or her little niece, calming herself only by reasoning that if that dreadful notion were true, he'd have called her to his country home, not London. Then she fretted that it might be that Charlie had got word of something dreadful befalling her younger brother, and then, her breath catching in her throat at the very idea, she wondered if anything awful had happened to dear Charlie himself. She didn't even have the dubious comfort of knowing she didn't have much longer to torment herself with these terrible visions of disaster for her loved ones, since she'd soon be far more concerned about herself.

She hadn't had much time to think when she'd flung her clothes into a carpetbag, ordered her maid to come quickly, scribbled a note to Warwick, and clambered into the waiting carriage bound for London. But Charlie's note was terse, and so not like him at all, and she'd not stopped to wonder at it when it had been delivered into her hand. Instead, she'd known she must go to him at once. Her only immediate worries had been because the contessa wasn't there to accompany her, Julian had gone as well, and Warwick wasn't there as usual to see things through so that she could take a step without dread of stepping wrong. It was only when she was within the dingy coach and on her bumpy way to London, trying to ignore the shocks the badly sprung vehicle registered with every rut in the road, and painfully aware of the cracked leather seats, musty smell, and dirty windows, that she let herself question the dire reason that necessitated the impromptu journey.

The horses flew down the twisting, narrow roads with such speed, the coachman never sparing them, his whip cracking so continually, that she was tempted to lean her head out the window and shout for mercy for the poor brutes, until she paused, wondering in sudden sick shock if there might not be indeed some terrible urgency spurring him on. But on the first stop, when they paused at an inn to change the foaming team, he wasn't very forthcoming. He wasn't a sight to inspire confidence either. He was something in the style of the coachmen she'd seen at the Swan the night she'd met Julian, which meant that he looked nothing at all like him, but instead resembled all the other stage and mail coachmen she'd ever seen. But although he was large and heavy and red-faced too, he was more of each than was ordinarily found in those men, and was slovenly, a thing none of them ever were, since they were generally proud to the point of arrogance, and were so careful of their clothes they were almost dandified in their absurd costumes.

This fellow, her maid noted darkly, had a nose as red as his neckerchief, a welter of food and snuff stains on his boldly checkered waistcoat, his Benjamin cape had rents and patches, his jockey boots were scuffed, his broad-brimmed hat was dented, and the linen at his neck and wrist was far darker than the team of grays the carriage was transferred to. And, he said, around the foaming tankard the ostler had brought out to him at the first stop they'd made, he knew ''nuffink about anyfink, missy, 'cept 'e was to get to Lunnon, and quick-like.''

She fretted and stewed and fidgeted as the miles went by, and though her body welcomed the pauses, she resented every stop the coach made for food or comfort as the long, anxious day passed. She was relieved when they pulled into the courtyard of the Crimson Cat and she was told it was their last stop before the journey's end. At that, she exchanged weak smiles and sighs with her maid, and after she'd sought the ladies' convenience, she relaxed enough to order a glass of cider and some light refreshments for them both. Then, since her maid always quite rightly saw to her mistress's needs and comforts first, she sat back and waited for the girl to return from her own toilette. It was then that the coachman stumped into the common room to insist she hurry back to the coach, as they were ready to leave again.

Susannah cast a longing look back to the pitcher, bread, and cheese that were being brought out even as she left, for now that she'd admitted her thirst and hunger, they seemed all the keener for having to be abandoned so soon after being acknowledged. She plunked down on the coach's peeling, flaking cushions with a sigh, for though the coachman had promised that her maid would bring "them victuals" along with her, it was hard to imagine how she'd get a drop into her mouth when the coach began to buck and jounce along the roads again. So when the carriage started up with a jolt and she was flung back in her seat with the backward thrust of it, she was too winded at once to shout what she had to. And then she discovered that she couldn't pry the windows open any longer, and that none of her frantic thumping on the ceiling seemed to have any effect either. Thus she had no way of telling the coachman that they were off and down the road despite the fact that her maid was still somewhere in the Crimson Cat ladies' necessary.

At first, she was horribly sorry for poor Millie, picturing her beside herself when she returned to find her mistress gone, and herself alone and stranded in a strange place, miles from home. And then she remembered poor Millie had a head on her shoulders and a fairly big mouth in that head at that, and she actually found herself smiling as she pictured a truer version of her maid's reaction. And then she recalled her own situation.

She continued to shout and rattle and exhaust herself making futile noises as the carriage reached the outskirts of London, but there wasn't an indication that the coachman had heard a sound. She was frightened then, worrying about herself, wondering if the coach was going to tip over, nervous about being alone. The only solace she had was in the thought of what Charlie would do to the fellow when she was delivered to him. And if, for one moment, the thought occurred to her that it was not a mistake, that the action was deliberate, and that it had not been Charlie that had summoned her at all and sent her off on this mad journey, then she found the perfect retreat from that absolutely hideous unthinkable thought. She refused to believe it. And like so many people who refuse to be cowed by fate, she got angry instead.

It was even easier for her to become enraged than it was for her to dissolve into tears when she discovered, as the coach slowed to almost a standstill in London traffic, that the doors had been fastened and barred from the outside. And when she tried to clear the windows with a handkerchief so that she might signal and wave to passersby to attract attention to her plight, and found that they'd been uniformly filthied, again from the outside, she found herself more comfortable trembling with rage than she would've been had it been fright she quaked with. Which wasn't to say that she wasn't roundly terrified by then. She was. But she wasn't ready to submit to defeat, because her da had taught her that fear was in itself defeat. For once, she was happy that she wasn't a true lady. A lady, she believed, ought to have subsided into tears and lain trembling on the cushions, awaiting her destiny. Susannah raged, and looked about for a way to deal death and destruction to the author of her difficulties, if only so that she wouldn't deliver herself to useless, helpless terror.

So when the coach at last rolled to a stop in a rubbish-strewn alleyway so hemmed about by high crooked houses that it was twilight at teatime, and the door was finally flung open, the three men who peered into the shadows of the carriage to see where the girl had tried to hide herself were forced to take an unplanned step back as the young woman, her eyes blazing fury, marched out. She almost believed herself mistaken in their motives, since for that second all three were too dumbfounded to do more than gape at her. She was, although she didn't know it, a perplexing if awesome sight to them.

They saw an absolutely lovely young lady, wearing a gown of celestial blue that did nothing to hide the perfection of a slender, but ripe form, and that emphasized her fair skin and the yards of flaxen hair that had come down from its pins during her wild ride. Her features were delicate and piquant, she was an altogether entrancing female, if one could ignore the fact that her fine brown eyes were slanted in a feline cast and filled with pure and glowing rage.

She saw three dangerous-looking grubby men of assorted size and height, all of whom would have announced their presence to her even if she were blind, they smelled so badly, some from simple dirt, some from the application of too much cheap perfumery. For as she stood and stared, she began to sort them out and saw one who was tall and filthy, one who was lean and ragged, and one fat one who had put on all the airs and graces of a gentleman half his size, so that his clothing fit badly, where it fit at all.

She was so fierce-looking in that moment when she left the coach that they simply gawked as she stepped out. But then, just as her expression wavered as she began to realize that she was in deeper difficulty than she'd known, they began to remember that however furious she looked, she was only a woman, and only one, at that, and there were three of them. It was the thin one who broke the silence.

" 'Ere, she's a treat," he whispered in awed tones.

"I knew me luck was changin'," the tall one said happily. "Come to Daddy, luv, there's a good girl."

He reached out for her, and involuntarily Susannah recoiled. This pleased him very much, and he smiled widely, giving her the benefit of the stained teeth he still possessed. He giggled, and reached for her again.

But Susannah observed a great deal and learned very quickly. This time she didn't cringe, but when he touched her arm, she swung her other hand and caught him soundly on the ear. He swore and reached for her, but before he could touch her again, the corpulent man said hastily:

"She's not yours, idiot, leave off. She's his, and we'd best be quick about getting her inside before she attracts too much attention. Miss," he said anxiously in what may even have been sincere tones, "come with us, please, or it will go hard for you."

She hesitated. The coachman called down nervously that he had to be off, the fat man looked unhappy, the thin one seemed stricken into silence by her beauty, and the tall man leered and said merrily, "I'll take her in, not to worry," as he reached for her again. This time he captured her arms, and placed one hand widespread on her bottom, as though he were about to lift her and fling her over his shoulder, although all he did was grin. She struggled with him, to his growing amusement, as she soon discovered it was hard to fight with someone taller and stronger, especially when she'd never been taught to fight, and when every time he touched her she was shocked into a temporary paralysis of shame and disbelief because of where he touched her, and when she was handicapped further by having to hold her breath as well, the closer he held her.

"Fool," she managed to spit at last, writhing in his grip, "do you think this is what Lion would approve?"

He released her so suddenly she had to steady herself against the side of the coach, and the fat man stopped arguing with the coachman about his fee for services. All of the men swung around to stare at her then.

She'd mentioned Lion, she supposed dazedly, only because that was the name that had naturally come to her when she'd thought of crime. She'd never expected such a gratifying reaction. But in truth, their reaction to her words was as nothing compared to the way she was surprising herself more each minute. In no way was she acting as a lady. In stress, in her moment of deepest need, she discovered herself reverting to an instinct she hadn't known she possessed, behaving as what she really was, whether she'd forgotten, or had indeed ever even known what that self was or not. If she'd inherited no business sense from her da, she was yet his daughter, and there were things, she discovered, that if not bred in the bone, were at least learned at his knee. Those things came to her now, unbidden, and she was grateful for them.

She raised her chin and tried to look ferocious. Da had always said the world believes what it sees, and a man can sell anything he can make the world believe it sees.

She'd been angry, she'd fought back in every way she knew, and now it seemed she knew still another way, since the right words were coming to her lips by bypassing her brain entirely. Her decision was made so lightning-fast she was scarcely aware of it. But one second she was merely encouraged and the next wholly decided, even as she stood glowering and panting for air at the side of the coach. She rejected all the expensive things learned at Miss Spring's academy. They were for ladies. She was, after all, just as the world always took pains to tell her, not one. And at any rate, ladylike recourses such as fainting, weeping, praying, and pleading seemed pointless now. Coolness, cleverness, some deceit, and pure brass, all the ingredients Da had sworn made for successful business, might yet save the day. At any rate, it made her feel better, and even if that were all it did, that was how she meant to go on.

"Er . . . Lion?" the corpulent man breathed. "You are acquainted with him?"

She paused. She thought furiously. If they were working for the King of Thieves, they'd not ask that. If they weren't impressed by his name, they'd not ask that. If they weren't terrified of him, they'd not look as though she had conjured up a demon at the mention of his name. She set her jaw, and set her bridges afire.

"*In*timately," she breathed, in the lowest, most vulgar fashion she could manage.

At least, she thought a little while later, as she stood and looked out at the blank wall her barred window faced, her tactics had gotten her off the street without further molestation or pain. The coachman had pocketed his coin, tipped his hat, forgotten to wink, and lashing his horses, had fled. The other men had held a whispered conference and then the fat man had offered her his arm, his apologies for the mistake, and asked her as nicely as you please, to please follow him. Since she hadn't any choice, because she couldn't outrun them, she'd agreed. He'd led her into a wretched hovel, up a flight of stairs so filthy her slippers stuck to them, and then, with a flourish, had shown her into this room. Once she'd swept past him, head high, he'd slammed the door on the hem of her skirt and she'd heard it bolted soundly enough to keep in elephants. Then she'd been left alone.

At least the tall man hadn't touched her again, though his leer, she decided, trying to cheer herself up, was, just as her nurse had threatened would happen to herself when she was little and refused to put off a silly face she'd made, now probably frozen to his nasty face permanently. She gazed at the blank brick wall and held her hands tightly together, and having no watch, decided she'd been waiting in this room for either an hour or an eternity. That was the worst part of it. The longer she stayed locked in the room, the more her courage ebbed. She was cursed with an active imagination but blessed with enough good sense to know that the horrors she envisioned were working against her. She tried to brace herself by turning her thoughts to other things, believing that if she weren't distracted she'd be capable of dreaming up far worse than what was actually awaiting her. Then the door opened and she discovered that she was wrong.

At first she was so relieved she almost wept the tears that anger had held back. The gentleman that came into the room was just that, a gentleman, there was no mistaking it. He was tall and well-proportioned, well-dressed in a tight blue Weston jacket, with scrupulously clean white linen at his neck, and he wore well-fitted dove-gray pantaloons and high shining boots, his only adornments a golden fob and a quizzing glass. He was also well-brought-up, for he bowed when he saw her, and then took her hand. She looked up into a face as fair as her own, but what she saw in those cold blue eyes caused her own eyes to shut as tightly as the door did behind him. When she opened them again, he was smiling, and she knew that all the rest was prelude and she had never, ever, been so frightened.

"Miss Susannah Logan," he said pleasantly, "what a happy accident to make your acquaintance here."

This comment amused him very much, and when she didn't reply after he'd done laughing softly, he went on, "I could have scraped up your acquaintance at Brighton, you know, but then, I'd have had to contend with those churlish fellows you've been living with, and I didn't care to. I decided to bring you to London and introduce you to society instead, just as your friends attempted to do. Do you like the gentlemen you've already met? They are eager for your further company."

He frowned at her then, and putting a gloved finger to her cheek, he looked into her face. She resolved not to blink or look away, and she kept her countenance immobile, but she couldn't control a sudden shudder at his touch, and he smiled again.

"But are you a mute? Is that why they had such difficulty launching you into the *ton*? And here I had heard it was only because you were a common baggage masquerading as a lady, a fishmonger's daughter foisted on society for love or money. Which was it, my child? One of the gentlemen needs money badly, and the other might have tired of your charms, for I understand he grows bored rapidly with his conquests, and so he might have used you to play his little joke on us. He was always fond of jests," the gentleman said, suddenly angry, suddenly glaring at her.

She tried to be brave, and stared back at him steadily.

"But to whom am I speaking, sir? We've not been introduced. I was abducted, carried here, I assume you to be my rescuer, and I'd like an explanation."

She knew she'd said the right things, for he seemed taken aback, but she knew she'd said them wrong, because what was meant to be cool and brazen came out weak and bewildered, in thin, trembling tones. Then she realized it hardly mattered, he had some plan in mind that words would not unravel, and when he spoke again she understood that what she'd seen in his eyes was so, and something had gone badly wrong in his mind itself that perhaps no mortal thing could unravel.

"My name is Lord Robert Moredon," he answered, smiling at her again, "a name that ought to be well-known to you. One of your gentlemen wanted to sully that name, the other attempted to muddy it. Both have failed. I have you, you see. And from what I hear, and from what I know, and from what I think," he said with a twinkle, putting his forefinger to the side of his nose, "that will distress them very much.

"But tell me," he demanded, annoyed again, "why should that be so? You are pretty, yes, but the world is full of pretty girls, what is it that you do so well to be so important to them? I think," he said charmingly, teasingly, coming close to her and putting his hand on her neck, "that you shall have to show me."

She drew back, fighting against his hand, and that he let

her do so without stopping her told her that he was enjoying himself.

"Oh," he said with a great deal of mock sorrow, "she doesn't want my touch. Perhaps it's because there's only one of me, and she's used to two gentlemen. How do they do it, child?" he asked with great curiosity, seeming so sane and interested that she found it difficult to believe she had heard what he said correctly. "Both together, sandwich style? But which one front, and which one back? Ah, I know. The beautiful blond boy in front so that you can gaze at him in his pleasure, the other round the back where he belongs. Or do they hand you back and forth? Hmm? Why so shy?" he teased. "Is it that you'd rather do it than speak it? Why, that's no problem, and if you'd like, I'll call in some of the fellows in the next room so that you can show us the way, and it will feel just like home to you.

"But I am not so perverse as those two, no, who could be? For I've heard," he whispered, "and I do believe it, that when you're not available, they manage to do wonderfully without you, the Adonis and the Highwayman. And I am never so lost to cleanliness. So I think I'll try you alone and then call the others in for their deserts."

He took her in his arms, but then paused to look into her face again. And in that moment she feared his embrace so much that reason fled and she gave way to hopelessness. But when his kiss didn't come, she opened her eyes to see him wearing the same sort of avid look that she had surprised briefly on Warwick's face that day in the wood just before he'd released her. But Warwick had acquired that intent, tensely concentrated expression only after many long sweet embraces. Innocent of such matters as she was, when Lord Moredon still made no move to touch her as he greedily drank in her appearance, and when she remembered that even the foul-smelling brute in the next room had let his hands rove all over her whenever he could, and would have done far more if he could, she dimly perceived that this man would never know that sort of desire for her. And that he neither wanted nor needed her body for his gratification, since it was only her distaste and fear he fed upon. Then she vowed that since that was the one thing she could control in all this nightmare, she would die rather than continue to give him such pleasure.

"You will not," she announced coldly and distinctly, her mouth inches from his, "get either of them this way, you know. No, for I am not Warwick Jones, nor am I the beautiful Viscount Hazelton, so having me, you still will not have either of them."

He dropped his hands and stepped away from her at once as though she'd stung him. He frowned, for it seemed he heard her words in some altered fashion, from afar or with an echo, for it took some while for him to make sense of them. Then he gazed at her with such hatred that it took all her resolve not to shiver.

"I don't want them," he said scornfully, "I never wanted either of them! Don't you understand? Why can't you understand?" he whispered fervently. "I keep telling you, I don't desire either of them, never, not even back at school. It's not just that it's a hanging offense, it's an offense to me, I'm a man and a man doesn't want other men, no matter how beautiful, how strong, or comely, or clever he is, with all his fair hair and golden skin. Let his sly, knowing friend Warwick have him, I don't care, I'm not jealous in the least," he snapped. "No. Not I!" he shouted.

He answered what she'd never meant to ask, but it told her more than she wished to know. He'd gone through a gamut of expressions as he'd spoken, wheedling, shouting, posing. Now he grew red-faced and writhed in distress, holding his hands tightly together as if he knew it was the last of his sanity he held there. She did not honestly think she would survive that moment.

But there was a tentative tapping on the door, and a meek but audible voice asked, "Your lordship, be you all right?"

"Yes," he said, "oh yes," he repeated, "yes!" He nodded. "Better and better than ever. I would not," he said loftily, sneering at Susannah, "dirty the lowest part of my person on you. No, I'll leave you to them, they have no honor to besmirch by wallowing in your foul body. I've better ways to pass my time, better ways to have my little jokes. Oh, I enjoy a good joke too. I'll be very merry when they're both gone, I shall laugh for hours. And then I'll have peace and honor and pride again too," he said reverentially, before he smiled once more.

"But for now it's very amusing, for the Highwayman rides again," he laughed. "Didn't you know? Oh yes, and all the king's men are concerned at how Gentleman Jones's ghost has risen from the grave, don't you know. And the beautiful Julian drives a coach, too! Oh heavens," he giggled, "how dangerous for him.

"But the first jest, little trull," he said, sobering, and smoothing a glove over his fingers, "is on you. Gentlemen," he said airily, throwing open the door and surprising the three men clustered close, who'd evidently been trying to hear all that had transpired within, "she's yours. Have her with my blessings. Hearty appetite. Then kill her."

The three looked at each other, then at Susannah.

"Ah, but, your lordship," the fat fellow said, grinning like a dog begging for a scrap, "she said—"

"She lies," Lord Moredon said, taking out his wallet, handing out bills to them as if they were calling cards. "Believe nothing she says. Or shouts out." He grinned.

The tall man took his payment and slipped off a battered boot to briefly display a bony grime-edged ankle before he hid the money beneath his foot without looking at it, he was so busily eyeing Susannah. As he pulled on the boot again, he laughed.

"Good sport here," he said to his companions, who were counting over their money. "I tole you she never knew Lion, lying bitch."

"Oh, Lion," Lord Moredon said, pausing as he was leaving the room. "Oh good. Yes. I'd forgot. I'll have my joke on him too. Be sure I'll tell him of your fate, little trollop, I think I'll even have your demise laid at his door. Literally," he said thoughtfully. "Deliver her to the Lion's door when you're done," he said lightly, as he started to leave once again. "That will be amusing, yes."

The tall man stopped in his tracks as he approached Susannah. His hand had been reaching out to her. She would, she thought, remember that cadaverous, filthy hand in all her nightmares forever, but at Lord Moredon's words, he lowered it.

"Lion knows her?" he asked, even as the fat man stopped counting his money and swerved around, crying, "He knows her and you want us to lay her corpse on him?" and the thin man visibly shook as he asked slowly, for it seemed he thought that way, "The beautiful lady is a friend to Lion 'isself?"

"If either one can be called friend," Lord Moredon scoffed. "But what matter?"

"But, your lordship—" the tall man began, as the gentleman wheeled round and stared at him.

"I have paid good money, in good faith, I want my will done," Lord Moredon said coldly, slapping a tattoo with the glove he carried against his palm, his eyes wide with anger.

"Oh, never fear, never fear, your lordship, your will be done, all right and tight, never fear," the fat man babbled, stepping down hard on the tall man's toe, before he walked the mollified gentleman to the door, continually murmuring, "Never fear," even after Lord Moredon's footsteps had stopped echoing on the stair. Then he came back into the room and sighed heavily, looking at his two companions.

"He's a crackbrain," he said, "mad, entirely. Bedlam-ripe. But he can make trouble. The Lion can make more."

"I don't want nothin' to do with the Lion, I don't," the thin man keened, shuffling his feet. "I din't know this 'ad to do with Lion. You never tole me," he accused the other sullenly.

"I didn't know. But I suppose that's why we got the hire," the fat man said sorrowfully, "it's likely no one else would take it, that does make a certain sad sense to me. So, since we can't take a step right, we'd best take none at all, except in the direction of the door. I suggest we take the money and leave the premises, and don't come back until this is all history."

"Oh, good, thankee, Nipper," the thin man breathed.

"Well then," the fat man said happily, "that's it, deeply regret your inconvenience, my lady, be pleased if in all charity you'd forget the incident, and the name my friend let slip, and we'll be done with this. Good day to you."

He turned and put his arm about the thin man and they went to the door, but then he stopped and looked back.

"I want her," the tall man said, staring fixedly at Susannah, "whatever. You go on, it don't matter to me."

"But, dear fellow," the fat man said nervously, "it is known that we are comrades. Even the rats in the walls in this hovel tell tales. It is known that we snatched the young lady. We shall be judged as one and the Lion will be very angry with us all."

"Let him. I can hide out after having her, or afore. Might as well have her then, eh? I won't kill her, 'cept with happiness," he laughed.

Susannah tensed. She knew no words would stop this man, and had no other weapons, but vowed she'd fight until he had to kill her. But as he smiled and swaggered toward her pulling at his makeshift belt, the thin man came up behind him, extracted a weighted bag from his floppy sleeve, and with no more fuss than a man putting out a lamp, swung the bag down at the base of the tall man's neck and sent him crashing to the floor. Then he carefully replaced the bag, bent, picked up the tall man's ankles, and began to drag him to the door.

"Impetuous. Foolish," the fat man said, shaking his head, staring down at the unconscious man. "The cosh was the only remedy for it. Not that you're not lovely," he said hastily, "but our respect for the Lion surpasseth beauty. Tell him that, please. Good afternoon," he said, bowing as he ducked out the door to the stair.

It was a long time after the sound the tall man's head made as it bumped down the stairs had faded, and a long while after the muffled curses of his friends' bearing up under his weight as they carried him from the alley were stilled before Susannah dared to move at last. And then she ran.

After she'd fled down three ragged streets, she paused, winded, her exhaustion finally allowing her brain to get control of her feet again. She realized, as she gasped for breath, that not only was it idiocy to run when there was no longer anyone to run from, it made no sense at all to run when one didn't know where to run to. She paused against a wall and tried to reclaim all her higher reasoning from whatever dark recesses it had scurried into when sheer terror had sent her winging out into the streets.

She had no idea of where she was, but had little doubt that it wasn't the sort of place she'd ever drive through, much less venture on foot, alone. Looking about at the deserted crumbling buildings crowded close to the filthy streets and scenting the ripe odors the wind blew to her nose, the purest of which was garbage, she realized she was a very long way from home. But, she decided, she'd had enough of fear for one day. She'd have to make do with her wit. It was her only remaining asset anyway, she discovered. Her portmanteau had gone with the carriage. And not only would it take a major modern miracle to get her to retrace her steps to the vile place where she'd been held captive, even though she hadn't thought to look when she fled it, she very much doubted if her reticule or anything in her purse had been left for her use. She'd been freed, but was certain her money had been redistributed the moment she'd been taken captive.

It was then impossible to get back to Greenwood Hall straightaway, even if she found a way out of this maze of hideous streets. And all her friends were there, or en route back there by now. Dear Charlie was, of course, even further from her. And she knew no other soul in London. And night was coming on. She almost wept then. But she looked up to see that she'd attracted some attention, and a thievish, dangerous-looking boy was eyeing her with considerable interest. Then she remembered that, of course, there was someone she knew. So she walked up to the boy, alarming him considerably, for he'd thought that if she were in her right mind she'd be picking up her skirts and running in the opposite direction. Even as he backed away from the madwoman, hoping none of his friends could see him now, she asked, as politely as she was able:

"Excuse me, young man, but can you tell me where the gentleman called Lion lives?"

Everyone, Susannah thought wearily, as she dragged down increasingly dark streets, knew the Lion. No one, however, wanted a word with her after she inquired after him. In one way she was glad of it, for she'd encountered a great many unsavory people in the last hours, from outright bad men and wicked women who'd tried to buy or menace her until she'd held up that one name, which like a flaming sword dispersed them—to the miracle of a shabby one-legged beggar who sprouted another leg to run with at the mention of that dread name—to one sweet, kindly older woman who had looked as misplaced as herself in these mean streets. The woman had appeared like a comforting angel from out of a handsome coach to offer her tea and charity, but then looked as if she were about to have a heart spasm when the Lion's name was brought into Susannah's grateful acceptance speech. The last Susannah saw of her was her back as she popped right back into her carriage. Tealess and terrified, Susannah then realized that however kindly the old dame had been, she must have actually been the living embodiment of what she'd always thought was a fabulous creature, talked about in girls' schools only in the night in whispered cautionary tales: one of the infamous females like the notorious Mother Carey or Madame Felice, who dealt in other females' services and resorted to kidnapping new employees right off the streets themselves now and again.

She'd almost decided that the Lion himself was a fabulous beast, and had paused to inspect a slipper to see if it had any sole left at all, when she heard a hoarse voice whisper:

"If you be lookin' for Lion, foller me, miss."

The ragged man was thin and shifty, for one horrid moment Susannah though he might be her erstwhile captor, but this man was thinner, and even more nervous. She hesitated only a second, and then decided that since the Lion's name had frightened men twice this man's size and twice his number, he was scarcely likely to defy him and mislead her. Anyway, she was weary. And she really had little choice, she thought as she followed him.

But when she finally came to the neat house he led her to on a better street than she'd been traveling, she entered it and after she'd passed the muster of a series of grim guards, she found herself in a spacious, cheerful, comfortable set of rooms. And there in the center, ensconced in a huge leather chair, looking as ruddy and cheerful as the firelight reflecting on his wide, craggy, smiling face, was the most welcome sight she'd seen all day.

"Oh, Lion," she sighed, her eyes filling with a mist of

happy tears, "how glad I am to see you. I've been searching for you everywhere."

"Yes, so I understand, Miss Logan. I am flattered, believe me. Now, what is your pleasure, beautiful lady, or is it," he asked, beaming, as he arose, "the same as mine? I devoutly hope so," he said enthusiastically as he approached near enough for her to see how largely he leered, "for that would save me a great deal of trouble tonight."

At that, Susannah did the first ladylike thing she'd done all during the long, distressing day, although she hadn't planned to. She crumpled, exceedingly gracefully, and fainted away at his feet.

19

"The trouble with females," the Lion grumbled, "is that they've no senses of humor. If Eve had laughed in the serpent's face, what a happier place this miserable old world would be."

"The serpent," Susannah replied from the depths of her mug, "was a male."

"Exactly," the Lion said, giving her an approving glance to cover the smile he'd almost given way to. "How was he to know the silly wench didn't have an ounce of humor in her body—it comes with the original rib, you know—and so couldn't appreciate his jest?"

"Genesis according to St. Lion. Interesting," Susannah commented as she put the tankard down and settled back in her chair. She yawned and then asked, all at once, sitting bolt upright and staring at him, "Whatever was in there, Lion? Are you trying to make me bosky?"

"It's only enough rum for a mouse to paddle his toes in, the rest's all juices. I wouldn't dare toy with you," he said smoothly, "for if Mr. Jones didn't come for my skin immediately after, with the handsome viscount tripping over him to get to me first, then you'd be sure to do the job for them."

"You quake," Susannah observed wryly, settling back again.

"In a way, my dear, I do," he answered, gazing at her reflectively.

She knew it for a compliment, and found that she couldn't jest at that. It hadn't been very long since she'd come back to consciousness, the Lion chafing her wrists, and damning himself under his breath three times over. Then he'd ordered one of his men to get her a mug of something bracing as he settled her in a chair to hear her story. She'd told it briefly, as it wasn't a thing she wished to linger on, and he'd frowned. Then he'd called for another man he'd whispered something to, even as he hastily scrawled out something on a sheet of paper. Whatever he was about, Susannah felt secure in the knowledge that it would all be to her benefit, and so she could relax for the first time since morning, content and safe and grateful to be in the company of the greatest villain in London.

"You'll send to Gloucestershire for Warwick?" she murmured groggily, all the frights and diversions of the long day interacting with the mouse's jot of rum to make her pleasantly sleepy.

"No need," Lion answered briefly, as he sanded another note and handed it to another minion. "It goes to his London address. If I know my man, if he's not there at this moment he'll doubtless be there before long."

She nodded, trusting herself to him completely, and he smiled at her bravery as he gazed at her. He was amused at her faith in him and very impressed with her courage at the hands of Lord Moredon's hirelings. He knew few women, and no ladies, who would have kept their heads so well. But then, in both instances, although he didn't mean to demean it, any more than he'd ever tell her of it, he wondered how much of that courage came from ignorance.

Could she know, for example, that in this part of the city she was far more than delicious-looking, she was a profitable piece for anyone to get his hands on in any sense? Fair, shapely, and beautiful, there wasn't a part of her that couldn't be sold or enjoyed, from her lovely body to the clothes that covered it, from her masses of bright hair to the slippers on her feet. In a world where there were those who scratched out brief existences by every low means known to man—from selling the teeth from a dead man's mouth, to creating him— even her lifeless form could be used for profit, provided one knew where to sell it. Only her cleverness, wit, and courage were worthless, extraneous to the matter, except to herself and those who loved her, like the song of a lark meant to be prepared in a pie.

"I was startled, that's why I behaved so badly," she suddenly said reflectively, although he'd thought she was done with that. But she'd been so brief in her account of her travails that he'd known she'd come out with more when she'd recovered herself further, so he sat and listened, being a man who knew there was always some profit in listening closely.

"Lord Moredon said the worst things, I won't repeat them, those I understood were too awful to mention, those I didn't, I think I didn't want to. He hates Warwick and Julian so much he only wanted to harm me to harm them. Can it be that such hatred can turn a man's mind?" she wondered aloud.

"Aye, that, and reverses on the 'change. Yes," Lion said, "it's true enough, though it's been kept close. I think he himself doesn't want to believe it, but the baron's been losing his fortune at the same rate his wits have been going. Now, what's a toplofty gent like that to do when he sees all his funds slipping away? Not every nobleman's as daring as your viscount, willing to soil his hands with work to keep body and soul together. Some turn to selling off family treasures, sisters included," he added dryly, "some sell themselves in marriage, some turn to gaming, some find that all those things won't help, perhaps that's what turns their wits. A few swallow their pride and leave the country, a few try to swallow their pistols when they get to point *non plus*, and some, like our friend Moredon, find other ways to escape the reality of their predicament.

"Added to which, his dear sister was defying him, and at that, with someone who'd always troubled him, and then Warwick Jones trounced him soundly in front of all his world. That turned the trick nicely, I think."

Susannah sat very quietly, digesting all the new information. She almost felt sorry for Lord Moredon, until she remembered his eyes, his touch, and his words. Remembering those words precisely now, she sat up straight.

"Did I tell you?" she asked excitedly. "He was going on about 'the Highwayman riding again' and 'all the king's men looking for Gentleman Jones's ghost' so that Julian should take care because he drove a coach? He found it funny, but it didn't make sense to me. Has he gone so far that he makes no more sense? Perhaps then they'll see how badly off he is and put him away before he can do further harm.''

"No," Lion said thoughtfully, rising and pacing, "no, there is, as the fellow said, method to his madness. It's a cold, calculating mind that's been turned. He knows what he's about well enough, too well, in fact. How else do you think he knew enough to get your protectors away, and lure you to London? Mr. Jones's uncle was sick, true enough, he died the other day, you know," he commented, pausing in his pacing to note her surprise, and nodded as he continued, "but I'll eat your best flowered bonnet if the viscount had a real invitation from the coaching company, and have a pair of your gloves on the side with it, if your contessa has any inheritance coming to her this side of the grave. No, he must have had a spy in Brighton, a kitchen wench or a stableboy, it doesn't take skill, anything with ears and an open palm will do for such. I know he's been paying what little's left of his coin for information all over the kingdom. He believes settling with your two gentlemen will settle his own troubles, and so he'll spend every last shilling and effort to do it.''

It was late, the room was dim, she was weary, but something in the Lion's resumed steady pacing and thoughtful expression kept Susannah alert so that she might hear every word he uttered.

"The part about the highwayman's true enough," he said at length. "Some fool's trying to revive the trade on Hounslow Heath and sometimes Blindley Heath, but the outcome will be the same, only faster, than it was in the Gentleman's day. Bow Street's horse patrol's cleaned those places up, and the only good pickings to be had at the game are far up north now. But that bit about the viscount, ah," he sighed, "I don't understand it, or maybe I've gotten to be like you, and just don't want to.''

She watched him carefully. He was a burly, barrel-chested man but still he moved with certain natural bearlike grace. He was intimidating, in fact the aura of great power he emanated had concealed what she could see now that she believed herself to be his friend: which was that he wasn't an old man at all, and though his wasn't an easy face to read, he might actually not be too many years senior to her own gentlemen. He caught her looking at him, and grinned, with almost as effective a leer as he'd greeted her with this evening. But now she didn't fear him, though a sudden thought made her very fearful indeed.

"Lion . . ." she asked slowly then, hesitantly, and he sighed, dropping her a few inches in his estimation, wondering, from the way she'd dropped her gaze at the look he'd teased her with, if she was about to say something about how long she could stay with him unchaperoned. That would have occurred to her about now, he thought disgustedly, since with all her courage she was styled a lady, and she suddenly sounded unsure and fearful again.

"Lion," she asked soberly, raising grave eyes to him again, "do you think Lord Moredon can harm Warwick? And Julian? He thinks he can."

"He can," Lion agreed, pleased with how wrong he'd been about her question.

"How can such a man run tame in society?" she asked, shuddering.

"He can't, not really, not anymore. Eccentric and amusing behavior is acceptable, even admirable, but the man's gone too far, he'll present a problem to the *ton* now. He's too dangerous and disturbing to be let in polite company, but too noble to ignore, still too influential to be transported, and it's too embarrassing to trot him off to Bedlam just yet. In the end it'll be all pure profit for me; arranging a nice fatal accident for him will bring in a healthy sum. Ah yes, the Lion does have teeth, Miss Logan, don't look so shocked," he said coldly, annoyed at her sudden recoil and grimace of distaste. "With all my talents, I do occasionally act as a rubbish remover for society."

She put back her head and stared at him.

"The lion," she said, angrily, "does not deal in carrion. That is the jackal you're thinking of."

He tensed. The amused and tolerant expression left his face, letting her see the quick fury beneath. Seeing his reaction, she knew at once she'd done a foolish, thoughtless thing; there was good reason this man was so feared. But that wasn't all she saw. She'd cut him badly, and it had been selfish to do so, for it wasn't strictly his morality she protested. Her anger, she suddenly perceived, was more at herself than him. Because he'd never lied to her. She'd only been too much an idealist, or maybe just too much of a child, to want to believe that a man she could like and trust could kill for hire. It was never his fault she couldn't see him as he was because she needed her own comfortable illusions, it was never his fault, she then explained shamefacedly, that she hadn't been able to see that before her rash remark.

He shrugged off her apology, too amazed at the fact that her insult had stung to be angry with her, too astonished that her apology bothered him as well. However prettily put, it wasn't pleasant to know she wasn't angry at him for his crimes, as any decent woman should be, but because she'd been disappointed in her estimate of him. He was boggled, and didn't know if it was because it had been so long since any decent female had rated him high, or because it was that she now promised to rate him so low, and so he told her in his turn, laughing at himself to cover his astonishment at his own new estimation of her.

"You've changed, Miss Logan," he said with admiration. "This isn't the correct lady I met in Mr. Jones's drawing room."

"I know," she said sadly, deliberately misunderstanding. "Just look at my hair, my gown, I look a sad romp now. Abduction, imprisonment, and escape do nothing for one's looks," she said sadly, a little smile peeping out as he laughed with her.

"But what could have happened to you?" he persisted. "Mr. Jones is an extraordinary fellow, but no miracle-maker. And until recently the viscount was hotfooting it after his lady. I doubt it was the Sussex air, or I'd bottle it and make my fortune from the noble gentlemen that way, turning all their proper ladies into real women for them."

She tilted her head to one side, as someone she knew often did, taking his jest seriously, because she found she wasn't at all offended that he no longer termed her a lady.

"I think," she said, pondering deeply, before she grew a

look of amazement, finding the truth and then bringing it forth newborn, ". . . I think it is that I grew up."

"My dear Miss Logan," he said sincerely, "if you ever decide to give up respectability, I am yours, completely."

"Thank you," she said just as sincerely, "I'll keep it in mind."

"Then here's another thing to remember," he said seriously. "Keep your gentleman away from Lord Moredon. Dissuade him from seeking revenge. Go home and stay there, and keep him at your side until it's settled. Moredon's a madman, and that lends him more cunning and cleverness than even your gentleman has."

She didn't ask which gentleman he meant. Because a man like the Lion, she thought nervously, might very well know.

They would travel by night. It was a dangerous time to be on the road, and it would be slower going as well. But neither of them would sleep this night anyway, both were men of action and both found it equally unthinkable that they should go to their beds while Susannah was missing, while she might be in danger, and while their lovely little friend, as they both thought, but neither dared say, might already be beyond their help.

Their only disagreement was as to their mode of travel. In the end Julian prevailed through logic and the press of circumstance. For it was an overcast night, just as he pointed out, and so the moon and stars wouldn't show their mounts the byways as quickly as a coach could be driven up the Brighton Road by someone who was well used to it. By someone who, as Julian argued, knew the road back and forth from its least gully to its worst turn, having driven it so often, drunk and sober, day and night, that he could do it in his sleep.

But sleep was the last thing from both gentlemen's minds as they rode through the opaque night, the carriage lamps fore and aft the only illumination on the road, the steady beat and jingle of the horses' hooves and harnesses, the creaking of the coach, and the occasional snap of a pebble thrown as the wheels spun over it, the only manmade sounds in the deep cricket-filled summer dark. Until Julian spoke.

"There's no sense springing the cattle, you know," he explained defensively after many miles of silent concentration on his driving, although his companion on the high hard coachman's seat hadn't spoken a word. "That's all flourish, done for an extra coin from the topside passengers, impressive, but to no avail, and no good coachman will do it unless he needs the money badly. They're only animals, and they only have so much in them, and what you take out now for a burst of speed you'll lose later in the long run. I suppose if you could change teams every five miles there might be a point to it, but then there's the changing that would eat up time. No, springing them is all show and no go, so don't fret, Warwick, we're going as fast as we can even though we're not racing to the wire."

"Never have I seen such horsemanship, my boy," Warwick said gently. "My silence came from the depths of my admiration, not vexation, believe me. There's no way we could get to London town faster tonight, and I'm grateful for your expertise, don't doubt it."

They drove on in silence, and then in concert they turned and looked at each other as best they could in the swaying, wavering yellow glow of the carriage lamps, and then they both laughed for the first time since they'd been handed the note when they'd arrived at Greenwood Hall that afternoon.

"Very nicely done," Warwick agreed. "You reassured me, I complimented you, and we're both comforted. But there's truth to it, Julian. There's good in it as well, since there's nothing else we can do but keep each other's spirits up just now. I'll confess I don't remember when I ever felt so helpless," he said with barely suppressed agitation, "so much at a loss, or so much at the mercy of time. And I don't like to be at anyone or anything's mercy. I realize I've never been. It's a new sensation, and so much as I've sought novelty all my life, I don't think I care for this particular feeling in the least."

"It's what you get for loving people, Warwick," Julian said, turning his attention to the leaders of his teams just then, and so missing the sudden grimace of surprise his words caused his friend to make, "but I'm glad you care for Susannah so much, you're a close fellow and I know you don't take up with many people. I'd hate to think you disliked the one woman I intend to spend the rest of my life with.''

"One?" Warwick said in more normal, aloof tones. "Dear Julian, last week you were ready to open a vein for the sake of your lady's smile, now you plight eternal love for little Sukey? Who shall it be next week, I wonder.''

"Susannah and Susannah and Susannah,'' Julian replied calmly.

"And all your yesterdays have lighted you the way to loving her?" Warwick misquoted coolly. "I wonder.''

"Have you never loved?" Julian demanded angrily, "that you mock me for finding it?"

"Patience," Warwick sighed, "I only jest because you find it so very often, my friend. And it's a wonderment to me. I'd caution you to take care of where you next place your heart, or if not care, then at least careful counsel before you do.''

"Why, there's your problem," Julian retorted, "you take too much counsel. Love's not a dry, debatable thing, it's not a thing you can reason out or decide intelligently.''

"There's where you're out," his friend argued wearily, "unlike impulse and infatuation, if there's no rhyme or reason to it, then it's never love at all.''

"Going to give me lessons about love, Warwick?" Julian asked icily.

"I'd sooner give the cat lessons in how to make kittens," his friend sighed. "I'm only attempting to make conversation, it's a long night.''

"It won't be much longer," Julian promised, slowing the coach as he took a bend in the road, for the lamps lit only an immediate path and what lay beyond each drastic turn was as secret as the dreaming night itself, "but I'm glad you care for her, for all that you hadn't any choice. Even a flint-hearted curmudgeon such as you can't resist her. But who could?"

"Who, indeed?" Warwick said softly.

Then they fell silent again as Julian guided them on, concentrating to the point where he began to believe that he was feeling his way along the road with his leaders' own hooves, and Warwick did everything he could as well to prevent thinking about what had happened to the young woman no one could resist.

There were four main roads to London; Julian took the new one most of the way, cutting over when he could to his old coach run when he thought inquiries might bear results, despite the time wasted for the diversion from the fastest route. The sleepy ostlers at the King's Head regretted they hadn't seen any spectacularly beautiful blond young lady passengers that day, and neither had anyone at the Goat and Compass or the Crown, the Maiden's Head or the Castle, though many remembered and had a greeting for the handsome viscount-coachman. But some old acquaintances of his at the Silver Swan recalled spying her briefly—''Who could forget such a stunner?'' a stableboy breathed in wondering memory. And so then they were off again without a pause for a drink or a reminiscence or a handshake with anyone there, or even a word for the serving wench who pelted pell-mell from out the kitchens when she heard of their arrival, and was just in time to see them go.

And then, at last, when they came to the Crimson Cat, they found Millie, still basking in the taproom in the sudden celebrity she'd achieved with her tale of abandonment and abduction. They swept her up with them and drove away with her so quickly, that for all that she'd seemed to know them, it almost appeared to all the envious servant girls that the lucky mort was being snatched all over again, but this time by two amazing handsome knaves.

Warwick joined Julian on the high driver's seat again when they stopped at the last toll before London. He'd left Millie in the coach in the care of Mr. Epford, the valet having insisted on accompanying them with such violence of feeling that they'd let him, if only to prevent his hanging onto the back of the coach along with the stout footman they'd taken to ride guard.

''She was taken by hired help,'' Warwick reported, ''and bad sorts, at that.'' To Julian's sudden look of puzzlement, he added unhappily, ''A rogue's a rogue, but a professional one does his job and nothing else. And I'd rather she fell into that sort of hands than those of some riffraff hiring out for mischief or from desperation, for they don't know what they're about and don't care about their reputation. Of course, there's honor among thieves.'' He laughed bitterly at his friend's surprise. "Men of any worth are proud of their name and skill in any line of work. Just look at the Lion. And I shall do that," he vowed, "as soon as we get to London. So we'll divide it, each to his own level: I'll track our Lion in the lower regions; you, Julian, will prowl the more fashionable watering holes to seek out Lord Moredon's direction."

"Be sure I shall," Julian said grimly.

"No, no, only seek it out," Warwick insisted, his voice deadly serious. "You must swear to me 'pon honor to do nothing else about it until we meet and compare information, or else we'll confound each other and not him."

He continued to caution his friend until as the coach rattled down through the familiar streets of town, he got his promise on it at last.

"Past midnight. Good. Neither of us will be hindered by the hour," Warwick announced, taking out his watch as they came to his own street, "since neither the lowest nor the highest in the land sleeps at the height of the night. One plays, the other preys on them, and as to which is which of them," he sighed sadly, "it would take a wiser man than I to know."

They were puzzled when they saw that the town house was glowing with light as they approached it, and pleased but surprised to find a stableboy ready to receive the dusty coach and horses from them. Before Warwick could raise the knocker to his door, Mr. Fox swung it open wide for him. Mr. Epford delivered Millie to the care of Cook, and Julian was about to take the stair to find a change of clothes in his old room so that he might scour the better clubs and gaming hells in proper attire, when he heard Warwick, in a peculiar tone of voice, sweetly inquire of his butler as to how he'd been so prepared for their arrival. As he'd been wondering the same thing, he paused to hear the reply.

"No message could have arrived from Brighton faster than we did, or have you developed new powers of observation? I'll hire you out for the Hungerford Fair and make our fortunes with your telling fortunes if you predicted it from a dream, but then how else could you know, Mr. Fox?"

The voice was idle, amused, but his master's face was not,

and yet Mr. Fox was not insulted, for he knew that his employer was a suspicious man and had good reason to be.

"This note came for you this evening, sir, and the singular person who entrusted it to me instructed me to hand it to you the moment you arrived. He seemed to expect you momentarily," the butler explained, more pleased by the obvious correctness of his decision to believe the shabby fellow who'd delivered the message than by his employer's absently muttered apologies as he took the note and scanned it anxiously.

Warwick smiled a thin smile and handed the paper to Julian, who stood arrested, with one foot on the stair.

"My dear friend Mr. Jones (if it is still correct for me to style you so)," Julian read aloud, "It may interest you to know I have in my care one prime article recently lost, strayed, and stolen. I hadn't thought you would be so careless, sir. But if you're interested in recovering this piece of goods, please come at once, day or night, to the southeast corner of Gray Eagle Street betwixt Spitalfields and Shoreditch, and wait upon events. Your most obedient servant, Mr. Brian McCulley Tryon."

As Julian looked to his friend, momentarily perplexed, Warwick grinned at last, and said with real relief and some small annoyance, "Two rhymes, I suppose, for emphasis, or luck. Lion, of course, it's our charming Lion."

After the usual trip down false alleys and around blind streets, a passage of time made bearable by the thought of the outcome, and unbearable by it as well, Warwick and Julian were told to leave their coach in a cobbled courtyard behind what appeared to be a decent-looking house. Then, again following the thin man they'd come to recognize as a harbinger of the man they sought, they went into the house. They were admitted to a tasteful study, where a beaming, sleepy-looking Lion, resplendent in a silken dressing gown, greeted them as hugely as if they were his lost brothers and not two grim, dust-covered, bone-weary gentlemen.

"How good to see you, Mr. Jones, my dear friend," he said, smiling hugely and putting out his hand. "Or," he asked in sudden coy alarm, "ought I, may I, still call you that?"

Warwick took his hand. "For now I'd much prefer it, Lion," he sighed, his voice slurring with his exhaustion and anxiety, "but damn your hide, is there nothing you don't know? Where is she?"

"How gracious," Lion said with pleasure, extending his hand to Julian then. "My lord, well met, how do you go on?"

But when Julian only looked hard at him, the Lion dropped his air of bright conviviality.

"Oh, put up your swords," he said in an altered voice, gesturing for them to take chairs as he sat down, "she's well, she's fine, in fact. Untouched, if that's what's concerning you. It concerned me as well, and I promise I didn't alter that happy state. She's safe, upstairs, I just talked her to bed, and now I suppose since I've sent word, she's waking and primping so you can take her back again. Pull in your tender sensibilities, gentlemen, it's all in order, as much as it can be. It's my Sally sharing her bed tonight, as much to protect her from me as it is to protect me from the temptation of her charms, because if I so much as glance at her cross-eyed, Sally will have my liver on a skewer. And not for Miss Logan's sake. A possessive chit, my Sally, not a moral one," he explained.

"Lord Moredon had her," he said harshly, unsettling his recently calmed visitors as he changed his tone with his topic, as he often did. "Or rather, I'm pleased to report he didn't. That she escaped is all due to her wit and courage. She's an admirable creature. But Moredon's completely mad now. Take her home, gentlemen, and don't let her out of your sight. As to that, don't let each other out of your sight. He means mischief, and it's not clear what it's to be. But he was babbling about that poor idiot who's riding the high toby on the Brighton and Bath roads again, and he ranted on about your ancestor, Mr. Jones, and your fate as a coachman, Viscount. I don't know what it all means, whether it's slander or accusation for other crimes he's got in what's left of his mind, but if I were you I wouldn't like any of it. For all I've just welcomed you to London, I'd advise you to leave it now, and stay away. London's a wonderful city. It's easy to buy anything you want here. Especially revenge.

"As to that," Lion said, stretching luxuriously, "his three handpicked helpers are my meat, gentlemen, forget them, they're no longer in the game. Don't pity them neither," he said coldly, as he saw the viscount's involuntary expression of distaste, "as Miss Logan does. She's all full of excuses for two of them because they aided her by coshing the fellow who wanted to sample her on the spot."

Now Lion seemed to be having some deliberate sport as he watched the viscount's ashen face for reaction, as he added:

"I didn't enlighten her, your lordship, because I'm a kindly man, but it's clear it was only healthy respect for your obedient that caused their courtly gesture. The chipper fattish one she described is notorious for liking the ladies in diverse ways, and the other, the silent respectful slow-witted one she championed to me, is quick enough when it comes to females, and well-known for especially liking those who don't care for him."

"Is there any other sort of diversion you enjoy, Lion, bull or bear baiting, perhaps? Have you any other hobbies, I wonder," Warwick asked easily, and as the man he addressed turned his head, he went on smoothly, "aside from rescuing fair damsels and tormenting their admirers, that is?"

"Well put, sir," the Lion replied with amusement. "You note that I do like to have my little sport with the quality. But well taken too, and I'll leave off, since the viscount doesn't disdain so much as he don't understand me."

"Ah, but who could ken the workings of that labyrinthian mind?" Warwick asked, as Julian interrupted him to say stiffly:

"I'm grateful for your intervention, Lion, again, although I don't understand it either."

"My father was the fifth son of an earl, and though I grew up in poverty, he drilled an outsize respect for my betters into my head," Lion confessed sadly.

"What a crowded orphanage the good fathers ran," Warwick marveled, "that they had room for your dear mother, your father, and, no doubt, for your old gran as well."

"Yes," the Lion said happily, "it was cozy."

But their banter was cut off when Warwick looked up and saw Susannah as she entered the room. Her gown was crumpled, her glorious hair in sad disarray, her face pale and still sleep-fogged, but so filled with gladness that even Warwick's thin, melancholy features lit with a reflection of her joyousness as he rose to his feet and stared at her. But Julian arose as well, and his fair face glowed with happiness, and being nearer as well as less constrained, he stepped forward and closed her in his arms and hugged her hard in greeting.

Warwick stood and stared at their glad reunion, and Lion watched as well, but it was never Miss Logan and the viscount he studied so intently. When Susannah stepped from Julian's embrace she came forward to give her hand to Warwick. He took it gravely and gazed into her face, and what he saw there made him nod and he said only:

"You relieve my mind, Susannah. I'll not let you come to harm again, I promise."

"I didn't come to harm," she corrected him, "but thank you for coming for me."

"Oh well, it was tedious," Warwick said lightly, "but we'd nothing better to do, true, Julian?"

"Very easy for you to say," Julian answered peevishly, taking his cue. "I had a good seat at a hazard table myself."

When they'd done laughing, Lion complained:

"Ah, the quality think they're the only ones who had sport spoiled this night. I missed a good ratting and a cockfight. Well," he said innocently, "falconing's passé, and there's seldom cricket matches hereabout. The hunting, however," he said slyly, "is always in season."

On that somber note Warwick ordered Susannah to the coach, after looking at his watch and exclaiming in horror at the hour.

"I want you home and asleep within minutes of getting there," he said sternly, "for like it or not, you've had enough of London's nightlife for a while, and we're going back to Greenwood Hall tomorrow."

But she only smiled at him and they shook hands all around, and Julian gave her his arm and led her out to the coach.

The Lion stayed Warwick with one touch of a finger.

"We were talking of your family, the little lady and I," he said, and as Warwick's heavily lidded eyes opened in alarm, he added at once, "Only your ancestor that swung for his sins, that is. I tell no tales you've omitted to tell, reasoning that as a reasonable gentleman you've some good reason for whatever you do, or don't.''

"Thank you, it's early days yet, and I choose to pick my time for revelation, true. But there's nothing you don't know, is that the point?'' Warwick asked carefully.

"No point to it at all,'' Lion answered thoughtfully, "except to let you know that I've never held a female in higher esteem, for all that she's too tender a heart. She had tears in her eyes when we spoke of Gentleman Jones's sad fate, and so I told her she'd never have suited that antique gent. To divert her from sentiment and acquaint her with reality—for there's nothing romantic about a hanging, nor should a man's hard death be taken lightly even after a century—I let her know that sometimes the bravest bad fellow to walk out on the air at jack Ketch's prodding won't drop down quick enough to eJnd it clean. That's when he expects his loving lass to help him by helping him into eternity the faster. I told her that what he needed most then wasn't tears or a fine lady to hang on his arm, but a female who loved him enough to jump up and pull on his legs as he dangled on the end of his rope in the sheriff's picture frame, so that he wouldn't be all day dying. And she, I said, was clearly too much the lady to have done it for him. The diversion worked. Because she agreed. Not a tear in sight. She was in a fine rage instead, and said she'd have jumped all right, but it would have been the hangman's legs she'd have gone for.''

The ginger-haired man roared with laughter before he subsided and said seriously, "Oh, Mr. Jones, do you know what a treasure she is? I myself offered for her, in a joke. But if she'd have said yes, there'd have been no joke about it. 'Struth, a man ought to aspire to such a female.''

"Indeed,''Warwick answered softly, "my friend Hazelton is a lucky man.''

"Ah yes,'' the Lion replied, his eyes growing distant, suddenly bored, suddenly too weary to speak any longer, as he yawned a farewell to his guest. "Yes, sir, if that's the way of it, good night and good-bye and much luck to you.''

It was a good night for most of them, since weariness brought sleep to everyone in the Jones town house almost as soon as they laid their heads down upon their pillows. But although Susannah sank into the familiar bed with a heartfelt sigh of gratitude, her sleep was uneasy, clogged with bits and pieces of odd, unresolved themes. She dreamed of highwaymen and hangings, and wakened from sleep only to fall back to be menaced by lions and leering madmen, and cried out once in the night before she turned on her pillow to dream of lords and ladies, and then at last found herself lost in a sweet embrace she didn't want to wake from, until she did, only to find herself alone, staring into the dreaming night, weeping, bereft of terrors as well as love.

So of course she was hollow-eyed and subdued the next day, giving Julian a good-morning in the same sad voice she gave Warwick her condolences in. They were so understanding that she wanted to weep again, for they never knew it was her own teeming brain that had frightened her from her rest, and not the memory of her dangerous adventure.

They left London after a light luncheon, after Warwick had left all sorts of instructions for a great many persons, including the absent contessa, should she ever admit her folly in leaving her charge so precipitately and return to them again. Mr. Epford had gone on ahead to prepare Greenwood Hall for their arrival, and Warwick sat with Julian again as the coach returned the way it had so lately traveled. Susannah shared the interior of the coach with Millie, and as the maidservant was not one to miss out on her rest, she deserted her mistress in sleep as soon as the coach wheels began turning. Yet though Susannah was so tired it seemed to her that she was moving in a haze as she headed back to Brighton, she sat awake and tried to face her phantoms, so that she wouldn't doze off and have to face them that way again.

It was after a stop on the long deserted road down from Blindley Heath that the coach door opened and Warwick joined her. He looked at her exhausted face and almost left her again, with advice that she should sleep, but she begged him to come in and keep her company. When he entered the coach he asked her straightaway about her weariness, and too weary to dissemble, she admitted to her crazy-quilt night of dreams. He nodded, as though he understood her very well, and then, pointing out the dozing Millie, and claiming in a whisper that their friendship transcended propriety, he began to extoll the benefits of his shoulder as a pillow. He'd gotten around to vowing that his left shoulder had actually been written up in a learned scientific journal for the amazing soporific qualities it possessed, when she submitted on a low chuckle and laid her head against him and closed her eyes at last, feeling, if not precisely safe, then at least comforted, at last.

Yet as the coach rolled on, her eyelids rolled up. She couldn't sleep. She was too acutely aware of where she was. His shoulder was hard and wide and reassuringly firm, and the velvet jacket she laid her cheek against was soft, yet she couldn't ignore the fact this was a breathing pillow she rested against, and she breathed in the slight spice of the woodsy fragrance she associated with him with every breath she drew. She found herself wondering what his expression was, what he was looking at now. She soon found that being close to Warwick prevented the relaxation she'd expected, and she was about to raise her head when she thought, in some confusion, that she was only dreaming that she was about to raise her head from that shoulder.

It took a second more before she was entirely sure that what she had heard was real and not another of the disjointed dreams claiming her once more. But the pistol shot was clear and loud enough to rouse the dead and shake off any fantasy. Yet the words she heard next were the very stuff of her nightmares.

For: "Stand and deliver," the voice called out, as cold as truth, as fantastic as a dream.

20

The coach halted on a stretch of the dusty country road just where some ancient oaks touched branches above it to give shade to what went on beneath them, and just where the land otherwise stretched away to endless heath after that one verdant pause, giving a clean sight line to whatever else passed up or down the road. It was an excellent place for a highwayman to ply his trade, it had always been so. Gentleman Jones himself had been hanged and gibbeted on a high branch of one of the ancient oaks to commemorate his favorite haunt. But the grisly crop the tree had borne didn't seem to discourage the two men who sat astride their horses beneath it, pistols at the ready, waiting for the passengers to step out and deliver all their goods into their hands, as ordered.

Susannah watched in dreaming wonder, the thought of what was happening too fresh and incredible to be terrifying as yet, even though she'd heard a shout and a scuffle soon after the voice had called out. She gazed in silent wonderment, not fully comprehending, as Warwick reached for a pistol he'd concealed in a pocket in the side door. But then, as though the walls of the coach were glass, she heard the same voice command from without:

"I hold a primed pistol at the ready, so pray cast yours out on the ground before you set a foot out the door. Otherwise, the weapon aimed at the jolly coachman goes off even as you go out. Fair enough, sir?"

Warwick was tight-lipped and his eyes blazed contempt but he threw the silver-handled weapon out the half-open window. As he rose, and bent to step out the door himself, the voice cried again, "Bravo! Encore, encore!" and after a pause, went on glibly, "I know there's more, my lord. You're too cautious a gentleman to trust to only one firearm. But I see. You've had a squabble with your handsome coachman. Ah, well then, where should you like me to give him his due: in the heart, or face, or have you some other preference? Ah!" the voice shouted in triumph as the second pistol followed the first, to hit the road in a small puff of dust. "Well done, your grace, how gracious. I await you. Come, come. I haven't all day."

"Stay here," Warwick commanded Susannah in an urgent whisper as he stepped out into the road.

She didn't move, since it was still the case that none of this had reality to her. It wasn't only the shock of it that made her doubt her senses, it was the fact that daylight highway robbery wasn't a thing one expected to meet up with any longer, at least not on any of the Brighton roads.

Traveling was no easy undertaking, a thousand bad things might happen on a long coach ride, the price paid for the modern luxury of speed was often too high: the horses could bolt, the carriage itself might tip over, axles could break, wheels could spin off to send one spinning off the road, accidents with other, reckless drivers were legion, there were floods and bridge-outages to worry over, but highwaymen, at least on these near roads from out of London, were now more a memory than a threat. The horse patrol Bow Street had established had chased them from their favorite haunts years before. Not only had they gone further afield, even their numbers had shrunk amazingly since the high days on the high toby, the days when such notorious bold rogues as the Cavalier Captain Stafford, the rapist Captain Howard, the ladies' joy and grief—courtly young Claude Duval, foolish Jack Sheppard, foppish Sixteen-string Jack, the legendary Dick Turpin, and Gentleman Jones himself—had prospered. These days such fellows were only the stuff of ballad and fable, and Susannah hadn't expected to encounter any of their sort, any more than she believed she'd ever meet up with any of the dragons and unicorns that she'd also been taught once had roamed her England.

Now Warwick Jones, descendant of one of the most famous of that ilk, stepped unarmed from out of his coach to face a modern man of the fraternity. But surely, Susannah thought, her confusion being dissipated by her feverish reasoning, surely this road pirate would accord Warwick the same courtesy those of the Spitalfields slums did upon hearing his name, if only for sentiment's sake, if only as a tribute to that odd kindred ancestry. Then she heard the highwayman's laughter as Warwick approached him, and then she knew there would be no honor of any sort in this, and certainly no mercy.

Nor was she surprised when the glad voice called again:

"Miss Logan, sweet slut, come out, come out, wherever you are," and above Warwick's imperative order of "No!" the voice sang, "Yes, I insist, or I'll kill them both first and then you, my dear. Don't you want to plead with me? Don't you care to beg me for favor? I might, I might relent, if asked sweetly enough. But you've no choice, Miss Logan. Cowering, you'll die cowering. Brave, you might yet brave it out. Come," he said approvingly, nodding as he sat his horse and watched with satisfaction as Susannah descended the coach's stair, head held high, "join the grand finale, Miss Logan, you and your maid both, yes, do."

He'd gotten a length of black silk and cut eyeholes in it, and wrapped it about the upper portion of his face. But it clung to his features, outlining them so there could be no mistaking his identity even if she were deaf and so couldn't recognize the variable, exultant voice, she thought, looking up to meet Lord Moredon's glittering eyes. He wore a greatcoat and a beaver hat, and his boots and linen and fine steed bespoke the gentleman. Even wearing his mask and with his pistol now aimed at Warwick's heart, he looked more like he was on the strut at a masquerade in Vauxhall than in all deadly earnest upon the deserted heath. His companion wore a stained bright handkerchief about his face, but the unkempt, ill-cut strawberry thatch of hair, his shabby garb, and his pied farmhorse made him seem a deliberate parody of his companion, like the satire that follows the tragedy at the theater. But there was nothing amusing in the way he kept his pistol pointed straight at Julian on the driver's seat.

The footman who'd ridden guard, Susannah noted with the first real jolt of horror she'd felt since the mad interruption of her journey had begun, lay senseless or dead in the road near the coach, the blood trickling from his forehead testimony to the blow which had felled him from his high perch. Millie, who'd crept out of the coach in her mistress's train, took one look at him and then fainted dead away in a heap on the ground.

"She's yours to dispose of when I'm done," Lord Moredon said negligently to his companion, before he turned his attention fully on the three remaining conscious members of the party.

"Oh, this is wonderful," Lord Moredon said with a great sigh of happiness. "The only problem I have is as to which of you I should remove from the world first. It is a question of consequences now," he said ruminatively.

"Speaking of consequences, the horse patrol guards this patch," Julian spoke up then, and though Susannah could swear she saw Lord Moredon's eyes flicker, he didn't look away from Warwick to answer him.

"Of course they do," he said in a harsh voice, "none know that better than I, Hazelton, I, who summoned them. Or rather, who warned them of the danger I might face on this road this afternoon. Danger from that rascal highwayman seeking to emulate Gentleman Jones upon this road these past weeks. Oh heavens," he said, smiling wolfishly, "just look, why, here he is, just as I paid him to be for all these weeks! Oh, wicked highwayman, spare me, do," he begged, pursing his lips to suppress his laughter, as the ragged redheaded youth grinned shyly at his mockery.

"My ancestor!" Warwick exclaimed, with what Susannah thought was, under the circumstances, unnatural calm, as he stood on the dusty road gazing up at the mounted man and raised one winged brow to signify his outsize astonishment. "Hardly. If that's your plan, Moredon, it's insufficient to the purpose. Only a blind man would see this fellow as even a poor copy of Gentleman Jones. Overlooking his rooster's crest, he's got all the airs of a barnyard, not a salon. A mask doth not a gentleman highwayman make. Best let us go our way, and rethink some more fitting prank."

"What cool composure," Lord Moredon caroled on a grin, "what a clever attempt. It should be even more amusing to see if you really regard death as a prank. As to resemblances, why, when a man sees death in the barrel of a pistol held to his head, he'll swear he's seen the devil himself behind it. Had I the time, I'd show you, I'd make you see whatever I chose before I cleared the world of another 'gentleman.' And never fear, this poor copy of your ancestor shall be the one blamed for it before he disappears from the scene, his most important role well done.

"The valiant men of the horse patrol will see only what he's accomplished when they ride by within a matter of hours to speed me safely along on my journey to Brighton, as I requested them to do, being such a nervous gentleman, you understand. Finding you dead, they'll regret they left it so late, as will I when I happen upon you even as they do, and then loudly lament your loss."

"This is a favorite coaching route," Julian said in a steady voice, "and five day coaches ply it. We'll not be alone long, Moredon."

"I know, and I've learned the schedules as well as you, Coachman, we've time yet, don't be so impatient to answer for your sins, I intend to get on with it," Lord Moredon replied testily. "It won't take long to kill you all, it's only taking me a bit to make up my mind, don't you see. You can't blame me for lingering over my sweet, can you? Rest easy, by the time I see dust in the distance, you too will be dust, golden youth. But in what sequence?" he asked himself, frowning.

"If I remove you first," he brooded aloud, "the pretty trollop will languish. She's been all eyes for you for weeks, it's been a famous joke in every drawing room, how the fishmonger's daughter yearns to catch herself a coachman."

Susannah took in her breath and lowered her eyes; to be on the brink of being destroyed was unbelievable enough, but to be told that the emotions one thought were so secret were common knowledge and the butt of common jests was another sort of death, surely.

"But then," Lord Moredon went on morosely, "the highwayman's proud heir might think he'd have an opportunity to comfort her then, and everyone knows that's what he's been after, yes, Hazelton, it's likely he's been warming her bed the moment you've gotten up from it, or so it would appear he aches to do, from his eyes.''

Warwick didn't move a muscle at that, he continued to gaze steadily at his tormentor, waiting for that one sidewise glance, that blink, that one flickering of his attention that might give him the opportunity to move. But all the while he stood straight and still, he writhed inwardly, wondering if it were true that it had been so easy for anyone to see where his heart lay, or if it were only true that the mad had certain heightened sensitivities and powers of observation beyond the range of the sane.

''And yet if I take him first, you'll think you have a free road to her and her funds, if not her body. That vexes me. I don't want you rejoicing, not for a second,'' he explained, as Julian stiffened, for though his fortunes had improved, his shallow pockets still weighed far too heavily on his mind, and the thought that Susannah might even for a second believe this madman touched him on the raw.

''But,'' Lord Moredon said gaily now, smiling, thrilled with his discovery, ''if I take her out first, you two will both suffer. Enormously. Not as much as I did with all the injury you did me, but enough. Yet, then,'' he said, crestfallen again, ''you two might think to console yourselves with each other as you doubtless did at school.''

''We were friends then, Moredon, only friends, even as we are now, and I think you know that. Whatever you might say now, you know that much at least,'' Warwick said flatly.

''Only that,'' Julian echoed. ''Whatever made you believe else?'' he asked, genuine puzzlement coloring his voice. ''For though we weren't precisely friends to you, we were never enemies of yours, Moredon, you know that.''

''You dare say that!'' Lord Moredon shouted, causing his horse to take a nervous step that made Warwick tense his muscles in readiness to spring. But then the masked nobleman quieted his voice and his mount, and leaning forward, he said in a hissing whisper, ''Always together, always laughing, always joking about things I was not supposed to know, lowering your voices when I came by, changing the subject when I walked past, the beautiful blond boy and the dark elegant youth slipping from out of each other's arms as I passed them by, pretending they didn't know how they tormented me with their words and their secrets, their faces and their bodies, never letting me in, never asking me in, I can't forget. And then after ignoring me, to attempt my sister? Not me, but only that simple whore, my beautiful noble sister?''

He paused. He had finally heard himself. A look of great dismay crossed over his face, clear even beneath the black silk mask. And then, not wishing to hear anything more, he acted, if only so that he wouldn't continue to hear that hateful voice so like his own issuing from his own mouth, saying such unspeakable things for him to hear. He raised his pistol to the level of Susannah's eyes.

"No more of this!'' he cried. "I won't hear any more. Do you think to unsteady me? Here, I'll take her down so smoothly, you'll see my hand don't even shake!''

And then Susannah could see no more.

Warwick took her shoulders in both hands and in an instant had spun her around and wrapped his arms around her to hold her fast against his heart, interposing his long back between herself and Lord Moredon so that whatever was aimed at her would have to pass through himself first before it could touch her. She could see nothing but his shoulder and the side of his face as he turned his head to see what was coming, even if it were only his ending. In that same instant, she heard a new harsh voice boom:

"Warwick Jones! Kinsman! To me!''

There was one moment of absolute silence. She looked to her left, even as all the others did, to see a huge black-clad gentleman upon a huge black horse, his many-caped cloak flowing over the saddle like a draped shadow, his high black hat and black mask concealing all his face, and his two gleaming silver pistols pointed straight ahead. Then there was deafening noise. All at once Susannah saw fire and blue smoke erupt from the pistols, but when she turned her head to see the source of the other thunder, she saw Julian standing on the driver's seat, a long carbine in his hands, spewing smoke, and turning yet again, she saw fumes rising from Lord Moredon's pistol too.

And then Lord Moredon, amazed and appalled, opened his mouth to protest, but only his life's blood issued forth and he fell from his saddle to the road.

The only other sound then was that of the hooves of the farmer-highwayman's mount as it turned tail, its rider bent low over the saddle urging it on, as it fled, ears flat back, off down a trail to the side of the road and on into the distance.

"You left it a little late," Warwick said coolly, but as he still held Susannah close, she could feel his heartbeat deny his poise.

"It was interesting. Better than a play. If I rode all this way and togged myself out in uncomfortable clothes—damme," Lion muttered, untying his mask, "I don't know how your ancestor bore it, a man could perish from the heat beneath one of these vile things—I think I deserved some sport."

Warwick seemed to recall how closely he held Susannah then and so he released her shoulders. Although he was reluctant to leave her, once he saw that she could stand unaided, he put her aside. Then, on legs he was surprised to find reacting to his possible extinction, as he'd not yet done, he strode to Lord Moredon, and with Julian, knelt beside the fallen man.

"No need to study him," Lion commented as he strolled up to them and looked down at the man they inspected, "unless you want to claim bounty. Then it would take some of my medical friends up in Scotland to take him apart well enough to see which of us it was that did him. My pistols made their point," he said, squinting down, "but I do believe that carbine answered the question. It would have done for the side of a barn. I'm all over admiration. Not exactly a dueling piece, my lord," he commented, looking at Julian, "but damned effective."

"A coachman," Julian answered, rising from his knees, "has no time for the niceties. I always keep a blunderbuss behind the seat. One never knows when a driver on the line might find a nice fallow deer, for instance, and a silver-handled pistol won't do him any good in the night, on the road, if that deer has mischief on his mind. But thank you for giving me the opportunity to use it. I might have been able to get him after he'd altered Warwick's jacket for him, but this way when you appeared all his attention was for you. Even I believed for a moment that Gentleman Jones had risen to avenge his great-grandson.''

"Yes, Lion," Warwick said, rising and looking at him curiously, "not that we're not grateful, and you may impersonate the Gentleman anytime you choose, although I do believe you've too much chest and not enough nose for it, though I certainly won't quibble about the results. But whatever caused your presence here today?"

"Ah well, I hear things in my line of work. Easy enough to find out about that poor lout Fred Stevenson who was being paid to play at highwayman on the Brighton Road, the idiot was drinking himself under the table every night on the proceeds and bragging from here to London about his exploits. Professionals don't take kindly to amateurs, so I heard about it soon enough from some coves who were interested in retiring poor Fred and trying on the post in his stead. But it's a lost art and a loser's ken I wanted no part of, the horse patrol is accomplished and has done for the game, and so would've done for Fred in a week or two.

"So I came down to interview the lad for a different position, but since he didn't care for the post of featured player at a funeral, he agreed to give up life as a land pirate after this one last run, and I doubt he'll trouble anyone but his livestock again. Still, so long as I was about it I thought I'd be in at the kill, so to speak. Say I did it out of curiosity, or as a tribute to Gentleman Jones, or to save his descendant's fine jacket, or for the sake of beautifying England's roads by keeping such handsome coachmen on it. But whatever you do, gentlemen, never say"—and here he dropped his voice to a stage whisper that clearly carried to Susannah—"that I did it all for Miss Logan because I thought she graced this old earth and believe it needs all the grace it can hold. No, never say that, or I'll deny it if only to save myself from all those impassioned kisses she's sure to want to cover me with.''

"As to that," Julian replied as he walked to Susannah's side and took her hand, "I think that since you've given my carbine so much credit, I can claim those kisses as my reward. Only not here," he said, no longer to Lion, but only to her as he gazed down at her, "and not just now," he whispered, as a promise.

"And as to my lord Moredon?" Warwick said as though thinking out loud, as he abruptly turned his attention from Susannah and Julian.

"Oh, I'll lug the guts," Lion said.

"Will Shakespeare was obviously a favorite at the foundling home," Warwick mused as Lion bent to hunker down near the fallen nobleman.

"Indeed," Lion said, "and he'd be the first to say that if it were done, it would be best that it were done quickly. I'll leave my lord on another, less-frequented road to Brighton, near to Dorking, I think, and by the time he's found with this silk on his face and his pistol in his hand, the horse patrol will be pleased to settle the matter by jumping to decide he was the gentleman highwayman they sought, come to his just reward. A few questions will show he hadn't been himself lately, and they'll soon find out he needed the money well enough. And then the thing will be over."

"He has a sister, he once had honor," Warwick said softly, as he gazed down at what had once been his enemy. "It would be just as easy to strip him of his mask, and leave him that at least. A name's not much, but all any man can bring whole to his grave. Let them think he fell afoul of the highwayman he feared. His pistol's been discharged, and when there are no further incidents, they'll think he either got his man or discouraged him from the trade forevermore . . . 'the quality of mercy,' as the man said, you know," he said with a sad smile. "Now, Lion, please, I own a debt. How may I repay you?" he asked on a sigh.

The large man looked at him at that, and smiled.

"You have," he said quite simply, very sincerely, "recently, when you told me I might still call you 'friend.' Now I see it's more than reward. It's an honor."

And then he took his cloak and covered over what remained of Lord Moredon before he went with Warwick to see to the fallen footman, who was moaning in the dust.

By the time that Julian cracked the whip and started his teams again, the footman had been restored with some brandy and a bandage round his head, and Susannah could see Lion so busily securing a large black bundle to the back of Lord Moredon's horse that he didn't even have time to wave good-bye as they drove away. Since she'd already thanked him so often he'd finally ordered her off and into the coach, she settled back and watched him grow smaller as they pulled away.

Millie was burbling with excitement as they resumed the long drive home. She'd not missed a thing, she said thrillingly, having never really fainted at all, but having only followed her older sister's advice, which was that whenever threatened, a clever female should swoon, since it's harder to take advantage of an unconscious girl.

"Not harder," Warwick said, cutting her off, "only less enjoyable."

And as she blushed at that, he cautioned her so seriously and severely to hold her tongue about all that she'd seen and heard that she almost wept and then promised on the heads of all her unborn children that she'd never breathe a word.

"No one would believe her anyway," he whispered in Susannah's ear when Millie had subsided. That ear was close to him, since as soon as he'd seated himself next to her again, before he could repeat his invitation, she'd decided to rest her head upon that amazingly therapeutic shoulder he'd bragged about less than an hour ago, but what seemed to them both to be days before, when he'd first joined her in the coach.

"Warwick," she said sleepily as the coach rolled on, so muted that he had to bend his head to hear, thus brushing his cheek against her soft honeysuckle-scented hair, "thank you, there's no way to say thank you, but thank you."

Before he could protest that it wasn't necessary, he saw that she was asleep at last, after all her wild journeying, as though this last incident was the last thing she could take in, and so in her wisdom, she'd simply shut herself off.

Millie remained silent too, although it was some time before she slept, since she was well-rested and still buoyed up by excitement. But as promised, she didn't breathe a word. Not for fear of disturbing her mistress, since she was fast asleep against Mr. Jones's chest. But out of consideration for the gentleman, who looked as though he was lost in thought, and sat never moving a muscle, except for now and again when he unconsciously stroked a strand of Miss Logan's bright hair away from her forehead. And all the while he bore a look of such tender sadness upon that elegant face of his that Millie wished with all her heart that someday, someone would look just so at her, if only for once, if only for a moment.

When they arrived at last at Greenwood Hall it was late in the afternoon. But for Susannah, who was refreshed after the deep and dreamless sleep she'd enjoyed for the rest of their interrupted journey, it was as if it were a bright new morning. She dashed up the stairs to her rooms and ordered a bath to get the last of the dust of the road from herself, and she sang softly as she scrubbed and lathered her hair. She was alive and hungry for everything now, and having not eaten all day, was so ravenous that she was looking forward to her dinner almost as much as she was looking forward to her entire life.

The gentlemen went to change clothes and wash as well.

Julian, having done, went downstairs to see where his friend was, only to find he'd finished first and so had already left his rooms. The viscount walked with a springy step, he felt lighter as well as light-headed with happiness, and almost a little ashamed of feeling so good about another man's demise. But just as it seemed that all his recent heartache and trouble had swirled around the name "Moredon," now that Lord Moredon was dead it looked like the last of the difficulties associated with the time in his life when that name had been important to him had been lifted from his shoulders as well.

His money would have been gone even if he hadn't thought himself in love with Marianna, but his desperation to recover it so that he could claim her as his wife had made life wretched for him. Ironically, now that he knew he was well rid of her, he was well on the road to recovering himself financially as well. With no more to fear from her mad brother for himself or those he cared for, it seemed to him that the world, as if in apology for all his recent unhappiness, could not now offer him more. He'd worked, he'd planned and plotted, and all to no avail, and suddenly all good things came to him unsought. Warwick had unexpectedly come into his life again to help him from his financial morass. And

Susannah had been a special gift, bright, beautiful, entirely good, and only waiting for him to turn and see her so that she could light up all his future.

He was, he knew, a very lucky man. So he was surprised enough to stop in his tracks and leave off the low merry whistling he'd been doing when he saw Warwick at his desk in his study. Warwick's lean face was so gloomy and intent as he scratched out some note he was writing that his friend thought for a moment that someone else had recently died, aside from his worst enemy and an old, unknown uncle who'd left him a fine legacy. Then Julian remembered something he'd recently heard and was momentarily ashamed of his own happiness. For whatever else, one thing was immutable. Warwick was his friend, and what touched upon his life touched upon his own. Even if, he thought uncomfortably, as he stared at his solemn-faced friend, it couldn't be helped that as sometimes happens with close friends, precisely because of their commonality, one's happiness might be the ruin of the other's hopes for it.

"Clean linen, smelling like a field of heather, working at your desk already—is there no end to your energy, Warwick?" Julian asked as he ambled into the room and took a seat near the desk.

"None," Warwick agreed, adding a last line, blotting the paper, and liberally sprinkling sand over it. "But then," he said, sitting back and gazing at his friend, "you appear to be entirely recovered from our ordeal as well. Now that all the running and rambling is done, you look as though you were ready to start all over again. And that's as well. Because, my dear energetic lad, you'll have to do just that, and pack again—tonight, I'm afraid. As will I.

"Julian," Warwick laughed with genuine amusement at his friend's startled reaction to his words, "our casual style of life of late has clouded your wits. But only think, the contessa is still sulking somewhere on the outskirts of Edinburgh. I received a message from her in London and she claims she's still making inquiries about her mythical legacy, although I suspect she's twigged to the truth by now and is simply too embarrassed by her foolish dereliction of duty to return straightaway. It hardly matters, there's no way she can fly down from the North to us tonight. And, for all our derring-do and skirting the outer limits of respectability of late, we can't stay on here overnight with Susannah, without a proper chaperon. She's been seen in local society now, so she'll continue to be watched. We can't do that to her reputation, in the name of friendship or good sense. So I propose we take off for Brighton and stay at the Old Ship for the night, or at least until my great-aunt Harriet, my late uncle's sister, arrives from Cheltenham for a visit. I've written to her, the note went off from London before we left. Even if she responds as speedily as I think she will—she's an incurable snoop and lonely, I should think, now that the old man's gone, for she loved to fight with him—the soonest she can arrive here is in the morning. The Ship has tolerable beds, if that's what's bothering you," he added when Julian looked down to his fingers, and then to the floor.

It was as Lion had said to him, Julian remembered, as Warwick gazed at him quizzically: if it were done, it would be best if it were done quickly. Yes, if there must be pain, Julian thought, it would be best for it to be given quickly and be done with it. So he took in a breath and with as much care as a surgeon trying to make a quick, clean incision, said as steadily as he was able:

"I don't see the need, Warwick. Because I don't want to leave Sukey now, not tonight, not after what's happened today. And I don't think I have to, for there's no harm in it if we're an engaged couple, is there?"

Warwick sat very still. Julian could swear that he'd stopped breathing; the only sign that he'd heard was the way his thin brows flickered and swooped for a moment, as though he'd registered some sudden pang.

But, "Indeed?" he replied as coolly as if he'd been told it might rain. "And are you?"

"No," Julian said softly, "not yet. But I wish to be. And I see no obstacle to it now. I think it's no secret what Susannah's feelings are in the matter, I don't believe there's ever been any doubt of that. It didn't need that madman to say it, you yourself told me, in fact. But as to that, Moredon said something else today, and because we're friends, and because we've been for so long, and because I want us to continue to be, I feel I must know—is it true?''

Warwick paused. Then he looked at his friend, his eyes so brilliantly dark and blue and both amused and pained that it was hard to look back at him.

"Would it make a difference?" he asked quietly.

"No," Julian answered steadily. "Would it to you, if you were me?"

"No. It would only take some of the joy from it, but there'd be so much joy in it, it would scarce matter. And as for our being friends, it's important, but there comes a time when a man ought to put down his toys and put aside his boyhood, friends and all, and take to him his greatest friend, his love, and let her supersede all others. That is more than you asked, but it is indeed how I should feel if I were you, if I were so loved.''

He rose from his desk to look out his window, to conceal his face, his hands laced behind his back, a back he'd turned once already this day to a man he'd expected to put a bullet in it. Now he turned it again, this time to his friend, who felt as though he'd placed a knife in it.

"You're very silent," Warwick said at length, as Julian struggled for the right words to end this conversation with. "Does it surprise you so much then that I speak about love? I, cold, odd, eccentric Warwick Jones? But I do feel things, if not precisely often. And perhaps I think now and again about love, just as other men do. Perhaps sometimes I think that it would be very good to love and be loved in return. Very pleasant not to have to pay to be touched, for example, for that's what all this business of mistresses and light females comes down to in the end, if you'll forgive the pun," he laughed lightly, "you know.

"And even if one loved a female one could never touch, for some reason, why then, even for a fellow such as me, who loves such touching very well, as well you know I do, I sometimes think it would still be more than any man could ask of life—to simply love someone more than himself. Especially if he were able every now and again to let himself believe such love might be reciprocated. Oh yes, I sometimes think these things, you know.

"But what are you to do, poor Julian?" he asked sympathetically, turning to give his friend his whole sad smile. "Offer me first try at her hand? You might. I could go in and offer for her first, so that when you came in she'd be laughing merrily, or weeping, she's that tenderhearted, you know. Or shall I come in after you do, like the farce, to round out her triumphant evening with laughter? No. There's nothing you can do, my dear beautiful friend Julian. The moment she clapped eyes on you, she was yours.

"Go to her with a whole heart, offer for her, and please, for the sake of friendship, never tell her about this conversation. I should like to always be at ease in your home. There's nothing worse than a female who thinks you've a passion for her," he said on a crooked grin; "it instantly erases all naturalness, the best of them can do nothing but primp and giggle and make fools themselves forever after, knowing that, whenever you show your nose. Can you see Susannah in fifty years, plump and gray, with a covey of daughters looking as she does now, and yet preening and simpering every time I hobble in on my cane to inquire after your gout? It's not to be thought of," he said with a friendly smile.

"But, Julian," he added, after they'd wordlessly shaken hands and the blond gentleman had turned to go, "please be sure it's what you want, and be entirely sure. Never cause me to regret not making a fool of myself in order to give her a choice. She's a remarkable girl . . . a remarkable woman," he corrected himself.

"I am entirely sure," Julian said quietly. "Can you doubt it?"

"No," Warwick said, "how could I?" And then added to the empty room when his friend had gone, "But then how should I know the way of it? I've never been in love before, at least not since I came to be a man."

Susannah was surprised to see only Julian awaiting her in the drawing room. Usually both of her gentlemen passed the hour before dinner with her, chatting and gossiping over sherry. This evening, when there was so much to talk over, only Julian stood waiting for her by the window seat. But he wore such a glad look when she entered the room that she felt assured that nothing was amiss. He was, in fact, radiant this evening, that was the only word she could think adequate to describe him. She was glad she'd worn her best green frock by way of celebrating the end of their woes, if only so she could feel she belonged in the same room with him in his present splendor. But it wasn't so much a matter of his clothes, as of his entire presence.

His handsomeness, which always approached the epitome of classical beauty, transcended that now, for no classical sculptor, however talented, could have infused his marble work with such human warmth, gaiety, and sheer healthy joy as his face held as he held out his hand to her. His golden hair was newly washed and slightly damp, his light eyes alight with laughter; for all his shocking beauty, he appeared altogether real and completely mortal as he put his warm lips to her hand.

"Sukey," he said, as if he couldn't wait to share a secret jest with her, "come, sit. No, stand. Ah, well," he laughed in some excitement, "it hardly matters. I've something to say, and if I formally pose you or position you to my liking before I do, I'll make a worse botch of it than I threaten to do right now. So hear me out, at once, and then choose your stance."

He stood directly before her and held her hand tightly as he spoke.

"Warrick reminds me that the contessa is gone. And he, being a proper gentleman, insists you must be chaperoned or we'll lose you your good name by staying on here with you tonight. That's Warwick, of course. He forgets you were abducted to London and passed a day and a half the night in the company of assorted thieves and murderers, and the other half in London alone with us, and forgets you're no flossy highbred Lady of Fashion to begin with. But he remembers your good name in Brighton. Well, the short of it is, Sukey, that I've told him it doesn't matter since I want to change it for you, whether it's good or bad. Oh, badly put." He grinned and shook his head and then he said more soberly:

"I want to marry you, Sukey, my love, there's the point of it. I do love you, and I do need you, and I do want you. And I was only an idiot for not having known it long before now. I don't know how else to tell it to you. So if you say yes, it'll all be settled, and I'll stay on, and it will scarcely matter if the contessa stays in Scotland so long she grows a beard.

"Sukey?" he said softly when she only stared at him. "That was poorly done, wasn't it? Not very romantic, and I know you're a romantic sort of a girl. But I've done with high romance, thank God, and have opened my eyes to what real love and real worth are, without the flowers and trimmings and sighs. You've been here, watching and waiting through my terrible protracted childhood, and I think that's the one thing I regret, that I couldn't have met you after I'd made a fool of myself so you couldn't see it. But perhaps I needed you right here all through it to point up the enormous difference between love and a dream of love. I think you understand me very well. That's only one of the ten thousand reasons I love you entirely, Susannah Logan.

"As to that name," he said quickly, before she could speak, "the fact of our different stations doesn't signify. If society can accept a viscount who was a coachman as soon as his fortune's mended, be sure they'll accept whomever he takes to wive, and I want you. And never fear, I vow that fortune will be repaired without your dowry. Will you marry me? There. There's nothing more to say."

He looked down at her. Her brown eyes were so wide he could make out the separate shadows of her upper lashes against the dazzlingly fair skin above them, and looking closely, he could see a small image of himself looking down at her in their dark depths. So he hoped he would always find himself, and since she didn't answer, he took her in his arms and held her gently and close, and brought his lips to hers, and explained before he kissed her:

"That's all I can say. But not all I can do."

And she went dazedly into his embrace, and felt his warm lips against hers, and it was exactly as she had always dreamed it would be.

21

The door to the drawing room stood open; as it wasn't a room meant for privacy, it never was closed when the master of the house or his guests were in. There was no way Warwick could avoid looking in when he passed, just as, despite all his better judgment, there was no way he could have avoided forcing himself to pass by the room. He glanced in for the space of a heartbeat, and stayed at the door staring when it seemed his own heart stopped.

The blond gentleman held the blond young woman in his arms, he kissed her, she seemed content with that. There was no reason for the master of the house to then back away as though he'd gotten acid in his eyes. There was no reason for him to flee to his study and sit at his desk, shaken and somewhat shamed, feeling like a voyeur, feeling displaced and out of place in his own home, as he'd once been made to feel so long ago. These were, after all, people he had elected to have in his house, these people he loved wholly, if too well.

They'd actually looked exceedingly decorative as a matched pair, he thought mirthlessly, the gold and the flaxen head finally joined at the mouth, fair skin against fair, like differently shaded lengths of the same bolt of cloth. But there was nothing incestuous about the sight of the two of them locked together in passion, there was instead something entirely natural and inevitable about it, reminding him of a pair of yellow butterflies he'd once seen mating, connected, their separate wings beating their same slow pulse.

He'd known what he'd see, he thought savagely, but he'd

needed to see it in order to give up at last. He'd rationalized that staying in his study while Julian proposed to the woman he loved would be like lurking or sulking or hiding, and he refused to be so childish. It wasn't until he saw them, of course, that he knew how he'd deceived himself: how he'd held out one foolish hope that perhaps she'd refuse Julian, because, perhaps, he thought humorlessly, there was a chance she'd caught a bad case of madness from Lord Moredon. Of course, she'd loved Julian forever. And if in some small part of his mind he still believed that he would have been the better man for her, why then, he was after all, he realized, an odd eccentric man, given to strange fancies.

Thank God, at least, he thought, rising and going to his decanter of port, he'd not given in to his strongest urge, to let her know completely how he felt, making an idiot of himself entirely by offering for her when he knew she loved another. He'd tried that once after he'd failed to keep his hands off her, and even then she'd looked at him in such shock he'd had to pass it off as a jest. His only chance to win her would've been to act as her comforter; he only wished that he had one now. He hadn't known, he thought in some wonder, that it would hurt quite so much as this.

He poured himself a generous glass, but then set it down without taking it to his lips. That *would* be childish. Instead, he'd sit and wait and come out of his study at their happy announcement, and then smile and jest and wish them every happiness. He'd shake Julian's hand and kiss her cheek. He'd had an old uncle, he knew the way of it. Then, after watching them for a space, he'd discreetly retire for the night. In the morning he'd find some wonderful excuse to go to London, or to Paris, or to hell with himself. But until then, he vowed, sitting down again after taking up a book for the look of it, he'd be grown-up if it killed him. And he had the oddest notion that it would.

Julian's lips were warm and gentle, his body strong and comforting against hers; when he pulled back from her for a moment, only to hold her close again in a wordless embrace, Susannah rested her cheek against his and saw the fair tendrils of his hair curling like some tender boy-child's would against the strong column of his neck. She was entirely astounded. For once the books and stories hadn't lied, his kiss had been exactly as she'd always dreamed it would be. Just as sweet and gentle as all the fairy tales had promised the handsome prince's kiss would be when he woke the dreaming princess from her sleep. It was only too bad, or too good, she thought, as she began to step from out of that perfect embrace, that she'd already been aroused, and so had been wide-awake when he'd come to her at last.

He drew back, feeling her withdrawal, and looked his question at her. Her response to his kiss had been everything he'd dreamed it should be: pure and gentle and innocent. Her response after it confused him; she looked grave and regretful and was decidedly not glowing with happiness or blushing with delight. For all his past history, he'd had little traffic with inexperienced girls, and so wondered if he'd stepped wrong. She clearly wasn't happy with his embrace, and that was a thing entirely beyond his experience; even Marianna had pretended some pleasure at his light kisses. But seeing her unease, all at once he remembered her secluded life and damned his insensitivity. Rather than something he'd done wrong, it was more than likely she had some foolish notion of what he'd expected from her. He'd set that right at once, he thought with fond compassion, but she spoke before he could.

"Julian," she said softly, lowering her lashes, looking so exquisitely abashed that he took heart again, but before he could reach for her again she said quietly but clearly, "I am very sensible of the honor you do me, but I cannot be your wife."

"But you love me," he blurted in his amazement, and wished he hadn't, for it sounded nothing like what he wanted to say, although it was absolutely true.

She grew very still. This was terrible, she thought, for she did love him and never wanted to hurt him, indeed, he didn't deserve insult and he looked very hurt indeed. But how could she tell him that precisely because his kiss had been exactly as she'd dreamed it would be, it was no longer enough for her, because she was a very different girl now from the one who'd dreamed that particular bright dream? It was never his fault that she'd lain in his arms waiting for a sensation that had never come, that she'd found his embrace pleasant, not thrilling, and his kiss incomplete, when she knew all that was lacking was her reaction to it. All it had given her was confirmation of a truth. It would be better if she could make up some comfortable lie and avoid the further truth she owed him as much as she'd owed him that kiss. But he was her friend and she was never a coward, and if there was only one truth, there were a dozen ways to say it.

"I did love you," she confessed. "I do still, in a different way. If you'd asked me weeks ago I should have said yes before the words were out of your mouth, if I believed I heard them right, that is. I suppose everyone knew how I felt, poor Lord Moredon was probably absolutely right. But, Julian, you spoke just now of a 'protracted boyhood,' and I understood you very well, just as you said I did. For all that you're a man and a nobleman and I'm a fishmonger's daughter, we're very alike, you know, you and I—that may be why we're such good friends. And so we are, never doubt it. I don't believe we'd be good lovers, though. But you see, I didn't want a lover then.

"I wanted a dream prince," she explained earnestly, looking beseechingly into his confused eyes, seeking his understanding. "I wanted a beautiful noble fair-haired fellow who had a white horse and fought dragons and bled ichor and lived between the covers of a book. And you exceeded all my expectations, you were . . . are, incredibly beautiful, and you had *two* teams of horses," she said on a sudden irrepressible smile, "and you bravely fought adversity and bad men, and treated me with just the right blend of grace and casual politeness. I would've snapped you up then, Julian—you fitted my fantasy perfectly."

"And now?" he said stiffly, unbelievingly, for still in some way he thought it all a jest, and that in a moment she'd give up this odd exhibition and cast herself into his arms, laughing. But it had better be a very good jest, he thought with growing displeasure, for he was disappointed with this display, it was unbecoming, very unlike her.

"Now," she said ruefully, "I see you're altogether too nice to labor under that burden for the rest of your life. What would I do if you got a streaming head cold, how would you explain a rash on your back to me? Oh, Julian,'' she giggled then, unexpectedly, as he gazed at her in startlement, ''how could you wed a bride who'd be appalled to discover you snored?

''Julian,'' she said, smiling up at him warmly, ''the oddest thing happened to me when I least expected it. I grew up. Just as you say you did. But if your growing up made you realize you wanted to marry me, my growing up made me see I couldn't marry you. I don't know if it was being with you and Warwick that prompted it, or being out in the world at last, or being mistreated by bad people for the first time, or being well-treated by them for that matter, that did it. But I achieved my dream, and when I did, I found it was like all dreams, wonderful to live in my mind, but as nourishing as the stuff of the clouds I built it from. I was accepted in society—oh, I'll grant it wasn't high society, only a little provincial part of it. But I danced and was feted and was permitted to be what I always wanted to be, and I found it was very pleasant. But only that, not worth half the trouble I went to attain it.''

''And I,'' he said, surprised at how aloof his voice sounded, shocked at how staggered he was at her refusal, more incredulous still at how her amused account of it stung, ''having been attained, am also deemed not worth half the trouble?''

''Oh, Julian,'' she sighed, ''you're worth far more than anyone's trouble. And I haven't attained you at all. Because I begin to believe you don't know me any more than I knew you.''

He gazed down at her, mute and troubled. She looked into that dear, beautiful face, made even more attractive by the bright intelligence she now knew lay behind it, and she sighed for the vanished girl who once would've given all she possessed to see that want in his eyes for her.

''There's someone else?'' he finally asked, groping for understanding.

''Oh. Yes,'' she said, looking down, quiet, embarrassed, flustered at last.

That, at least, he thought, incredible as it was, of all of this, that made sense.

*   *   *

Warwick looked up as Julian strode into his study. He put on the best representation of a fond smile that he could and rose to his feet, laying aside a book on insects he'd been engrossed in, and that he'd have been alarmed to find himself reading. But then his smile vanished, for Julian was white as talc and clearly upset.

"I'm going now," Julian said abruptly, "for the night, as you suggested. In the morning perhaps I'll have calmed myself enough to know if and when I'll ever return here. I feel rather a fool, you know. And I'd like the time to think this out. She refused me."

There was still wonderment in his voice as he said that, for he'd never been refused before. Even Marianna had granted her favors even as she'd rejected his name. And yet, he realized, though females had given him "yes" for answer every time he could recall having asked them for answer in his life, the two times he'd offered wedlock, he'd been turned down: once with a sop to his masculinity, once with what was definitely sympathy. All those easy affirmatives, and two such devastating negatives? It was a profound revelation he'd need time to consider.

Warwick stared at him until his words took on meaning. His first impulse was to offer to intercede, to find where the problem lay. It might be that Julian had put a word wrong. Susannah was sensitive, and like many such people, might've had some odd, hidden reason for having said no, meaning yes, all the while desperately wanting someone to winkle the true answer out of her. Then he paused. Julian was his best friend, and he loved him well. But he couldn't, not for the sake of his soul, offer to help him in this. Not when doing his task right would mean doing so much wrong to himself. He hesitated; then, deciding he must let Julian find his own way, he echoed:

"Turned you down?"

Julian thought for only a moment. There was a strong supposition that he was already considering, and this man was his closest friend, and he well knew where his heart lay. But though he might damn himself forever for being petty and cruel and small-minded, he couldn't bring himself to hand over that which he'd wanted, even to his best friend. If it were to be his fortune, let him seek it, he thought, as he replied, giving only half a loaf, but at least giving that:

"She says there is another."

Then, after looking steadily at Warwick, Julian chose not to stay any longer. So much as it was good to see dawning hope brighten that melancholy face, it was painful as well. Then too, he thought in his own defense, it mightn't be true either; she'd changed, so much so that he couldn't swear to anything concerning her. And though unlikely, he might be wrong, she could have had some entirely different gentleman in mind when her eyes had grown so soft, and her color had risen and she'd ducked her head at the thought of him, and he'd hate to stay to see that resurgent hope dashed. So, beset by too many hopes and fears and too much sympathy and envy for his friend, he decided to leave while there was still enough doubt in his own mind to make the rest of his night barely bearable.

"I'll be at the Golden Horse, outside town," he said over his shoulder. "It's a coachmen's stop, there's a pretty red-haired wench there who could make a man forget his own name, if only for a night."

And then he picked up his hastily assembled portmanteau and let himself out.

When his butler scratched at his door moments later, Warwick looked up.

"The viscount's left, sir, and so Cook was wondering when you'd like dinner laid. And as Mr. Epford generally has this night out, he was wishful to know if you needed him."

Mr. Fox, in London, would have known all these answers, but Warwick was glad that his country butler had broken his reverie. This was, Warwick decided quickly, amused at the thought, not a time for thinking, after all.

"As I don't know what I'll be needing, tell Cook to lay out a cold collation and then take the night off. Mr. Epford may leave whenever he wishes. I'll not need him this evening," Warwick said, realizing he needed neither valet nor cook, nor butler, nor baker, nor candlestick maker. Because all he needed now, and very badly, was wisdom, good fortune, and a miracle, he thought as he took a deep breath, arose, and left his study to try his luck.

She wore a green frock, and with her bright hair done up in high curls, she looked, he mused, very like a daffodil. And so he would have told her when he came in the drawing room, despite the fact that her high breasts, slender waist, and rounded hips gave him far more than a flowery image, if he hadn't seen her face when she turned to him. She looked so woebegone his hopes sank, and wondering if she were already regretting her decision, he reported tonelessly:

"Julian's left."

"Oh dear," she said sadly, "I'm sorry. Would it have been better if I'd left and you two stayed on here? I mean," she said at once, seeing his surprise and remembering Lord Moredon's ugly accusation, and never wanting him to do so, "since there are two of you and only one of me, it might be better if majority ruled. That is to say, Julian said it was my reputation that concerned you the most."

"No," he said quietly, "your happiness concerns me most."

"I couldn't marry him," she said, turning her head from those watchful eyes. "I'm not a great lady, after all."

"Ah, unequal stations in life and so on, so that's why you denied him?" he asked with a small laugh, thinking, yes, she refused to save him from gossip, and the clunch never guessed it, it's only a simple misunderstanding after all, they'll have it patched up within hours after they meet again, why have I left myself open to such unhappiness?

"No, of course not," she protested, spinning around and staring at him. "I only meant that ladies are trained to take marriage as a business arrangement, and I've not been. I've grown up quite a bit, but I've still got some romantic notions. Because some of them are good. I couldn't marry where I didn't love."

"Oh," he said, "yes, now I recall. Julian said there was another man on your mind."

He grew still, with the quiet, listening tension that was his hallmark. His eyes were half-lidded, yet she knew he missed nothing in her expression as he waited for her to speak again, and she wished he'd speak instead. She was not a fool. She knew, now that she permitted herself to know how she felt about him, just how he'd always felt about her. Yet here he stood, cool and watchful, and she began to wonder if she and

Julian were not the only ones who'd changed in these past weeks. Although she believed Warwick had been grown-up from the start, perhaps because he'd not been allowed to be a boy for very long, and so had always been more constant than either of them, it might be that because of it he'd also had no use for futile yearnings and so had already found another who reciprocated his love. If, she thought in sudden shock, it had been love, and not another, simpler sort of yearning he'd felt for her.

"But you've been under careful observation here," he said, when it seemed she wouldn't speak, "so I wonder who the lucky fellow could be. And the only name I can come up with is Lion's. I do hope that's not true," he said wistfully. "I'd like to come to your wedding, but I think having Bow Street as your witnesses is a trifle much, and it's more than a bit risky having 'my Sally' as your flower girl. But then, who else?" he pondered, putting his hands behind his back and staring at her, his head held to one side. "Mr. Epford? Mr. Fox? Not Lord Beccles?" he gasped in horror. "You'll never find a marriage bed big enough for him, his mama, and yourself."

"No, of course not," she laughed.

"Who then?" he asked quietly, very seriously.

There was no sense in running anymore, she was weary of it anyway. It seemed she'd passed too many years running after ephemeral goals, too many years running from reality. And too, she realized, whatever happened after today, this part of her life was over. Even as she stood in the drawing room with Warwick Jones, she saw that she must leave soon, or he would, and like a traveler about to depart forever from some well-loved place he knew he might never return to, it was then as if the very room she was in lacked reality, and was already fading into memory.

"You, of course," she said sadly.

Before he could step closer, she added, "You, always, I think."

He studied her face closely as he came up to her and put his arms about her.

"Would you say that again, please?" he asked, amazed,

his dark blue eyes searching her face for mockery, or jest, or truth.

"You, Warwick," she said, finding it simpler now that she'd admitted it the once. "I do so love you. At first for the way you made me laugh, and then for the way you made me think, and then at last for the way you made me feel. When I couldn't sleep at night, it was you who teased my mind. When I was in danger, I thought only of you. When I looked upon death, it was the loss of you I feared most. Oh, Warwick, Julian was a dear, safe dream. I thought I loved him when I first looked upon his face. And for all you're very handsome," she said so earnestly he knew she thought she spoke the truth, "I knew I loved you only when I came to know you. But you frightened me very badly, you frightened me straight into growing up, I do believe."

"Do I frighten you?" he asked as he drew her closer. "Beauty and her Beast, is it?" He smiled.

"Oh, you make me angry," she cried. "Can't you understand that you're very attractive? Why, even Sally told me that she fancied you and said she preferred your looks to Julian's because she'd never keep company with a fellow who looked like he just stepped off a pedestal in a museum, because she'd always worry if she matched him."

"I see," he said, deliberately, wickedly obtuse. "I make you look magnificent by contrast."

"If you didn't persist in befriending someone who looked like an oil painting," she said furiously, "you wouldn't always be going on about being a 'gnome,' you know."

"That's 'goblin,' " he corrected her, while he still remembered, for the word already sounded alien to him.

"Whatever," she said, calming. "Your looks please me very well, it's you yourself that frightened me."

"Odd, you absolutely terrify me, you know. Yes," he said with a wistful smile, "and with good reason: you can be fatal to me. You can annihilate me with a word: that word is 'no.' You can kill me with another: 'good-bye.' What an arsenal, my love. Do you know your power? No one's ever had such power over me."

"And what if I said yes?" she asked, her lips inches from his.

"I don't know," he answered honestly. "You never have."

And then he gave her no chance to, and as he dared not say another word lest she change her mind, or lest he'd heard wrong, and because he could no longer think at all when he held her so closely, he kissed her. Then he had no more doubt. She clung to him as if she needed him as much as he did her, and had longed for him fully as much, although he knew that wasn't possible. Her mouth was welcoming, her body completely yielding against his, her arms came up around his shoulders to hold him closer. He never wanted to end their embrace, and when he did, he knew why. For when he looked down at her to enjoy the felicity of seeing that lovely face before he kissed her again, he saw she was weeping.

"Changed your mind so soon?" he asked, hoping for a chuckle, hoping it was a jest.

"Oh, no," she managed through all her tears.

"Susannah, love, please," he said, "what have I done? Or not done? Or ought to do? You're destroying me, you know," he said helplessly. "At least tell me, however bad it is."

"It's stupid," she said wretchedly, "but knowing it makes it no better. I t-told you that I love you."

"So you did," he said. "Is it that I didn't tell you how much I love you? But I expect, I hope, I presume," he added anxiously, wiping away a tear that started up at his words, "that you'll give me at least the next fifty years of your life in which to do so. I expect you'll marry me," he said at once, wondering if she thought otherwise for a moment, horrified at that thought of her estimate of his morals, of his affection for her. "In fact, I'll keep you here at gunpoint if you don't. It's not right to toy with my affections, I'll have Mr. Epford swear out a deposition saying that you've dishonored me, else. Or is it that I didn't vow fidelity? But how could I ever betray my own heart? Susannah, please," he said desperately, "what is it?"

"I've given up a great many childish illusions, Warwick," she said at last, as best she could with quivering lips, "but some cannot, will not leave me. I've never read a romance, Warwick, nor have I ever heard of one, in which the heroine declares for the hero. No, I have not," she said bravely as he gazed at her with dawning understanding and what looked like rare delight, "and don't smile, for it's not foolishness. Why, just think," she said on an indignant sniff, "of a few decades from now."

"All right," he said wonderingly, "I shall. I am. Now what?"

"If you grow angry with me, if you grow vexed, why then, you've only to throw it in my face. 'You,' you can say with perfect justification, 'declared for me, after all, and I, in all courtesy, had to accept.' And the point is, Warwick, you *are* a gentleman, and decades hence or no, how shall I ever really know you're not just being kind and overly n-nice about it?" she concluded, new tears falling.

If she began to realize at that point that it was her own nervousness at her incredibly profound reaction to his touch that had unsettled her, as well as maybe being her own last defenses being thrown up at the thought of abandoning fantasy forevermore to actually take to herself such a live and vital love and lover as Warwick Jones, it was still too late to stop the trembling, much too late to stop the tears. And if he saw the same thing, and perhaps a little more, realizing she might very well be as unsure of love as he was, if not more so because she'd never experienced the physical part of it, he knew for the sake of that future pleasure, he must stop, if not her weeping, at least her fears.

"Ah," he said, thinking deeply as she blotted her cheeks with the handkerchief he'd handed her, "yes, it will do. Susannah," he said with a mysterious smile, "say nothing, ask nothing, but only come with me now."

He put out his hand, she took it, and he led her from the room. She followed him up the long curving stair and walked with him quickly along the long, carpeted upper hallway. They went down a corridor she'd never seen, her room being at the other side of the great house, and then he opened a door and led her into a chamber, shutting the door behind them. He gave her only enough time to look about the huge, high-ceilinged room, and then he led her forward again, this time to a huge canopied tester bed. Then he put two hands on her slim waist and picked her up, seating her on the high bed. He took a long step and sat down beside her.

"This," he said, a little breathlessly, for he'd taken the journey speedily, "is my bedchamber. This is my bed. This," he said, putting one hand against her cheek and the other in back of her head, as he bent to her, "is my kiss." It was a long while before he raised his head again, and this time he was even more breathless than he'd been before.

"You see?" he said softly. "Not just simple lust. Although, heaven knows, there's a great deal of that going around these days. No," he said as he kissed the base of her throat and recovered himself enough to try to ignore the shapely white breasts he could so clearly see from this new vantage point, "not just that. For now, you see, I've compromised you. No doubt of it. I've emptied the house, lured you to my chamber, placed you in my very bed, and compromised you thoroughly. Now you must marry me. So when I'm villain enough to claim a few decades hence that you declared for me, you've only to retort, 'Ah, but, wretch, you compromised me, remember, and thoroughly.' "

He sat back and smiled at her in triumph. That smile, she thought, looking at him in the late-afternoon sunlight that came in his high windows, that endearing smile transformed that thin aristrocratic face and made him truly more beautiful than any other man she'd ever seen. But for all he smiled, his eyes were worried. And for all his worldliness and facility and charm, he was, she realized in that one moment, very anxious for her approval, entirely bent on her happiness, and as totally vulnerable to her as she was to him. She hadn't thought she had that much more growing up to do until that moment, when she saw that love was precisely this, this equal thing of giving and fear and want. And then she felt as though she'd come a long way and finally come home to herself.

"Warwick," she said gently, no longer afraid of him, or even herself, "no. It won't do. Because," she said, lowering her lashes, even as his dismay showed, for grown-up or no, she had a rigid code to surmount, "I don't see where you've compromised me . . . thoroughly."

"Oh," he said, entirely at a loss for words.

But then he realized that he didn't need them. He took her back in his arms and answered her, for a long, delicious, thorough time. It was when he realized how very thorough he'd been that he recalled himself again. By then, she lay back against his pillows, her flaxen hair spread out over them like another silken coverlet, the lovely green gown down to her waist, her white, pink-tipped breasts against his cheek, the taste of them burning on his lips, his hands slowly slipping the green gown further down so that it would impede them no more.

"Susannah," he said, raising himself on his elbows, trembling a little with the effort, but then quickly covering her nakedness with himself so that he'd not be tempted by what he saw, before he realized how unbearably tempted he would be by what he felt, "Susannah," he said in an agony of desire he tried to conceal, "it began as a jest. I've gotten a bit carried away and though I'm delighted at how well I can carry you away, I think I've compromised you fairly thoroughly by now."

"Oh," she said, her mind still scattered by the new things she'd felt, her senses still taking control of her sense, "have we done that?"

His body trembled, but with laughter now. "No, love," he sighed, moving a regretful inch away, but convinced by her question that it was the right, if not the most comfortable, move to make, "we have not. And in a week, at the most two, for I won't wait longer to marry you, you'll understand why that might have been construed as an insult. Or at least," he laughed, "I hope you will."

It was the laughter that decided her. For it was his laughter that she loved as much as anything he gave her.

"I don't consider myself compromised thoroughly, then," she said stubbornly.

"Susannah," he said seriously, his eyes searching her face a breath away from hers, "I can wait, you know. I don't have to take this further unless you're sure, I don't want to hurry you, I only want what you want."

"I'm sure I want you," she said just as seriously, "and perhaps I want you to be sure as well. And perhaps I want to show you that without a doubt."

She was terrified, of course. As staggered as he was by her answer. This went against everything she'd ever been taught.

She'd always known what Warwick seemed to want, but in these last few days since she'd grown up, she'd come to see what he needed. And that—reassurance—was a thing she knew she could provide him by giving him herself, without reservation. But she quaked, and hoped he'd take it for a tremble of passion as he took her in his arms again.

The look he gave her as he did made her forget her terror. For she thought she'd never seen such an expression in any man's eyes, and had never expected to see it in Warwick Jones's sad face, but it suited him, that incredulous look of tender joy. Worldly as he was, it was likely he knew the difference between fear and desire. Perhaps he also knew her purpose, and knew that with her upbringing she could show no greater trust than to give herself without wedlock, and knew that to deny her because of his own moral reservations was to refuse to understand the enormity of her gift to him. Or it may have been that he was too moved by her now to put her aside for any reason.

But in this at least he was supremely confident; here he knew his own skills as well as he knew his own heart. He only regretted, and told her so, that it was all too new for her to enjoy fully or find as fulfilling as he'd wish it to be for her. The green gown and her shift and her slippers were discarded, and he delighted in the slender but lavish body she shyly presented him with as he slowly brought her to readiness. Whatever she would have been, she would have pleased him; that he found her to be so lovely, so faultlessly made, almost overwhelmed him.

She only protested once, and then he drew back in astonishment, when she explained very primly that she thought it wrong for him to keep his shirt on after he'd removed all else, whatever he said he'd been told about virginal sensibility, for if he took pleasure in seeing her body, she thought it only right that she might see his. Then he forgot all his expertise and felt like the merest boy in his anxiety, as, against all popular wisdom, he disrobed as completely as he would if she were not the pure young woman of his heart, but only a woman of the night. When she looked, and then averted her eyes, and then peeped again, only to tell him wonderingly at last, her eyes wide and shining, as he held his breath in fear of having made a horrible misjudgment, that she thought he was entirely beautiful, he found it difficult in that moment to remember any of those skills he was sure he had.

But so she did find him wholly handsome, entirely thrilling, every perceived difference on his strong clean muscular frame, however unimagined, seemed apt and perfect. His body was long and well-shaped, from narrow hips to broad shoulders, she was amazed that a grown man had so many grace notes about his person. His hair was softly silken; although tight sinew moved beneath his smooth clear skin, she was bemused to discover that dusky skin to be as exquisitely sensitive to the touch as her own was. And there was delicacy in his touch, for while never tentative, he was always gentle with her.

His skill was undeniable, but it was true her heart was beating so fast with the shocking nature of what they were doing and what she was permitting him to do, that she scarcely registered more than bits and pieces and parts of wild sensations as he touched her and kissed her, and found places that she hadn't known existed for her to feel sensation upon. It was all, as he'd said, too new to judge. Still, she was entirely glad of her decision, for aside from the fearful delight she found in his arms and at his hands and lips, there was the grander pleasure of seeing how much she delighted him.

He never left her alone to wonder or worry, for he watched for her every response and told her often exactly how much he loved her as he enjoyed and prepared her. His love and desire were so intermixed that when at last he came to that final barrier, he swore he felt the pain that she did, and he held his breath and hated the moment when her pleasure stopped and she gasped in hurt surprise. She smiled at him after that, and tried to kiss away his expression of dismay, whispering that it was better, it was fine. This first time then, he tried to forget his art and attempted brevity for her sake, and was grateful he could save her further discomfort, when, realizing how much he valued her even as he gazed down and saw their joined bodies, for the first time in his life mind and body linked to bring him joy on every level, and he gave himself to her as completely as she'd given herself to him.

She'd been surprised by the sudden burning ache that interrupted their idyll at the moment of profoundest intimacy, because his every touch had been tender and nothing in his gentle embrace had prepared her for pain. But even as she stiffened and gasped in startled astonishment she remembered all the tales she'd heard. He paused then, and seeing his distress, she tried to console him for his dismay at her reaction to the inevitable wound he'd dealt her. When he continued, she forgot the discomfort, being overwhelmed herself by the intensity of the pleasure she felt him experience. In some fashion, then, she found her joy in his, discovering such pride in her ability to transform her cool, amused, distant Warwick into a totally absorbed lover racked with transports of delight that it brought her to a form of fulfillment as well.

He held her close for a long while after, and when he found himself again, he kissed her as he waited for the tears he thought inevitable. But he understood that popular fancy had nothing to do with his Susannah when she put her lips to the hollow of his neck and sighed with contentment, and said she thought it was all lovely.

"Liar," he said gently as he rose and went to the washstand to get a cloth and some water.

"Nature's unkind to you females," he told her as he returned to her side. "It won't be wonderful for you for a while yet, but then, I promise, 'pon honor, it will be. It was nature's fault," he said suddenly, "you do know that?"

"Yes," she said simply, "the girls at school said it's the gentleman's assurance that they're opening a new bottle, and they expect it and enjoy it."

"Rubbish," he scoffed. "The girls are idiots. Or their gentlemen are. I don't care if the wine enjoys my drinking it. And I could've done without hurting you. In fact," he said as he applied the cool cloth, "I don't know if we gentlemen would be so eager to begin our careers in such matters had we your barriers to surmount. Time," he assured her as he took her in his arms again, "time will equalize us, you'll see, I promise."

After a while they lay silently, but just when he thought she'd gone to sleep she murmured drowsily:

"You don't have to marry me, you know."

"I know," he replied, gathering her even closer. "I don't have to breathe either, it just makes it possible for me to live. Silly creature. As if there'd be any point to it without you, now that I've found you."

"Not so silly," she whispered contentedly. "I knew you'd say that. I just wanted to hear it."

She drifted off listening to his chuckle where it began in his chest. Then secure in his clasp, she slept against him again, as dreamlessly and peacefully as she'd done in the coach, this time through the night. And thus never knew that he watched over her all the rest of the night, never closing his eyes except to refresh them for an instant, afraid that if he did he might sleep to wake and find her gone, and find it all had been a dream. She awoke only once, and seeing him gazing at her, reached for him. And then, though what quite naturally followed next was still novel to her, it convinced her that whatever else her new husband would be, he'd not be a liar. For she began to perceive that there would be a great deal more to this new activity than she'd ever dreamed, just as he'd promised her, and so she confided in his ear to his further delight when they'd done.

She woke again to find him gone from her side, and sitting up abruptly, saw him standing by the bed, dressed, only just tucking in his shirttails.

"Where are you going?" she wailed.

"Morning's coming," he explained gently, looking down at how she was rising naked from the bedclothes, and tucking a sheet around her to firm his resolve, "and for all my jests, I don't want to start this marriage with gossip. It wouldn't ordinarily matter so much, but I think my great-aunt Harriet will be arriving with the dawn, and I want your reputation spotless for her. Come, get dressed, and I'll speed you to your room before the servants wake."

"Warwick," she begged, her eyes wide, "don't leave me now. Not just now."

For all her newfound maturity, it was still all too new for her. She was afraid that once he'd left her, she'd feel guilty, and wrong, wronged and somehow shamed. He brooded as though she'd said all this instead of thinking it, and then his face brightened.

"Very well, even better," he said, "I'll put on my lovely morning robe, and spirit you into your room to fetch one of yours. We'll sit together in the east salon, in high state, sober and righteous as puritans, too principled to have gone to bed in an unchaperoned house. Yes, Aunt Harriet will adore it, come.

"I intended to speak to you alone before she arrived, anyway," Warwick said, once he'd settled her on a couch, deep in his arms, in the east salon, where, as he'd said, they'd be able to see any coach come down the drive, and disengage in plenty of time.

"There was a thing I wanted to tell you before you met her, but somehow it slipped my mind," he said, smiling and taking her hand to his lips.

He held on to her hand and toyed with her fingers, and seemed a trifle nervous as he went on, "We can't have a grand wedding, since I'm in mourning. So I thought we'd have a simple one, by special license, as soon as possible. Do you mind missing out on all the fuss?"

She assured him that she didn't, but he seemed even more anxious, and so she became a little ill-at-ease as well.

"My uncle left me some funds, the rich get richer, you know," he said quickly, "and a magnificent home, near Gloucester, I'd like to live there, if only for his sake, all his energy went into it, and it is the family seat."

She was too nervous now to do anything but nod, and so he went on rapidly, suddenly very serious, "He left me something else."

She held her breath, hardly knowing what to fear.

"And I can't refuse it, if only out of respect for him. You'll be marrying Warwick Jones, of course. But don't take alarm when the minister unites you with the Baron Ives too."

"You, a baron?" she gasped after a moment, as realization dawned.

He nodded, and as she pondered this startling development, added, "And though you'll be no bigamist, you'll be wedding the Viscount Kimberley as well."

Before she could speak again, he gazed at the ceiling and uttered, ". . . and the Earl of Dartford."

"Warwick," she cried, sitting bolt upright in alarm. "An earl? You're an earl now? However shall I marry an earl? The fishmonger's daughter and an earl?"

"Don't worry about it," he said soothingly, taking her back in his clasp, "I'm still Warwick Jones, the highwayman's heir. Eccentricity runs in my family. No one will be the slightest put out, believe me. Uncle talked to his pond carp, all I'm doing is marrying someone whose father made his fortune from them. Anyway, don't let the earl bother you. For then the minister will say, 'Marquess Holyrood,' but pay him no mind either, for then he'll say, 'Duke of Peterstow.' And that's all, I promise, I promise."

"A duke!" she gasped. "A duke! Me, a duchess? Oh, Warwick," she grieved, "whatever shall I do?"

"This, I think," he said gently, distracting her.

"Oh," she said, distracted, enchanted, "yes."

Lady Harriet Jones arrived at dawn and was shown into the salon to meet her great-nephew, the new duke, and his promised bride. She was anxious to meet the girl; she'd heard about her when she'd seen Warwick last, and had been thrilled that he'd her to talk about. It had given her hope. There were too few close-connected, documented Joneses about, and she'd worried that bachelorhood would run in the family until it ran out entirely. It was a curse to them. Now, he'd won her. And she was well pleased with what she saw he'd gotten. Pretty as she could stare, nicely mannered, and with a great deal of money, Warwick had assured her. No title, but then, manner had always meant far more to Lady Harriet than title, and money was always welcome, she was a Jones, after all.

Warwick said they were glad to see her. Doubly so, he explained, since they'd sat up all the night, sleepless, in the salon, afraid of retiring for fear of offending sensibilities because there was no chaperon in attendance on them. Lady Harriet sighed to herself. That was entirely like her great-nephew and all the Jones men: icy, bloodless eccentric. And yet, there the pretty child was, hanging on his arm, gazing into his face as though she saw the sun itself rising there. She felt sorry for the girl. For Warwick was, as everyone knew, an odd, haughty, peculiar gentleman. She shrugged; it took all kinds.

Then Lady Harriet left to be shown to her rooms. It was just as well she didn't look behind her as she did. For like Lot's wife, she couldn't take life with a pinch of salt. So she wouldn't have cared for what she'd have seen, if only because she was a strong-minded female who loved her convictions, and hated to be contradicted.

22

Nan watched him as he lay sleeping, as she'd done for hours, and was yet again astonished at how young and innocent he appeared when those light, speaking eyes were shuttered. But then they opened, and were blank in that half-second before comprehension flooded back to him, and she held her breath in fear of what he might say in that moment when he recalled where he was, and whom he was with. For if he could hurt her with a glance, she dreaded the wound he might inflict with a thoughtless word.

She didn't know if it would be worse if he remembered or if he didn't. Last night he'd suddenly appeared in the doorway of the Silver Swan again, coming in out of the fog like a wraith, looking as pale, wild, lost, and tormented as any mist-born wandering soul. He'd been soused, of course, she knew that the moment he'd leaned close to her to whisper his greeting, and it had been evident in the taste of his kiss, the moment after that. She'd been looking forward to this meeting with him for months, so that she might soundly snub him. Her triumphant walking-away speech had been rehearsed in too many lonely nights as she lay in this bed alone, or with others, for her not to know it by heart. But she'd looked into that beautiful, tortured face and she'd said yes, if she'd bothered to say anything at all, as she'd led him carefully down the stairs to her bedchamber.

Although he'd been so disguised he could scarcely speak without slurring, or step without foundering, he'd been capable enough to delight her, but she believed he'd be able to do that even if he were at death's own door, and not just so badly jug-bitten. He'd turned to her many times in the night, and whatever his state, he'd been so tender and gracious she hadn't needed to hear him mutter something about celebrating his wedding night to know that someone had lately cut out his heart, and that he was, somewhere, bleeding badly, if invisibly. It hadn't been herself that he'd spent himself with last night, she knew that. But she no longer cared. He'd needed her, she'd served him. That, after all, had always been the only foundation of their relationship.

The light gray eyes grew aware. He closed them. And then groaned.

"Aye," she made herself sneer, hopping out of bed as briskly as if she'd never passed the hours staring down into his face like a witling, waiting for him to wake and come back to her in any way he chose, "you deserve it too. Drunk as a wheelbarrow. An' prolly feel as though you ort to be in one on the way to the boneyard now. Here," she cried as he sat up, winced, and then tried to stand, "don't need you fallin' an' havin' to be put up in splints. Take your time. Hang on, I'll get you the landlord's finest, tastes like he did sumthin' nasty in it but it'll set you right. Have a wash while I'm gone, it'll help," she said as she shrugged into a plain frock and eased slippers on.

"Need help?" she asked then, dropping her air of insouciance, as she hesitated by her door.

"No, thank you, Nan," Julian said, looking up at her with a rueful smile. "You've given more than enough already."

There was payment enough, she thought as she raced down to the taproom. The landlord of the Silver Swan was only just checking out his supplies for the coming day at this early hour, but he was good enough to mix up his cure for a surfeit of spirits for her guest, and kind enough to say nothing until she took it in her hands. And even then, "You're a fool, Nan, but a good one," was all he told her.

When she returned to her room, he'd obviously washed; his golden hair was still wet as she saw it emerge from the shirt he pulled over his head. He grinned when he saw her, and drank down the cup she handed him with a huge grimace, but swallowed it all. She said nothing as she handed him the razor she'd kept for him, but after he'd lathered his face, she took it from him again, saying only that she scarcely needed a bloke with a cut throat littering her room, and shaved him in silence, forbearing to say another word until she was done.

Then he took her hand as she began to move away.

"I'm going away, Nan," he said.

"Thought you'd already been," she answered, looking to her hand, and never to his eyes.

"Further, this time," he said. "I'm giving up the coachman's game," he explained, "England itself, for a space, too. I've made a little fortune actually, with the help of a friend. But I'm off today to seek a better one, and won't come back until I'm richer than I need to be. I don't know where I'm bound, or when I'll be back."

She stared at him in silence. She might be only a serving maid, and no better than she should be, and she knew that herself. But there'd never been any man like him before, and she knew that when he left her, there'd never be any like him after. It was more than his face and form; she appreciated manly beauty and it came in many guises to her—she accepted that that had always been her downfall. It was his air, his speech, his courtly manner, it was, she realized, he himself. He was unique, her viscount-coachman lover.

All of this might have shown in her face then. She didn't take care to conceal it, she was so taken with what she now saw in his face in the daylight. He'd changed, something had altered. The morning light showed the lack of sleep and the amount he'd drunk the night before, but it wasn't only the slight smudges under his eyes or the sadness to the set of his lips, it was something that shone from his eyes, it was a change in his very soul she saw in the full glare of day. But it made him no less beautiful to her. So she used the last of her rehearsed renunciation speech at last, to save some remnant of her soul from his possession:

"Then, good luck to you, my lord," she said, "and goodbye, and a good life to you as well."

"Would you like to come?" he asked.

She gasped. It was not only at his words, for he'd said it expressionlessly and she didn't know if he jested or not, but at some terribly lonely thing she glanced for just one moment, something she knew quite well, having found it at the bottom of her own soul whenever she dared to look.

"Oh, aye," she scoffed, for she knew how to fend off honest feeling better than anyone, "it would be wise of me, nice secure post, that, runnin' off around the world with a noble gennleman."

"I'll sweeten the pot," he said, still emotionless, still as sincere or insincere as he'd been. "Marry me, then. Why not?" He spoke as much to himself as her as he added, with a new, small twisted smile quirking his lips, "It would be pleasant to hear 'yes' for a change, and I'm about to change my entire life." Then, at last, he laughed. "You'd be valuable to a roving man, even that black-haired wench at the Crown hasn't got your talents, nor can she shave a man half so smooth, I'll warrant."

Once, when she'd been young, in that brief hour, Will, from down the road, had asked her to come berrying with him, though she'd known very well what he'd meant. And she'd been afraid. So she'd asked that stupid Annie Hanks to come with her so that she'd not have to face it all alone, not yet. But soon she'd tired of Annie and left her on the road, and gone on with Will and what was to be her life. She knew too well what it was to want something so badly that you ran away from it, and so much that you couldn't stay away from it neither, and how it felt to try to avoid what you knew you must do. And she'd never be any Annie Hanks, not for any man, especially not if she cared for him.

And she was a realist. She knew he never meant it even if he thought he did. Pain made anyone say foolish things.

"Oh, lovely bride I'd be for you, my lord," she laughed. "I couldn't sign the marriage register, I'd have to make my mark. Can't read, nor write. I can shave you just fine, and do a great many other fine things for a man, the only thing I know good is carin' for a man's body," she added, just to see him wince, even as she did saying it. But when a thing had to be ended, it had to be sure.

"So thank you, my lord, but no thank you," she said, laughing, making it all a joke for both their sakes, "and I hope you don't compliment all your barbers that way."

"All things come in threes, my luck's bound to change

soon," he said, making no sense to her, and he bent and kissed the tip of her nose. "Thank you, Nan."

After he'd dressed and gone downstairs to eat and said good-bye to the landlord, he asked Nan to come with him to the door. He gave her a purse, over all her denials, but though it weighed far heavier on her heart than it could ever in her hand, she took it at last, when she realized he must end things in his own way too. The payment, she thought, would certainly make his proposal a jest. But then, she had to reconsider, and she had the rest of her life to do it in. For at the last, before he left her, he looked down into her eyes and whispered:

"You know, Nan, you're exactly the sort of girl I most like."

"And just what sort is that?" she asked saucily, knowing the answer and hating that he needed to erase everything tender this way.

"Why," he said seriously, watching her closely, as closely as he'd observed her that long-ago night when she believed he hadn't, "the wise, and kind, and loving, generous sort, of course."

"Did you tell him about Ben Compton?" the landlord asked as she stood at the door and waved at her last look at the Viscount Hazelton as he rode out of the courtyard.

"No need," she said flatly, for indeed there'd been no need to tell him she was marrying another coachman on the Brighton run, "he ain't coming back for years. And when he does, I'd be too old for sport."

"Ben's dark as a Gypsy," the landlord commented, for all it was none of his business, he was a friend and knew he could pry. "Last night might have been pleasurable, but was it wise? Be something fierce to pay if you presented Ben with any kind of a golden baby that wasn't in a purse."

"Ben's already started 'is own, why do you think I'm marrying 'im?" she said savagely as she turned away, bitter at being reminded that there again she'd lost him, and so had no chance to ever have anything to remember him by, except for all her dreams, for all the rest of her life.

*   *   *

It was a macabre place to wait, but Warwick, Julian thought, on a shake of his head, had an unusual sense of humor. When he'd heard that his friend planned to visit the Silver Swan one last time before he left England, Warwick had made him promise to wait here on this last morning so that he might send a farewell gift to him. He'd agreed to the odd request, Julian thought, if only because he'd been so anxious to leave that wedding yesterday he'd have promised to wait at the gates to hell in order to escape the merriment, and not just beneath the hanging oak where Gentleman Jones and Lord Moredon both had met an end.

He sat his horse in the shifting shade and waited, glancing up and down the long road, and at length, he frowned. It wasn't for the futile waiting; he had, after all, nothing better to do now. His scowl was for the painful reminder of how Warwick must have passed his wedding night last night, for Warwick never forgot anything, drunk or sober, and yet this time he clearly had forgotten that last word he'd had with his friend. Pleasure, Julian thought with the uncomfortable admixture of hurt and happiness he felt for both his friends since he'd seen them wed, evidently could make Warwick forget his word in a way that everything else he'd experienced in his life had not. If he felt some consolation in the thought that Warwick had previously encountered very little real pleasure, after all, and certainly deserved some, he soon forgot it as he tried to block the next natural images that occurred to him when he considered the subsequent activities of the happy bride and groom. He was so busily doing that that he didn't lift his head to see the rider coming out from the trees behind him until he heard the hoofbeats.

"Three times dead, and buried twice over. I could've had you down and out before you turned round the first time. Good God, my lord, have you an army at your back that you can be so casual of life?" the rider said, drawing rein as he came up beside him.

"No," Julian answered, embarrassed, for he was right, "it's only that I didn't expect more blood to be let at this tree's roots. And," he added, deciding to give truth because it was due, "I was deep in thought and blue-deviled, and perhaps didn't care very much for my neck just then. But thanks for sparing it, Lion. But never say Warwick's pulled your teeth?'' he asked, his amazement growing as the large man's appearance began to register upon him. ''You're not his messenger now?''

''They're bright and shining as ever, my lord, but I do bring his message as a favor,'' he answered, and taking a paper from the bag at the side of his saddle, he handed it to Julian, adding, ''Best if you read it now.''

Julian scanned the paper and looked up to find the other man studying him just as closely.

''But,'' he said in confusion, looking from the paper to the larger man, ''you? You are the gift Warwick gives me, as he says, '. . . to take with you on your travels, for your comfort, safety, and future success'?''

''So it would appear. He gave me you, by the by, when he gave me a similar letter.''

Julian checked, as the Lion went on ruminatively:

''And I too would've refused his generosity at once, if it weren't for the fact that I admire the duke very well, damned if I've ever met a cannier fellow, and if he claimed you'd be of worth on a journey, I was forced to think it over. Then I determined at least to carry out his first wish in the matter. For as it happens, I'm leaving dear Mother England on the first fair tide too.

''Yes,'' he said on a sidewise smile, ''I too have some notion of rising in the world, if not,'' he added, looking pointedly up to the tree they rested beneath, ''quite so far as all that. Which is almost the reason entirely. It seems Lord Moredon left me a hard legacy, for some of the information he laid with Bow Street interested them far too much. And then, our friend, the new duke, was entirely right. 'Lion,' he said, 'uneasy lies the head that wears a crown, and uneasier the one that makes too many crowns at your game.' Quite right,'' the sandy-haired man brooded, ''and when I considered that not only Gamy Leg Bob and Whitey Lewis were after my position, it gave me some pause. I only took on my post by accident, I'm not a Londoner born, but it was such a ripe tasty ken that I fell into it, so to speak, and never gave a thought to the future.

''But I'm versatile. And tired of the game. It might be,

too, that I grew even more tired when a certain lovely lass who lately became a duchess let me know she thought I was too good for it. I'm not a sentimental fellow, but I never met her like before, and I think I might like to again.''

"You never shall," Julian said softly, "she has no like."

The large man looked steadily at the fair-haired young man and saw the sudden pain glance in those astonishly light eyes. The lad had changed, he thought, and it added something to him, not that anything had been lacking. But now he'd grown a look of vulnerability that no Grecian statue could attain, and it made his beauty more human, more heartbreaking and accessible, and so perhaps even more invulnerable to age and time. Did he know, the man known as Lion wondered, that that face of his, unleashed against the world, could build or topple empires?

"Don't tease yourself, my lord," Lion said sincerely, his voice sounding so different in that mode that Julian stared at him. "You never had a chance. She was born for him. From the moment she first drew breath, she was his. If you'd asked for her at once, she'd only have discovered it later and so brought pain to everyone."

"And so, then, I'm to be left with you?" Julian laughed lightly as he put the thought away to think on deeply some other time.

"So, at least, the duke would have it," Lion answered, continuing to gaze at him appraisingly, "for he took care to give me both letters, one for myself and one for you, before I left the wedding."

"You were there?" Julian asked, completely astonished. "But you're far too large to overlook. I never saw you. Where were you, beneath the altarstone at the chapel?"

"Rude fellow," Lion said on a grin, "didn't you note the chap who took Great-Aunt Harriet's fancy at the wedding feast?"

"But he was an old gentleman, heavyset, in stays and laces and a great moth-eaten periwig . . . he had her in raptures . . . good Lord, Lion," Julian said sincerely, "I'm all over admiration. You might have proposed to her and run off on the spot, your impersonation was so complete."

"No impersonation, I liked her very well, had I twenty years more and she forty less, I'd have made a match of it."

Julian stared at the other man, now taking care to examine him aside and apart from either his occupation or reputation. Today he looked a solid, amiable, prosperous man of business. And yet last night he'd been a creditable octogenarian, and before that, a convincingly ruthless criminal, and a dashing highwayman too. Today he seemed of an age with himself and Warwick, and the easy air he'd adopted overlaid all hint of his strength and cunning, but then, he could obviously be any age, Julian thought, or anything, he wished. Realizing this, he was as impressed with Lion now, for the first time, as Warwick, he conceded, had been from the very first.

"Our mutual friend said that you were bound for parts unknown, seeking your fortune," Lion commented slowly.

"I'd thought perhaps the Indies or the Caribbean or the colonies," Julian said just as slowly, still assessing the other's reactions. "Aside from warmth and little yellow birds, I'd had a mind to meet up with some of the undiscovered jewels and trade and riches to be found in the East and in the New World."

"And how did you think to earn them?" the Lion asked carefully.

"By luck, but failing that," he said on a white-toothed smile, "by the labor of my back and my wit and wisdom."

"Not a bad idea, but I had thought of the Old World myself," Lion said thoughtfully, "and of the riches and opportunities changing hands as the world's boundaries are changing. Bonaparte may be on Elba, but there's a great many unsettled things to be saved and sold and settled in the courts of the Russias and on the Continent."

"And how had you planned to settle those matters?" Julian asked with interest.

"Less with luck than with skill, more with wit than wisdom, yet with luck to lead me, with some hard work as well. The work I've been doing was lucrative, but far too dangerous. I've a sudden yen, it seems, for respectability. I've a mind now to build me a manor house right here in England someday, find an interesting bride, and infest the world with evil children."

Julian laughed. "And Sally?" he asked.

"Ah, Sally's an ambitious chit, but has no daring. She elected to keep her throne by going with the new king, and belongs to Gamy Leg Bob now, or Whitey Lewis."

Julian laughed; he'd been so intent on his conversation that he was surprised to find that his horse had begun walking, and that he rode down the road slowly now, with Lion by his side. It felt, he thought, companionable.

"Are you entirely set on the Old World?" he asked conversationally.

"No, I thought I'd ride to the docksides and tarry there, picking up gossip and lending an ear, until I found which way the wind was blowing more fair. And you, my lord, are entirely decided upon those little yellow birds?"

"Not at all," Julian said. "I hope I'm not so stubborn as that. I just wish to make my fortune, and return home some-day to . . . whatever I'm ready for then, I suppose. I've recovered my fortunes somewhat, with Warwick's help. I'd like to do the rest on my own. Even this lovely animal I ride is a gift of his, a beast I rescued after Moredon sold him into coaching, and that Warwick saved again for me. Moredon tried to master the poor brute with pain and anger; I found he yielded to patience and hard work. The world's more frac-tious than this horse, but I reason if I could alter him, there's hope I can alter my own state as well."

"The duke said you could learn," the Lion said after a silence as the two horses ambled on together.

"He was right," Julian replied, "but he ought to have added that I have to."

The other man eyed him with growing approval.

"I have some education, write a fair hand, can fence and spar, wrestle and play cards with the devil without going to hell, and I've some Latin, passable German, and exquisite French," Lion said negligently.

"I have less education than I should, but I can fence and spar, and though I'm a disaster with cards, I can dice, I've Latin, Greek, French, Italian, and some Spanish. And I can drive a coach through the teeth of hell," Julian replied.

"I see, my lord," the Lion said thoughtfully.

"Friends call me Hazelton, friends of my heart say 'Julian.' You may call me what you wish," Julian said at length, never looking up from his horse's ears as he did.

"Ah. Well, Julian, my lad, friends call me by what they knew me as when they met me, and that has changed frequently. Friends of my heart are so scarce I can hold them all in that one organ and still give them room to dance, but they call me Arden, believe it or don't, when they do. Whatever you call me I will answer to," he replied, at once, for a large fierce man, looking very conscious as he concentrated on tending to his mount's reins.

"Well then, Arden," Julian said, "that's a mountain of horseflesh you've got there, do you think he can put on any speed? It's a fair way to Portsmouth, but there's an inn there that has a way with beef, and invariably obliging twin, would you believe it? Twin bar wenches. Of course, one's uglier than the other," he mused, "but the novelty of it draws from miles round."

"This fellow," Arden replied, much offended, "is never such a work of art as that black gentleman you're astride, but like his master, if he's told there's a meal at the end of the road, you may believe he can move. Twins, did you say?"

"Aye," Julian laughed, as he spurred his horse, and then Arden did, and so they raced down the long road, side by side, as if someone had just reminded them that the sooner they arrived at their destination, the sooner they might, someday, be able to return.

Amorous Escapades

☐	THE UNRULY BRIDE by Vanessa Gray.	(134060—$2.50)
☐	THE DUKE'S MESSENGER by Vanessa Gray.	(138856—$2.50)
☐	THE DUTIFUL DAUGHTER by Vanessa Gray.	(142179—$2.50)
☐	THE RECKLESS GAMBLER by Vanessa Gray.	(137647—$2.50)
☐	THE ERRANT BRIDEGROOM by Vanessa Gray.	(141598—$2.50)
☐	THE RECKLESS ORPHAN by Vanessa Gray.	(143841—$2.50)
☐	ORPHAN'S DISGUISE by Vanessa Gray.	(145631—$2.50)
☐	THE LOST LEGACY by Vanessa Gray.	(149580—$2.75)
☐	THE ABANDONED BRIDE by Edith Layton.	(135652—$2.50)
☐	THE DISDAINFUL MARQUIS by Edith Layton.	(145879—$2.50)
☐	FALSE ANGEL by Edith Layton.	(138562—$2.50)
☐	THE DUKE'S WAGER by Edith Layton.	(145666—$2.50)
☐	LOVE IN DISGUISE by Edith Layton.	(149238—$3.50)
☐	RED JACK'S DAUGHTER by Edith Layton.	(144880—$2.50)
☐	LADY OF SPIRIT by Edith Layton.	(145178—$2.50)
☐	THE NOBLE IMPOSTER by Mollie Ashton.	(129156—$2.25)
☐	LORD CALIBAN by Ellen Fitzgerald.	(134761—$2.50)
☐	A NOVEL ALLIANCE by Ellen Fitzgerald.	(132742—$2.50)
☐	THE IRISH HEIRESS by Ellen Fitzgerald.	(136594—$2.50)
☐	ROGUE'S BRIDE by Ellen Fitzgerald.	(140435—$2.50)
☐	SCANDAL'S DAUGHTER by Margaret Summerville.	(132750—$2.50)
☐	FORGOTTEN MARRIAGE by Ellen Fitzgerald.	(142241—$2.50)
☐	LESSON IN LOVE by Ellen Fitzgerald.	(143817—$2.50)
☐	HEIRS OF BELAIR by Ellen Fitzgerald.	(146514—$2.50)
☐	VENETIAN MASQUERADE by Ellen Fitzgerald.	(147782—$2.50)
☐	A STREAK OF LUCK by Ellen Fitzgerald.	(148819—$2.50)

Prices slightly higher in Canada.

**Buy them at your local
bookstore or use coupon
on next page for ordering.**